THE NOVELS OF ROSS MACDONALD

THE NOVELS OF ROSS MACDONALD

MICHAEL KREYLING

University of South Carolina Press

Published in Columbia, South Carolina,
by the University of South Carolina Press

Manufactured in the United States of America

09 08 07 06 05 5 4 3 2 1

Library of Congress Cataloging-in-Publication Data

Kreyling, Michael, 1948–
    The novels of Ross Macdonald / Michael Kreyling.
        p. cm.
    Includes bibliographical references and index.
    ISBN 1-57003-577-6 (alk. paper)
    1. Macdonald, Ross, 1915– —Criticism and interpretation. 2. Detective and
mystery stories, American—History and criticism. 3. Noir fiction, American—
History and criticism. 4. Private investigators in literature. 5. Archer, Lew (Ficti-
tious character). 6. California—In literature. I. Title.
    PS3525.I486Z75 2005
    813'.52—dc22

                                                                    2004027811

For permission to quote from the published works of Ross Macdonald, grateful
acknowledgement is made as follows:
    From *The Moving Target* by John Macdonald, copyright © 1949 by Ross (John) Mac-
donald. Used by permission of Alfred A. Knopf, a division of Random House, Inc.
    From *The Barbarous Coast* by Ross Macdonald, copyright © 1956 by Ross Macdon-
ald. Used by permission of Alfred A. Knopf, a division of Random House, Inc.
    From *Archer in Hollywood* by Ross Macdonald, copyright © 1956, 1967, by Ross Mac-
donald. Copyright © 1949, 1951, by Alfred A. Knopf, Inc. Used by permission of Alfred
A. Knopf, a division of Random House, Inc.
    From *Archer in Jeopardy* by Ross Macdonald, copyright © 1958, 1962, 1968, 1979,
by Ross Macdonald. Used by permission of Alfred A. Knopf, a division of Random
House, Inc.
    From *Black Money* by Ross Macdonald, copyright © 1965 by Ross Macdonald. Used
by permission of Alfred A. Knopf, a division of Random House, Inc.
    Grateful acknowledgement is made as well to the Perseus Book Group for permis-
sion to quote from *Selected Letters of Dashiell Hammett, 1921–1960,* ed. Richard Layman,
with Julie Rivett (2001); to Universal Music Publishing Group for permission to use
"California Girls," by Brian Wilson and Mike Love, copyright © 1965 Irving Music, Inc.
(BMI); to Special Collections and University Archives, UC Irvine Libraries, for permission to use the Kenneth Millar Papers; to Harold Ober Associates for permission to
quote from the published works of Ross Macdonald; to Mr. Norman Colavincenzo,
Trustee for the Margaret Millar Charitable Remainder Unitrust, for permission to quote
from the materials in the Kenneth Millar Papers and from the published works.

For Chris, after all the years and all the words

CONTENTS

ACKNOWLEDGMENTS

It has often seemed to me that writing a book about other books is a sign of madness. If I am right, then there have been several people who have encouraged me in the malady.

Prof. Matthew J. Bruccoli, of the University of South Carolina, a friend of Ken Millar's, a collector of Ross Macdonald's work, the author of a biography of the writer and the definitive bibliography, might have been the first to suggest to me a project on Macdonald. It was generous of him to allow more room in the field.

In Santa Barbara, Millar's hometown, and still the home of many of his friends, I found welcome and support. The late Donald Pearce, a graduate school friend of Millar's and later a member of the English faculty at the University of California, Santa Barbara, took my wife and me to lunch and talked enthusiastically about his friend's life and work. Mr. Norman Colavincenzo, trustee of the Margaret Millar Charitable Remainder Unitrust, opened the files of the trust's research materials to me and has granted permission to use all the material for this book. Norman also took us to lunch at a restaurant with such a beautiful view that I could understand at once why Macdonald's characters would commit murder to live in Santa Teresa (Santa Barbara). Eleanor Van Cott and the late Robert Easton gave us time and interest; Mr. Easton was especially moving in his memories of Millar's last years. Also in California I met, albeit only over the telephone, Tom Nolan, whose biography of Ross Macdonald is cited frequently here. He was nearly finished when I was beginning archival research at the University of California, Irvine; we have followed much the same path but looked at different traces of the author.

A paragraph of their own is not enough tribute to Carol and Ralph Sipper. Both were friends of the Millars, and Ralph, a.k.a. Joseph the Provider, a dealer in first editions and literary collections, was extraordinarily generous to two strangers (my wife and me) when we called to introduce ourselves and the book project. If Carol and Ralph like the book, we do not need any other approval.

At the Special Collections and Archives of the University of California, Irvine, Libraries, head of Special Collections Jackie Dooley and her staff were unfailingly generous and professional. Bill Landis even kept the reading room open on the Wednesday before a Thanksgiving so that we could stretch our research time on an academic schedule. He could have been at the beach; it is only minutes away.

In New York City Mr. Ashbel Green, Millar's editor at Alfred A. Knopf, now Random House / Bertelsman, took me out for a literary lunch and all the good talk that goes with it.

At the University of South Carolina Press, it has been a gift to work with my acquisitions editor, Barry Blose, and the managing editor, Bill Adams. I hope this book repays their efforts and the press's faith in it.

This book is dedicated to my wife, Christine, herself an author, who helped with the research, read the drafts, won some arguments, and lost others. I could not have written the book without her; in fact, without her there would have been no point in writing it.

THE NOVELS OF ROSS MACDONALD

Prologue

Who Reads Ross Macdonald?

Jacques Barzun, for years the dean of the Columbia University Graduate School and the highest of brows championing "modern" philosophy, music, and literature, was also, like many cosmopolitan intellectuals, a devotee of detective novels. He sandwiched his admiration for Dorothy Sayers between layers of Darwin and Berlioz. Barzun wrote more than one defense of the time he spent reading in a lower brow, and in them all he shied away from claiming full literary status for the genre. In "The Aesthetics of the Criminous" (1984), Barzun is scrupulous to label the detective writer a "practitioner of the genre," not a novelist or an author. In the same essay he concedes that since "one or another element of good fiction must be sacrificed" to the needs of the genre, no detective novel ever rises unscathed to the level of literature.[1] In "A Catalogue of Crime" (1989), he makes a strategic retreat: "Stories of crime . . . are not, properly speaking, novels at all. They are tales."[2] Tales may be spun by rustics or the naive; their meanings are simple and may be conveyed in bold print. Novels are made by literary artists with sophisticated intellects; they capture the complexities of the times. The highbrow knows the difference. In his reluctance, Barzun is like many "defenders" of the detective novel: very careful *not* to attribute too much cultural value to what, he fears, is ultimately a guilty pleasure.

In "Why Read Crime Fiction?" (1999) Barzun shows that he is well aware of the periodic skirmishes over the literary status of the genre and that he knows the scorn literary critics have been known to heap upon the genre and its defenders. Edmund Wilson's infamous antagonistic essay "Who Cares Who Killed Roger Ackroyd?" charged that the entire genre lacked an intellectually respectable reason for being and that regular readers were fooling themselves with claims to the contrary.[3] Barzun, although he writes decades after Wilson's salvo, defends his years of reading in the genre by slipping around the original charge. Detective novels are meant not to exercise the mind but to entertain it. "Entertainment, then," Barzun continues, "is the prime intention of the tale and it is a pity that in our times people are so addicted to entertainment that they must restore their dignity and self-respect by pretending that some things they like are not for pleasure, but uplifting, informative, *educational*."[4]

Detective novels are for idle hours, with the intellect at half-speed or less, and it is a mistake to call upon them for more than simple rest and relaxation. Besides, Barzun claims, the Golden Age of the detective novel spanned the years from 1920 to 1970 and was governed by Sayers, Allingham, Heyer, Christie, and Marsh—not an American among them. Not only, then, is reading detective novels harmless to the properly cultured mind, it is nostalgic as well, for "the art form has reached exhaustion and nothing more can be done with it . . . [except] to recall its best days and reread the classics."[5]

Even such a staunch defender of the "art" of the detective novel as John G. Cawelti is ambivalent in his claims. In *Adventure, Mystery, and Romance: Formula Stories as Art and Popular Culture*, Cawelti likens the experience of reading in the genre to the simple pleasure of childhood reading, when all "conventional expectations" were fulfilled. Rather than argue for the inclusion of the detective novel, as novel, in the category he calls "mimetic fiction" (18), Cawelti proposes a separate classification, "a specialized literature of escape," with its own rules and protocol[6] (13). Separate, though, is never equal. Moreover, in discussing the American counterpart to the British Golden Age, Cawelti devotes a chapter to "Hammett, Chandler, and Spillane"; although he mentions Ross Macdonald with praise, he omits his novels from the mainstream of his discussion.

I spend so much time debating critics with whom I disagree because the temper of Barzun's understanding and the heft of Cawelti's theorizing are exactly wrong for reading Ross Macdonald's detective novels. Although raised and educated from elementary school through college in Canada, Kenneth Millar (1915–83)—who published under his own name and pseudonyms John Macdonald, John Ross Macdonald, and ultimately Ross Macdonald—adopted the specifically American literary tradition of the detective novel practiced in the twentieth century by Dashiell Hammett and Raymond Chandler, "practitioners" wholly omitted from Barzun's literary history. Macdonald also did more to merge the formulaic and mimetic novels than Cawelti seems to recognize. On the strength of eighteen novels featuring his detective Lew Archer, Macdonald stretched the power of the genre well beyond Hammett and Chandler; in some individual novels in his series he closed the supposed gap between "formula" and literature, far surpassing the need for a default defense as talespinner rather than novelist.

One of the earliest and still one of the strongest critical studies of the three writers in this American tradition, George Grella's "Murder and the Mean Streets: The Hard-Boiled Detective Novel," analyzes the genre in search of identifying themes and styles and ranks Macdonald as superior in several respects to Hammett and Chandler.[7] Yet Macdonald's status in the "trinity" of Hammett-Chandler-Macdonald is too often overlooked. Cawelti was not the only critic to look away from Macdonald when he was in plain sight. Two recent critical studies of the contemporary American crime novel offer convenient examples. Andrew Pepper acknowledges Macdonald as one of the three founding fathers of "the apparently unitary figure of the white, male, hard-boiled detective"; nonetheless, he shuffles Lew Archer offstage in favor of Hammett's Op or Chandler's Marlowe when an example is called for.[8] Hans Bertens and Theo D'haen add a layer to the neglect of Macdonald by clearly unintended slights such as tracing Chandler's influence in the 1980s and 1990s as "modified by Robert B. Parker," and by assaying the influence of Chandler and James Ellroy but not the obvious presence of Ross Macdonald in Michael Connelly's series of Harry Bosch novels.[9]

This book proposes to explore more fully the relationships among the three major figures of the twentieth-century American detective novel, and argues that Macdonald's novels call for the same quality of literary attention we customarily reserve for "the novel." They "aim at the representation of actions that will confront us with reality"[10] rather than ease us into a parallel world of weightless, imaginative escape. Three book-length critical studies of Macdonald's fiction have been published, and two biographies trace his life.[11] Tom Nolan's *Ross Macdonald: A Biography* is indispensable, especially so in Macdonald's case because he used his life so intensively in his fiction. Nolan's work is, however, a biography: In a biography the life envelops art. In this book I want to reverse the relationship, to give the novels first claim on biographical data. Macdonald did, at the end of his life, rank "writer" as the first among his many identities. Matthew J. Bruccoli's *Ross Macdonald* stresses the publishing history of Macdonald from juvenilia to the final novel in the Archer series. Bruccoli's biography follows and is clearly based on his earlier *Ross Macdonald / Kenneth Millar: A Descriptive Bibliography;* he leans to the bibliographic history of the novels rather than to literary criticism. No one who reads Bruccoli's works on Macdonald will ever underestimate the grit, determination, and sacrifice of the writer's profession. But the novels as art still elude us.

There are literary studies of Macdonald-the-novelist, but each of the published literary studies of Macdonald's fiction seems pinched in one way or another. Peter Wolfe's *Dreamers Who Live Their Dreams: The World of Ross Macdonald's Novels* was researched and written with Macdonald's full and generous cooperation but still channels one thematic approach (the psychological one signified in the title) through the entire body of work, restricting our sense of the diversity (albeit limited) of Macdonald's writing. The "world" thus evoked is too hermetic and interior; there is very little sense that Macdonald's novels occupy the public world, often with tension between the need to represent that world fairly and the need to stick to the genre.

Jerry Speir's *Ross Macdonald* is a brief introductory book in a publisher's series, and it seems truncated, as if an editor arbitrarily hacked off sections to make the manuscript fit the requirements of the series format. Bernard A. Schopen's book in the Twayne series suffers a similar series fate, coupling plot summary with the record of published reviews. There is room for a book that strikes out after the novels with a diverse set of literary-critical approaches, aiming to see how Macdonald the writer responded to both interior and exterior "worlds"—the nature of his consciousness and the influences impinging on it from the outside. Late in his life (1977), when it was evident to him that he probably would not write another novel, Macdonald wrote in a journal: "Though I have attempted over the years to seek or invent other uses for myself, other reasons for living—husband, teacher, father, scholar, officer, environmentalist, grandfather, all of which have their validity—I am forced back to the ultimate recurrent realization that I am a writer." This book attempts to pay tribute to that writer, for writing was the ultimate "use" Macdonald found for his life on earth, and the one by which he asked to be judged.

For various reasons, then, none of the existing books satisfies the various challenges Macdonald's work presents to us. How does the mutual bond of text and life actually work? Is the transfer of information from lived life to printed page as one-dimensional as a bank deposit: you give ten dollars to the teller and your balance is increased by ten dollars? How did Macdonald's full-scale adoption of Freudian theories advance the genre? Many modern novelists have been critically explained in Freudian terms, but how many accepted the Freudian paradigm as a palpable fact, as "given" as one's genetic coding or genealogy? In general, using Macdonald's novels as examples, how does a popular genre marry with "literature," and does the marriage last? Can the "genre novel" ever graduate to the status of "the novel"? In other words, is Cawelti's distinction between mimetic and formulaic ultimately the most reasonable way to appreciate Macdonald's achievement?

Additional challenges face Macdonald's readers because of the deliberate choice of literary tradition he made. Most published critical discussion (and passionate conversation) tends to analyze Macdonald's novels on the basis of internal structure alone; that is, does he fairly develop the case, disclose and camouflage clues fairly, motivate good and evil to realistic standards, keep the pages turning without coy posing or outright deception? More often, critical discussions deteriorate into partisan battles between Chandler loyalists, who still resent Macdonald's corrections to Chandler's preference for style over plot, and Hammett aficionados, who regret that too little blood and liquor are spilled in Macdonald's novels.

Such questions bring us back to Barzun, who prudishly declared: "Thus we can accept a private eye who thinks about political corruption and the vices of the rich, and who is keen about jazz; but when he drinks and fornicates incessantly we cease to believe in his capacity for consecutive thought." [12] Macdonald's Lew Archer stands out in his time as a private eye who seems to err on the side of self-control; the novels of which he is the central character seem, therefore, not to deliver the vicarious experience of the mean streets and the self-destructive hero who walks them. Archer drinks, but only beer; and he fornicates, but far short of "incessantly."

It is important to read Macdonald in his time, and both Barzun's moralistic point of view and Cawelti's Aristotelian classification do not point us in this direction. As Macdonald's work progressed, he pressed the formula toward engagement with reality: the travails of his own family, the social and moral upheaval of the 1960s, America's and California's obsession with race, the environmental sins of unreflective development, and (finally) aging. My position will become clear as the chapters roll forward: I think that Macdonald took the American detective novel further than either of his twentieth-century predecessors, that his debt to Hammett was more benign than the one to Chandler, and that Macdonald ought to be read by the standards he projected rather than by those he eclipsed.

There are, as the history of criticism of the detective genre amply shows, many traps and pitfalls in the way of those who write about the genre. I cannot hope to avoid the pitfall of partisanship in the comparative discussion of Macdonald and his dual fathers (Hammett and Chandler). My position is that Macdonald eclipsed them both—one in a kindly and the other in an antagonistic contest. My argument in this dispute is confined principally to chapter 4. There is a second pitfall, perhaps larger than the first. Any author of a series of novels with the same characters and setting inevitably resorts to established patterns. James Fenimore Cooper moved Natty Bumppo from upstate New York to the edge of the Great Plains in his Leatherstocking series, but Natty was still Natty wherever he landed. William Faulkner moved Compsons and Snopeses all over Yoknapatawpha County and from one novel to the next, sometimes revising individual histories. Readers then come to expect, even demand, consistency of development. It often follows that critics fall into a monotonous, repetitive pattern too, following discussion of one book with discussion of the next, like beads on a rosary, relentlessly murmuring the same thesis. To avoid droning one thesis through a quarter-century of novels, I have (sometimes arbitrarily) used historical and cultural topics or themes for each chapter (for example, Freudian family romance, the myth of California, intimations of mortality, and others). Some of these choices reflect influences Macdonald consciously chose to engage, others simply enveloped him. The discussions of Macdonald's novels are arranged chronologically, but the novels themselves are bundled with different thematic twine in each chapter. The twine might pinch at some points. (For example, is *The Goodbye Look* of 1969 the last novel of the 1960s or the first of the "master" phase of the 1970s?) But, in a contest between critical thesis and novel, the nod always goes to the novel.

There is a third pitfall, peculiar to writing about detective novels: giving away the endings. Trying to withhold crucial information in preliminary drafts of the chapters resulted in stultifying coyness; there are simply no interesting ways to be vague. Be prepared to be told whodunit. I apologize in advance for spoiling some of the pleasure of narrative by assuming the reader knows the name of the murderer. Macdonald's novels are so durable that you can read and reread them with renewed pleasure until the paper and glue wear out. I have, and I know I am not the only one.

[1]

Constants

In 1928 Dashiell Hammett (1894–1961) wrote a letter to Blanche Knopf, who was editing his first novel, *Red Harvest* (1929), a novel that would speed the hard-boiled style into American literary history, make the Op the reincarnation of Natty Bumppo in the urban wilderness, and propel Hammett from the pulps to literature. Hammett was ebullient: "I'm one of the few—if there are any more—people moderately literate who take the detective story seriously. I don't mean that I necessarily take my own or anybody else's seriously—but the detective story as a form. Some day somebody's going to make 'literature' of it."[1]

Ross Macdonald made good on Hammett's promise. Not yet thirteen years old when Hammett wrote to Knopf, Kenneth Millar (1915–83), the writer's legal name,[2] published his first novel in 1944. In 1949 he published with Knopf the first of his detective series with Lew Archer as the investigator, and he continued the series through *The Blue Hammer* in 1976—eighteen Archer novels in all. In the Archer series as a cycle, and in a handful of the individual novels, Macdonald refined the ore that Hammett and Raymond Chandler (1888–1959) after him had staked out. Of the eighteen Lew Archer novels, perhaps a half-dozen as individual works fulfilled the vision Hammett predicted. They brought "genre fiction," usually praised for uncluttered page-turning, to the level of literature: texts to be read and reread, not touristic walks on the wild side but examinations of the state of human nature in its personal and social moment. As a body of work the Archer novels stand as one of most illustrious achievements in American novel writing.

Hammett was cool in his letter to Blanche Knopf, shying away from taking himself or his work too seriously, possibly for fear of forfeiting the hard-boiled mystique. Seeming to try too hard, to feel too deeply, or to strive too openly for the respect and status of the literary establishment is treason for the detective and the detective novelist. But Macdonald bucked the rules, taking himself and his work, sometimes, all too seriously. Seriousness of intention, a mixed blessing Macdonald freely acknowledged, is the hallmark of his work and life. He seriously interrogated his own life experience for the fundamentals of its structure, settling in the crucial midpoint of his career on the Freudian model of action and motivation. He repeatedly made the themes and events of his private life the subject matter of his novels. Human imagination, he maintained, works within "structures," and those structures constitute the language by which we understand each others' experience.

The loop connecting life and work was tight, and the more often Macdonald retraced the lines, the more fully realized his work became. In his mature novels, from *The Goodbye Look* (1969) through *The Blue Hammer* seven years later, content and form merged. Nor was Macdonald averse to readings of his life into his work. "I don't see any objection to a writer openly discussing himself because it's what we're doing anyway. We might as well admit it and learn from it and help other people to learn from it," he told an interviewer late in his life. "The art of self-discussion, self-understanding is the route by which we are going to get somewhere. If we do get somewhere. I don't mean as individuals but as a culture."[3] Macdonald was as serious as any critic drawn to his work.

It was "as a culture," as a collective, that Macdonald viewed his relationship to subject matter, self, and the audience. What makes his work of enduring interest in the wide and expanding field of the detective novel is the deliberateness with which he chose the genre, the clarity with which he judged the form and himself, and the "somewhere"—the expanded range and quality of communal understanding—to which he pushed his complex burden. "New" entrants in the genre (Joseph Hansen and his gay detective Dave Brandstetter, Walter Mosley and Easy Rawlins, Sue Grafton with Kinsey Millhone) could not have grown the voices of their previously "marginalized" detectives if Macdonald had not reinvigorated the genre. As detective novelist, then, Macdonald was curiously positioned both inside and outside the lines, both renegade dissenter and responsible spokesman for a genre in the tight grip of a white, male band of brothers.

In her foreword to *Self-Portrait: Ceaselessly into the Past* (1981), a collection of Ross Macdonald's occasional writings, Eudora Welty, who admired Macdonald's work and understood his vision, sums up the "constants," the inevitable and inescapable structures running from his life into his writing and back again.

Welty observes the emergence of major factors, for example how the sea became, very early, the most deeply felt element in Ken Millar's life. She explains how the sense of family became the generative force of his work and its true subject, not by way of a happy and secure childhood but through the uncertainties of being moved about constantly during his formative years, of knowing very young the unsettled lives of his parents, and of his father's desertion of the home. We learn that his belonging in two different countries—by birth and by raising—brought him, through his own deliberate struggle with it, to the profound and liberating recognition of what place meant. We find how the same migrations planted in that lively and curious mind a lifelong interest in the North American *colloquial* language, which became the closely studied instrument of his work.[4]

Welty saw that Kenneth Millar's life fed Ross Macdonald's writing, and that the writing, at certain crucial or crossroads moments, revealed the meaning of the life. Not all breakthroughs were partings of the ceiling; often the floor gave way, and Macdonald had to haul Millar out of troubles as deep as trenches on the ocean floor. In the end, Millar slipped into the final trench, from which Macdonald could not rescue him: Millar lived seven years after Macdonald finished his final novel, trying unsuccessfully to write another, thwarted by Alzheimer's disease. His friend, poet and critic Donald Davie (1922–95) wrote about Macdonald's latter days, physically living a life he could no longer intellectually pilot:

> Wonderful all the same, or
> Wondrous, there in the thresh
> Of the directionless lengths
> Of days. . . . [5]

Welty struck the keynote to understanding the complementarity of the Millar-Macdonald mutual egos. For good and ill, the writer took up and refined the only subject matter he had, his life, using learned literary tools and ingrained habits of being to understand and endure it.

In his own life—which he called his "inward journey" after one of his literary heroes, Romantic poet and critic (and unlikely patron for a detective novelist) Samuel Taylor Coleridge (1772–1834)—Millar identified "structures" larger than personal ego into which that personal ego could safely flow, archetypes like the search for the lost father, the return of guilt for repressed crimes in the past, the history of California (like Coleridge's imaginary Xanadu) as an allegory for yet another botched dream of the earthly paradise, the always-failing symmetry between the "natural" cohesiveness of the family and the sharply angled egos of the individual members.[6] As an academic intellectual, a career he sampled but did not pursue (he earned a Ph.D. in English at the University of Michigan in 1952, several years after he had pledged himself to the vocation of professional novelist), Macdonald identified his themes with literary constants: the obsessive confessional tale, as in Coleridge's "The Rime of the Ancient Mariner"; the abandoned son reinventing himself on his own, as in F. Scott Fitzgerald's *The Great Gatsby;* the Oedipal conflict in its many manifestations —the family romance played out from Abraham's household to Freud's consulting rooms. These larger, more comprehensive, time-spanning structures gave his cases more reach, more depth than the average caper but (in the minds of disapproving critics) more erudition than the shamus should profess.

As the son of an absent father, father of a troubled daughter, and grandfather of a boy who died of a drug overdose, Macdonald ransacked Freudian psychological structures to harness what he sensed as a destructive vortex of panic and error in his own "family romance." As a bona fide "popular" writer (his earliest model was Charles Dickens), he deliberately chose the detective novel (after experimenting with other popular genres) to be the form through which he would fulfill his obligation to art and his deeply felt responsibilities to audience. Macdonald clung to structure, not as a performer seeking the latest innovation but as a believer repeats a liturgy or prayer in the belief that eventually he will become that prayer. Macdonald's faith in literature was secular but no less moral for that, and he believed that to foster the greatest communication among the greatest number was the writer's moral and cultural duty. Hence the choice of a popular form and the constants of theme.

Such a high public and moral purpose is not generally the reason for readers to browse the mystery shelves in libraries, bookstores, and airport newsstands. The disjunction between serious moral purpose and temporary escape makes for a wide crevice, and Macdonald's work far too often has fallen or been pushed into it. Ross Macdonald is the foremost author of the detective novel in American literature. He is the author who, recognizing the tradition of Poe, Hammett, and Chandler, raised the bar so high, with nearly two dozen novels published between 1944 and 1976, that writers in the tradition during his lifetime and since his death in 1983 pay him the tribute of not claiming to have raised it any higher. And yet, too often Hammett and Chandler are acknowledged and Macdonald is neglected.[7]

To return to Welty's insight: the constants of Macdonald's life woven into the constants of his work. The most basic of these is Macdonald's belief in structure as a constant itself. To questions from more than one interviewer over the years of his writing career, Macdonald consistently maintained that when he began a novel he aimed at the structure of the whole, not at an intermediate target such as a colorful character or stand-out scene. "I invent the life [of the character] to fit the structure," he replied to one interviewer. "The two things go together, you have an idea of the life and that suggests the structure to you too. The structure and the life, it's what art is, making a structure that corresponds to the life and finding a life that will fit into the structure" (Kaye, 14). The cases that his detective, Lew Archer, investigated, therefore, are not random sequences of beatings, chases, and badinage with obtuse cops and feral blondes. They are problems in the collective unconscious, and Archer's pursuit of understanding them brings us closer to our enduring situation rather than an escapist distance from it.

In the terms of the tradition into which Macdonald inserted himself, his insistence on structure makes him an anti-Flitcraft. The Flitcraft "intermezzo" (chapter 7) in Hammett's *The Maltese Falcon* (1930) articulates the philosophy of the hard-boiled hero. Early in the chase, Spade takes time out to explain to Brigid

O'Shaughnessy the ground rules: mind and world are radically disconnected. It makes as much sense to plan for chaos as it does to plan for a predictable future, so the rule for the hero, the private eye with the clarity to see the truth, is never to think beyond the immediate situation. Spade never theorizes beyond the here and now. He concocts stories to lend any moment a temporary, if outlandish, plausibility, then waits alert for the next moment. This makes him a successful detective; he does not so much "solve" cases as discipline himself to be present when they reveal themselves. In this way he is superior to his dead partner and Lew Archer's namesake: Miles Archer made the fatal mistake of thinking beyond the immediate moment and imagining himself in bed with Brigid.[8] Lew Archer is the antitype to the Flitcraft inspiration: there is one, reliable structure, not a proliferating list for a series of present moments.

If Macdonald did not articulate this departure from Hammett, he did so in the case of Raymond Chandler. Early in the cycle of Archer novels, Macdonald explained to his publisher, Alfred Knopf, that he believed he was superior to Chandler (then, in 1952, on the lee slope of his productivity) because Chandler could only do parts—scenes—whereas he, Macdonald, could do entire plots. "Chandler practices, and has stated, the opposite theory: that a good plot is one that makes good scenes. I don't wish to give the impression that he's my *bête noire*. Hell, he's one of my masters. But I can see around him, and am in growing disagreement with much of his theory and practice."[9]

Chandler was notorious for his loosely constructed plots. Tales of trying to make *The Big Sleep* into an intelligible screenplay are well known in biographies of Howard Hawks (the director) and William Faulkner (who worked on the screenplay).[10] Macdonald's belief in structure was his "opposite theory," and he never began writing a novel until he had the entire structure planned. He would fill spiral notebooks with sketches of relationships, events, motivations—and, in the margins, question himself about plausibilities. Gradually the notebooks would become drafts, and the drafts would be taken to his typist to become the typescripts sent to his editor at Knopf. He wrote mainly in the afternoon, carefully but steadily; he was a writer of stamina rather than inspiration, of solid wholes rather than flashy parts.

Further using Chandler to distinguish his own practice, Macdonald repeatedly insisted, even to his own potential detriment, that as a novelist he had no interest in individual character except as it had a contributing part to play in the overall structure of a novel:

> Everything is controlled by the structure of the book, really, but the structure of the book is created to a great extent by the sense of the character. The sense of character is one of the basic drives, one of the basic energies, that makes the structure of a book, and I suppose sometimes a book will start with an inkling or a conception of a character and then I have to find out what the book about

the character is. Generally, though, I don't start out with a character, I start out with an idea, which is generally a moral situation. (Nelson, 10A-1)

"Moral situation," for Macdonald, meant more than violation of a written ordinance or even a religious commandment. Morality, for the secular Macdonald, was embedded in the expressive structures that cultures used to tell stories and make sense out of panic and chaos. The audience at large knew the moral because it knew the structure in its collective consciousness by virtue of having told itself certain stories over and over: The beautiful daughter of the king will face false suitors before she finds the true one. Young men who wish to rise above their station will be rejected, initially, until they prove their mettle. Freud put the family at the intimate center of this cultural process, for kings and queens, their daughters and sons stand in for the family and the drama of membership. A "mandarin" like James Joyce or Samuel Beckett might devise a structure so intensely convoluted that only a special disciple would or could find the way through.[11] In Macdonald's scheme, such rarefied literary performances failed in their duty to reinforce the public's moral sense of itself because they moved the structure out of common ground and into an elite refuge.

Choosing an example from his own work, Macdonald cited Albert Graves's murder of his client, Ralph Sampson, and his misdirected desire to marry Sampson's young daughter, Miranda, in *The Moving Target* (Nelson, 5A-4). Graves's actions are meaningful both in content and in form, for the audience will know that to kill is wrong and will further recognize the path to transgression, because Graves, over forty years of age, usurps the formal role of the "young" man justly entitled to marry the rich man's daughter after surviving a series of challenges. Using this early and elementary example from his first Archer novel (1949), Macdonald argues for the inherent moral content of narrative form and, by necessity, for the writer's moral obligation to honor such forms in their entirety. "Truth is within a context or within a form," Macdonald insists (Nelson, 22A-1). And the number of these forms is both limited and well-known; persons in the general population may not be able to name Freud's catalog of forms, but they live them.

This is just the sort of tight-quarters challenge that prompted Macdonald to select the detective novel for his life's work. Feeling, as he did once he began to reflect consciously on his life circumstances, that a human being could be dealt only so many permutations of the cards in fate's deck, it was obligatory for the artist who spoke to and for all human beings to trim his imagination to the finite number of narrative forms.

There is another, autobiographical, reason for Macdonald's emphasis on form. One of the most familiar structures both in the lived experience of any people and in the stories told and retold at all levels of sophistication is the loss or denial of the father. The plot of Oedipus is retold in *Hamlet* and again in the novels of D. H. Lawrence, whom Macdonald read at a crossroads in his college years. Macdonald acknowledged that the loss of the father was the central structure of his own life:

> Well, it's really the basic, the original story of my life. My original sin, so to speak, was to be left by my father when I was going on four and there's no doubt at all that that's why the subject is so personally important to me. But you see the personal importance when you work on it imaginatively over the years becomes something more than personal, it becomes almost—well, it doesn't become more than personal, but it becomes what might be called a personal myth rather than a personal experience. . . .
>
> But it's sort of my central area, and it's the central original fact of my life, so to speak. You see, I'm not just talking about what happened when I was four, I'm talking about what happened throughout my childhood. And the theme and similar themes have been reinforced by my experiences as an adult, and as a father, and as a grandfather. (Nelson, 6A-3)

Macdonald's tortured syntax, the false turns and self-corrections in his explanation, mirror the tortured process by which being left by an adult when you are only four years old becomes an "original sin," and then by working and reworking becomes a structure larger than experience: a myth. Only by suffering experience and doubling that suffering by working it into myth does, in Macdonald's view, the private person become the public artist. The way being wronged becomes being guilty and the way guilt brews over time—but not beyond memory and recovery—evolves into the situation, or case, that Lew Archer investigates.

John Macdonald Millar (1873–1933), the novelist's own father, was a rover who failed as a newspaper editor in California and the Canadian Northwest before taking up other occupations. He was working as an editor in Los Gatos, California, when his only son to survive infancy, Kenneth, was born in 1915. By the end of the decade the elder Millar was a harbor pilot in Vancouver, British Columbia, and some of the son's most vivid memories (and some of the most harrowing dreams in his old age) involve town life in Vancouver: the sounds and smells of the sea, the tang in the air left by his father's pipe, his sheer physical presence standing close to the helm as his father piloted a tugboat. These intense physical memories return in *The Galton Case* (1959), a frankly autobiographical novel, when Lew Archer opens a dead man's suitcase and inhales the mingled odors of the man's loneliness and the salt sea.

Macdonald raised his father to mythic stature by skirting abandonment and remembering him through the archetype of James Fenimore Cooper's Natty Bumppo, a white man who in his younger days spurned the comforts of civilization and lived in the wilderness with Indians (Kaye, 30–31). The elder Millar, in his son's mythic reconstruction, stepped out of the epic story of the

Canadian Northwest, a bringer of poetry into the wilderness just as one of his father's friends, the Canadian painter John Innes (1863–1941), brought the wilderness myth to life in history painting.[12] "My father was a poet," Millar claimed in tribute decades after his death, all memories of abandonment forgotten or repressed (Kaye, 29). And he further paid tribute by using his father's name in the various stages of his own pen name: John Macdonald, John Ross Macdonald, and finally Ross Macdonald.

The son could love his father only by wrapping him in a myth, a structure; not by facing the actual wandering man who deserted son and wife and left them to wander, as poor relations, from one dour kinsman to another. In fact, Macdonald used the writer part of his father to blur the wanderer part. Apropos of life and writing, Macdonald often gave similar statements: "Fiction is a handling of pain" (Kaye, 33), and the original pain is being left behind.[13] The essentially tortured birthright of father to son is summed up in a scene that Macdonald described at his father's deathbed. Suffering the debilitating effects of a series of strokes—the vascular condition that Macdonald himself would suffer (gout and high blood pressure) in his adult years as a kind of physical "constant"—John Macdonald Millar returned to Kitchener, Ontario, to die in the charity ward of a public hospital. There he was visited by his high-school-aged son, who would slip into the hospital on the sly so as not to be seen by his classmates. He was publicly ashamed of, but privately attached to, his father. Crippled, shaky, unable to talk, the elder Millar wrote out his last words to his son, but the marks on the paper were all but indecipherable.[14] When Macdonald in the late 1940s tried to write the autobiographical novel of his own life, which he called *Winter Solstice*, he repeated the theme of inscrutability: he never let a publisher see the manuscript (Kaye, 24).[15]

Macdonald's childhood, full of misery and anxiety, forms the thematic center of the reciprocal structures of his life and fiction. Archer is consistently involved in cases in which he tries either to put a family back together or to understand how it came apart. He acknowledged that the search for the lost father "recurs through all my books, beginning with *The Moving Target* and before the Archer series ever started in *Blue City*" (Kaye, 55). In fact, rooting his early growth as a writer in his reading of Charles Dickens's *Oliver Twist*, Macdonald further enmeshed his own youth in the story of the abandoned son. In a real sense for Macdonald, Dickens's own unhappy childhood and the unhappy childhood of his character reinforced the archetypal structure of the unhappy childhood that prefigures the writer. Structure, both lived and aesthetic, gave shape and meaning to MacDonald's life by seeming to appear wherever he looked. What you lived you could read about; what you read about you could, in turn, use to understand your lived life. "An unhappy childhood," he said, "is practically indispensable to a writer of fiction. You don't have the impulse to write fiction on a large scale and spend your life at it unless (1) you have been hurt, hurt into expression in a way that most people are not, and (2) [you are] somewhat distanced by experience from the 'joys and sorrows of life'" (Kaye, 21). Each time Macdonald used the missing father structure in his novels, he reapplied myth to his own life, incrementally merging actual experience with aesthetic form. This made the act of writing, for Macdonald, both real and imaginative, public and private, academic and vernacular, since we are each and all either sons or daughters in some kind of family intact or dispersed. As Macdonald put it in "Down These Streets a Mean Man Must Go": "A man's fiction, no matter how remote it may seem to be from the realistic or the autobiographical, is very much the record of his particular life. Gradually it may tend to become a substitute for the life."[16] But never an escape. It was a small step for Macdonald, in life and work, to accept Freudian psychiatry as a valid, universal structure since it is based so deeply on family interaction in the production of the relationships to others and the self that define consciousness:

> Of course I was psychiatrically oriented long before I talked to a psychiatrist [in 1957]. Freud was one of my early and most important masters. And not just Freud, I've read and been influenced by a lot of psychiatry. More than influenced by. It's been quite central in my life. I think the perceptions of modern psychiatry are just central for us. (Nelson, 5A-2)

Sometimes, as in his "failed" attempt to come to terms with his life in *Winter Solstice,* his autobiographical novel, the contours of the Freudian explanation were too searing to handle without a thicker heat shield of structure. Full self-confrontation was delayed until he underwent analysis in 1957, as part of his coming to terms with the troubles of his own daughter, which came to a head in 1956 and again in 1959. In less than a full year of therapy, Macdonald experienced (or forged) a liberation that, in his own view, showed the way to his greatest work. He ultimately came to think of modern psychology, informed by Freudian psychoanalysis, as the "modern mythology" (Nelson, 23B-1), the comprehensive myth into which all personal experience fits. Insofar as Freud, for better or worse, relied so heavily on Oedipal patterns of behavior—departed fathers, the power of the incest taboo, the return of the repressed—Macdonald also relied on them. In his Archer series he increasingly relied on psychoanalytic patterns to guide his detective's movements and analysis. In his doctoral dissertation, on Samuel Taylor Coleridge, he positions the Romantic poet/critic on the historical threshold between Thomas Aquinas (the last hero of the age of faith) and Sigmund Freud (the equally great hero who systematized knowledge in a secular age). And in the twinned story of his and his daughter's lives, which he wrote for his analyst in 1957, Macdonald is clinically frank about the way he acted as a carrier of neurosis from his own ruined youth to his daughter's.[17] In other words, he did not only know the Freudian paradigm as an intellectual hypothesis, he lived it as daily experience.

Closely connected with the loss-of-the-father myth was the place where Macdonald's father myth was enacted: the West, specifically California, and yet more specifically Southern California, the "island on the land," as Carey McWilliams[18] called it. In the works of Dashiell Hammett and Chandler, in later followers of Macdonald such as Sue Grafton, T. Jefferson Parker, and Michael Connelly, and especially in Hollywood's appropriation of all American places to itself, California has run the gamut from paradise to pseudo-place. In the long arc of Macdonald's novels, from World War II to the Bicentennial, California has been central to America's imagined identity, evolving from stereotypical "mean streets" into what writer Mike Davis calls an "ecology of fear,"[19] a site for confronting the multiform extinction of human life—by our own hands. Macdonald weathered a peripatetic childhood of suffering and shame, largely on his mother's Delphic promise that he had been born in California and was therefore entitled to its golden future:

> A lot of bad things happened to me in Canada—bad things in the sense of poverty and so on, being pushed around quite a bit from one place to another, one family to another, one house to another—and I was supported by the idea that, let's say, my life in Canada wasn't the only potential life I might have. Now of course it was more of a dream than a reality but the dream actually did come true so that lends it more validity than it would otherwise have. I did make my way back to the U.S. and became an American again. . . . And in fact a Californian. I came back home and sort of started over, and I did so not entirely by my own volition. (Nelson, 10A-3)

California, then, possesses a kind of super-psychic attractive power, drawing energy and individuals to it when personal experience loses the challenge to shape itself. Macdonald sensed California's power in and around his work. One of his foundational writers, F. Scott Fitzgerald, ended up in California after his crack-up. *The Great Gatsby,* like Dickens's *Oliver Twist,* gained importance as a "structure" in Macdonald's life and work because its author touched down in California and died there (Kaye, 1).

California, however, is mixed redemption, just as the dream of starting over is for Gatsby. "Starting over," the deep structure of the myth of California in the American imagination, is as often as not a temptation to trample on place and people. Nick Carraway indicts Tom and Daisy Buchanan in Fitzgerald's novel for trampling others simply because they have money but forgives Gatsby because the latter believed so completely and naively that wishing for a new life could make it so. Macdonald's novels are full of reinvented selves. Manuel Torres recreates himself in Hollywood as Lance Leonard in *The Barbarous Coast* (1956) and ends up dead. So does Pedro Domingo in *Black Money* (1966). Our sympathy for Ralph Sampson, the murdered man in *The Moving Target,* is chastened when we realize that he has exploited migrant workers to finance his new ego as the king of a California paradise. Jack Biemeyer, in *The Blue Hammer,* has mined a mammoth hole in Arizona, the proceeds of which buy him a secluded canyon home in Santa Teresa, Macdonald's fictional version of Santa Barbara. Similar "moral situations" keyed to place serve as covert and overt structures in each of Macdonald's Archer novels. The ways his suspects and victims connect physically to the California landscape—the houses they live in and the way these structures are engineered to touch the earth—often function as shorthand for moral and historical disconnectedness.

Macdonald the citizen loved the privileged part of California where he lived: Santa Barbara, the model for fictional Santa Teresa. Although he declined to believe the whole state was a model for the flowering of the future of American civilization, he clung to the myth of Santa Barbara as a Periclean remnant of classical culture in a miasma of sprawl (Nelson, 5A-1). Santa Barbara's size and its location, nestled between Pacific Ocean and mountains, protected it from the excesses that had poisoned the possibility of civilized life a hundred miles to the south in Los Angeles. In two late novels, *The Underground Man* and *Sleeping Beauty,* a forest fire and an oil spill, respectively, add environmental transgression to the formula for evil and break the spell of the enclave. Indeed, the heavy human tread on the fragile ecology of California can be heard much earlier—in, for example, in the steel forest of Homer Wycherly's oil derricks in *The Wycherly Woman* (1961) and in the predatory land acquisition and agricultural practices of Carl Hallman's father in *The Doomsters* (1958).

The edenic beauty of California—to which the myth of the second beginning naturally seems to fit—is deeply embedded in American mythology. European settlers who landed in Massachusetts and Virginia in the seventeenth century were drawn to the New World by the same myth of the new start. America's history of westward expansion, our "manifest destiny," is as much the story of the translation of the new-beginning myth by successive waves of western pilgrims as it is the story of the technological advance of steel rails, steam power, and the repeating rifle. For the first version of the American myth, Massachusetts Bay and Plymouth Rock function as the sacred spots, and John Winthrop and Cotton Mather are the spokesmen. For expansion westward from the seaboard, James Fenimore Cooper and Francis Parkman solidified the myth, and the lone hero with a gun became its icon.

When Macdonald claimed his birthright by moving to California permanently in 1946 and situating his literary life there, he knew he had to answer to senior writers who had defined the twentieth-century version of the myth of the new beginning and turned its gunfighter icon into the private eye. He had an advantage, though: his father had been the real thing.

There were two established writers of the myth of California in the genre of detective fiction, two who had effected the transformation of the plainsman into the urban gunslinger: Dashiell Hammett and Raymond Chandler. These

writers were both role models and icons to be replaced. "Weaker talents ideal-
ize," Harold Bloom has written in *The Anxiety of Influence,* "figures of capable
imagination appropriate for themselves."[20] Macdonald proved his own "capable imagination" in his engagement with his precursors by appropriating what
he needed and jettisoning the rest. But not without anxiety.

Hammett and Chandler were not the only precursors of Macdonald's "capable imagination." Fitzgerald, on the grounds that he had come to California to
begin again after his crack-up in the East, played this role for Macdonald, as
evidenced notably in *Black Money,* a novel that appropriates all the themes of
Fitzgerald's *The Great Gatsby.* Macdonald even included Frank Norris among
his California fathers, a Northern California novelist, not known widely beyond
graduate school seminars as the author of a statement of principles called "The
Responsibilities of the Novelist" and a novel, *The Octopus,* about the vast wheat
fields of the Central Valley and the industrial capital drawn to them. Norris
argued that "the People" had a kind of lien on the novelist's work. "It is all very
well to jeer at the People and at the People's misunderstanding of the arts," he
wrote, "but the fact is indisputable that no art that is not in the end understood
by the People can live or ever did live a single generation."[21]

Chandler and Hammett, however, occupy Macdonald's forebrain. To make
any beachhead at all in the detective novel genre, he knew he had to come to
terms with these two "masters." Macdonald was a disciplined, sometimes even
facile, imitator of established literary styles and genres. From his college years
until the debut of Archer in 1949, Macdonald "tried his hand at various forms"
ranging among "boy's life" didactic stories, satirical squibs, espionage novels,
autobiography, and scholarly dissertation (Kaye, 24). His engagements with
Hammett and Chandler, however, were neither experimental nor academic. He
struggled with his forerunners as Jacob struggled with the angel—for his very
name and standing. When he came to write detective fiction he had decided to
make it his genre by fitting himself into what he considered to be a serious literary tradition with longevity and popular recognition but with a potential only
he could exploit.

The nature of his engagement was, in other words, not merely a question of
besting Chandler at the net in a match of similes, nor of echoing Hammett's
tough-guy melancholy by rescuing Archer's name from the trivia bin (Miles
Archer is the name of Sam Spade's murdered partner in *The Maltese Falcon*).
Macdonald believed, and with scholarly rigor argued in "The Scene of the
Crime,"[22] that Hammett was more deserving than Chandler to hold the torch
for the American detective novel, and therefore it was Hammett Macdonald
located at the genesis of his development. Chandler achieved this distinction
only much later. Hammett had invested the form with moral meaning and sociological scope that his American predecessor, Poe, had only hinted at accom-
plishing. Poe's detective, C. Auguste Dupin, is an intellectual, detached from

"the People" and the lived experience of evil. He solves crimes as problems, not as ongoing narratives of human lives. Conan Doyle's Holmes, Macdonald granted, by virtue of his drug addiction and his brief infatuation with Irene Adler, was minimally more human than Dupin. But it was Hammett, the inventor of the detective novel's "hard-boiled" style and content, who declined to "hold the problem of evil at arm's length." Macdonald explains, "But Hammett does what Hemingway never attempted. He places his characters in complex situations, in great cities like San Francisco and New York and Baltimore, and allows them to work out their dubious salvations under social and economic and political pressures."[23] Chandler, Macdonald concluded, had failed to live up to the obligation of representing a wide range of "dubious salvations" situated in the diversity of public life. Hammett wrote from life, Macdonald told an interviewer in 1970, and Chandler wrote from literature (Kaye, 11). Frank Norris was called in for further support. "It is not now," he charged in "The Responsibilities of the Novelist," "a question of *esthetic* interest—that is, the artist's, the amateur's, the *cognoscente's*. It is a question of *vital* interest."[24] Macdonald reinforced his critical verdict with his own autobiographical record. As a lonely and troubled teenager, he had first read Hammett, and Hammett's prose had shown him a way out of his personal maelstrom. Chandler was a later acquisition, picked up when Macdonald was in college and graduate school (Nelson, 5A-4, 5B-1).

Macdonald harbored large ambitions for the Hammett and Chandler models. He obliged them to speak to "the People's" need for an image of its true character: its *"vital interest."* This is what he meant by testing the "colloquial" styles of his mentors, and what Eudora Welty confirmed in her foreword to *Self-Portrait.* The purpose of a colloquial tradition in a national literature, Macdonald explained (possessing perhaps the zeal of the convert, since he did not seize his Americanness until he was an adult), was "to carry over into fiction the oral tradition, the spoken language which is actually the carrier of our social and cultural meanings. It's what people say to each other in their own tone of voice that really counts in life and if you get such a tone of voice and a sense of actual speech in your writing, you've got something better than literary prose" (Kaye, 39). Macdonald dreamed of "a classless society where there will be one language spoken by all men so that they can understand each other. Such a dream requires a language in print which is not so different from the way men talk. People should read a book and recognize themselves talking in that book. . . . In order to perpetuate and maintain and glorify the language, which is the highest product of any civilization, you have to write fiction in which the language is written more or less as it is spoken" (Kaye, 39). Ultimately, to paraphrase Macdonald further, the work of fiction fulfills a public yet metaphysical purpose by bringing into palpable reality the sense of community to which, he believed, all men aspire in their social relationships. Hammett fulfilled this democratic mission; Chandler took a kind of *"esthetic"* road and cut himself off from "the People." Hammett's colloquial style "is a clean useful prose, with remarkable range and force. It has pace and point, strong tactile values, the rhythms and colors of speech, all in the colloquial tradition that stretches from Mark Twain through Stephen Crane to [Ring] Lardner and Mencken, the Dr. Johnson of our vernacular." Chandler's Marlowe, by contrast, is democratic at one remove; he speaks "an overheard democratic prose."[25]

Hammett served yet another vital purpose for Macdonald: he connected the writer, through American literary images, to his own elusive father. We have already seen that Macdonald mythologized his father as a latter-day Natty Bumppo of the American and Canadian Northwest. Macdonald identified Hammett's detective-hero as Natty Bumppo as well:

> Shorn and urbanized, he became in Hammett's best novels a near-tragic figure, a lonely and suspicious alien who pits a hopeless but obstinate animal courage against the metropolitan jungle, a not very moral man who clings with a skeptic's desperation to a code of behavior empirically arrived at in a twilight world between chivalry and gangsterism.[26]

Rather than remember his own father as the man who abandoned wife and son for whimsical or self-serving purposes, Macdonald invests him with the qualities he admired in Hammett and his heroes. One of those heroes in particular, Sam Spade, Macdonald sees as a vehicle for Hammett's "radical philosophy" of rejecting and satirizing the modern, urbanized (San Francisco) "values" in which he had to live. Hammett, the literary father, and John Macdonald Millar, the biological one, merge in the son's imagination: "I'm sure it was the radicalism of the area that took my father there and caused me to be born in the San Francisco area" (Nelson, 21A-1). Macdonald's projection of his distant father's radical philosophy, of which the son knew but little, suggests that Hammett was just as important autobiographically as he was literarily. Macdonald used Hammett as the hammer to nail down with one stroke literary and autobiographical structures.

Circles, like the one that runs through Hammett, John Macdonald Millar, and Kenneth Millar were far from mirages of coincidence to the son and writer. Indeed, one of the constants of Macdonald's life and work was return, movement along a line that seemed straight, only to curve like Einstein's universe and "repossess" the past in the present. In his introduction to *Archer in Jeopardy,* a collection of three novels published in 1979—his last published title—Macdonald acknowledged: "The underlying theme of many of my novels, as I read them now, is the migration of a mind from one place and culture to another. Its purpose, like the dominant purpose of my young life, was to repossess my American birthplace by imaginative means and heal the schizophrenic pain."[27] He candidly admitted that he repeated basic plot structures in his novels: lost sons in *The Far Side of the Dollar, The Goodbye Look,* and *The Underground Man;* lost daughters in *The Way Some People Die, The Wycherly Woman,* and *Sleeping Beauty.* A "cynic," he imagined, might say he had only one fundamental novel that he wrote over and over" (Kaye, 55).

But the pattern of departure and return comforted Macdonald. He was reassured by a strong presence of circles in his own life. Born in California, he traversed a long-arcing circle back there when the navy sent him to San Diego in 1944. There, before Kenneth's birth farther north in 1915, his parents had buried a child who had died at or very soon after birth. Becoming a writer in California repeated his father's abandoned career as newspaperman and sometime poet in the same state. The death of his only daughter, Linda, by cerebral hemorrhage in 1970, repeated his mother's death by the same cause in 1936. The circle is perhaps the immemorial structure, repeating itself from womb to cosmos. Macdonald was comfortable in the circle of his life's work:

> Over a long period of time, the novelist writing a book is a man who is willing to wait for his effects, wait for his payoff and make the reader wait too. This has been characteristic of my life and I've spent a great deal of my life waiting and working towards a distant goal. The tendency has been to pick up loose ends and complete circles that have been begun. An arc of a circle leaves me unsatisfied. I ultimately want to complete the full circle, and, of course, I'll complete the fullest circle of all when I die. (Kaye, 73)

Ross Macdonald imposed a great literary and autobiographical burden on a form that had, he believed, been underused and undervalued by the public. He made a passionate but deliberate decision at the beginning of his professional life that the detective genre harbored potential that had not been fulfilled, although excellent writers from Poe to Raymond Chandler had worked the lode. And he had the writer's faith that the detective novel could and should do what any good novel in the traditions of fiction did: "give a picture of life as it is lived over a period of time and span of space" (Kaye, 44). He knew what he was doing when he set out. Macdonald possessed the intellectual scope and depth, the dedication, and the stamina to take a so-called minor genre and "make 'literature' of it."

"An Unhappy Childhood Is Practically Indispensable"

"Happy families are all alike," so begins Tolstoy's *Anna Karenina;* "every unhappy family is unhappy in its own way."[1] Ross Macdonald's collected works might be engraved with an even more sobering epitaph: "Unhappy families are all alike; even happy families are unhappy most of the time." But, spinning lead into gold in his Archer novels, Macdonald transformed a truly unhappy childhood into the foundation for his fiction.

Born in Los Gatos, California, December 13, 1915, Kenneth Millar was the first and only surviving child of John Macdonald Millar and Anna Moyer Millar (1874–1936). His parents had been married September 13, 1909, in Calgary, Alberta, and thereafter "Jack" Millar and his wife, trained as a nurse, led a peripatetic life up and down the West Coast from British Columbia to San Diego County. One of Kenneth's older siblings who had died in infancy was buried near San Diego, the mythic California territory of Helen Hunt Jackson's novel *Ramona* (1884). Jack Millar had tried and failed to publish a small local newspaper there. Business failure and personal sorrow sent the parents on the road.

Determined to follow his own father's (the novelist's grandfather's) profession of publishing a newspaper, Jack took his wife north to the Bay Area. His fortunes seemed to have turned when his son, Kenneth, was born in 1915. Jack Millar's poem "To Kennie's Mother on receipt of Kennie's photo, 1916," three ballad stanzas of iambic tetrameter, was published in the Los Gatos paper Millar edited. Jack wrote, his only son recalled, in the bonnie rhythms of Robert Burns.[2] The first stanza of the poem marks a high point in family harmony:

> Few men are blest as I have been
> Though gilded stores have been withheld.
> This wondrous gift of perfect love
> Is Life's own evidence fulfilled.[3]

Before marrying Anna Moyer, daughter of a clan of Pennsylvania Mennonites who had migrated to Ontario, Jack Millar, whose folk had settled the Bruce Peninsula in Lake Huron, also in Ontario, led the bully life of a frontiersman among the Indians and hunters of the Northwest. He is said, by his son, to have accompanied "The Painter of the Canadian West," John Innes (1863–1941), on one of the artist's sorties into the romantic British Columbia wilderness. If so, Jack Millar must have come back gilded by the association. Innes was a legendary figure. Like his contemporary Theodore Roosevelt, Innes was larger than life. In his twenties Innes ranched in Alberta, lived with the Blackfoot Indians, started and lost small-town, frontier newspapers (like Jack Millar), went off with Canadian troops to the Boer War in 1902 and came home decorated. In the teens and twenties of the new century he returned to the West, expanded his cartooning skill into historical painting, and is known in Western Canada as the creator of several series of historical paintings commemorating the romance of exploration and the stirring enterprise of commerce.[4] If Millar's father was a minor player in the epic of the Canadian West, Innes, his father's friend, was a titan.

Heroic stature once removed could not guarantee domestic happiness. In 1919, the Millar marriage was close to crack-up. Jack had given up the newspaper life for an undomestic life of adventure. He became a harbor pilot in Vancouver, British Columbia, and one of Kennie's most vivid memories is holding the helm of a harbor boat with the bulk and smell and sound of his father hovering over him. He remembers, too, the diversity of the playmates the port city and wharf life supplied: a source, he later speculated, of his democratic (small d) politics (Kaye, 30–31). The year 1919 was the last one in which the Millars lived together as a family.

After the crack-up of their marriage, Jack stayed in the West for a time, and Anna Millar took her four-year-old son back to Kitchener, Ontario, where her strict and poor Mennonite relatives took them in, seasoning their charity with a sense of resentment that her son was never able to purge. Years later he was to remark ruefully that he "must be the only American crime novelist who got his early ethical training in a Canadian Mennonite Sunday School."[5] In fact, when Archer comes of age as a moral detective, his pronouncements more often than not mirror early lessons: the hope of mercy deferred over the certainty of justice and suffering.

Kitchener became the Dickensian, coal-fired, industrial, cloud-shrouded, cheerless city that embodied all that was desperate, terrifying, and dehumanizing in the broken modern life Macdonald portrayed in his later work: the dystopia to the California utopia. Whenever Archer leaves sun-washed California for the purgatory of a trip to the Midwest, particularly in *The Galton Case* (1959) and *The Chill* (1963), it is to a version of satanic Kitchener and its grotesquely miserable souls that he goes. No doubt when he read *Oliver Twist* at the age of eight, it was not only the model of Dickens as professional author but also Oliver's life in the blacking factory that seemed to fit Macdonald's experience and memory. The past was nothing to go back to—or seemed so to the young Kenneth Millar. Jack Millar could stomach none of that past, either, and so was reluctant to return to Ontario. His son was torn by sharing his father's rejection of the urban hell yet resenting his father's distance from him. That psychic fissure between love and resentment focused the anger Macdonald remembered as the constant temperature of his youth.

For the first couple of years in Kitchener, Macdonald attended Mennonite Sunday school and absorbed a moral and spiritual dourness along with material poverty. Anna Millar had converted to Christian Science but seems to have taken the "scientific" aspect of her new religion off into the territory of sideshow "cures." In one revision of his autobiographical novel *Winter Solstice,* completed after his military service in World War II, Macdonald includes an episode in which a Dickensian character named Dr. Roderick Cantell demonstrates his healing lamp, the Cantellamp, which "transmutes the murderous rays which devastated Hiroshima into health-giving, life-giving power."[6] The Cantellamp succeeds only in blowing a houseful of fuses, and the boy who narrates the story is plunged into darkness and shame that his mother could entertain a charlatan.

Poverty grew so desperate that Anna Millar actually took her young son to the gates of an orphanage in 1921, only to give in to the boy's cries and return to their mean rooms for another try. Kenneth was rescued from Kitchener relatives for two years by his father's cousin Rob (Uncle Rob) Millar who still lived on the Bruce Peninsula, territory that the Millar clan had settled when they emigrated from Scotland. Uncle Rob was the town electrician in Millarton and on weekends the projectionist for the only movie palace in town. In those years, the early 1920s, Kenneth grew to like Uncle Rob and the silent films he showed every weekend. Actress Pearl White and serial melodramas like *Plunder* were his favorites.[7] The *Boy's Life* idyll was cut short In 1925, however, when Rob's wife died unexpectedly during an operation. Kenneth had no choice but to return to his mother's Mennonite kin in the city.

The bull market of the 1920s raised many boats, and one held young Kenneth Millar. His mother's sister, Aunt Laura, rising on the economic tide, volunteered to pay her nephew's way back out west, to Medicine Hat, Alberta, and there to enroll him in St. John's, an Anglican private school, the poshest school he had yet seen. Macdonald remembered St. John's for reinforcing in him the difference between haves and have-nots. He was always conscious of being among the latter, and his shame and resentment boiled beneath the surface. He vented his anger, he recalled, by doing some things he was ashamed even to remember until psychoanalysis freed him in middle age: he stole, drank, smoked, and engaged in what he called homosexual contacts with other students. He considered most of his youthful vices ordinary except the last, which left a thick residue of shame. When he adopted the detective genre as his profession in 1949, he had to take with it its inherent homophobia. Macdonald was customarily cruel to his gay and effeminate characters; not until the final Archer novel, *The Blue Hammer* (1976), did he call for tolerance.

The stock market crash in 1929 sent him back to Ontario, where he graduated from high school (Kitchener Collegiate Institute, where he would later teach) in 1932. Disorder and sorrow followed him as usual, but sardonically mixed with threads of good fortune. His father, broken in health at the age of fifty-nine, had come back to Kitchener to be cared for in the charity wards of the local hospitals. He had suffered a series of strokes that serially destroyed all his faculties. His son kept his father's condition and even his presence in Kitchener concealed from his peers. But Jack was still fond of Kennie and surprisingly provident, too, for an adventurer and itinerant poet: when he died in 1933 his son was informed of a life insurance policy with a benefit of two thousand dollars, just enough to pay for four years of college. Not exactly the "gilded stores" Jack Millar had envisioned at his son's birth, but enough for the moment.

Kenneth enrolled in Waterloo College, one of the affiliated colleges of the University of Western Ontario, and majored in English and history. In his sophomore year, 1935, he came home from classes to discover his mother naked on the kitchen floor. Anna Moyer, it was later determined, had suffered a cerebral hemorrhage. When she died soon after, Kenneth took a year's sabbatical from college and, funded by a small inheritance from his mother—another cruel surprise—set sail for England, Ireland, and the continent. He was in Munich in 1936, watching a Nazi rally, when a Hitler supporter, interpreting the foreigner's continuing to puff a pipe as the Fuhrer motored by as a sign of disrespect, knocked the pipe out of Millar's mouth and roughed him up. Millar used the episode in his first novel, *The Dark Tunnel* (1944), in which a American professor breaks up a Nazi spy ring at a university in the Midwest. Literature is often the best revenge. On his way back to Canada, he flirted with the idea of going to Spain to fight against the fascists with the Abraham Lincoln Brigade. It was the thing for young, committed liberals to do, but he was unable to arrange transport.

Millar returned to college a world-traveled young man who had brushed up against the headlines. Before leaving on his sabbatical, he had met Margaret Sturm, a brilliant student in classics, the daughter of a well-to-do coal merchant in Kitchener. Both aspired to become writers and both placed their first publications in their high-school student magazine, *The Grumbler.* Millar had, perhaps not wholly facetiously, invited Margaret to go with him when he took his *Wanderjahr* in 1935–36. She declined. But their relationship resumed when Millar returned, and they were married on June 2, 1938, the day after Millar graduated from Waterloo College. He commemorated the event by using June 2 as Lew Archer's birthday.

Both his mother and father had told him repeatedly that he was a U.S. citizen by virtue of his birth in California, but he had traveled to Europe on a

Canadian passport. Jack's "testament" to his son, written in 1928 when he came back to Kitchener too old to wander the Far West, begins: "Kenneth Millar. Birth registered at Los Gatos, California. 1915. At 21 you can claim U.S. citizenship by right of birth. It has advantages."[8] Those"advantages," however, seemed mostly imaginary in the FDR 1930s when the United States appeared unable to take care of most of the citizens already within its borders. Material circumstances never dimmed the myth, however. The narrator of Millar's autobiographical novel, *Winter Solstice*, cherishes the idea of California as "a land of light" beyond the acrid and dark Canadian city of his purgatory. But he never makes the trip.

Millar, fresh B.A. degree in hand in 1938, applied for a graduate fellowship to Harvard. It was not forthcoming, but in the process he learned again that U.S. citizenship was his for the asking; he need only supply a legal birth certificate. Millar, now a husband and a citizen of both Canada and the United States, took a job teaching at his old high school and spent summers in Ann Arbor doing graduate work in English at the University of Michigan. On June 18, 1939, his one and only child, a daughter, Linda, was born.

Teacher, graduate student, husband, father: As if these multiple obligations were not enough, Millar also began to make himself a professional writer. He tried almost every form a publication would pay to print. He sent the *New Yorker* an Ogden Nash–type satirical poem on world leaders from Neville Chamberlain to Chiang Kai-Shek. The editors returned it; after all, they already had the real Nash. He tried a ballad about Paul Bunyan and Babe, the Blue Ox. It, too, came back. A few years later, he tried a poem on the Detroit race riot of 1943. None of the poems made a dime, but Macdonald kept them in his archive.

Short fiction and essays seemed, however, most likely to bring in the money that he needed to supplement the meager salary of a high-school teacher. He wrote and began to place boys' and girls' outdoor stories with morally didactic conclusions in *The Canadian Boy* and *The Canadian Girl*. He sent a Poe-esque story, "The Red Parrot," to the pulp *Strange Stories* in 1939. He tried *Collier's*, *Onward*, *Story*, *Saturday Evening Post*, *Esquire*, Mencken's *American Mercury*, and others with all sorts of stories: sophisticated high-society vignettes, gothic tales, psychologically realistic stories of character, O. Henry–type stories with neatly tailored endings. He had perhaps his most consistent good luck with the hip Toronto magazine of satire and humor, *Saturday Night*.

Millar compiled an amazing record of rejections and acceptances, all written while teaching full-time at Kitchener Collegiate Institute, parenting an infant daughter, and spending his summers in graduate school at the University of Michigan. No doubt he felt a motivating kick when his wife, writing as Margaret Millar, completed a novel, *The Invisible Worm* (1941), during a few months of rest and recuperation following the birth of their daughter. It was to be the first of her more than two dozen novels of mystery and psychological suspense. For more than a decade after her first novel, Margaret Millar was the writing spouse with the critical reputation and royalty checks. Her novel *The Iron Gates* (1945) was optioned by Warner Bros. and took Margaret Millar to Hollywood as a studio writer while her husband served (and wrote fiction) in the Pacific.

Millar tried full-time graduate work in English when the combination of summers in Ann Arbor and teaching high school in Kitchener became onerous, but he was never keen on becoming a university professor. Millar was an accomplished graduate student with bright promise, but he soon saw that university professors in the war and postwar years had to subsist on high prestige but meager wages. In those years the profession was rigidly hierarchical, and although Macdonald liked structure as a novelist he preferred more liberty as a worker. Moreover, he wanted a wider audience than the faculty office, classroom, and professional symposium could provide. When World War II interrupted his graduate studies, Millar was anxious to break the boundaries of academia. He served as a communications officer in the U.S. Navy from 1943 to 1946. He wrote two novels—espionage thrillers, self-consciously tailored to the genre—during off-duty hours in cramped shipboard quarters. Discharged in 1946, he tried a psychological suspense novel, the genre in which his wife excelled. He went back to graduate school, over his spouse's objections, to finish his dissertation on Coleridge, not so much to prepare himself for a professorial career as to clear his agenda of an unfinished project. In the process of writing about Coleridge he wrote three Lew Archer novels, the first of which, *The Moving Target*, Alfred Knopf published in 1949.

Millar's career as a novelist did not run as neatly from imagination to publication as his wife's did. In hindsight, of course, it seems that anyone would have recognized Lew Archer as a classic from the opening sentence, but Millar did not take to the detective novel right away and was not sure of Archer's staying power during the first several years of the series. Before Archer appeared in *The Moving Target*, Millar published two espionage novels; a third, titled "Return to Berlin," cowritten with James Hans Meisel, a member of the University of Michigan faculty when Millar was finishing his dissertation, was never published. Millar then tried a realistic novel in the manner of Hammett's *Red Harvest: Blue City* (1947). A psychological suspense novel, *The Three Roads*, followed, and then the autobiographical novel he felt to be almost obligatory, *Winter Solstice*. He abandoned it as "pretty hopeless" before *The Moving Target* was published in 1949 (Kaye, 24).

The espionage novels are deeply invested in the genre and the politics of the 1930s and World War II. John Buchan's *The 39 Steps* (1915) was a particular influence since Buchan was a Canadian; it pits the lone, heroic, and reluctant amateur against organized foreign agents and obtuse homeland security. Graham Greene's "entertainments," such as *The Confidential Agent* (1939) and *The*

Ministry of Fear (1943) appealed to the young writer because Greene wove ethics and cultural debate into the tried and true pattern of suspense. In Millar's debut, *The Dark Tunnel* (1944), Robert Branch, a young professor at a university modeled on the University of Michigan, smashes a ring of Nazi spies in the Midwest. There is, of course, a femme fatale, lost when Branch (smoldering after some of the same indignities Millar had had to swallow in 1936) flees Munich, but found again in the final pages when Branch cracks an elaborate cross-dressing scheme by which Nazi agents have infiltrated the United States. There is an evil German professor, a strong and handsome FBI agent who rescues Branch, and casting-call Nazis with evil white Aryan hair, green eyes, and homosexual proclivities that jab Branch in his macho solar plexus. A reviewer found it "a thrilling story told with consummate skill."[9]

In *Trouble Follows Me* (1946), Branch metamorphoses into Ensign Sam Drake. Drake can quote Stevie Smith's poetry (*Trouble*, 34) while cracking a ring of "Jap" spies who have eluded the FBI. In the process, Sam ponders some of the events of his time—the Detroit race riot of 1943, African nationalism as an answer to "the Negro problem" in the United States, and the evil that seems to lurk in the mysterious allure of women. Tall, blonde Mary Thompson turns out to be a black widow, a Japanese agent in an all-American body: "I saw that like all true criminals she was abnormal. Part of her sensibility was missing and part of her mind was blank. She could not see herself as evil or depraved. Her ego stood between her and the rest of the world like a distorting lens" (*Trouble*, 202).

As she holds a gun on Sam, Mary is shot to death by a disaffected African American, Hector Land, dupe of Japanese agents who manipulate him with the false promises of black nationalism as the remedy for racial insults. Then, as Land turns his gun on Sam, the hero must shoot him—a grand blood-letting climax releasing floods of ethnic, racial, and sexual anxieties. Ensign Kenneth Millar, writing all of this aboard the USS. *Shipley Bay* "somewhere in the Pacific" in 1945, made no claims to great literature: "It's going to be a strange book," he wrote to his stateside wife on April 12, 1945. "I don't like it but I'm sort of fascinated by it—a mixture of sex, action, the negro problem, love, tragedy, melodrama, about five murders, in some places quite good writing, and farce. God knows what to make of it, I don't."[10] As long as it was "good enough . . . for the trade," Millar was satisfied; getting started as a writer was his overriding purpose.

A more accurate prediction of Millar's future literary course was his next published novel, *Blue City* (1947). *Blue City* is just as violent, homophobic, and macho as the early espionage novels, but Millar's consciousness of paying a debt to a particular writer, Dashiell Hammett, whom he took as a model, partially rescues *Blue City* from the oblivion that has generously engulfed the earlier novels.[11] Hammett's first novel for Knopf, *Red Harvest* (1929), is very similar in hero, plot, and title. The Continental Op, Hammett's precursor to Sam Spade, has been called to Personville, a mining town filthy with smelter smoke, labor tension, and ownership corruption. The Op rechristens the town "Poisonville" and undertakes a complete purging and reformation, sometimes straying outside the law to accomplish the redemption.

The precedent of *Red Harvest* gave Millar an opening. *Blue City,* he confessed, was a conduit for "a lot of anger in me"—anger at the city where he had suffered the indignities of poverty growing up and the hierarchy that pressed its will upon him (Nelson, 5A-4). Taking on Hammett's influence deliberately for the first time, Millar channels his anger into a redemptive plot and literary project he felt would be publicly useful: "It was certainly an expression of anger, although there was more in it than anger, there were positive elements, too" (Nelson, 5A-4). The "positive elements" are not just those that helped Millar direct his anger at specific targets—targets more real than a ring of cardboard Nazi spies working on the faculty of a midwestern university. With *Blue City,* Millar began to explore ways to graft popular literary form and what he called "colloquial" language to the main trunk of literary history he had studied as a graduate student. *Blue City* is "Hammettesque, to put it mildly" (Nelson, 5A-4), but it is also Hamlet-esque because Macdonald tries to weld hard-boiled and hard-hitting realism to the one of the most familiar plots in English literature: Hamlet. At times the welds are awkward, but most of the time the novel works.

Johnny Weather, the estranged son of the "blue city's" deceased kingpin, J. D. Weather, returns to the midwestern industrial city of his birth to avenge his father's murder and to come to psychological terms with blemishes on his father's character. Like the son of wandering Jack Millar, Johnny Weather simultaneously loves and hates his father. J. D. controlled the slot machines in the blue city, and had, like biblical Abraham, put away his first wife (Johnny's mother) and replaced her with a trophy wife, Floraine. Yet, in spite of his immersion in the rackets, J. D. was loyal to the have-nots (34–35). Johnny seems fated to relive his father's socially responsible side, for the first thing he does after hitchhiking into town is to defend one of the dispossessed against the power structure, embodied in a couple of bullying cops (13–14).

Parts of the mythology with which Millar surrounded his own father, especially the "radical philosophy" that linked him (in the son's imagination) with Hammett, come into play in *Blue City.* As in Hammett's works, the fault line in civic honor runs through its official custodians, the police: some are good and some not so good. Above the dividing line, virtue gives out and power corrupts; below the line, virtue is where you find it and there is no power except hand-me-down power to corrupt the downtrodden. Johnny Weather works his way up from below the line to the puppeteers at the top.

The prime suspect in the murder of J. D. Weather—the Claudius to Hamlet's murdered father—is the man who supplanted Johnny's father in the local rackets and in the bed of his stepmother. For a name, Millar gives him an abrupt monosyllable, Kerch. As a character, Kerch is a primer of simplistic vices. His physique symbolizes an inner, moral flaccidity: his flesh is sickly white and "bovine." "In spite of his huge head and torso his legs were very short and his feet were tiny" (85). His dandyism calls attention to the illegitimacy of his power. The royal purple of his silk tie accentuates the crime behind his illegitimate claim to the "throne" of Johnny's father (81). His sexuality is repellent: One of the bar girls, compelled to endure Kerch's attentions, compares him to a frog because of his bulbous eyes (67). Johnny, like Hamlet, is disgusted morally and sexually by the man who has eclipsed his father.

Kerch's body is not the sole reason for Johnny's repulsion. Millar harbored a lot of anger at himself for homosexual episodes in his youth, and he used *Blue City* and other early novels to exorcise the guilt. Kerch's henchmen are sexually "abnormal." Johnny instantly identifies Garland, Kerch's enforcer, as homosexual when he interrupts him and another gang member, Joey Sault, en flagrante. Their stag party "sounded like a kennel, though some of the voices were lap-dog voices, high and querulous" (54). Garland is the type of epicene "fag" that the early Millar, and his model Hammett, could seldom resist bashing. Garland's thin and delicate features and his "lilting" voice drive Johnny to the brink of sadism (55). Johnny cannot contain his disgust, calling Garland "Gloria" to taunt him (59). When the two meet later in the novel, Johnny beats Garland with special ferocity (137). Some of the homophobia comes with the genre; Hammett's Spade cruelly tortures Joel Cairo and "the boy" Wilmer in *The Maltese Falcon*. But much of the homophobia in Millar's early novels fends off private guilt, too. Not until his last novel almost thirty years later, *The Blue Hammer*, does Macdonald begin to redress the balance by allowing Archer to argue, albeit silently, for tolerance of a gay relationship.

Women characters fall into the stereotyping mill too. Floraine, Johnny's stepmother, plays the Gertrude role at full sexual volume. She sets out to seduce her stepson on their first meeting, almost as if she cannot help herself: "She leaned forward to touch my knee, and I could see the single young line made by the separation of her breasts in the V of her neckline" (31). Johnny resists, not solely because of the incest taboo, but also because signs of death and decay cluster around Floraine as if she were Medusa herself: "She seemed neither shocked nor displeased. She leaned back in her low chair and stretched her arms over her head. Her live, stirring body in that still room was like a snake in a sealed tomb, fed by unhealthy meat" (32). Floraine's polluted sexuality is typical of the misogyny integral to the hard-boiled style and imagination. To the perennial question "What does woman want?" the perennial answer is "To devour men." Millar was not alone in sensationalizing the female character as devourer. James M. Cain was responsible for several of the most memorable maneaters of the time; Ensign Millar had seen the film version of *Double*

Indemnity (with screenplay by Raymond Chandler) several times while at sea in 1945.

The "moll" in the hard-boiled genre has few options between a heart of gold and poisonous treachery. Millar grants Floraine some Shakespearean overtones, though, and in showing her literary mercy he gives an early indication of the blend of popular and academic discourse that will come to mark his fiction. When Johnny asks her about his father, her late husband J. D., Floraine temporarily ceases to act the black widow and becomes a sorrowful wife: "She was sitting straight up now. Her white hands on the arms of the chair and her crowning hair made her look like a tragic queen" (32–33). The chains on female characters in *Blue City* are loosened even more by Carla Kaufman, who plays the virtual role of Ophelia. She is the daughter of an intellectual Jewish shopkeeper, whose portraits of Marx and Engels Johnny recognizes when he visits his shop. Karl Marx is one of the writers "radical" Jack Millar had recommended to his son in his 1928 "testament."[12] Old Kaufman as the garrulous Polonius figure provides Johnny with all the local history he needs to distinguish trustworthy from untrustworthy contacts. Carla, like Ophelia, is wary of Johnny Weather's attentions, for he seems more "antic" than sane—especially in a city controlled by Kerch. In a reversal on Shakespeare, however, Millar has his Ophelia rebel against the controlling power of Kerch/Claudius. Instead of going under, she helps Johnny expose Kerch as the murderer of his father.

The revenge plot of *Blue City* mirrors the one in *Hamlet* just as the cast of characters does. Johnny openly pursues Kerch, as Hamlet does his uncle, until, in a final scene of exposure and slaughter, the truth comes out, the killer of Johnny's father is named, and the poison in the civic bloodstream is purged. Unlike Hamlet, however, Johnny does not die and give way to Fortinbras, who then disposes of the bodies and cleans up the public arena. Johnny is his own Fortinbras. With the help of Carla, Johnny wipes out the gangsters, exposes the neurotic and cowardly district attorney, and tells off, rather than physically whips, the industrialist puppeteer who runs the city from the sanctuary of his library—where he reads Veblen's *The Theory of the Leisure Class* (1899) and Henry George's *Progress and Poverty* (1879) but does nothing to alleviate actual economic and class antagonism in his city.

If the Shakespearean aspects of *Blue City* lend it the structure of a revenge tragedy, the way Millar deals with Allister (the neurotic and failed district attorney) and Sanford (the sinister industrialist who owns both cops and crooks) works as the "Hammettesque" angle of the novel. Through Hammett's voice, Millar vented years of personal anger against real and supposed frustration. But he also stepped beyond personal emotion into the public arena, where class issues are legitimate public policy. He found specific permission in Hammett's work, where Natty Bumppo metamorphosed from frontier myth figure into the Op and Sam Spade, "the urban tracker of man":

I think Hammett really invented the modern metropolitan man. . . . This is one of the reasons he is, at least in my opinion, a writer of first rank and of considerable importance. He was really the first writer I can think of who wrote about our cities the way they actually were. The first fiction writer who wrote about cities as they actually were in terms of crime and corruption and the inner workings of cities. (Kaye, 8)

Millar's obligation to Hammett is not elegantly paid in *Blue City,* but the intention is robust. Instead of inventing a dramatic turn of plot in which action might carry the message, Millar uses a static scene in which Johnny lectures the industrialist Sanford on his failure to nurture the human values of the modern metropolis (192).

Coupling two "structures," revenge tragedy and hard-boiled realism—each one fully equipped with a cast of characters, a fixed set of events, and an appropriate language—Millar tried to achieve something more with *Blue City* than an inarticulate scream of anger or the simple replicating of a literary type. By welding high and popular forms and discourses, Millar tried to make the combination more relevant to the public purpose. Johnny and Carla, for example, end the novel in love, and the consummation of their love in promised domestic harmony symbolizes the reinstatement of "normal" sexual and civic relations in the city. The "deviant" sexuality of Kerch and his gang and the psychosexual neurosis of Allister (222), the failed official redeemer of the city, are both eradicated as extremes. Even though Johnny has killed and beaten several villains on his way to triumph, he ultimately renounces violence (230). Johnny's gift of ethical, heroic responsibility to his city, however, is ambiguous. In terms of plot, all things end happily; thematically, there is lingering indecision:

> I flung open a window and leaned out over the sill. The sickness I had was more than physical, a spiritual sickness that turned the real world crazy at the edges. . . . It was an ugly city, too ugly for a girl like Carla. . . . If Carla and I wanted to make anything of each other—and that would be hard enough— we'd have to get away from this city. When her shoulder healed, I knew she'd be ready to go. . . . But then I couldn't be sure that I'd be ready. I had a chance to stay and stick in the monster's crop. I was hardly the man for the job, and I couldn't do it alone, and you couldn't build a City of God in the U.S.A. in 1946.
>
> But something better could be made than an organism with an appetite for human flesh. A city could be built for people to live in. (230–31)

The ambivalent resolution to *Blue City* indicates that the simplistic generic types and plots Millar was testing would not, probably, satisfy his sense of the public, ethical novelist's responsibility in the long run. If he were to become the kind of novelist he honored—Dickens or Hammett or Fitzgerald—then his novels must instruct the city, transform it from a dark warren in which individuals devoured one another under the Kafkaesque control of unseen powers, into a "City of God" in which the interpersonal relationships of the citizens rose to the level of redemptive, civic love. Old Kaufman's Marxist preachings suggest a materialistic way to reach civic compact under one universal— class struggle; but Millar holds out for a transcendent, rather than historical, universal. Fleeing the corrupt police, Johnny escapes on foot through the public library. He picks up some abandoned clothes that make him look like an old Jewish peddler and a discarded library book, Augustine's *City of God,* in Latin (155). The message, echoed in the novel's final paragraphs, if billboarded, is nevertheless clear: the Augustinian City of God is the ideal to which we humans ought to aspire, to which our heroes should lead us and our authors instruct us.

Millar continued to try his hand at popular genres after *Blue City.* His next novel, *The Three Roads* (1948), is dedicated "To Margaret [Millar]," a husband's attempt to join his wife in the genre—the novel of psychological suspense— which she had taken to success. *The Three Roads*—with an epigraph from *Oedipus Tyrannus*—follows the struggles of Bret Taylor, a U.S. naval officer, who is haunted by repressed memories of the murders of his wife and his mother. Images of the murder of his mother originate in his childhood and suggest his father's revenge for her adultery. Images of his wife's murder seem to be his own memories of repeating his father's violence on his own wife. It is the kind of plot Alfred Hitchcock ably directed in films like *Spellbound* (1945).

Bret's lover, Paula West (like the character Ingrid Bergman plays in *Spellbound*) tries to guide him through the underbrush of his repressed memory and the residue of incomplete Freudian analysis performed by navy doctors, but her energy for the task is undermined by her nagging suspicion that Bret's memory of killing his wife might in fact be authentic. Like the contemporary champion of psychological suspense novels, Daphne Du Maurier's *Rebecca* (1938), in which the second Mrs. DeWinter must live with the realization that her husband did indeed kill his first wife, *The Three Roads* holds its breath for the climactic revelation.

Alfred Knopf, who published *The Three Roads,* thought it Millar's best work and urged him to settle into psychological suspense as his metier. Bennett Cerf, the enterprising publisher of Random House (Margaret Millar was one of his authors then) visited the writing couple in Santa Barbara in 1948.[13] The unhappy childhood must have seemed light-years in the past.

But Millar had another genre to try. One of Millar's college professors at the University of Western Ontario had introduced him to the novels of D. H. Lawrence, which at the time—the middle 1930s—would have qualified as avant garde fiction. The meeting was not as felicitous as Macdonald's earlier encounters with Dickens and Hammett. When he had read *Sons and Lovers,*

Women in Love, The Rainbow, and other Lawrencean novels, Macdonald was the age, social class, and psychological profile of Lawrence's protagonists. Given his own troubled sexual past, his love/hate relationship with mother and father, his ambition to raise himself out of provincial obscurity and poverty by becoming a writer, it seemed to the young Kenneth Millar that he was reading his own bildungsroman when he read Lawrence. Later he admitted to having been intimidated:

> For a budding writer to be introduced to D. H. Lawrence is a curse as well as a blessing because he's a writer of such overpowering genius and originality that unless you are extremely assured and bold in your own ideas, you're likely to be completely silenced. As I was. In reading D. H. Lawrence, instead of encouraging me to write, it made me feel it was hopeless. (Kaye, 66)

He identified Lawrence's muting mystique as one of the eventual reasons he chose to work in a form other than "the mainstream novel as it's called" (Kaye, 66). But first he had to try.

After experiments outside the "mainstream novel" in genre fiction, Millar tried his talent and his publisher's patience, with an autobiographical novel, *Winter Solstice,* in which he planned to deal with the sorrows of his youth: his vexed relationship with his mother and father, his life on the mean streets of Kitchener, his plans for escape through education and writing, his sexual encounters. He tried several stylistic approaches to the material. In one draft the story of his life is told through the mediating point of view of a young, psychologically restless high-school teacher (which Millar had been very recently) who keeps obsessive watch on the life of the youth who represents the young Millar. That version quickly bogged down in the teacher's panting fantasies of his young student's sexual exploits with "whorish" and "heavy-breasted" classmates. Another version is told through the third-person point of view of the young man himself; the teacher disappears. This version focuses much more closely on the street life of the city (unnamed Kitchener). The central, autobiographical character (named, in this draft, Billy Felding) meets an adventurous older boy, named Albie White, in a poolroom. Albie has plans to enroll at UCLA, and Billy sees that "California was a land of light" (16). The murky darkness of Kitchener prevails, however, and neither Albie nor Billy leaves town.

As this draft of the autobiographical novel continues, Albie metamorphoses into another male companion, Jim, who is more unsavory. With Jim, Billy nearly gets into serious trouble for shoplifting. The reasons for Billy's desperate misery are plain: the in-laws who take care of him and his mother are parsimonious in hospitality and censorious in religion. Billy feels doubly impotent: unable to leave, powerless to do anything in place. The bars of his cage are not only financial. Billy's love for his mother is half erotic, half fatalistic—wholly Lawrencean. He cannot save her from her own and her kin's ignorance of the outside world (they are, for example, swindled by the inventor of a revolutionary lightbulb who claims it will shine forever on practically no electric current). And yet Billy hates the higher social classes, represented by the doctor who treats Billy's terminally ill father in a local charity ward. Billy, predictably, is attracted to the doctor's daughter but senses that the doctor himself cannot stand the idea of anything approaching physical contact between his daughter and a lower-class boy. A similar relationship and subplot will return later in *The Galton Case* (1959), *Black Money* (1966), *The Instant Enemy* (1968), and *Sleeping Beauty* (1973).

Millar progressed on *Winter Solstice,* the title he gave to this draft, to the point of paying a typist to prepare the manuscript. But he never submitted it to Knopf. In retrospect, he explained that he was dissatisfied with *Winter Solstice,* that its subject matter was too dangerous, and that he turned to the detective novel as more insulating and more successful at shaping raw material into plot.[14] It is just as plausible that he found, in the first place, that D. H. Lawrence had already written Kenneth Millar's life, and that Millar himself possessed a creative imagination that thrived on rules rather than the open field of the "mainstream novel." Not for a decade, at least, was he equipped to handle the pressurized tangle of his youth and early maturity—not until he entered full-blown Freudian analysis in 1957. And then he had the thick rulebook of Freudian psychoanalysis to shape his expression: a slot to receive every sensation and mood. The deep tensions and anger of his childhood and youth seethed like a subterranean oil and gas deposit whenever he tapped them. He capped a lot of his inner tension with the Lew Archer novels.

[3]

Literary Fathers and Archer's Debut

The Moving Target

Discussions of Millar's novels, like those of any American writer in the detective genre, usually begin with the bloodlines of the two twentieth-century fathers: Dashiell Hammett (1894–1961) and Raymond Chandler (1888–1959). Hammett's heyday was the 1920s and 1930s, Chandler's the 1930s and 1940s. Together, their work brought hard-boiled detective fiction within hailing distance of mainstream literature in the middle of the twentieth century. Kenneth Millar decided to join this tradition at its highest point. He was not drafted; he enlisted.

Millar approached the genre with deep and sophisticated literary knowledge—not always an asset to a writer who must turn out a novel every year or eighteen months, with no other steady means of support. Before he wrote his espionage novels Millar was a graduate student in one of the top programs in the country, his literary landscape groomed to professional academic standards. He never, though, seems to have envisioned a career as a scholar or teacher. Millar himself described his periodic returns to academia as "relapses" (Kaye, 8-b-3). When Millar re-created himself as Ross Macdonald, detective novelist, then, he took the step with no safety net.

For his first full-time stint in graduate school, 1941–43, Millar was saturated in another tradition: the high-culture, academically enshrined "canon" of the writers more recently known as "dead white males." If Hammett served a gritty apprenticeship on the job as a Pinkerton and Chandler toiled among the pulps and Hollywood movie studios, Millar served in the library. For better or worse, his "great books" foundation shaped, sometimes intrusively, his writing as a detective novelist. Sometimes, it seems, Lew Archer is a National Merit finalist.

Millar made the canon of great books and great ideas associated with "the Christian West"[1] his lifeboat in high school and college. When he was in graduate school, that canon was coin of the realm. In interviews, he has consistently made a point of praising the Canadian educational system, in which he spent the first two thirds of his training, for its concentration on great books and great ideas. Indeed, in graduate school in the American system at the University of Michigan (1939–52, with several years off for service in the United States Navy during World War II), Millar wrote a doctoral dissertation on Samuel Taylor Coleridge as scholarly as any published by the academic professionals of his generation. As late as 1959–60, with the encouragement of his friend, poet and critic Donald Davie, Millar was hoping a university press would publish it.[2] He reviewed academic books, often for the *San Francisco Chronicle,* under the byline Kenneth Millar when he was far more widely known as the novelist Ross Macdonald. His academic background makes Macdonald tough to digest among a cohort of writers with grittier resumés.[3]

Now a pockmarked battleground of the culture wars, the canon of the Christian West was standard issue for the college student of Millar's generation. The decades of the 1930s and 1940s, when Millar was in high school and college, were decades of unquestioned prestige. The values embedded in the great books were seen to be threatened by the Axis powers in World War II. All the more so in the era of the cold war after the Allied victory: the Western canon became the vehicle of cultural reconstruction for the European and American victors. National literatures, and individual writers within them, expressed the central themes of the victorious West: the ethical conscience of the individual, the sanctity of the social compact under democratic humanism, government by consent of the governed—the basic human rights enunciated in the charter of the United Nations as part of postwar reconstruction.

If Millar sought to advance the more homegrown version of these values developed in Chandler and Hammett, he did so not only by improving their episodic plot mechanics and flat presentation of character. He advanced the genre by carefully grafting it to the main trunk of Western literature not merely by having his hero, Lew Archer, drop a canonical name or title here and there. Millar took the very great risk of conceiving of Archer's cases as moral and ethical equivalents to the predicament of modern humanity. It had always been Millar's intention, from the moment in childhood when he recognized Dickens as the public writer he wanted to emulate, to make himself into *l'homme engagé.*

In an interview at the time of the publication of *The Underground Man* (1971), Millar still held that belief: "There is nothing like the life of your own times, there is nothing like being in direct contact with the central events of your own time" (Kaye, 68). As a young man he had seen Nazi Germany first-hand, and tried without success, during a sabbatical from college, to get to Spain (with Orwell, Hemingway, and other heroes of the generation) for the civil war (Kaye, 68). To understand his novels, individually and as his life's work, we have to see how his fully conscious choice of the popular form meshed with his fully conscious sense that literature engaged in its particular times could be "great." In other words, we have to see how both roads, the one taken into the popular realm of the detective novel and the one not taken into academia, make Millar's novels distinctive.

Millar determined to make himself a writer so that he could address the public on the issues the pubic needed to ponder if it were to preserve its humane traditions. As a boy reader in the Kitchener public library, he first identified Dickens in the role of public writer. As a college student, he ran the gamut from Greek drama to D. H. Lawrence. Millar's literary thinking came into focus in graduate school at the University of Michigan; as the collision of academic and public literary life approached, he identified the detective novel genre as his way to survive the wreck.

His dissertation, "The Inward Eye: A Reconsideration of Coleridge's Psychological Criticism" (1952), is, in hindsight, a hint to the way Millar's intentions evolved through high- to popular-culture literary forms and language. Two fundamental themes emerge in Millar's 455-page dissertation. First, he subscribed to the consensus belief that Western civilization had undergone a wide and deep loss of metaphysical underpinning when the ages of Augustine, Aquinas, and Dante were displaced by the Enlightenment—the ages of Descartes, Marx, and Darwin. Unlike most cultural conservatives, Millar did not lament the passing of the Age of Faith and its champions, Augustine, Aquinas, and Dante. In a way, he thought, they had it easy: all the answers were in fact one answer, God's will. In spite of all the things you could not see, there was one unseen force you knew to be certain: the hand of God. Even though a rampant materialism had become "the Frankenstein monster of our age,"[4] there was no way to reverse history and return to the past. Descartes, Marx, and Darwin proved to be the materialistic replacements for faith. The regime of materialism did not make life more pleasant, but it did make it more human.

Millar chose Samuel Taylor Coleridge as the subject of his dissertation because he understood Coleridge to be the crucial stress point of this shift, and the inventor of a method of dealing with a new linkage between the seen and the unseen: psychological criticism. Millar's insight into Coleridge was built upon his (Millar's) investment in Freud. Millar knew where Coleridge was going better than Coleridge did. Freud, in the twentieth century, made the inside of human consciousness a replacement for the loss of the metaphysics of the outside by replacing the hand of God with a universal model of the unconscious. Millar saw Coleridge as Freud's indispensable precursor, groping toward the universal model of the unconscious by way of humans beings' response to stimulation of the imagination.[5]

Millar imagined the Coleridge who wrote his poems (especially "The Rime of the Ancient Mariner") as the inward, or private, eye who in seeing harm and telling it as story (or "case") initiated the process of healing. In his dissertation, Millar called this the "suturing" of the historic wound.[6] He certainly had enough "historic wounds" of his own to understand the need for suturing. Millar read

Coleridge's poems, letters, and essays as "gestalts," or cases, in which the poet or the Mariner used "fancy" the way the private eye uses hunches: thinking from disconnected, concrete images toward reintegrative "constants."[7] A century after Coleridge, Freud would supply us with a more definite map of these gestalts—origins and destinations—in the form of narratives adaptable to literature (the family romance, the return of the repressed), or complexes (Oedipus, Electra). Coleridge is, however, indispensable because he first mapped the territory of the "inward Odyssey" and stated the necessity of healing the ruptured modern soul by working out a partnership between Romantic individualism and the "human values" of "reality."[8] When Archer explains that Albert Graves, in *The Moving Target,* or any murderer in a subsequent case, fell into crime by losing the human dimension, Millar draws his detective's ethics from the core of his work on Coleridge. The criminal does the tearing, Archer's eye spots the need for suturing.

The exhausting scholarly work on Coleridge might have given Millar a deep foundation in moral and psychological themes. But from the time he had heard John Buchan's address to a high-school graduating class in Kitchener, Macdonald sought a more personal mentor and a more public vocation. He found one in Ann Arbor: W. H. Auden (1907–73), who taught Millar for only one semester, fall 1941, in English 135: "Fate and the Individual in European Literature." Millar remembered Auden's influence as definitive. "Auden . . . legitimated the kind of writing that I wanted to do. He was the first important critic to take detective fiction seriously. . . . It was his personal discourse that—he said things that sort of liberated me" (Nelson, 12A-1). Auden also projected an aura. He had been an ambulance driver in Spain in 1936–37, living the life the younger Kenneth Millar had found to be just beyond his reach. To Charles H. Miller, another student in English 135 that same semester and Auden's housemate, Auden was "the most committed poet of the times," and his course "an individual monument at the University of Michigan."[9] What constituted Auden's "personal discourse" is a calculated guess, but his required reading list was exhaustive, ranging from Augustine, Sophocles, and Shakespeare, to Kafka and T. S. Eliot. The "recommended reading" was no less impressive, from contemporary anthropologists Ruth Benedict and Margaret Mead to the poet Paul Valéry. Millar annotated his reading list (more than fifty titles altogether) by checking off those he owned and those he borrowed from the library. This graduate course and the exposure to Auden was vitally important in Millar's intellectual career—the kind of Oedipal motif of meeting the unknown father at a crossroads that Millar used obsessively in his subsequent fiction.

Millar's notes for English 135 reflect a passionate reader and driven student who was less interested in performing appreciations of the aesthetic forms of the works he devoured than he was in the moral and ethical truths they dramatized.[10] His attraction to these themes was largely autobiographical; he could apply them to the gnawing questions that had haunted his childhood and young adulthood. Millar was drawn to the darker aspects of "Fate and the Individual" because he saw his life crowded by fate and his individuality in jeopardy.

His reading seems "fated" now because it often came to him branded with his own initial: K. The two works that ignited Millar's most extensive note-taking were Soren Kierkegaard's *Fear and Trembling* (1843) and Franz Kafka's *The Castle* (1926). He addressed interpretive notes to himself in the margins of his class notes with his own initials, K. M.; the visual effect on the notebook pages creates a virtual conversation among interchangeable Ks.

In his notes for *The Castle,* K. M. seems intuitively identified with the fictional K's (Kafka's protagonist's) blundering in the literal and metaphorical dark city supervised from the sinister castle. K. M.'s notes debate the sexual relationship of K. and the barmaid Frieda, who eventually leaves K. for one of his "assistants"; the relationship between K. and the messenger Barnabas (which K. M. judges to be male friendship rather than homosexual desire— dangerous territory for K. M., given his boyhood guilts); and the nature of the "community" under the power of the castle—clearly another example of the "monster" society he would discuss in his dissertation and, before that, blast and begin to reconstruct in his early novel *Blue City.* The castle cannot foster the Augustinian meaning of "the City of God" because the castle keeps people chained to a meaningless round of bureaucratic, worldly duties. In a paper for Auden, Millar linked the sinister power of the castle to the surreal comedy of the Marx Brothers in *Duck Soup* (1933), a madcap story that ridicules espionage, bureaucracy, and patriotism. The Marx Brothers mocked what Kafka suffered. In his marginal comments Auden expressed enjoyment with the comparison.

The theme of society fostered or deformed by the way power is wielded over it is relevant to Millar's early novels, up to and including the 1949 debut of Archer in *The Moving Target.* His travel in Nazi Germany had verified this theme in current history and personal experience. And Millar's ingrained liberalism meant that in the most general terms he envisioned a remedy in the future rather than in a return to the past, however idealized. In notes for a comparison of Dante's *The Divine Comedy* and *The Castle,* Millar favored the latter, even though it seems to diagnose only discord and sorrow. Millar, as detailed in notes from an English 135 class taken in 1941, saw Dante as working "to a great extent with ready-made materials: Ptolemy, Aquinas, the medieval world." Kafka is, however, "a pioneer (Dante was in art but not so much in theol., ethics. philos.) . . . (tho' he learned from Kierkegaard.)" Kafka's "pioneering" in ethics and psychology for a world denuded of metaphysics places him over Dante's more systematic and affirmative canonical views and suggests further that Kafka's dark system of unfulfilled sexual relationships, paranoid estrangement from authority, and seemingly permanent alien status within the diseased community of the castle served both to objectify Millar's personal past and to furnish a moral arithmetic for his own novels that was more in keeping with "the times." Johnny Weather's fate in *Blue City*, for example, seems to be imagined on the same lines, although arguably not as deeply, as K's in *The Castle*. Johnny's love for the prostitute Carla ends happily, and Johnny (unlike K.) not only succeeds in subduing the powers behind the Blue City's corruption but ends on the brink of a new regime based on the ideals of Augustine's *City of God*—a book that makes a cameo appearance in the novel.

The other K important to Millar was Soren Kierkegaard. His *Fear and Trembling*, blending philosophical and religious seriousness, autobiography (his love affair with "Regina"), and his concentration on the story of Abraham and Isaac (a father/son story of the type that Millar considered central to his own life and work) made Kierkegaard as crucial as Kafka. Kierkegaard's "knight of faith" is a man who struggles to live by faith in a world lacking all clues to a "gold standard" backing up the faith. In Kierkegaard's existential universe, a human being has only his or her own serial actions as the raw material of meaning. It is as if Hammett had paraphrased, and reduced, Kierkegaard in the Flitcraft parable. There is no certainty of a purposed beginning, much less a guaranteed reward at the conclusion. Abraham, heeding Yahweh's command to kill his firstborn, is the model for existential modern humanity in need of meaning and faith. He is not certain of the divine origin of the order, nor is he serene in the belief that his son will be better off as sacrificial victim. Faith is a leap in the dark. Kafka's answer to the bind was surrealist dream work; Kierkegaard, alternatively, outlined an existential heroism in which absurdist action was not only possible but redemptive. There might be no "sanity clause" in the human contract (as Chico and Groucho negotiate it in another film, *A Night at the Opera* [1935]), but the knight of faith has to act as if there were. The alternative to absurd action is despair and suicide. Kierkegaard's hero is a blessed fool standing beside Kafka's doomed fool in K. M.'s notes; they both operate in the metaphysical dark.

Millar pushed the detective hero in this direction, with guidance from Auden. In his notes for Auden's class, Millar outlined a short paper:

Sherlock Holmes. the detective hero. think of the detective story as an alle-
gory about human nature in general.
"A Study in Scarlet" essential.
The Sign of the Four } recommended
Hound of the Baskervilles Paper on above. Quality not quantity (5 pp. really
good.)
You can bring in other detectives.
Detective-hero = a form of the ethical hero.
Certain relations to the Quest (Golden Fleece, Grail, Moby Dick)[11]

This outline has the basic formal and thematic qualities Millar would later invest in his Archer series. Archer's cases are allegories of the quest for ethical action in a world all but devoid of such possibility; Freud would supply the particulars. *Noir* California would serve as the solid frame to which Millar could affix the metaphorical darknesses of his various Ks. And Archer himself develops quickly in the series from the hero of physical action common to the tradition of Hammett and Chandler into a hero of moral and ethical discrimination who seeks answers to why people do evil rather than ways to punish them.

In "The Comic Hero," one of the essays he wrote for Auden's course, Millar scouts the territory of the hero from Aristophanes to the Marx Brothers. From the wide range of comic heroes suggested in Auden's syllabus, Millar chose the democratic comic hero:

> One kind of comic hero I am not going to try to fit into my definition, although I may use him for illustration, is the hero of comedy of manners.
>
> Comedy of manners is class-comedy, and the comedy I shall chiefly concern myself with is what I shall call democratic comedy, for reasons that will appear. Democratic comedy is destructive of appearance and hails you back to the sources of life; comedy of manners is preservative of appearance and conventionalizes the sources of life, so that its highest excellences are formal.

Millar's preference for the common or democratic over the conventionalized is a choice that runs true in Lew Archer's cases. The comic hero as Millar sees him always exposes the hypocrisies of the establishment, and connects right and wrong to a real social fabric—"the central events of your own time" told in the language spoken by real people.

The difference between conventionalized morality and democratic morality was important to Millar, and he drew the distinction in his novels in several ways. An early scene in the second Archer novel, *The Drowning Pool* (1950), is an apt example. Archer enters the case at the rehearsal of a very mannered play in which amateur actors at a community theater conventionalize emotions onstage while backstage the "real" versions of the same emotions are being acted out by two real people not in the cast. As *The Drowning Pool* develops, the fundamental either/or of this theme is elaborated: in a three-sided relationship, a woman is caught between her "conventionalizing" husband, who pulls her toward empty forms of public appearance, and her "democratic" lover, who "hails [her] back to the sources of life." Archer sees his case as separating the conventionalized from the genuine, a quest in which he is not entirely successful.

In "The Comic Hero," Millar pursues the significance of the democratic hero by making the kinds of distinctions Auden himself would later make in his own study of the literary hero, "Ishmael—Don Quixote" in *The Enchafed Flood: Three Critical Essays on the Romantic Spirit:*

All, or nearly all of the comic quests end in a final irony which combines success and failure, that is, two kinds of reality. Because he is no Galahad the comic quest hero cannot succeed; because he lacks the obsessed moral single-ness and pride of an Ahab [hero of Melville's *Moby-Dick*] or a Brand [Ethan Brand, hero of Hawthorne's short story of the same name] he cannot fail tragically.[13]

The mixed, middle ground—where the irony of uncertainty and survival take the place of certainty and tragic death—Millar identified as the turf of his comic quest hero, the path Lew Archer is fated to take as his cases unfold before him. From the vantage of *The Blue Hammer* (1976), the last published Archer novel, Millar saw his hero as comic because he survived cases that had proven tragic to the direct participants (Nelson, 21A-1). Dismissing Shakespeare's Hamlet as lacking the motivations of "the ordinary social man," Millar concludes his essay for Auden with a fanfare for the common hero: "Thus he can act as our cham-pion, the vicar of the sceptic in all of us, against convention, marriage, Emily Post, the four hundred, and the rights of property. Like the Democratic mob at Andrew Jackson's inauguration, he stands on the chairs in the White House."[14] Auden praised his student's work, giving the essay an A[+]. He even offered to introduce Millar into the New York City literary circles in which he moved. A combination of Millar's trouble distinguishing male friendship from homosex-ual attraction and his inchoate suspicion of himself as a professional academic prompted him to decline Auden's offer (Nelson, 12A-1; Kaye, 8-b-3).[15]

Auden's critical attention to detective stories—he called it "addiction" in his essay "The Guilty Vicarage"—doubtlessly smoothed the way for a Canadian student in an American graduate program looking for a popular literary form in which to invest a career. But Auden's taste leaned to the British country house variety perfected by Sayers and Christie; and as much as he liked read-ing them, he ranked detective novels lower than art, something that "may throw light. . . on the function of art,"[16] but not art in themselves. Much of what Auden wrote about detective stories in "The Guilty Vicarage" and in reviews of individual novels actually sheds reflective light on Millar's Archer novels. What Auden calls "the milieu," for example—the social surround of village, country house, weekend parties into which murder intrudes, only to be suavely excised by the gentleman-sleuth—represents an innocent society in a state of grace which must be set right by the savior-detective. Auden, that is, saw the crime of murder as a metaphor; the real "crime" is the disturbance of the social idyll.[17]

Such an innocent state of grace hardly applies to Archer's Southern California milieu; and the label *savior* seems wrong for Archer. For Auden "The detective-story society is a society consisting of apparently innocent individuals, i.e. their aesthetic interest as individuals does not conflict with their ethical obligations to the universal."[18] Not only does Archer find more guilt the deeper he delves, but Millar was totally unconcerned with writing memorable, stand-alone characters (Nelson, 10A-2). He was obsessively concerned with the "structure" of his novels (Nelson, 10A-1). Auden, albeit less directly, encouraged Millar's attention to structure by asserting that the detective story was deeply linked to the literature of the Christian West through a fundamental structure of narrative. The quest for the Grail and the detective story, Auden argued, were the "mirror image[s]" of one another.[19] Auden also insisted that the theme of the detective story is "ethics," and he keyed the meaning of *ethics* to the literary and philosophical works of the Western canon of great books and great ideas. "The job of detective," he concludes in "The Guilty Vicarage," "is to restore the state of grace in which the aesthetic and the ethical are as one."[20] Archer could never be seen as restoring the state of grace to a community already irreparably betrayed by ethical breach; the meaning of California, as we shall see later, is the always-already ruined state of grace as part of Millar's American heritage. Yet Millar did—if perhaps only in the retrospective view from *The Blue Hammer* —see a kind of redemptive, metaphysical mission in Archer's work. To this question: "What are the philosophical, psychological, personal implications of A[rcher]'s repeated statement in many books: It's all one case?" Millar replied:

> Well, he would only be saying it about the case in that particular book.
> He wouldn't be saying that his whole series of cases are all one case. But in general, although there are major plots and subplots in the books, they're all related to each other and you can't solve the main case without also—solving is the wrong word, let's say understanding—the others. And this reflects my feeling that we're all members of a single body to degrees that we have no idea except in moments of what might be called revelation. (Nelson, 23A-4)

Millar's response suggests that he intended both less and more (not solution but understanding) in his carefully structured books than the ordinary cathartic satisfaction of finding out whodunit; he intended a moment of communal revelation very similar to the climax of a religious ritual. In that moment of recognizing our unity in "a single body" lay the basis for Millar's private detective as ethical hero.

Eight years after teaching Millar in Ann Arbor, and in the same year *The Moving Target* was published, Auden delivered the Page-Barbour Lectures at the University of Virginia. These lectures were published in 1950 under the title *The Enchafed Flood: Three Critical Essays on the Romantic Spirit.* Auden's lectures cover many of the works he had taught in his graduate seminar at Michigan. His lecture on the Romantic hero, "Ishmael—Don Quixote," is particularly relevant to Millar's hero Lew Archer, for in it Auden elaborates on the figure of the "ethical hero"—a type Millar had suggested to himself in his class notes— and suggests another source for Archer's name.

Auden, like a true Aristotelian, classifies the range of Romantic heroes from the Quixote-type who knows his desire for truth does not have a prayer of fulfillment in the real world, but who chooses that world anyway, to the Ishmael of *Genesis,* the son not chosen by God or Abraham and therefore doomed to become a wanderer on the social margins. Auden, however, locates Ishmael closer to the center of the Romantic tradition, where ethics defines the middle ground between tragedy and comedy. In comedy, nothing means anything in the long run; in tragedy, everything does. In between is the ethical hero of Romance, not knowing for sure where the meaning lies. Auden explains the middle type: "The ethical hero is the one who at any given moment happens to know more than the others. This knowledge can be any part of the truth, not only what is commonly called ethics."[21] This is Archer, or any modern private eye (not Poe's Dupin or Conan Doyle's Holmes, both of whom know it all from the outset), understanding more about how the plots and subplots connect than his clients or the police. In his initial conversation with Mrs. Sampson in *The Moving Target,* for example, Archer learns more about her than she intentionally discloses, enough to wonder who her analyst might be (8). But he never knows enough to stop the evil from happening.

Further, Auden sees that the hero does not expect "any ultimate relief" from his search or quest. He concludes one search in sight of the beginning of the next, and, like the Ancient Mariner, solves his problem by telling his story, not by ridding his society of evil.[22] He is a wanderer not only in geography, but also in inner spaces; "something catastrophic has happened in [his] past" that keeps him restless, alone, and searching.[23] Auden finds the original type of this restless, "neurotic," wanderer in Abraham's unacknowledged son by the discarded slave woman Hagar—another part of the same story Kierkegaard had ransacked for the key to existential ethics. Auden found in the disowned son the type of the ethical nomad—the wanderer who had been abandoned by his father and had become, in compensation for the loss of the patrimony, an archer. "And God was with the lad, and he grew up; he lived in the wilderness, and became an expert with the bow" (Gen. 21:20–21, RSV). Millar might have consciously adopted the name of Spade's murdered partner as homage to Hammett. But unconsciously, to a writer and less-than-favored son who felt himself exiled from the privileged land of his birth (California), a wanderer in a wilderness both geographical and psychological, "Archer" was also a secret name under which he could try to tell his own inner story.

In 1967, for the foreword to *Archer in Hollywood,* an edition of three of his early Archer novels (*The Moving Target, The Way Some People Die,* and *The Barbarous Coast*), Ross Macdonald located the origins of Archer in an author's crisis.[24] After Knopf had published *Blue City* and *The Three Roads,* Macdonald recalled, he felt it was his "duty to write an autobiographical novel about my depressing childhood in Canada." He gave it up, though, fearing that the material was too "radioactive." Instead, he invented (crediting Raymond Chandler for the suggestion) a protective shield: a private detective. "I was in trouble, and Lew Archer got me out of it" (Hollywood, vii). Macdonald simplified the genesis of Lew Archer; the essential elements of the character were a complex web in his imagination, waiting for the name to bring them into focus. "Archer" in a real sense has multiple fathers. The name itself is lifted with deference from Hammett; the professional decision to begin a detective series is attributed to Chandler. The pseudonym he chose for the first Archer novel, John Macdonald, borrows parts of his father's name. It is no surprise, then, that Archer's cases, from the first, invoke the father's responsibility in the family and the father's responsibility to put the family back together when it fractures—a task that falls to Archer in the father's default.

The central crime of The Moving Target, the kidnapping of Ralph Sampson and his eventual murder, are related crimes, and someone has to pay. More deeply—maybe more deeply than Macdonald understood in the first of his series—the crimes give way to the problems of disorder when the father is forcibly removed or, as Archer is quick to learn, when he was a dysfunctional authority in the first place.

The theme of the father emerges slowly in the gradually coalescing picture of the Sampson household in disarray—roles and functions denied, mistaken, or simply not fulfilled. The wife is loose and discontented, the daughter both too old and too young, her suitor of the wrong generation, the son not natural but surrogate. The established genre entails certain compulsory steps before improvements can be made. Macdonald begins with place and style. The Moving Target opens with a compact metaphor that sets this course. Hard-boiled similes and metaphors—conscious moves to appropriate a style—set up a swirl of imagery, and the central moral situation barely escapes: "The light-blue haze in the lower canyon was like a thin smoke from slowly burning money. Even the sea looked precious through it, a solid wedge held in the canyon's mouth, bright blue and polished like a stone. Private property: color guaranteed fast; will not shrink egos. I had never seen the Pacific look so small" (Target, 5). Despite the natural beauty of California, the innocence of origin myths is going up in smoke and hard-boiled tough-talk. Auden's and Macdonald's concepts of the genre are similar and dissimilar at this stage: both require a myth of innocence at the origin (Auden's is social, Macdonald's is natural or environmental), but Auden's is susceptible of rehabilitation if damaged while Macdonald's seems always already broken beyond fixing. Original sin in the California eden is always already too big to be fixed by a savior/sleuth.

Archer moves in a "fallen" California eden. The haves appropriate the earth and its comforts, leaving a large and diverse class of have-nots invisible from the cliffside enclaves where the rich hole up with their money. These acts of appropriation, prior to and almost invisible in the plot of the novel, create gorgeous comfort for some (the Sampsons), and misery for many, represented in the novel by the migrant workers exploited by the kidnapped father and his criminal associates, Beat losers Archer encounters on the trail of the missing man, and finally by the simian thug Puddler, whom Archer has to kill.

The problem that gnaws at Archer from the outset, however, is more complicated than finding a kidnapped man. The man, Sampson, is the hub of a tangled system of desire and greed that orbits far beyond simple crime and punishment. Archer, to be sure, follows clues, overcomes physical obstacles on the trail of the kidnapped father, even kills a man (an episode over which Archer as character and Macdonald as novelist brood until both can live with it). But he never holds out a ray of hope that he or anyone else can set the world right again, for human concerns have put the world out of kilter, made the Pacific seem "small." Like the Coleridgean model on which he is partly based, Archer senses the complexity in the situation in his first conversation with the "carnivorous" Mrs. Sampson, whose real or feigned immobilizing injury initiates a pattern of split characters living outside the lines of familial roles. She tries to appropriate Archer when she asks him what he thinks of her as a client. With instinctive stubbornness, he protects his autonomy: "'I never think about my clients'" (*Target*, 6). Most of his clients, like Conrad's heart of darkness, do not bear much looking into. When Archer fends off Mrs. Sampson's offer of a drink before lunch with "'I'm the new type detective'" (9), his remark is not only a sly criticism of Chandler's Marlowe or Hammett's Spade, who never seem more than an arm's length from a bottle,[25] but also a comment on the inappropriateness of the offer. If Archer says he does not think about his clients, Macdonald does think about his writing fathers.

In *The Moving Target,* the "structure" of evil develops like a photographic negative from the first contact in the case. Mrs. Sampson, whose questionable paralysis signifies a more probable "psychological" crippling, reveals the nature of the dysfunction before she utters a word. Her bedroom is a "high white room too big and bare to be feminine. Above the massive bed there was a painting of a clock, a map, and a woman's hat arranged on a dressing table. Time, space, and sex. It looked like a Kuniyoshi" (6). The "new type detective" not only does not drink before the traditional cocktail hour, he is even something of a connoisseur of contemporary painting. The painting that hangs above Mrs. Sampson's bed is an example of what Macdonald called a "real symbol," not an "echo" supplied by a writer who deals in surfaces only (Nelson, 5B-5). And it is a clue too—not a piece of forensic evidence like tobacco ash or lipstick on a highball glass, but a "life clue" (Kaye, 20). Yasuo Kuniyoshi (1889–1953) was working in a "late" period when Macdonald chose one of his works for Mrs. Sampson's boudoir, a period during which his paintings were characterized by "psychological tensions," "duplicity," "imaginative charade and make-believe."[26]

The subtext of the painting cues the subtext of the novel, but with signs embedded in a level of the text that not all readers are going to find, or like.

Archer immediately senses sexual dissatisfaction as the subtext of Mrs. Sampson's facade of command. Her remarks about another couple, for whose divorce Archer had done some investigative work, set Archer on edge. "'Millicent and Clyde are dreadfully sordid, don't you think?'" She tempts Archer to indiscretion. "'These aesthetic men! I've always suspected his mistress wasn't a woman'" (6). Archer refuses the bait, and as he looks back at his new client he sees "something frightened and sick hiding in the fine brown body" (7). The question that surfaces by the end of the conversation, or "session," is whether the wife is not the cause of the husband's disappearance, for Archer suspects that her "normal" sexual appetite has been diverted by greed for her husband's money. The strong implication is that her paralysis from the waist down is not the cause but the effect of the "something frightened and sick" this Delilah conceals under her healthy tan. Archer knows enough Freudian psychology to wonder who her analyst might be; he has no doubt she needs one (8).

Macdonald had used the character of the paralyzed wife a few years earlier. In "Death by Water," a short story he wrote while in the navy, Macdonald made a wife dying of Lou Gehrig's disease the murderer of her rich husband. The story won fourth prize in the 1945 *Ellery Queen Mystery Magazine* contest.[27]

The other characters in the house of Sampson are similarly dysfunctional and cued to the subtext of charade and duplicity. Alan Taggert, the pilot of Sampson's private plane and the putative "son," is a youngish man who left the mainspring of his life in the South Pacific when the war ended. His nostalgia for barracks and flying days is inflected, as Archer-the-analyst hears it, with sexual longing. Remembering his plane, a P-38, Taggert speaks with "loving nostalgia," as if speaking a girl's name (*Target,* 10). He pays make-believe attention to Sampson's daughter, Miranda, who appears at just this moment in Archer's interrogation of Taggert to underscore the point that she cannot compete with an airplane. Miranda is twenty-one, nubile, desirable; Archer recites her complete sexual history before they exchange more than a few words. Miranda, Archer decides, "was worth waiting for," the only human being in the Sampson entourage not yet terminally enmeshed in its duplicity (10). Her future, however, might not hold the fulfillment Archer anticipates. Albert Graves, the Sampsons' lawyer—at forty years of age approaching the category of father rather than suitor—hopes to marry her. The prospect of this match fills Archer with acute discomfort. Graves, who ran a town in Bavaria as an officer in the U.S. military, blushes when he discusses Miranda. The mismatch in age, class, and experience seems to Archer to doom the girl's chance for happiness—as if Graves is Caliban to Miranda, a Caliban who succeeds in his threat to kill Prospero (17–18).

Archer is drawn into the web of duplicity himself when he meets Fay Estabrook, a washed-up actress whose twin refuges are liquor and astrology. Archer feigns interest in Estabrook in order to get information on the missing Ralph Sampson. Estabrook had decorated Sampson's cottage in a local residential hotel with a lavish array of astrological signs. After a little cocktail lounge badinage, Estabrook warms up to Archer's attentions and asks him his birthdate so she can cast his horoscope. He tells her June 2, "Really? I didn't expect you to be Geminian. Geminis have no heart. They're double-souled like the Twins, and they lead a double life" (36–37). Archer is in fact duplicitous with Estabrook, fending off her questions with questions of his own. In the end, Estabrook gets so drunk that her own double life pokes through the surface: "Her voice had dropped its phony correctness and the other things she had learned from studio coaches. It was coarse and pleasantly harsh. It placed her childhood in Detroit or Chicago or Indianapolis, at the beginning of the century, on the wrong side of town" (40).

Archer learns next to nothing from Estabrook and succeeds only in making himself feel soiled by his own deception. Several hours of drinking and inconclusive questioning only get him inside Estabrook's house, where she passes out. He intercepts one telephone call, allowing the caller to believe he is Estabrook's husband, Dwight Troy. Troy himself soon shows up on the heels of the call, a dapper hoodlum with "a trace of south-of-England accent" and "epicene hands" (47, 48). Troy's pistol-wielding machismo splits on the edge of his epicene sexuality, an echo of the homophobia in Blue City and in the genre more generally. Troy's phony accent might also be a swipe at Father Chandler, whose Anglophilia saturates his novels.

Archer talks his way out of trouble with Troy, but back into it when he sets out for the Wild Piano, a bar which is the source of the phone call to Estabrook. The Wild Piano connects the Santa Teresa eden to the Beat underworld of smuggled migrant workers, a phony religious seer, heroin, and Puddler— the first man Archer kills. The bar serves as the hinge between the psychological and sociological structures of evil that Macdonald saw as distinguishing his work from Chandler's. Whereas in the Santa Teresa world evil appears as the sufferings of the rich, in the Wild Piano, evil appears in the lives of the victims of the too-rich. To project this contemporary sociology in The Moving Target, Macdonald took on the world of a Beat generation novelist. The bar girl who serves him at the Wild Piano, for example, is feral, a genuine angelic Beat who could have stepped full-blown from the pages of Kerouac: "She leaned forward to let me look down her dress. The breasts were little and tight, with pencil-sharp nipples. Her arms and upper lip were furred with black" (51).

At the Wild Piano, Archer finds Betty Fraley, whose keyboard talent still shines through the Beat crust of addiction, jail time, and age. As "moved" as Archer is by her playing a "psychosomatic blues," he keeps his distance from her physically: "When I lit it [a cigarette] for her, she inhaled deeply. Her face unconsciously waited for the lift and drooped a little when it didn't come. She was a baby with an ageless face, sucking a dry bottle. The rims of her nostrils were bloodless, as white as snow, and that was no Freudian error" (53). Archer knows a heroin addict (a "snowbird") when he sees one. Unlike Kerouac, the Beat laureate, Macdonald does not celebrate Fraley's addiction; he sees nothing angelic in this hipster. As in his posing as a fan of Fay Estabrook, his act for Betty Fraley pulls him across the line of genuine human connection. Fraley sees through the charade and summons Puddler, the club's bouncer, to take care of Archer. He cannot talk his way out of this tight spot, and Alan Taggert has to rescue him (a rescue that turns out to be trumped up). In the end, however, Archer has to kill Puddler.

Archer's killing of Puddler functions in *The Moving Target* both as a suspenseful scene of physical action and as a kind of meta-novelistic point on which Macdonald works through his intentions for violence and outlines his revisions to the ethical field of the detective novel. Macdonald uses violence thematically, not merely to indulge the reader's desire to walk on the wild side. "I can write an ordinary hard-boiled mystery with all sorts of shenanigans and gunplay with my eyes closed," he had written to Knopf in a letter protesting comparisons with Chandler.[28] Macdonald wants the action (even the deaths) to register morally and ethically on the common reader, not merely to function as a bang-zam comic-strip panel.

The second time they meet, Puddler is Archer's captor, ordered by Dwight Troy—the evil presence behind an immigrant smuggling ring and the disappearance of Sampson—to keep Archer out of circulation. Archer knows the only way to get loose is to use his brain over Puddler's brawn:

> Lit from below by the yellow flaring light, his face was barely human. It was low-browed and prognathous like a Neanderthal man's, heavy and forlorn, without thought. It wasn't fair to blame him for what he did. He was a savage accidentally dropped in the steel-and-concrete jungle, a trained beast of burden, a fighting machine. But I blamed him. I had to take what he'd handed me or find a way to hand it back to him. (114–15)

All of which is to prepare the ethical ground for the killing of Puddler. In Macdonald's earlier espionage novels, bodies dropped right and left. As we have seen in the previous chapter, he could even be blasé about them. But when he undertook the detective genre with intent, Macdonald would no longer be willing to let the action formula erase or obscure moral and ethical standards. Killing a human being is serious literary business; Macdonald carefully orchestrates. Always skeptical of resolution solely through action, Macdonald later wrote: "Archer is a man of action as well as an observer and recorder, but the emphasis is not on his physical exploits. He is less the hero of the novel than its mind, an unwilling judge who is forced to see that a murderer can be his own chief victim."[29] In fact, it is his deliberate sense of obligation to those standards that constitutes his "advance" of the genre. Macdonald championed Hammett because he took the corpses and the murderers back from the polite upper classes represented by Dorothy Sayers and S. S. Van Dine.[30] But, in taking crime back to "democracy," Macdonald knew, he was obliged to give it genuine moral weight. The killing of Puddler, then, is both a scene of suspense and part of a larger moral design in the novel, and in the genre. When the final fight comes, Macdonald tempers Archer's moral responsibility by stressing Puddler's muscular advantage as "machine," "bull," and "Neanderthal" (114, 116). To buttress his moral standing, the victorious Archer dives deep into the Pacific six times in vain attempts to save Puddler from drowning.

Macdonald's strong hint of Puddler's function as his mythic adversary is counterpointed by Albert Graves's killing of Taggert and later his killing of Sampson. By killing Taggert, Graves saves Archer's life and removes his rival for Miranda. Killing Miranda's father is a more complicated act, for, as Macdonald later stated, Graves's motivation lay in the structure of the story in which the king's daughter is saved for the heroic suitor. In the archetypal tale, the king gives his daughter to the heroic suitor who saves the kingdom from external threats. But Alan Taggert occupies (problematically) the role of the successful suitor, and Graves is wholly inappropriate, not to add guilty of murdering Taggert. Miranda is trapped between being a young woman and a part in a tale, not so much a person as the rich man's daughter. Thus Macdonald set about to accomplish one of the goals he had in view when he took on the detective genre: the connecting of a mythic or perennial structure to a historical time and place.

Several years after the publication of *The Moving Target,* Brigid Brophy summarized the myth of redemptive violence in her essay "Detective Fiction: A Modern Myth of Violence?" Brophy concentrates particularly on the tale of the hero who saves the king's maiden daughter from the threat of rape/marriage to the "monster," making the point that archetypal repetition takes the sting out of the violence in detective fiction by ritualizing it.[31]

Macdonald's first Archer novel certainly reflects this concept but suspends investment in it by giving it neither to Archer nor to the narrator. Negotiating the meaning of violence in his novels—historical/ethical fact or metaphor?— gives character to their moral themes. Archer had known Graves in Bavaria after the war; spending time in occupied territory should have taught Graves the difference between real and metaphorical violence. Mitigating his downfall, Macdonald sees, is the way the magic word *California* blurs the distinction between mirage and reality:

There may have been a time when Graves didn't care about money. There may be places where he could have stayed that way. Santa Teresa isn't one of them. Money is lifeblood in this town. If you don't have it, you're only half alive. It must have galled him to work for millionaires and handle their money and have nothing of his own. Suddenly he saw his chance to be a millionaire himself. He realized that he wanted money more than anything else on earth.

"Do you know what I wish at this moment?" she [Miranda] said. "I wish I had no money and no sex. They're both more trouble than they're worth to me." (*Target*, 166)

Miranda is young, fallible, and she gets the solution wrong. Archer knows the melancholy truth: in California there is nothing but money and sex, and the nostalgia for a lost wholeness, which Miranda feels as if it were an amputated leg.

The Moving Target juggles moral basics as it comes to a close. Archer prefers to believe that jealousy of the rich caused Graves to lose his moral innocence. But the DA, who comes on the scene at the end like Fortinbras at the end of *Hamlet* opts for a different view: that Graves had lost potential for moral innocence before any overt act marked him as Cain. The DA remembers Graves talking about Kierkegaard. "'He quoted something about innocence, that it's like standing on the edge of a deep gulf. You can't look down into the gulf without losing your innocence. Once you've looked, you're guilty'" (168). Archer, who had taken Puddler into the same deep gulf, insists that moral actions are empirical, not symbolic. They are grounded in reality—in this case, in the migrant pickers who are causing "trouble" (71) on one of Sampson's farms, or the Filipino houseboy who does his work unseen—except by the novelist (9). In Archer's view, Graves had lost sight of "self" in the real world of interconnection, where he bore responsibility for knowing those workers, the real (not the imagined) Beats. Graves had seen as much in wartime Bavaria; he should have known. He lost any chance of innocence long before he tumbled for the fantasy of money and sex: the seductions of Southern California.

Earlier in the book, Archer had confessed, "Once or twice before, I'd caught myself slipping off the edge of the case into a fairy tale. It was one of the occupational hazards of working in California, but it irked me" (71). Macdonald leaves the debate over Graves as a draw at the conclusion to *The Moving Target*, but he makes Archer a secret-sharer in the murderer's guilt. And he outlines the elements of the "newness" he aims to bring to the detective genre.

That newness was, at the outset of the Archer series, but dimly understood. Macdonald had forged it in a workshop, a university educational system, not unheard of for producing works in the genre. But he determined to produce those works with both hands, not only with the left—that is, never as diversions or "entertainments" or adjuncts to more serious work. The first installments in the Archer series are, therefore, rough and mixed in their effects:

there are fistfights and psychoanalytic explorations, tough talk and literary allusion. There are structural anomalies: like wholly unanticipated DAs who deliver lectures on Kierkegaard. And for the first cycle of Archer novels, Macdonald continued to seem to experiment, half in and half out of the formula, feeling his way through the occupational hazards.

[4]

The Rock and the Hard Place

Chandler and Hammett

Not least among the occupational hazards of undertaking the detective novel when Macdonald did were the rock and the hard place: Dashiell Hammett and Raymond Chandler. Until Macdonald finally came through the ordeal of disposing of the two fathers with *The Galton Case* in 1959, his work swerved from one model to the other. Hammett he acknowledged more readily and more happily. *Blue City* was a forthright *homage* to the twentieth-century inventor of the genre, who had done his best work in the 1920s and 1930s, then slowly succumbed to alcoholism and tuberculosis—not to mention harassment by a cold war U.S. government suspicious of his commitment to civil liberties. Hammett's presence in the Archer novels is largely benign, probably because Macdonald knew almost precisely what he wanted to borrow from Hammett: the spirit if not the actual lingo of the American vernacular, the modernized myth of the frontier solitary, the reclamation of the detective genre from the vicar's garden. Chandler's presence is a different matter. He was much more sensitive about being supplanted in the genre and was specifically critical of Macdonald. Macdonald, on the other hand, never seemed as sure of what he wanted from Chandler. When Chandler or the Chandleresque appear in the early Archer novels, the effect is grating, like fingernails on a blackboard.

Macdonald took Hammett in intellectual stride. Chandler made himself an obstacle. Raymond Chandler had revised Hammett's standard by the time Archer appeared, but despite his success was already a little paranoid about rising competition. For example, he did not much like *The Moving Target*, correctly figuring that the name on the title page was a pseudonym. In a letter to a friend, Chandler took issue with Macdonald's skill in metaphors, and he widened his criticism into a full-blown objection to what he considered to be the novelist's mistaken separation of the violence common to the genre from an attempt at literary sophistication.[1]

Whether Macdonald knew of Chandler's objections to *The Moving Target* at the time they were registered is unlikely. But a public clash was not long in coming. Macdonald's Oedipal frustrations with Chandler became critical in 1952, when the editors of Pocket Books, to whom lucrative paperback rights to *The Way Some People Die* (1951) had been sold, suggested to Alfred Knopf that the novel be rewritten in the Chandler style (Nolan, 133–55).[2] Macdonald responded with a manifesto:

> With all due respect for his [Chandler's] power, which I am willing to admit I do not match, but which I also insist I do not try to duplicate, I can't accept Chandler's vision of good and evil. It seems to me that it is conventional to the point of old-maidishness, that it is anti-human to the point of sadism (Chandler hates all women, and really likes only old men, boys, and his Marlow [*sic*] *persona*), and that the mind behind it, for all its tremendous imaginative force, is both uncultivated and second-rate.[3]

In Archer's cases, finding out who did it is not as important as finding out how many willful and accidental accomplices there were, and how far back in the history of a doomed family the evil began. "My subject is human error," Macdonald protested. "My whole structure is set up to throw insight into lives, not undramatically I hope; its background is psychological and sociological rather than theological."[4] Having Chandler out in the open, in the sense that another party (Pocket Books) had invoked his authority, actually enabled Macdonald to see his own world more clearly—its personal (psychological) density and its person-to-person (sociological) orientation replacing the vertical (theological) tendency of Chandler. An argument of just this sort had been brewing since his graduate school days when he championed Freud and Kafka over Dante and Aquinas.

By the time of Macdonald's manifesto to Alfred Knopf, Chandler himself was on the wane. And Macdonald's sense of obligation to his work had never been strong and immediate. Years later, assessing his debt, Macdonald placed Chandler later in his development, and shallower, than Hammett:

> But the first time that I read Chandler was about 1941 or 1942. He had published his first novel *The Big Sleep* in 1939 and I was onto him within a year or two after that and I was enormously impressed and thrilled by his writing as a great many readers were. It was just about the best writing that had ever been done in the detective story, it was so different. I think Hammett is a greater novelist, but I think Chandler's writing line by line is extremely fine. Or page by page, I don't think his books as a whole had the same strength. There is a difference you know between Hammett who was wrenching this stuff directly out of his own experience as a detective and another man who comes along and writes it from what is essentially a literary background.[5]

The Long Goodbye (1953), Chandler's novel closest to contemporary with the Macdonald of this period, was "written by a much older man" Macdonald said, and did not have "electricity and the tightness" although it was well written.[6]

Macdonald, whenever he discussed Chandler, walked a tightrope, for both writers shared significant elements of life history: American and British (or British by way of Canada) educations; "literary backgrounds"; even dislike for Los Angeles.[7] In a model of literary influence derived from Harold Bloom's *The Anxiety of Influence,* Chandler is the more difficult precursor than Hammett because he is so similar to Macdonald.

Chandler was, as Kevin Starr has said in *Embattled Dreams: California in War and Peace, 1940–1950,* essentially a writer of the 1940s.[8] Macdonald thought of himself as the writer of the next generation. Chandler's California is bounded by the "Hollywood Raj," expatriate British actors and movie industry types, who favored gin and lime, tweeds and pipes, and affected superiority to the natives.[9] Chandler's Hollywood was closer to a production of *Guys and Dolls* than a realistic city. In Starr's catalog:

> A city of cops, crooks, and defense lawyers; a demimonde of rackets, scream-
> ing headlines, and politicians on the take; a town of gamblers, guys and dolls,
> booze and sex; a place for schemers, also-rans, suckers and those who deceived
> them: the kind of city in which a private detective such as Philip Marlowe
> might make his way down means streets in search of the ever-elusive truth
> and get sapped with a blackjack for his effort by parties unknown.[10]

In other words, so perilously close to cliché that self-parody became a very real danger for the unwary writer. Macdonald was anything but unwary. Indeed, although he joked about being the only serious American novelist with a Mennonite-Canadian background, the joylessness in that background prepared him to disparage Chandler's Vanity Fair Hollywood, and to understand the deep temptations of the California myth.

The timing of Macdonald's manifesto was nearly perfect. In a letter to Knopf, who had published all of his novels before 1948 and who might have hinted at his returning in 1953, Chandler sounded a note of elegy, expressing weariness after just finishing a novel (probably *The Long Goodbye*), regret and sorrow that he had never been prolific, and resignation that Knopf already had his up-and-coming detective writer. Chandler did not mention any names, but it was almost certainly Macdonald who had replaced him on Knopf's list. Chandler was probably right, in one sense: one publishing house was not big enough for two top guns, himself and Macdonald. Macdonald's early experimentation with the espionage formula had cleared the underbrush of superficially defined evil, and almost wholly satisfied his hankering for "natural animal emotion." Archer would suffer his share of beatings in the early novels, but after killing Puddler in *The Moving Target* (and a particularly obnoxious client in *The Ivory Grin* [1952]), he shied away from physical violence. He has nothing like the masochistic appetite of Marlowe for absorbing beatings, nor the almost equally ardent desire to inflict them. Macdonald became more interested in emotions as they were intended or understood or blocked by human habit, not by muscle. The baton was passed, although neither writer was actually aware of the handoff, in the three-sided exchange involving both writers and Knopf in 1952–53.

If Chandler loomed like a forbidding father over the launching of Archer, Hammett was a more generous hovering spirit. Although Macdonald could be as keen a critic of Hammett's flaws (Kaye, 11) as he was, more often, of Chandler's, it was Hammett's democratic, American prose he wanted to emulate, not Chandler's mannerist artificiality. "But it is a clean useful prose," he wrote in "Homage to Dashiell Hammett," "with remarkable range and force. It has pace and point, strong tactile values, the rhythms and colors of speech, all in the colloquial tradition that stretches from Mark Twain through Stephen Crane to Lardner and Mencken, the Dr. Johnson of our vernacular."[11] Hammett's vernacular was crucial to Macdonald because it connected him to a wide reading pubic receptive, even addicted, to the detective genre but all too often put off by the kind of literary language that Kenneth Millar, Ph.D., was prone to use.

In "The Simple Art of Murder," Chandler himself betrayed more than an inkling of the ways Hammett had put the American detective novel beyond the purview of "fuddy-duddy connoisseurs":

> Hammett gave murder back to the kind of people that commit it for reasons, not just to provide a corpse; and with the means at hand, not with handwrought dueling pistols, curare, and tropical fish. He put these people down on paper as they are, and made them talk and think in the language they customarily used for these purposes. He had style, but his audience didn't know it, because it was in a language not supposed to be capable of such refinements. They thought they were getting a good meaty melodrama written in the kind of lingo they imagined they spoke themselves. It was, in a sense, but it was much more. All language begins with speech, and the speech of the common men at that, but when it develops to the point of becoming a literary medium it only looks like speech. Hammett's style at its worst was almost as formalized as a page of Marius the Epicurean; at its best it could say almost anything. I believe this style, which does not belong to Hammett or to anybody, but is the American language (and not even exclusively that any more), can say things he did not know how to say or feel the need of saying. In his hands it had no overtones, left no echo, evoked no image beyond a distant hill. He is said to have lacked heart, yet the story he thought most of himself is the record of a man's devotion to a friend. He was spare, frugal, hard-boiled, but he did over and over again what only the best writers can ever do at all. He wrote scenes that seemed never to have been written before.[12]

Chandler knew his opposite when he saw him. For a man who, elsewhere, in "The Simple Art of Murder," admitted that he liked "the English style better" (985), his praise of Hammett is slightly left-handed: he wrote better than he knew. Both served literary apprenticeships in *Black Mask* and other pulps in the 1920s and 1930s, and Chandler acknowledged that Hammett was the one who emerged earlier as the star performer, the one who, as Ezra Pound, acknowledging a tradition in American poetry, said to Walt Whitman in "A Pact" (1916): "It was you that broke the new wood, / Now is a time for carving."

For Macdonald, Chandler's "carving" was a little too filigreed. Hammett's ax left the "American grain" exposed, and that was all to the good. As an American by birth (who should have picked up Hammett's vernacular "naturally") but a Canadian by rearing and education, Macdonald could not simply fall into the idiom. Years of Anglo-Canadian education and an American doctorate made the vernacular something like a second language for him. He had to think deliberately to use it, and he relied on echoes of Hammett to confirm the "lingo." Beginning with Chandler's dismissive remarks about the author of *The Moving Target,* more than one critic has pointed out that although Macdonald professes the common language and the world it names, his private eye knows a lot that the ordinary person is not likely to know: history, art, literature, psychology. Very often, to give Chandler his due, Macdonald's readers do know that Archer's mentality is a cut above the democratic average person, leaving "overtones" and "echoes"—not of Marius the Epicurean, to be sure, but the "finish" of Macdonald's encounter with literature.

Hammett's prose, in any case, gave Macdonald a clearer American target than Chandler's, not only because Hammett had absorbed the salty speech of grifters and street people, but also because he had absorbed one of the foundational American myths—the homegrown moral virtue and practical survival skills bound up in Cooper's frontier hero Natty Bumppo. William Ruehlman has argued, in *Saint with a Gun: The Unlawful American Private Eye* (1974), that a "terrible duality" characterizes Natty Bumppo as "prototypical American hero": he is both deeply moral when he is forced into situations where he must kill (whether wild game for food or his Indian foes) and yet "trembles in his eagerness to get a shot off at an enemy." The main channel of this tradition of lawful unlawful violence runs through Hammett and Chandler, coming to a kind of sinister apotheosis in Mickey Spillane. Ruehlman finds Macdonald "an interesting exception" because Archer seems unfulfilled by violence, ether as victim or perpetrator.[13] The problem of violence troubled the early Archer novels thematically and structurally. On the one hand, overt physical violence seems not to have met Macdonald's test for genuine evil; it is presented as tangential to or as a remote symptom of the deeper malaise that Archer intuits. On the other, beating someone up never seems to solve any of Archer's cases; there is always more to the case. For Macdonald, Hammett's language was the way out of the problem with the violent hero, for the language had two dimensions: It could communicate the data of the story at the speed with which it actually happened, and it could Americanize mythic form.

A good example is "Fly Paper," one of Hammett's Continental Op stories. The Op is on the trail of a killer, Babe McCloor, who has just shot an important witness in a "wandering daughter job." Like Cooper's Deerslayer on the trail of Indian captives, the Op cannot afford to let the trail go cold:

> The big man [McCloor] was a yegg [thief]. San Francisco was on fire for him. The yegg instinct would be to use a rattler [freight train] to get away from trouble. The freight yards were in this end of town. Maybe he would be shifty enough to lie low instead of trying to powder [take a powder; flee]. In that case, he probably hadn't crossed Market Street at all. If he stuck, there would still be a chance of picking him up tomorrow. If he was high-tailing, it was catch him now or not at all.[14]

Cooper's Deerslayer never did a niftier job of gauging the psychology of crafty Hurons, nor could Hammett do a better job of resuscitating the myth of the frontier than by putting a self-reliant, plainspoken man in an urban setting that was supposed to have exterminated all natural allies to his survival. Deerslayer relied on nature—broken twigs, footprints in streamside mud, the ominous silence of birds. The Op tracks his prey by psychological spoor: the yegg's fevered thought leaves traces along his route, and the Op's sensors pick them up as if they were outlined in fluorescent paint.

Nor is it just the transporting of the Deerslayer myth from forest to the streets of San Francisco that is important. Hammett's diction rescues the detective novel from the drawing room and the vicarage garden. *Yegg, rattler, shifty, powder, high-tailing* season the Op's monologue with the tang of street talk and the urgent rhythm of his own stride in the chase. Chandler found this style, in Hammett, sometimes disingenuous, actually highly stylized when it pretended to be unprompted. Much is left to the ear of the reader. Is the Op's syllogistic thinking naively flawless, or is his cadence as deliberate as a Shakespearian line?

> If he stuck, there would still be a chance of picking him up tomorrow.
> If he was high-tailing, it was catch him now or not at all.
>
> There's special providence in the fall of a sparrow.
> If it be now, 'tis not to come; if it be not to come, it will be now; if it
>   be not now, yet it will come.
> The readiness is all. (*Hamlet*, V, ii)

To Macdonald's ear, Hammett's language was the poetry of the common. It was the combination of literariness (which delighted the Ph.D. in him) and new-minted Americanness (which served his public responsibility as a novelist) that drew him to Hammett—and pushed him away from Chandler. He wanted to reach a living, thinking, book-buying public through stories that would trigger their sense of being engaged in a moment—a moment that was in itself unique but also part of a continuum. This was one of the responsibilities of the novelist that, in Macdonald's view, Hammett fulfilled more democratically than Chandler.

Macdonald's years of formal education had implanted a deep indebtedness to traditions that seemed to ally him with forms and readers more attuned to Chandler than Hammett. It was no easy task to serve both masters. To an interviewer he described "keeping both of my lives alive" (Kaye, 26). Especially in his early novels, those between *The Drowning Pool* (1950) and *The Barbarous Coast* (1956), Macdonald's struggle to negotiate the difficult territory between the rock and the hard place, Hammett and Chandler, causes a kind of schizophrenia or lack of resolution in several of the early Archer novels. Indeed, he thought of giving him up at one point. To Henry Branson (1905–81), a friend from Ann Arbor days and the author of a series of detective novels featuring urbane physician-sleuth John Bent, Macdonald confessed in 1953: "Another Archer. I'd like to ditch that character, at least temporarily, as you would Bent, but he seems to be my bread-and-butter, and I can't afford to be bored with that."[15] Between 1949, when he wrote The *Moving Target,* and 1952, when he received his PhD in English, Macdonald wrote his 455-page dissertation and three additional Archer novels, *The Drowning Pool* (1950), *The Way Some People Die* (1951), and *The Ivory Grin* (1952). By 1952 he was understandably worn down, incapacitated by an attack of gout, and still on the fence about a career: he was not all that sure that Archer was a savior for the long haul. In fact, the next novel after *The Ivory Grin, Meet Me at the Morgue* (1954) was not an Archer novel, although it was a crime novel. In 1955, Dodd, Mead, publishers of his very early espionage novels, inquired about the possibility of a non-Archer series to alternate with the Archers, which were the property of Knopf.[16] Archer's survival through his early years was anything but guaranteed.

The second Archer, *The Drowning Pool,* Macdonald remembered wryly as teetering on the verge of being "silly" because of the combination of Hammett-like thugs and James Bond-ish gadgets in the hydrotherapy scenes.[17] But the flaws originate not only in Macdonald's never-repeated attempt to combine the gadgetry of one genre, the spy thriller, with the realism of another, the American detective novel. They stem also from the oil-and-water separation of two languages: one, a Hammett-like voice commenting on the grunge of public corruption; the other, the self-conscious literary writer loading his "significance" from the top. It is clear, from evidence internal to the novel, where his allegiance lay (with Hammett) but not clear how he could assuage the other voice.

The Drowning Pool is a schizophrenic novel. In one of its selves, Archer becomes a kind of psychoanalyst called upon to diagnose and treat a dysfunctional family. Maude Slocum, a young and attractive wife, calls upon Archer in his office because someone has been sending her husband anonymous letters accusing her of infidelity. One aspect of the schizophrenia is that the husband may not care. James Slocum, only son of a strong woman, Olivia Slocum, whose Valley property rests upon valuable oil deposits, is a "Peter Pan"—a no-longer-young man with attenuated tastes in theater and "a thin sweet tenor" voice (52). When Archer meets him at the beginning of the novel, Slocum is playing the lead in a mannered drawing-room comedy for a community the-ater, *The Ironist.* Slocum's picture outside the theater box office sends ominous signals:

> [He] was a man in his late thirties, with light hair waving over a pale and noble brow. The eyes were large and sorrowful, the mouth small and sensitive. The picture had been taken in three-quarters face to show the profile, which was very fine. Mr. James Slocum, the caption said, as "The Ironist." If the pic-ture could be believed, Mr. James Slocum's pan was a maiden's dream. Not mine. (16)

The delayed pun on pan—Peter Pan—is more Chandler than Hammett, as are the manner and content of the description, but the temperament of Archer is all Hammett, except that the corruption he detects, and detests, has moved from the public arena to the private psychology. Slocum is an effeminate man, his culture conventionalized rather than natural. To complicate matters, he is also a father, and the family over which he "presides" is infected by his own failure to grow out of being a son.

The author of the play, Francis Marvell, is another "aging Peter Pan, glib, bland, and eccentric" and fond of James Slocum in a way that rasps with warn-ings of homosexuality for Archer (37). Sexuality "ironized"—played to differ-ent scripts by different casts—psychologizes the novel and converts Archer from pure op to therapist. Early in the case, for example, Archer overhears Slocum's wife, Maude, warn her husband to leave their daughter, Cathy, alone. Maude's menacing tone of voice "made the short hairs prickle at the back of [Archer's] neck" (34). Archer's psychoanalytic intuition warns him darkly of incest and other unnamed violations of the daughter, a set of problems he has not been called in to handle.

Cathy Slocum herself, like nearly all of the at-risk daughters in Macdonald's plots, has more than an intuition of the unease rife among the adults. In their first conversation, Archer is attracted to her nascent sexuality and impressed by a glimmer of womanly maturity in an adolescent girl's body. She is the con-tinuation of Miranda Sampson: "I followed the tall fine body to the swing, amused by the fact that it contained an adolescent, though. The book in her hand, when she laid it down on the cushion between us, turned out to be a book on psychoanalysis by Karen Horney" (29).

Putting one of Horney's books on psychoanalysis in Cathy Slocum's hand is another mark of the dedicated academic in Macdonald, and an enormous risk for a detective novelist. For most practitioners, the book would be important for what it could physically hide: a purloined letter, a telltale timetable, a cryptic code. But Macdonald wants us to know what is written on the pages. What kind of shamus reads current psychoanalytic theory by one of the early, feminist dissenters from orthodox Freudian practice? Hammett's women (Brigid, Effie, and Iva in *The Maltese Falcon,* for example) don't seem to need a psychoanalyst to handle themselves—or Spade. Macdonald, out of his emerging devotion to Freudian psychoanalysis, begins to equip his daughters (like Miranda Sampson) with just enough knowledge of their situations so that their suffering, and their relief, call for an articulate rescuer with more brains than brawn. Cathy, for example, reveals to Archer in the final pages of the novel that she recognizes the relationship between her putative father and his mother (her grandmother) as an Oedipus complex: "She twisted my father from the time he was a little boy, she made him what he is." Archer bids up her revelation with a question about the Electra complex. Lucky for the analyst, the girl had not read that far. "She knew too much already, more than she could bear" (240). The problem in grafting Hammett's idiom to Macdonald's "brainier" sense of crime and evil is that when the experiment does not work, the result may be a two-headed calf. In which case, Chandler's charge of intellectual puffery seems all too valid. One schizophrenic half of *The Drowning Pool* swirls around the Slocum family as a protracted case of diagnosis and attempted therapy. The "crime" is James Slocum's injection of latent homosexuality into the "normal" family unit. It is not all his fault, of course. His mother, Olivia, is a mom of Wylie-an proportions.[18] His confused sexual loyalties ultimately lead his daughter to commit a crime, not completely unjustified or unmotivated—an act that calls for understanding and, perhaps, punishment.

In the other schizophrenic half of the novel, the half superficially more derivative of Hammett, a gangster named Walter Kilbourne tries to get control of the Slocum oil properties. Kilbourne's wife, Mavis, is the seductress who generates "the whirling vortex . . . the drowning pool" (117–18). Sex shapes this half of the plot, too, but Archer does not need a degree in psychiatry to figure it out. Mavis's impotent husband has hired a stud, Pat Reavis—"a fine American marriage," Archer smirks (196), and a fine hard-boiled foil to the Slocum family plot. Reavis has also seduced Cathy Slocum. Sex weaves the divided plots together.

The weaving, though, is structurally superficial. The crime in Kilbourne's half of the novel lacks a psychological angle: he is merely greedy for all the money the Slocum oil can bring him, and he will commit murder and mayhem to get it. To that end he employs an evil doctor, Melliotes, who runs the hydrotherapy tank with the help of a sinister nurse, whose character is so over the top one suspects irony in her construction—as if this novel had been written after rather than before *One Flew over the Cuckoo's Nest.* On this side of *The Drowning Pool* there are no characters with inward, psychological corners; there are the roughly drawn stand-ups that Macdonald must have remembered from his boyhood fascination with Pearl White cliffhangers,[19] or taken out of mothballs from his espionage novel days.

The problem in terms of the Hammett transfer is that Macdonald's clear attempt to complete it occurs in only one half of the novel. Mavis kills her husband (who doubtless deserved a thousand executions) after Archer had instructed her only to watch him, gun in hand. Before the killing of Kilbourne, Archer had been willing to let Mavis escape to Mexico; after the killing, Archer, like Spade at the end of *The Maltese Falcon,* revises his judgment and explains to the female killer that she has broken not only a moral commandment but also a code of honor (218–19). Hammett's conclusion in *The Maltese Falcon* works more effectively; Macdonald's seems contrived. But the situations are related: in both, the male had put the female in charge of honorable action and she failed.

Macdonald often forbore to mention his second Archer novel in interviews. It was not included in any of the three omnibus editions of his work, but it was, along with *The Moving Target,* one of the two "Harper" Hollywood versions of his novels starring Paul Newman (1975). It is not difficult to speculate on his motivation for silence. *The Drowning Pool* is unsubtle in its attempt to appropriate Hammett's language and the power of the frontier myth he used. In rendering Archer the latter-day Natty Bumppo of American literary myth in *The Drowning Pool,* Macdonald telegraphs his thematic pitch. Midway through the case, for example, Archer tracks Pat Reavis from Los Angeles to Las Vegas, finally running him to ground in rough terrain outside the city. Reavis recognizes him at once. "'Archer?'" Reavis says. "'The name is Leatherstocking,'" Archer replies, with a laconic brevity that Cooper's loquacious Natty could never have managed (138). The crucial point that Macdonald himself had made about Hammett was that he had absorbed the "language" of Leatherstocking—the entire evocative symbol system—so elegantly that no underlining was needed. Chandler had reiterated the point: when Hammett's style is working best, no one knows it is style at all. Macdonald, in the second Archer novel, was still working toward the Hammett ideal of a transparent style.

The way is not smooth. While the crimes of the gangster Kilbourne are conventional and therefore easy to grasp, the family crimes in the Slocum menage are more difficult. Olivia Slocum, the matriarch, has commandeered her son's mature sexuality. He has married anyway, as much for social cover as anything else. His daughter, not surprisingly, is not his natural child, but the child of his wife and the local sheriff. Cathy, like many sons and daughters in Macdonald's fiction, intuitively knows her real, as opposed to her public, parentage and resents her "grandmother" for emasculating her putative father. This is, in a very real sense, a case for a family therapist rather than a private detective. Until, of course, the daughter's resentment causes a murder and the two spheres —family relationships and public statute—collide. The possibilities for theme are rich, but the challenges to plot are daunting.

Macdonald's third Archer novel, *The Way Some People Die* (1951), is more successful in its homage to Hammett and more successful in plot because Macdonald keeps the action more confined to the sociological sphere. Once again, a missing or troubled daughter is the fuse to the case. Galatea Lawrence has disappeared from her job as a nurse, and her straitlaced mother hires Archer to find her. What Archer will learn is that, in the course of tending her patients, Galley made a connection with a gangster, and she traded in caregiving for easy money. So far and so quick was her fall that she had committed murder long before Archer could pick up her trail. At the outset, though, Archer has a premonition that it is not only the girl he must (but probably will not) find alive or intact, but the mother's image of her, too. After observing Mrs. Lawrence's obsessive household control and neatness, Archer already suspects he knows why Galley, her daughter, has fled and that she never was nor ever will be the paragon her mother imagined. In her nursing school class picture, she stands out: "With her fierce curled lips, black eyes and clean angry bones she must have stood out in her graduating class like a chicken hawk in a flock of pullets" (178). The vulnerable, victimized daughters in the first two Archer novels, Miranda Sampson and Cathy Slocum, have metamorphosed into a predator.

Sociology outweighs psychology in *The Way Some People Die,* and this adjustment produces a novel more responsive to Hammett's legacy than Chandler's. The search for Galley Lawrence takes Archer south from Los Angeles through Long Beach (where, in an early autobiographical aside, we learn he grew up) to Pacific Point, the second of Macdonald's fictionalized Southern California settings—this one resonant of Los Angeles while Santa Teresa echoes Santa Barbara. The drive gives Archer an opportunity to muse on the milieu of his present quest through a sociological cross-section of Southern California. From L.A. to Long Beach to Pacific Point, Archer moves from brown skins to white, from poverty to affluence, from hardship to privilege.

One of his first stops is the Point Arena, a seedy venue for rigged wrestling matches and other rackets where Joe Tarantine, a flashy grifter often seen with Galley, hangs out. "A social researcher with a good nose could have written a Ph.D. thesis about that air" in the arena: cigarettes, beer, sweat, and cheap cologne (186).

From the Arena, Archer's investigation takes him to Tarantine's mother's house:

Sanedres Street was the one I was on. It ran crosstown through the center of the Negro and Mexican district, a street of rundown cottages and crowded shacks interspersed with liquor stores and pawnshops, poolroom-bars and fly-blown lunchrooms and storefront tabernacles. As the street approached the hills on the other side of the ball park, it gradually improved. The houses were larger and better kept. They had bigger yards, and the children playing in the yards were white under their dirt. (189)

This is not only the gritty neighborhood of Hammett's urban Leatherstockings, it is also the gritty and stratified neighborhoods of Macdonald's own childhood in Kitchener and of his stillborn autobiographical novel, *Winter Solstice*. With its leaning to the sociologically concrete, *The Way Some People Die* seems less likely than *The Drowning Pool* to lose itself in caricature and contrivance.

In fact, Macdonald seems so much more comfortable with Hammett's influence in this novel that he actually has Hammett play a kind of cameo part. In chapter 3 Archer interviews Galley Lawrence's last known landlord, one Mr. Raisch, who bears more than a coincidental resemblance to the notoriously emaciated Hammett, the thinnest of thin men, worn by hard knocks and tuberculosis:

When I got out of my car a mockingbird swooped from one of the trees and dived for my head. I gave him a hard look and he flew up to a telephone wire and sat there swinging back and forth and laughing at me. The laughter actually came from a red-faced man in dungarees who was sitting in a deck-chair under the tree. His mirth brought on some sort of attack, probably asthmatic. He coughed and choked and wheezed, and the chair creaked under his weight and his face got redder. When it was over he removed a dirty straw hat and wiped his bare red pate with a handkerchief. (14–15)

Macdonald colors his Hammett cameo red and redder in sly verbal tribute to the author of *Red Harvest,* the novel that most directly shaped his earlier, pre-Archer novel *Blue City*. And perhaps it represented an anti-McCarthy wink to a fellow writer who had served time rather than name names.[20]

In addition to giving his character a general physical and political resemblance to Hammett, Macdonald has Raisch demonstrate that he is as good a detective—old and infirm as he is—as Archer himself. He spots clues to Archer's origins (the L.A. license plate on his car) and his occupation ("maybe you got a tumor under your armpit" [*Way,* 182]). And he tells Archer that he is not the first gun-toting visitor in search of his former tenant, giving a virtuoso rendition of the visit of two "poolroom cowboys" that could have come straight from the pages of Hammett (182–85). After all, Macdonald knew, Hammett often "puts a little bit of a comic spin" on his prose, just to remind himself and the reader that he made no claim to writing hallowed *literature* (*Nelson*, 13B-1).

The cast of *The Way Some People Die* would be comfortable in a Hammett novel, too. For the most part, they emerge from the underground of urban rackets. Danny Dowser is the kingpin of an Irish mob; Blaney and Sullivan are his muscle. Herman Speed is a kind of *über*-gangster, related to Dwight Troy in *The Moving Target* and Kilbourne in *The Drowning Pool*. It is Galley's stint nursing Speed that gets her involved in the underworld. But she is a willing Persephone.

Macdonald's thematic interest in urban corruption dates from Hammett's, when perpetrators had names like McCloor ("Fly Paper") and Yard, Thaler, and Quint (*Red Harvest* [1929]). Crime still vies with evil, and is still the purview of Anglo-Saxon miscreants. More diverse ethnic competitors lurk on the margins, however. The Tarantine brothers, representing a sort of sociological or ethnic inevitability—embedded in the urban landscape Archer traverses —seek to break into the Dowser rackets in the novel but end up as victims instead. Simmie, the African American boxer, is likewise more victim than empowered agent. Macdonald's hypothetical "social researcher" (186) would still find organized crime the cultural preserve of white people and poverty the default condition of the nonwhite.

Although Macdonald stays within Hammett's sociology in *The Way Some People Die,* his concept of a moral culture based in psychology rather than in the law of the jungle pushes the boundaries beyond where Hammett had stopped. Hammett was by no means unaware of the psychological roots of crime, but in naming causes he stressed the inequities inherent in American urban conditions. The town of Personville, site of *Red Harvest,* is a good example. Shrouded in smoke from the town's smelters when the Op makes his visit, Personville is known as "Poisonville" to those doomed to live there. The means of all wealth had originally been concentrated in one man, Elihu Willsson, now confined, like General Sternwood in Chandler's *The Big Sleep,* to his bed and attended by a major domo. Once upon a time the elder Willsson had controlled every financial enterprise in town capable of turning a profit. Then came world war and the rise of the Wobblies (IWW organizers unionized the mines that fed the smelters), and Willsson's control was splintered. He got old and the underclasses achieved enough organization to take on some of the corruption themselves. Outlaw crime replaced the overlord's "legal" exploitation of workers and capital.

Hammett's Op, although usually hired by the wealthy with possessions insured by the firm paying his salary, often becomes a class warrior: he takes the master class's money, yet conspires to short-circuit its exploitative practices. Macdonald departs from Hammett's paradigm on this fundamental level, substituting psychology for sociology as the vocabulary of his quest. In *The Way Some People Die,* certainly, thugs with superior power inflict pain on those who are powerless in order to take something of value from the weaker. In Macdonald's emergent plot (not the surface plot concerning the actual criminal rackets), the more powerful inflict pain and suffering on the weaker, not to gain a material advantage but to gratify an insatiable will-to-power. Thus Henry Fellows (in reality, the gangster Herman Speed on the lam), impresses Archer as the kind of violent man who will pass along all physical insults to someone lower in the pecking order. Archer would like to slug "Fellows" when he meets him, but he knows the man would only pass on the beating to someone weaker, probably his wife Marjorie. Archer makes the moral choice to stop evil as a condition, not crime as one or a series of actions, by denying himself the very real satisfaction of punching Fellows (62). The moral/psychological formula for Hammett's heroes is much more basic: slug away.

Archer makes a second, and confirming, moral decision a few scenes later when he refrains from roughing up a desk clerk and petty grifter named Ronnie who is running a scam at a motel where he sets up men looking for sex with an underage girl:

> He [Ronnie] was the kind of puppy who would lick any hand that he was afraid to bite. It was depressing not to be able to hit him again because he was younger and softer and too easy. If I really hurt him, he'd pass it on to somebody weaker, like Ruth. There was really nothing to be done about Ronnie, at least that I could do. He would go on turning a dollar in one way or another until he ended up in Folsom or a mortuary or a house with a swimming pool on top of a hill. There were thousands like him in my ten-thousand-square-mile beat: boys who had lost their futures, their parents and themselves in the shallow jerrybuilt streets of the coastal cities; boys with hot-rod bowels, comic-book imaginations, daring that grew up too late for one war, too early for another. (135)

Archer's world, as it emerges early in the series, is a bleaker moral wasteland than Hammett's crooked metropolis. There is always something the Op can do to redress the balance of good and evil: a crook to arrest or a hood to beat up. But for Archer evil is systemic: there is no way for him to bring an entire culture to justice. The sinners are more likely to rise than the saints. Abstinence from violence is more constructive than violence itself, but less dramatic.

The linchpin of *The Way Some People Die* is the problematic psychology of Galley Lawrence, the missing daughter. Dowser and Speed can be arrested and convicted relatively easily of nameable crimes: selling dope, fixing fights, murder. And Archer disposes of them efficiently. But Galley is a different kind of evil; she is the renegade cancer cell on a rampage in the body politic. Archer has trouble finding her because she does not want to be found. She has had a taste of easy money and the life it buys, and she will not go back to nursing. When Archer finally does catch her, he debriefs her as a psychoanalyst might initiate treatment of a patient (234). "'You're a good liar, Galley. You have the art of mixing fact with your fantasy'" (233). Archer knocks down one barrier of denial after another, finally getting beyond statutory crime and into the territory where will and power and desire destroy conscience. Galley is the "predator" she appeared to be in her class picture:

> "I have an idea you like killing men. The real payoff for you wasn't the thirty thousand. It was smothering Joe, and shooting Keith and Mario. The money was just a respectable excuse, like the fifty dollars to a call-girl who happens to be a nymphomaniac. You see, Galley, you're a murderer. You're different from ordinary people, you like different things. Ordinary people don't throw slugs into a dead man's back for the hell of it. They don't arrange their lives so they have to spend a week-end with a corpse. Did it give you a thrill, cooking your meals in the same room with him?"
> I had finally got to her. (236–37)

The "thrill" is also Archer's, for he is a psychoanalyst whose quest for the key to behavior, not the final empirical clue to a chain of criminal actions, is gratified in an orgasmic rush. Galley Lawrence bears a strong but not complete resemblance to her murderous sisters in Hammett and Chandler novels: Brigid O'Shaugnessey in *The Maltese Falcon* and Carmen Sternwood in *The Big Sleep*. All three are inventions of misogynistic fantasy, versions of the black widow stereotype who copulates and then kills. But Macdonald gives his black widow a case history, a sketch of domestic upbringing, school friends. It is as if he is trying to say that murderers do not spring full blown from a dusty shelf of cliché, or even from the Jungian collective unconscious. Murderers are made by disturbances in human nature and in the society made from it. The crimes of Dowser and Speed (like those of Kilbourne and Melliotes in *The Drowning Pool*) are discovered and disposed of in a denouement that functions, in the respective novels, like false dawn. In both early Archer novels, however, after crimes are "righted," evil continues. And Archer keeps trying to understand how it begins and why it spreads. Each case requires two, complementary but not simultaneous, endings. In terms of narrative technique, the history of Macdonald's Archer novels is the history of narrowing the structural gap between nabbing the guilty party and understanding how she or he got to be that way.

The fourth novel in the Archer series, *The Ivory Grin* (1952), brings crime and evil into closer, nearly synchronized, orbits. Still, however, the case depends on a gangster and his evil deeds, although these deeds are confined to the past and the gangster to a kind of syphilitic madness that has forced his "retirement."

Macdonald wrote *The Ivory Grin* quickly in the early months of 1951, feeling the conscious influence of Nelson Algren's *The Man With the Golden Arm*. Then, sensing his graduate work like a nagging unfinished project, he drove to

Ann Arbor for the summer and defended his dissertation on Coleridge. In the fall he returned to Santa Barbara "totally exhausted" (Kaye, 8-b-7). Four novels and a dissertation in four years, plus the separation from wife and daughter that his sojourns in Ann Arbor required, left Macdonald susceptible to chronic health problems, mostly circulatory, which he shared with both parents. He was confined to a wheelchair for several months in 1952 by severe gout. But he had a strong doctoral dissertation *and* a strong novel, one to "expand my own horizons and . . . a bigger book than I had written before" (Kaye, 8–b-7). He was so confident of *The Ivory Grin* that he wrote his own promotional copy in a 1952 notebook: "[Macdonald's] characters have a psychological dimension, his stories have social range and moral meaning, and at their highest points an almost tragic passion. Instead of action for action's sake diluted with cynical sentimentality, here is human compassion for the broken patterns of life."[21] The sparring with Chandler continues, by long distance, in the second sentence; Macdonald had always faulted the older writer for not suturing his scenes into a viable whole. One obvious reason Macdonald claimed "social range" for *The Ivory Grin* is that, by registering the presence of "the Negro Problem" in America more strongly than in any of his previous novels (and, arguably, in the genre), he had turned a popular form toward a social problem rather than away from it.

Judging from evidence in his abandoned autobiographical novel, *Winter Solstice,* Macdonald had a complex sense of race as a public force and a literary theme. One of the most vivid and self-sustaining scenes in his unpublished manuscript involves the young protagonist, who has furtively entered the hospital where his father lies dying, confronting a black custodian:

> The friendly Negroes and the friendly dead, William thought wordlessly as he went up the fire-stairs; they were the ones you could count on not to kick you when you were down, because they were down too. He envied in a way the unworried underground existence of the dead, and the warm mystery the Negroes seemed to share with one another. Both were members of a group which could never cast them out. Negroes were Negroes, and the dead were dead. It was the sick people like his father, the poor people like himself who lived in suspense from minute to minute, because they seemed to belong nowhere. Cast out by the world of life and luck, they had no grave to hide in, no blackface mask to disguise their humanity and excuse their social death. He envied the underground fraternity of the Negroes, the subterranean democracy of the dead.[22]

The concept of the social death of blacks in an overwhelmingly white and racist society was still to be acknowledged on an open public stage in America, although Ralph Ellison was working with such themes as social death and "the black mask of humanity" in his fiction and criticism.[23] Almost three years before American racial practices were legally wrenched into change with *Brown v. Board of Education,* Macdonald expanded the detective novel horizon by including race. Critic and novelist Anthony Boucher, a friend of Macdonald's, wrote in 1944 about the inherent conservatism of the genre: "In most mysteries up to recent years, you could safely assume that a labor organizer was a racketeer, that a Communist had a bomb in his pocket, that a Negro was either sinister or comedic relief."[24] Neither proximate mentor, Hammett nor Chandler, had brought blacks further than such subordinate roles and flat stereotypes in their fiction, though Hammett had become president of the Civil Rights Congress of New York in 1946 after he stopped writing.

Macdonald worked with the material of *The Ivory Grin* in a short story before he expanded it into a novel. The fourth Archer novel began as "Strangers in Town," a short story for the 1950 *Ellery Queen Mystery Magazine* competition.[25] The short story contains most of the racial subplot of the novel in truncated form; Macdonald wrapped the black story with a white murder plot in the novel.

The Ivory Grin begins in Archer's office as he listens to a patently bogus story told by prospective client Una Durano, an unattractive woman repugnant to him morally (because he is sure she is lying) and sexually (because of her squat and masculinized figure). Una wants Archer to find Lucy Champion, a black woman light-skinned enough to "pass," who, according to Una, is a former maid whom she suspects of theft. Archer's sympathy, like the youth's sympathy in *Winter Solstice,* is triggered by a kind of underground bond with Lucy. Archer feels Lucy's "social death" the way Millar-surrogate William feels the social death of African Americans in *Winter Solstice.*

Lucy's trail takes Archer from Los Angeles to a hot and dry valley town, ironically named Bella City. Symbolically, Bella City is T. S. Eliot's wasteland: in a squalid room at the Mountview Motel, on the trail of Lucy Champion, Archer hears the thin and desperate voices of a man and woman having sex in an adjoining room:

> A woman groaned behind the wallboard partition in the next room, number nine.
> A man's voice said: "Anything the matter?"
> "Don't talk."
> "I thought something was the matter."
> "Shut up. There's nothing the matter."
> "I thought I hurt you."
> "Shut up. Shut up. Shut up." (24–25)

In the second part of *The Waste Land,* "A Game of Chess," lovemaking is just as disconnected and arid: "Speak to me. Why do you never speak. Speak." "What are you thinking of? What thinking? What?" Bella City is no place for sustaining human relationships.

The highway through town functions as "a rough social equator bisecting the community into lighter and darker hemispheres" (*Grin*, 11). Archer plunges into the latter, and there he does find traces of life that counteract the sense of wasteland: watered lawns, neat houses, paved sidewalks. Lucy and a young black man play with a hose while the young man washes his car. Pretending to be taking a survey of radio listeners, Archer melts into the thriving black neighborhood and happens to be next door when Lucy is evicted from the house where she rents a room. The young man's mother is skeptical of her morals. Before Archer can catch up with Lucy, however, she is murdered in the Mountview—confirming the symbolic signals he had picked up on his first visit: death is as likely as sex to lurk behind the thin walls. The young black man, Alex Norris, whose mother owns the house where Lucy had boarded, is arrested for the crime simply because white law assumes a black man committed the murder of a black woman: "His [Norris's] gaze was turned inward. He seemed to be seeing himself for the first time as he was: a black boy tangled in white law, so vulnerable he hardly dared move a muscle" (48). The massing of small-town "white law" against Norris simply because of his color adds to Archer's instant dislike of Una Durano, the woman who put him on Lucy Champion's trail, and he sets out to find the murderer as a stroke for racial justice—even though, as the case develops, the evil lies elsewhere.

The road is not smooth. Archer has to break through accumulated black distrust of whites so that he can persuade Alex Norris to talk to him. He has good luck with Alex's mother:

> "You are on our side, Mr. Archer?"
> "The side of justice when I can find it. When I can't find it, I'm for the underdog."
> "My son is no underdog," she said with a flash of pride.
> "I'm afraid he'll be treated like one. There's a chance that Alex may be railroaded for this murder." (133)

But Archer has less success with Alex himself, who is more stubborn and distrustful, and even less luck (so little, in fact, that he gives up trying) with the white powers in Bella City. One of the local deputies handcuffs Alex to the body of Lucy Champion in a cruel attempt to pressure him into confessing. Macdonald names the torturing deputy Schwartz, an ironic linguistic pun that puts two "blacks," one of skin and the other of name, in the interrogation room together.

Alex Norris and the subtheme of small-town white racism idle while Archer pursues the solution to another murder, one that had preceded and caused the murder of Lucy Champion. On the trail of the black woman, Archer meets another hunter, Max Heiss, a much cheaper private eye of questionable ethics. Heiss is on the trail of a missing local man, Charles Singleton, scion of a wealthy family, pampered son of an indulgent mother. Archer finds a notice of the reward for information on the whereabouts of Singleton when he finds Lucy's body. Both the trail of Singleton and the trail of Lucy Champion lead Archer to the office of Dr. Samuel Benning, a shopworn local GP, where he meets two principals in the case: the doctor's browbeating wife and the skeleton in his closet.

The challenge to Archer is formidable. But Macdonald makes a point of describing it in terms that distinguish it from the customary detective's work: "The pattern I was picking out strand by strand was too complicated to be explained in the language of physical evidence" (148). Discerning psychological markers as well as forensic clues, Archer seeks a "gestalt" (192) rather than a definitive piece of physical evidence. This kind of search requires a special set of skills, more like those of a psychoanalyst than a simple gumshoe. As Archer explains, ruefully, to a young woman who still hopes the vanished Singleton will be found alive, evil is not "in the world" but in "people's heads" (216) You cannot beat it out of them; the harder the blows, the more determined their silence.

Most of the evil in The Ivory Grin is in the head of one character, Dr. Benning. He is responsible for the murders of Lucy Champion and Charles Singleton, the skeleton in his closet. Dr. Benning, Archer learns, is a counterpart to the deranged hoodlum, Leo Durano. Although Durano in his right mind was a criminal with a long list of offenses, in his dilapidated mental state he might merit some limited measure of our sympathy. The same kind of random search for mercy and understanding shapes Archer's early thinking as he focuses on Dr. Benning. Even though Benning is a doctor who had used the instruments and skill of the medical profession to take life rather than to preserve it, Archer does not immediately condemn him. As a medical student Benning had wanted to specialize in psychology but could not afford the extra years of school (147). Added to his professional frustration is the emotional and sexual frustration of knowing that his wife, Bess, prefers another man (Singleton) and had been the sexual property of still another (Durano). Archer can feel something for this professionally frustrated and sexually insulted "underdog" (238). But he can also separate his feeling from his moral thinking.

In the end, the racial subtheme reappears and cuts the knot of Archer's dilemma. Benning had violated "the human idea" and must be held accountable, no matter how badly fate had treated him. Archer will not let Benning walk away, no matter what he has suffered in frustrated dreams and sexual insult. He must go into jail as Alex Norris walks out (239–40), although not before Archer takes out unspecified anger by shooting Una Durano to death—the second person he kills.

The Ivory Grin is a strong book, progressing beyond previous Archer novels by striving to connect parallel plots of crime on one track and evil on another

(Durano and Benning) and social justice (Norris). The weave in the early Archer novels is coarser, and the reader can, like Archer himself in *The Ivory Grin*, pick one strand from another perhaps too easily. Most of the Singleton plot is related in flashback, not wholly digested; and the character of Bess is forced to shoulder an immense load of sexual guilt. The character of Lucy Champion is the connecting thread in *The Ivory Grin*, and she, the femme fatale, need not have been marked with race for the novel to work. But Macdonald intended to expand the horizon of the detective novel by pressing toward social comment. The year Knopf published *The Ivory Grin*, 1952, was the same year Ralph Ellison's towering novel on race, *Invisible Man*, was published. Neither Macdonald nor anyone else would make the claim that *The Ivory Grin* merits ranking with *Invisible Man*. But Macdonald went beyond the standard scope of the detective novel to bring its readers to the color line.

Macdonald's homage to Hammett was sincere, but it had its limits. The gritty sociological and class realism of Hammett's work generated a language and a world of speakers that Macdonald needed in the construction and reception of his popular universe. But with the realism came Hammett's realistic sense of crime. His people committed evil acts by bootlegging, extortion, armed robbery, graft, and murder. As unsavory as such a roster of crimes might be, increasingly in the 1950s such felonies did not serve Macdonald's emerging vision of human disorder, frustration, and neurosis. The Singleton plot that Macdonald added to the race-based plot of the short story from which *The Ivory Grin* grew is overtly Freudian. Tracking Charles Singleton, Archer learns, is tracking the neurotic relationship between a "pre-Freudian" mother (92) and the adult son she has crippled. Still the two plots do not converge.

Meet Me at the Morgue (1953), Macdonald's next novel, gives Archer a sabbatical. Macdonald tested the character of Howard Cross, a probation officer in Pacific Point. Archer works alone; Cross works in an office. Like *The Ferguson Affair* (1960), a later non-Archer novel in which the investigator is married and soon to become a father, *Meet Me at the Morgue* functions as a referendum on Archer as a type. Can the strong mystique of the solitary private detective work as effectively when he is a fully connected member of a social group, a working office, or the nuclear family? In *Meet Me at the Morgue*, Macdonald uses the Howard Cross character to stand outside Archer, temporarily, and to take his measure before committing to the long run of an Archer saga. *Meet Me at the Morgue* provides one additional experiment: The plot is the most full-fledged Freudian "case" that Macdonald had yet attempted, involving Cross in a network of intersecting complexes.

Meet Me at the Morgue begins with the kidnapping of a young boy, Jamie Johnson. One of Cross's parolees, Fred Miner, the Johnson family chauffeur, is clearly implicated in the crime—so clearly, in fact, that Cross is reluctant to believe that Miner would actually risk parole by committing such an obvious crime. The original offense for which Miner was convicted had never been adequately explained, and nothing in Miner's character, to Cross, added up to the kidnapping of a boy of whom he was obviously so fond. The investigation of the current kidnapping leads Cross to revisit the crime for which Miner was convicted and paroled. Fishing out of an old and apparently cold case the loose ends of motive for the current one (an emerging Macdonald trademark), Cross finds himself in complex territory.

There are additional accessories to *Meet Me at the Morgue* suggesting that Macdonald was experimenting with changes to the detective formula he had begun with Archer. Archer is divorced, and although he notices attractive women in his early cases, he does not pursue a romantic interest. Cross's "Gal Friday," Ann Devon, a very young twenty-four-year-old, has a desperate crush on her boss even as she dates a young lawyer in Pacific Point, Larry Seifel. Macdonald uses this three-sided relationship to explore the psychology of romance without creating, for Archer, a relationship on which Macdonald might have to renege. Cross has, if anything, big-brother feelings for Ann, and Seifel is still sexually knotted to an adolescent fear and distrust of women: "'But even the best of them let their emotions get out of kilter now and then,'" he tells Cross, in boy-talk about Ann. "'They can never understand that business is business. They want to make everything into a personal issue'" (30). This is, in fact, what Ann does with the Johnson kidnapping by volunteering to stay with the missing boy's mother, Helen, for the duration of the ordeal. The two women bond over the missing child, and Cross is taken aback:

> It seemed to me that dealing with women was like playing blindfold chess against unidentified opponents. Ann had never hinted that she was in love with Larry Seifel, or even that she knew him. I had had a vain suspicion now and then that she was secretly rather fond of me. Now a shadowy triangle was taking shape between her and Seifel and Helen Johnson. I didn't like it. (34)

Seifel is the lawyer to both Johnsons, and yet more the wife's counselor than her older husband's. Complications set in when Cross finds himself attracted to Helen Johnson, too. Sex complicates many of Macdonald's Archer plots, but seldom does it entangle Archer himself. Macdonald seems to be using Cross as an Archer stand-in to measure the depth and degree of romantic complication his hero can tolerate. Perhaps the character's surname carries a pun: he is a "cross" between the celibate knight and the social male responsible for a relationship.

Cross's quest to find the Johnson boy leads him to another kidnapping years in the past. A character who begins on the fringe of the case turns out to be at the center, and what puts him there is the Gatsby syndrome: a certain naive and sometimes criminally savage faith in the American dream's power to transform hopelessness into successful second chances—and second selves. The mythic dynamo of California makes both the second chances and the savage implementation all but inevitable. Cross's case pivots on a Gatsby-like recreation.

A character from the industrialized Midwest (Macdonald's preferred venue for disruptive memory), carrying the ethnic name George Lempke, moves west and transforms himself into a "new" man under the symbolic name Art Lemp. Lemp, or limp, keys the character as part of the Oedipal paradigm. Indeed, Larry Seifel, Cross's sometime rival for Helen Johnson and the unwitting son of Lemp/limp, is dragged down by an Oedipal complex (146–47). Macdonald has his Oedipal complex and watches it, too. He even gives himself the rare privilege of "correcting" its tragic outcome, for Helen Johnson discards the Oedipal suitor, Seifel, emotionally young enough to be her son, and replaces him with a "healthier" mate, Cross himself.

Macdonald defuses the Oedipal myth by rewriting its tragic ending. Helen Johnson and Howard Cross seem destined for the sort of happy life together at the end of the case rarely if ever glimpsed at the conclusion to the detective novel. With her aged husband dead and her son rescued, they constitute an instant family. But happy families, as Tolstoy wrote in *Anna Karenina,* are all alike. Unhappy families are an endlessly rich supply of stories. The unhappy family in Macdonald's next novel is a perfect example.

The title of Macdonald's next novel, *Find a Victim* (1954), the fifth in the Archer series, acknowledges this thematic trend. Look in any family and find a victim. In fact, the title is deeply ironic, for it would be more difficult to find a character in the novel who is *not* the victim of bad luck or emotional deprivation. Tony Aquista, a man Archer finds dying of a gunshot to the chest on the roadside of a Valley highway, is only the first and most literal victim. Each of the suspects Archer meets in the case is equally victim and perpetrator. Even Archer shares the burden; a subplot recalls his own failure to be the Good Samaritan and surrogate father to a troubled young man in his Long Beach past. The precarious psychological condition of "the young man" as a type and Archer's failure to mentor the psyche in jeopardy loom significantly at this stage of the Archer/Macdonald alliance and signal the beginning of a definitive turn away from the Hammett/Chandler axis toward Macdonald's own reconfiguration of the detective novel. Macdonald returned to it again in a later novel, *The Doomsters* (1958). In *Find a Victim,* though, Macdonald struggles with a plot in which criminal activity is embedded in family histories and anchored to place.

The setting of *Find a Victim* is a Valley town with the suggestive Spanish name of Las Cruces. The crosses might be intersecting roadways (a reference to the crossing of three roads in the Oedipus story), but the allusion might equally suggest crucifixion, salvation through suffering. Indeed, a pattern of Christian religious imagery vies with the Oedipal/psychoanalytic in the novel. In the first scene, when Archer lifts the dying man Aquista off the ground, he seems to strike the *Pietà* pose: "Supporting his hip on my knee and his loose head with my arm, I turned him onto his back" (3). For this act of good Samaritan-ship, Archer is held on the road to Sacramento to solve the murder of Aquista in Las Cruces and the disappearance of a local woman, the younger sister of the local sheriff's wife. The person guilty of the case's multiple murders is eventually exposed, in the final scene of the novel, in the ultimate pose of Christian stigmata: her hands bleeding from stripping foliage and thorns from a lemon tree. Her married name is Hilda Church.

Las Cruces is a black hole of dysfunction in ways that the Christian imagery can only begin to depict. If the religious imagery seems too overdetermined for a story about sin and contrition, it accompanies Macdonald's interrogation of the disease of family life. Families, as is increasingly important in Macdonald's fiction, have ceased to nurture. In this land of cross-bearing, one of Archer's first stops with the dying Aquista is a motel whose proprietor is suspected of having an affair with the missing woman. The wronged wife ruefully admits to Archer that her marriage has been "seven lean years" (19), an image that works to link the biblical wordplay with the ongoing situation of famine in families. No fat years seem to loom on the horizon, and no characters seem provident enough to plan for the continued hunger.

The place where all of this suffering persists is both cause and effect, as Macdonald illustrates in his use of architectural setting. Driving the missing woman's older sister to her modern tract home, Archer senses that the architecture of the denizens seems as tentative as their grip on life:

> The road spiraled off among low hills whose flanks were dotted with houses. It was a good residential suburb, where people turned their backs on small beginnings and looked to larger futures. Most of the houses were new, so new that they hadn't been assimilated to the landscape, and very modern. They had flat jutting roofs, and walls of concrete and glass skeletonized by light. (49)

More is at play here than the proverb about people who live in glass houses. Broadly sensitive to architecture on the Southern California landscape, Macdonald makes a point in each of his novels of housing his characters in structures that either connect them to a moral base in nature ("assimilated to the landscape") or fail to engineer any such connection. More often than not, the houses his people build fail to represent their best dreams. This concrete and glass house, boasting in material and design of transparency between inside and outside, is in fact just the opposite. When Archer lets his passenger into her darkened foyer, she makes a desperate and highly neurotic pass at him, afraid of what might lurk in the darkness within the glass box (50).

Archer seems no stranger to a world darkened by so many victims. He initially notices its "Waste Land" aridity driving by an abandoned Marine base (4). And he sees himself embodied in the palm rat, a creature who "lived by his wits in darkness, gnawed human leavings, listened behind walls for sounds of danger" (52). This insight occurs while Archer searches the bungalow apartment of the missing woman, the younger sister to the woman in the glass house. Outside in the courtyard is a dry fountain over which presides a "pockmarked cherub" (51).

The unrelenting darkness seems to loosen Archer's characteristic terseness about his own life. He reveals to the widow of a murdered man the story of his own marriage's demise, and then, with her breathless cooperation, ends her seven lean years of marriage by making love to her (162–63). He remembers his former failure to come to the aid of Bozey, then a teenager in need of one gesture of adult help, now swallowed up in the quicksand of crime and evil that undermines Las Cruces. Archer deepens the moral fog by bribing a witness with marijuana and justifies his action by telling himself that even the cops bribe informers (70). He even remembers the wartime experience of charred human flesh from his time on Okinawa (176).

Find a Victim is the noir-est of Macdonald's early Archer novels. Each of the physical settings in the case is vaguely or overtly corrupt, whether from neglect or from the crimes enacted there. The dark contagion infects Archer, who confesses to tactics and motives that put him perilously close to the line where ethics curdle into expediency. In *The Ivory Grin* Archer could find relief from the wasteland by siding with and liberating the underdog, by achieving real justice in a system of de facto bigotry. In the earlier novel an innocent man walks out of jail as the guilty one enters. But the bottom line of *Find a Victim* is negative. Even the missing woman, who has been dead all along, is both victim and victimizer: the victim of incestuous assault by her widowed father but also the blackmailer of a married man she has seduced and a rival for her own sister's husband. If the family had failed her by allowing her to become the prey of the father, then she had in turn violated the familial bond by taunting her older sister with her sexual frigidity. The only system of accounting that Archer finds realistic in this less-than-zero game is to expect loss as the result of every transaction. Expect the worst, he tells us, then any good thing that happens seems that much better (140). *Find a Victim* is a significant intersection on a long path of departure from the tradition of Hammett, in which good and evil are rough-hewn realities and the hero can rely on quick wits and quick fists to separate the one from the other, and an anxiety-ridden engagement with the imaginative world of Chandler, where every look and every syllable of conversation is a veiled calculation of the other's readiness for sin. In *Find a Victim,* Macdonald finds the penal code next to irrelevant in describing or correcting human corruption. Sin is a kind of condition or atmosphere—as the network of Christian allusion in the novel hints, a darkness more than equal to the light. Even one of the murder victims, the missing woman, had been both sinner and sinned-against. "'She was thoughtless, but she wasn't consciously evil,'" her older sister pleads with Archer. "'She didn't mean to be bad." Nobody ever does,'" Archer replies. "'It creeps up on people'" (204).

The next Archer novel, *The Barbarous Coast* (1956), takes on Chandler's Hollywood, especially the attenuated and mannerist ship of fools of *The Long Goodbye* (1953), the Chandler novel that seems to have grated most against Macdonald's evolving practice. Archer is called to a gated community of wealth and privilege (the Channel Club at Malibu), just as Marlowe's infatuation with Terry Lennox in *The Long Goodbye* takes him inland to the moneyed enclave of Idle Valley. Approaching the gates of this Vanity Fair, Archer intercepts George Wall, a young Canadian who thinks his new wife, Hester, is held captive inside the dark fortress. Little does Wall realize that this Hester is literally living up to the worst suspicions of Hawthorne's benighted Puritans in *The Scarlet Letter:* his vagrant wife is as promiscuous as the good folk of Salem fear Hester Prynne to be. Archer reluctantly takes on Wall as an advisee, trying out a premise—the reunion of a young husband and wife—he would use in future novels, *The Chill* (1964) and *Sleeping Beauty* (1973). His motives are mixed. In part, because restoring husband and wife will vicariously fix his own loneliness, for Archer himself is forlorn in his "two-bedroom stucco cottage" with its empty beds (*Coast,* 61); and in part because he is not comfortable with his actual client, Clarence Bassett, the manager of the Channel Club, who wants to hire Archer to protect him from Wall.

Archer's discomfort with Bassett plays out Macdonald's discomfort with the enigma of Chandler. If Hammett was a fairly benign presence in his cameo appearance in *The Way Some People Die,* Chandler's cameo results in a kind of exorcism. First, Bassett's tweedy English affectations seem perversely out of touch with a beach paradise on the Pacific:

> He sat down at the desk, opened a pigskin pouch, and began to stuff a
> big-pot briar with dark flakes of English tobacco. This and his Harris tweed
> jacket, his Oxford slacks, his thick-soled brown brogues, his Eastern-seaboard
> accent, were all of a piece. In spite of the neat dye job on his brown hair, and
> the unnatural youth which high color lent his face, I placed his age close to
> sixty. (9)

The shot across Chandler's bow is obvious: Marlowe's pipe rituals, his sharp eye for tailoring, his Anglophilia are clearly set up in the introductory appearance of Clarence Bassett. In the mid-1950s, Chandler, born in 1888, was in his late sixties—the same decade but the distant end.

From the outset Archer tries to minimize his contact with Bassett by taking on Wall. George Wall treats Archer like a father confessor or lay analyst, admitting his guilty feelings toward Hester after she had told him of all the other men who had been her sexual partners. "'I don't know what that makes me,'" Wall agonizes; "'Human, I [Archer] thought'" (63). Typically, Archer does not say what he thinks, for Wall is not his son, penitent, or patient. Yet his thinking is evident: beyond the gates of the Channel Club, humanity struggles for a break; inside the fortress, "breaks" are as common as canapes.

The Barbarous Coast takes Archer into the cultural capitol of noir: the Hollywood Chandler loved and hated, and made his own fiefdom. In Macdonald's Hollywood, studio money and mob money cohabit in Las Vegas ventures. Mentioning Siegel and Cohen in the novel lends the fiction a kind of documentary spin. Chandler's own work as a screenwriter is also undercut in the novel. Screenwriters, originally of pure artistic intent, conspire in the cheapening of art into "product"—Flaubert's *Salammbo* for example, is being retrofitted with a happy ending (125–26). And not coincidentally, Flaubert is the one highbrow writer Marlowe knows. In a conversation in *The Long Goodbye* with the sexually impotent, violently alcoholic, and mentally blocked writer Roger Wade, Marlowe uses Flaubert as an example of a writer who worked through severe writer's block.[26] But if Marlowe drops Flaubert's name, Archer knows the plot of *Salammbo,* the difference between literature and Hollywood kitsch, and the difference between reading Flaubert in translation and in the original French (126). Archer cannot save George Wall's wife or other moths drawn to the Hollywood flame of celebrity, but he does succeed in saving George himself. However, in terms of the plotting of *The Barbarous Coast,* this salvation is awkward since George never gets to slay the dragon: He retires from the novel about halfway through after being beaten up by a gang of studio thugs. Whether Archer can save himself from the fog of corruption flowing from Hollywood to Las Vegas is one of the crucial issues of the case, for in pursuit of good the detective faces his own touch of evil. Confronting a woman he later learns is Hester's sister but at the time believes to be Wall's corrupt wife, Archer bears down. He is convinced this Hester is not above selling her body for studio perks or becoming an accomplice to murder and a blackmailer by stealing the weapon. But the supposed Hester turns the tables, calls Archer a "sadist," and blunts his attack. "I caught myself doubting my premises, doubting that she could be any kind of hustler. Besides, there was just enough cruelty in my will to justice, enough desire in my pity, to make the room uncomfortable for me. I said goodnight and left it. The problem was to love people, try to serve them, without wanting anything from them. I was a long way from solving that one." (119)

Love, used by Macdonald in the sense of *agape* not *eros,* is an anomalous term in the detective novel of the 1950s, about as appropriate as "a pearl onion on a banana split," as Chandler might say (499). But if Macdonald felt anxiety about the influence of Chandler, he felt more in his dedication to exorcising the genre of Chandler's mannerist control. The language he used for the push was risky; the private eye had to use the word *love* and not mean taking a witness to bed. In fact, Macdonald pushed "love" further from formula erotics in *The Barbarous Coast,* for he has Archer dream of a man who lived by himself in a landscape of crumbling stones. He spent a great deal of his time, without much success, trying to reconstruct in his mind the monuments and the buildings of which the scattered stones were the only vestiges. He vaguely remembered some kind of oral tradition to the effect that a city had stood there once. And a still vaguer tradition: or perhaps it was a dream inside of the dream: that the people who had built the city, or their descendants, were coming back eventually to rebuild it. He wanted to be around when the work was done. (182)

Archer's dream recalls Augustine's City of God, a trope Macdonald had used in more than one early novel. The dream puts Archer in an anomalous position as private eye. If he truly wants to be around for the rebuilding of the city, then he will have to drop his solo mystique: no more retiring from the field to his monastic cell of an apartment when the case is closed.

The Barbarous Coast is still far from solving the structural problem with the detective novel, for it concludes in a shower of murders. Archer counts them off: "So you cut Stern's throat. You shot Lance Leonard's eye out. You beat Hester Campbell's skull with a poker" (238–39). Stern is a homosexual mobster from Las Vegas; Lance Leonard is the former Manuel Torres (nephew of the security guard at the club), whom Stern grooms as his toy; and Hester is the vagrant wife, who prefers the fast lane of starlet/blackmailer to wife. The "you" Archer accuses is his one-time client, Clarence Bassett, the target of Chandler exorcism. "'You hate and despise me, don't you?'" Bassett counters. Macdonald invokes the novelist's right against self-incrimination: "'I don't think I'll answer that question'" (239). But he does answer in the denouement. Archer smokes out a longstanding, but apparently never-consummated relationship between Bassett and the rich, neurotic wife of a movie studio executive—perhaps a veiled reference to Chandler's affair with and eventual marriage to Cecelia Hurlburt Pascal, almost twenty years his senior. He further reveals that Bassett, like Chandler, is a terminal alcoholic. Almost beside the point, he makes Bassett a multiple murderer. For the coup de gras, he has Bassett's dying body produce a grotesque "mewling," like a child calling for his mother (245)—perhaps another veiled swipe at Chandler, whose allegiance to his own mother is one of the strongest themes in his life story.

The Barbarous Coast is not a pleasant novel; the attack on Chandler is as direct as the compliment to Hammett in The Way Some People Die. Macdonald's "early phase" from The Moving Target to The Barbarous Coast sails an irregular course, maneuvering between massive influences in Chandler and Hammett and trying out the equipment of the genre for what Macdonald wanted to keep and what he wanted to alter. Hammett's Op or Sam Spade could slug their way to a solution to any crime. Philip Marlowe's suave world-weariness helped him to slip through a few tough situations on style alone. With the evolving Archer,

Macdonald tested fundamental changes to the paradigm, and the early results were mixed.

Whether the exorcism of Chandler was necessary or successful is a moot point. Life circumstances overwhelmed literature. *The Barbarous Coast* was the last Archer novel before upheavals in Macdonald's private life—which he addressed through full-scale Freudian psychoanalysis—significantly changed the shape and character of his work. In a sense, if Archer got Macdonald out of an autobiographical jam with *The Moving Target,* Macdonald's own family ordeal got Archer out of the dead end of *The Barbarous Coast.*

The next phase of Macdonald's career is deeply influenced by his own experience with Freudian psychoanalysis, a territory he had known from a careful distance as a student, but one he would know from its deep interior from 1957. The Freudian structure became for him the structure of structures and clarified even as it absorbed his sense of guilt and correction. The Archer of *The Barbarous Coast* doubts himself, confirming a character trait that Macdonald thrusts against the typical cocksure demeanor of heroes like Marlowe and Spade. And although Macdonald will sparingly use the literal crime of rackets and mobs in future novels, none of them will depend on such situations for moral thematics or plot structure. Immersion in the Freudian universe would give Macdonald the way to see crime in the most "natural" and fundamental of human organizations, the biological family.

[5]

Freud and Archer

The Detective as Analyst

In one of his chats on writers and writing with Roger Wade, the bitter novelist he has been hired to babysit in *The Long Goodbye,* Chandler's Philip Marlowe delivers an amateur psychologist's diagnosis of what haunts his "patient." Wade scoffs at the whole approach:

> "Okay. . . . So you have read Flaubert, so that makes you an intellectual, a critic, a savant of the literary world. . . . I'm on the wagon and I hate it. I hate everybody with a drink in his hand. I've got to go out there and smile at those creeps. Every damn one of them knows I'm an alcoholic. So they wonder what I'm running away from. Some Freudian bastard has made that a commonplace. Every ten-year-old kid knows it by now." (562)

Whether or not Wade's tirade was aimed directly at Macdonald, who had published four Archer novels, each of which contained a modicum of Freudian psychoanalytic shaping to the evidence and the inquiry, it landed close to dead center. There was more than one "Freudian bastard" making the original paradigm of psychoanalytic theory and practice a "commonplace" in the 1950s, when Chandler dismissed and Macdonald sought to implement Freudian approaches to action and motivation.

For the writers and readers of Macdonald's generation, even fictional ones like Roger Wade, the conviction that unconscious motivations explained human actions on all fronts from (especially) the most intimate to the nationalistic, amounted to common knowledge. Freudian, Jungian, Reichian—whatever the particular patron, the structure of structure was psychoanalytic. In Alfred Hitchcock's *Spellbound* (1945) Ingrid Bergman plays a beautiful psychiatrist with a sexy European accent, and the dream sequence in the film (art design by Salvador Dali) gives the unconscious a visual dimension full of clues to veiled meaning. In the final scene, the villainous psychoanalyst, played by Leo G. Carroll, walks step by step through a dream interpretation that implicates himself as the murderer. Interpreting dreams could be that mechanical, and that inevitable, and the impulse to psychoanalysis that powerful in overcoming self-preservation.

Beginning with his first visit to the United States in 1909, Sigmund Freud had enormous impact on the American mind, both conscious and unconscious. Indeed, many Americans did not suspect they *had* an unconscious until Freud explained it, and the news was not universally welcomed. In the 1920s and 1930s the pioneering work of Harry Stack Sullivan became the foundation for orthodox Freudianism in the United States, and significant waves of professional refugees from Hitler's Europe solidified the ranks in the late 1930s and 1940s. One of these refugees, Karen Horney, provided the book that Cathy Slocum is reading in *The Drowning Pool.*

War and its aftermath deepened the need for psychoanalysis. Not only did many survivors of the war suffer from delayed trauma caused by what they had seen—and could not easily exorcise or describe—on the battlefield; the home front produced trauma as well. With so many men at the front, the traditional family was disassembled and the roles, freedoms, and prohibitions redistributed. When the men returned, there were rippling effects of readjustment to the prewar norm. Betty Friedan located large and deep pools of discontent among the women shanghaied into the readjustment, and charted the waters in *The Feminine Mystique.* McCarthyite politics in the 1950s also reinforced the hold of psychoanalysis. Joseph Schwartz, author of *Cassandra's Daughter: A History of Psychoanalysis,* notes that "in 1950s' McCarthyite America ego psychology became the dominant psychoanalytic theory . . . combining as it did an unchanged drive psychology along with a vision of mental health consisting of a satisfactory/unconflictual relationship with society at large."[1] In other words, conformity, the political and cultural password to the 1950s, was backed up scientifically on the couch.

If America in the 1950s and early 1960s was saturated with a psychoanalytic awareness—if not widespread obsession—California was the place where that obsession took physical shape and mass. Starting his California architectural career in Hollywood in the 1930s, and gaining success state- and nationwide in the following decades, architect Richard Neutra (1892–1970), claiming Freud as an influence, projected his theories into the design of living spaces:

The "family group," small or large, held together by bonds of closest genetic relationship, often also carrying the healthy seeds of centrifugal development and inner antagonism, has been studied by psychologists as humanity's basic element, just as thoroughly as the single individual. The snail's shell, the bird's nest, the wasp's hive, the ant's hill—all these, built quite reflexively, become the immediate physical surrounding of these animals and are no less important to them than is constructed housing to a family. With this environment our soul searchers have concerned themselves unjustifiably much less than with marital relations or those between parents and children. I well remember how Professor Freud used to smile at my statement that housing architecture, the daily and nightly impact of physical surroundings, decisively raises conditioned responses, as the reflexologist would put it.[2]

Archer from the outset had shown, like his creator, deep curiosity about his clients' nests, hives, and shells. In the 1950s he found a rich environment. Macdonald, a peripatetic occupant of four houses in Santa Barbara and one in Menlo Park, lived a life he could transfer to Archer's clients: a life saturated with "the family group" and the "conditioned responses" sparked by "housing architecture." From the 1950s to the end of his career, houses figure significantly in Archer's cases; both victims and perpetrators take parts of their characters from, and leave their traces, on the "psychotherapeutic architecture" in which they dwell.

American writers, of course, climbed on the psychotherapy bandwagon most conspicuously. Allen Ginsberg and Tennessee Williams—to mention only two—entered psychoanalysis in the 1950s. One of the most famous books of literary criticism of the 1950s, Leslie Fiedler's *Love and Death in the American Novel,* was openly Freudian in its reinterpretation of American "classics":

> To Freud and his followers, and also to Carl Jung, I owe a similar debt. Readers familiar with orthodox Freudianism and Jungian revisionism will recognize the sources of much of my basic vocabulary; I cannot imagine myself beginning the kind of investigation I have undertaken without the concepts of the conscious and the unconscious, the Oedipus complex, the archetypes, etc.[3]

Reviewers were divided over Fiedler's racy readings of *Adventures of Huckleberry Finn* and *Moby Dick.* Either Fiedler had sullied American literature by finding sex where it had been least expected or wanted—on the raft with Huck and Jim, or on the Pequod with Ahab and his crew—or he had saved it from benighted adolescence. Macdonald, writing as Kenneth Millar, reviewed *Love and Death* for the *San Francisco Chronicle.* Millar was divided in his opinion, too: as reductive as Fiedler's thesis could be, he argued, it could also open doors to hidden truths. For a novelist with his own "investigations" to carry out, Freud could be a major ally because his explanations of human behavior went well beyond the powers of "every ten-year-old kid" to understand.

Macdonald needed no initiation into the Freudian paradigm or its application to literature in the 1950s. From his college days in Canada he had been reading Freud and his rivals and disciples. His doctoral dissertation at the University of Michigan interpreted the Romantic poet and critic Samuel Taylor Coleridge as a precursor to Freud; Coleridge's type of "psychological criticism," Millar argued, hardly made sense without Freud in the wings. Archer was increasingly meeting clients who needed an analyst as much as, or more than, they needed a private detective. In hindsight it seems inevitable that the decade of the 1950s would make or break Archer and Macdonald. The audience was ready, the cultural mood was right, and Macdonald had the tools.

Barriers between art and life, theory and practice broke down for the Macdonald family in 1956 and brought psychoanalysis out of books and into their lives. On February 23, 1956, Macdonald's sixteen-year-old daughter, Linda, driving while intoxicated, struck two boys on a Santa Barbara street, killing one and injuring the other. Linda fled the scene and rear-ended another car. From the scene of the second accident Linda was taken to a local hospital, where her parents recovered her and gradually learned the magnitude of the trouble. The next day, Linda Millar was taken into custody for the hit-and-run death. She was arraigned a few days later. The spring and summer were a hell of court appearances, newspaper stories and publicity, psychiatric evaluations of Linda, probation, and civil suits.

By the beginning of the school year in September 1956, the Millar family had sold its home in Santa Barbara and moved north to Menlo Park to assess the damage out of the spotlight and to attempt to start over. Psychoanalysis for both father and daughter was the hub of the process. Beginning late in 1956 and continuing for almost a full year, Macdonald met weekly with a psychiatrist, researching his life and memory systematically for the plot that had led up to the disastrous family events of 1956. A true believer in Freud, Macdonald produced more than forty pages of handwritten apologia, explaining his life from birth to the present, including a blow-by-blow narrative of the rearing of his daughter and taking upon himself the guilt for the crisis in his family.[4]

The primary reader was his psychiatrist, but his motives seem to have been to control the outcome of the sessions. Producing the text of his own psychiatric history put Macdonald beyond the boundary of traditional analysis. In "On Beginning Treatment" (1913) and in other recommendations to practitioners, Freud warned against such textual production by analysands (patients):

> There are patients who from the very first hours carefully prepare what they are going to communicate, ostensibly so as to be sure of making better use of the time devoted to the treatment. What is thus disguising itself as eagerness is resistance. Any preparation of this sort should be disrecommended, for it is only employed to guard against unwelcome thoughts cropping up.[5]

Macdonald, however, seems to have written out his analysis specifically to flush out "unwelcome thoughts" that had been baying at the doors of his conscious mind for decades. There is scarcely a page on which he does not accuse himself of complicity in his daughter's trouble or trace the unhappiness in her life to causes in his. At the same time, however, taking blame for his daughter's misfortunes is taking her life under his control and useful therapy away from the professional. There is only one explanation, and Macdonald knows it, has known it, and will persist in knowing it: pathologies in families create pathologies in individuals. Like the brilliant student he had always been, Macdonald will earn this analyst's A⁺.

Freudian theory is an immensely complicated, evolutionary, and organic process of understanding. Any application outside an individual case of course risks reducing its operating principles to cliché. This is what happens in *Spellbound*. To give Chandler his due, Roger Wade is entitled to scoff at "Freudian bastards" who reduce the fluid complexity of Freudian conversation to the mechanics of a board game. Not all apertures (doorways, tunnels, open windows) are representations of the female, not all hard and cylindrical objects male. The final frames of another Hitchcock film, *North by Northwest*, in which the hero pulls the heroine into the upper birth of a sleeping car just as the train rushes into a tunnel, communicate with a Freudian wink just what transpires in that upper berth as the audience leaves the theater. If it were only that simple, Chandler's Roger Wade must wish.

Freudian theory, of course, is dominated by sex; our development of consciousness is not possible without the somatic, or bodily, development of sexualized anatomies, the realization of desires that grow with them, and the guilt that inevitably comes with learning the rules. Nor do we develop sexually and psychologically in isolation; for better or worse we develop in families. The first "others" we desire are family members; the first "others" from whom we hide those desires are the same people. Family tensions ripple outward from the intimate nuclear family to the extended family of kin to the neighborhood, the state, tradition (the family extended into past and future)—even into our houses, or so Richard Neutra thought. On their outward trajectories, our selves encounter the innumerable shocks to innocence that make the plots of our lives. In these collisions, Macdonald would find Archer's cases and his angst. "It is love," one critic of Freud tells us, "not justice, that is the first virtue of the family. The family is a naturally social, not a conventionally social, institution, but justice is a public or conventional virtue."[6] In the foggy middle-ground between love and justice, the family and the public, the natural and the conventional, Macdonald remapped the "mean streets" of the twentieth-century private eye.

The fundamental narrative of this development from family to public and back again outlines a central fixture of Freudian understanding: the family romance. In simplified form, the family romance assumes a symmetrical family group: a mother, a father, a son, a daughter. Symmetry is assumed to dominate the textbook narrative of the developing functions of adulthood and sexual identities; luckily for novelists and psychoanalysts, in the real world where the patients come from it seldom does. As infants, the son and daughter are to identify mother and father, respectively, as objects of sexual desire. As he becomes older, the son suffers rejection by the mother, who "naturally" favors the father. The son in turn rejects the mother as a traitor and rebels against the tyrannous will of the father, who then becomes The Father, the principle of denial of all self-aggrandizing desire: state, church, superego. Rebellion against all authority is the inevitable next stage. A confrontation between father and son occurs; as a result, the son is physically or psychologically ejected from the family. He may "kill" the father in some fashion, usually metaphorically. Hence the wide appeal of the Oedipus story as a basis for father/son narrative, for in the ancient tale the son actually but unwittingly kills his father.

After the break, the son begins a period of lost wandering (literal or metaphorical) until he can, by one substitute or another, reconnect his original desire for the mother to a woman who is not his mother. When and if the successful transference is accomplished, the perturbation to family symmetry is remedied. The son sets up his own family, and the cycle begins anew. A similar pattern of idyllic childhood harmony, followed by estrangement and chastened reintegration ("civilization and its discontents") was proposed for the daughter. The Greek story of Electra parallels the story of Oedipus.

Clearly, "failures" in the symmetry may occur at any point. The mother might not prefer the father to the son; she might keep the son close to her emotionally, stalling or altogether disrupting his growth to sexual autonomy. Archer "diagnoses" this problem in the Slocum family of *The Drowning Pool*. The daughter might never lose her original desire for her father; none of the men she meets will or can satisfy her. Either parent might be absent, physically or psychologically, and the son or daughter is then faced with the real possibility of a truncated emotional life if no surrogate can be found.

Many of the plots generated by the family romance are familiar in literature. Psychoanalyst Otto Rank analyzed many. Freud himself analyzed *Hamlet* as a version of the Oedipal story. For his analyst in 1957, Macdonald transcribed his own life according to the family romance narrative, identifying actual incidents to punctuate each constitutive element of the family romance and tie his own life to the formula; in the process he established an ongoing lend/lease agreement between autobiography and fiction. In a sense, Macdonald healed himself by willing the family romance narrative into his own life, and his life into the narrative.

In *The Doomsters*, the first novel he wrote under the heavy and deliberate influence of his psychoanalysis, the family romance is drowned in a handbook of Freudian motif and imagery, most of which it cannot digest. In the next novel, *The Galton Case* (1959), structural unity is mandated by the family romance, and content and form reach an almost seamless partnership. As *The Galton Case* concentrates on the Oedipal model, focusing on fathers and sons, *The Wycherly Woman* (1961) takes very similar material and concentrates on the family romance from the daughter's perspective. Scenes of therapy between a professional and Phoebe Wycherly, the damaged daughter of the novel, with

Archer looking on, seem heartbreakingly real in the context of the Millar family's immediate suffering.

The Freudian breakthrough of the late 1950s sealed Macdonald's course as a novelist. What had been hinted at in the earlier Archers with a wisecrack here or an aside to the reader there would become the standard: Archer left both Hammett's and Chandler's worlds and became the private eye as psychoanalyst.

The Millar family, having spent almost a year in Menlo Park, moved quietly back to Santa Barbara in the late summer of 1957. Two novels came directly from exile and therapy: *The Doomsters* was written during the difficult year of exile in the Bay Area, and *The Galton Case* was the work of a born-again Macdonald surprisingly happy to be back in Santa Barbara. Two novels, *The Ferguson Affair* (1960) a non-Archer detective novel, and *The Wycherly Woman* (1961) a return to Archer, followed hard upon these and were driven largely by the emotional and financial crisis of Linda Millar's second "breakdown": her disappearance without notice from college at the University of California, Davis, for about ten days in 1959. She was discovered unharmed in Los Angeles and returned to counseling and to college, but the expenses of a regional search plunged Macdonald into deficit both financially and psychologically. Rescuing missing daughters thereafter became an urgent theme in almost all of his novels and an equally urgent cause *for* them.

The novels of this pressurized period of Macdonald's life were crucial to his career and to the genre at large insofar as he was leading its evolution beyond the prevailing mode. He called *The Galton Case* "a breakthrough" novel, and what he meant becomes clear in a comparison between it and *The Doomsters*. If *The Doomsters* is a loosely constructed novel with a heavy Freudian accent, in The *Galton Case* Macdonald almost ruthlessly merges the Freudian drama of lost and found identity with his own life story and the narrative form of the detective novel. *The Wycherly Woman* is, under the burden of immediate personal trauma, a poignant penitential novel in which a lost daughter is rescued and her real father's suicide closes his account payable to her. The result of the four novels of this hinge period was a remodeled detective story form that, without dispute, was Macdonald's own, a form that put him out of reach of Hammett and Chandler—but a form that could be as repetitive as it was incisive.

The Doomsters (1958) and *The Galton Case* (1959) are representative of both the times, saturated, as Chandler's Roger Wade growls, with Freudian knowledge and pseudoknowledge, and of Macdonald's determination for personal breakthrough. In *The Doomsters* Macdonald struggles to impose the voluminous wardrobe of psychoanalysis upon a cast of characters of differing sizes and shapes. A student used to excelling, Macdonald seems to want to prove that he (or Archer) knows more than any other "Freudian bastard" out there. He mostly loses the contest; *The Doomsters* is an interesting but flawed novel in which Macdonald failed to find a principle of structural unity for the Freudian ensemble. In *The Galton Case,* however, Macdonald subdues the competing claims of novelistic structure and psychoanalytic theory. "In writing *The Galton Case,*" he recalled in the preface to *Archer at Large* (1969), "and mastering its materials, I felt an exhilaration which I hope the book communicates to its readers. For me, in its indirect way, it stated and made good the right to my inheritance as an American citizen and writer. . . . I was a real pro now" (ix–x). He felt he had finally occupied a platform from which he could understand himself and be understood by the collective mind of the public. He had found a personal, not just an academic, justification for the Freudian model. Like Hammett he had finally come into possession of personal experience he could use to back up his fiction. And more than Chandler, he had a story that operated as a whole, not just line by line: a content as well as a style.

The *Doomsters,* Macdonald's final semipro novel, eluded his mastering intention; the parts do not add up to a whole. Archer is awakened just before dawn by an escaped mental patient, Carl Hallman, who is sane enough to seek Archer for help in proving that he did not, in fact, murder his father. Archer reluctantly takes the challenge, at first just to get Hallman back inside the walls. But Hallman escapes Archer's custody, thereby sealing the detective's responsibility for him. The case then takes Archer into the murders of Hallman's father and mother, his older brother, the brother's wife, a shady doctor who treats the Hallman family, and very nearly Carl Hallman himself. Multiple deaths are not Archer's only problem; his own psychological state becomes a problem as well.

Because character, dialogue, imagery, and theme take several paths to the Freudian goal, Macdonald's first schematically complete Freudian detective novel seems more like a helter-skelter charge to the objective rather than a programmed march. Too many of the characters, including Archer himself, operate on the thin edge of depthless caricature. Things tend to migrate from their undeniable thingness into the territory of Freudian fetish. Mrs. Hallman's gun, for example, "a short-barreled little thing with a pearl handle set in filigree work," sent to her by her father "all the way from the old country," (167) reads more like an overdetermined symbol that an actual murder weapon—a fetish, representing Mrs. Hallman's arrested sexual growth somewhere between daughter and wife. Clearly it is appropriate that her character should be associated with such an object, but its gun-ness is overawed by its fetish-ness. Dialogue in *The Doomsters* is often presented with marginal dramatic meaning for character and plot; rather, it glosses the overriding Freudian theme of the novel as the characters seem to recite lines from a textbook. And the plot concludes not with a tense flick of plausible revelation or with a pursuit and capture, but with a deflating, largely nondramatic narrative of explanation.

The *Doomsters* begins with a ceremonial bow to Freud: a dream ripe for interpretation. Archer, both analyst and analysand in this novel, describes it briefly: "I was dreaming about a hairless ape who lived in a cage by himself. His trouble was that people were always trying to get in. It kept the ape in a state of nervous tension. I came out of sleep sweating" (3). Dream-work, as Freud himself described it in *The Interpretation of Dreams,* is often a complex, but never meaningless, interweaving of unconscious and preconscious wish-fulfillment.[7] In dreams of nakedness, of which Archer's is a prime example, forces of sexual desire and inhibition struggle to a checkmate. Almost transparently, Archer's dream figures his own blocked sexual appetite (his caged and hairless body) and the inhibitions preventing satisfaction (the spectators who constantly keep surveillance on him). As Macdonald the novelist well knew, Archer's dream sets the detective's body and mind, in the ensuing case, in a tense conflict between desire and satisfaction. Like Macdonald the patient in 1957, Archer is caught between inhabiting the paradigm as analysand and understanding it from the outside as analyst. Quelling his own "nervous [sexual] tension" complicates the solving of the case.

Archer is awakened from his dream by a figure who steps right out it—a double, or doppelganger, a secret sharer of Archer's condition. Carl Hallman is "a very large young man" with fair hair and light blue eyes, whose collaboration with Archer's dream is signaled in the text by the "naked" garage lightbulb illuminating him when he and Archer meet (3). As Macdonald knew from Freud's own interpretations of dreams, words as well as things can carry the latent meaning in dreams, and attributes repressed in one area can be displaced to another without compromising meaning. The nakedness of the lightbulb illuminating Hallman connects with the nakedness of Archer's dream-body. Hallman is the detective's alter ego, and taking on the young man's case is clearly a way of taking on his own.

Hallman has just gone over the fence of a psychiatric hospital where he had been committed on suspicion of murdering his father. The family romance narrative surfaces early and without camouflage in *The Doomsters.* Hallman's father plays the role of the heavy and forbidding Father Principle. A wealthy landowner and powerful political figure, Hallman Senior has enforced a sexual embargo on his younger son, Carl, by barring him from "excessive" identification with his mother. Trying to make a man of Carl has resulted only in the son's self-imposed exile from the family kingdom, Purissima, anything but the "most pure" setting for this California version of the family romance.

A savvy, lay analyst, Archer talks Carl into returning to the hospital in return for his, Archer's, pledge to investigate the details of the elder Hallman's death. The patient does not make it back to the hospital; within sight of the walls he dumps Archer out of his own car and speeds away. But Archer the analyst does make it to the asylum, and once there is drawn more deeply into the case, not only by his own investment in the son's innocence but by his own neuroses. What better place for a neurotic, albeit an unwitting one, than a clinic? In badinage with the doctor treating Carl, Archer archly deflects his own complicity in Carl's escape when he "denies" that Hallman had actually driven off with his car: "'I confess, Doctor. I never had a car. It was all a dream. The car was a sex symbol, see, and when it disappeared, it meant I'm entering the change of life'" (25). Archer's wisecrack falls flat for the simple reason that it reveals too much of its neurotic origin. The point of the jokes Freud himself used as examples of neurotic revelation was always that the teller was never aware of the subtext; that was the work of the analyst.

Archer's unconscious anxieties are revealed again a few pages later when he meets Rose Parrish, the psychiatric social worker handling Carl Hallman's case: "She was tall and generously made, with a fine sweep of bosom and the shoulders to support it" (27). When she leaves the room, her body seems almost too large and female to be contained in it: "Miss Parrish went out rather hastily, bumping one hip on the door-frame. She had the kind of hips that are meant for child-bearing and associated activities" (28). Representation of the female body in the detective genre (because it was overwhelmingly masculinist when Macdonald practiced) is almost always coded by exaggerated sexual attributes: breasts, hips, legs, lips. But Macdonald doubles the coded meaning by having Parrish's hips bump against a door frame, an aperture which, in the Freudian dictionary, is often identified as a female sexual symbol. Clearly, Archer's sexual appetite is as tightly caged as the hairless ape's in his initial dream. Perhaps more of the embedded meaning in the character of Rose Parish can be appreciated by noting that in the short story from which *The Doomsters* evolved, "The Angry Man" (1955), the character of the psychiatric social worker is male.[8]

Archer's own neuroses further complicate his handling of the case when he meets Mildred (née Gley) Hallman, the wife of the incarcerated boy/man who had stepped out of (and into) Archer's dream. Archer's attraction to Mildred is more oblique than his voyeuristic lust for Rose Parish. (*Gley* is an old Scottish word for *slanted, off-center,* and Macdonald might have rummaged in his Scots-Canadian unconscious for the witty word clue.) In his first interview, Archer seems drawn to Mildred's arrested, oral-stage development, "biting one knuckle like a doleful child." The look she gives him, however, holds "nothing childish" (38) and prompts his fear that he is far too personally engaged in this case than he wishes to be. He cannot, must not, acknowledge to himself the hidden motive for his involvement: "I couldn't be sure, though. Perhaps that was my reason for coming there—the obscurest motive that underlay the others" (39). Although a detective can sleep with his female suspects (in fact, it is something of a tradition), an analyst must never sleep with his patients.

Archer's analysis of the case of the Hallman family becomes, in the terminology of Freudian Karen Horney, "self-analysis," a process that justified a comparison between the analyst and the detective. Archer works on both tracks, but keeping his bearings requires that, as Horney states, the analyst be "straightened out in his relations to self and others."[9] On one track, that of the conventional private eye, Archer is "straightened out." When, for example, he meets the conventional pinup woman in the plot, Zinnie, the wife of Jerry Hallman, Carl's elder brother, Archer is on firm ground. As Zinnie shows Archer around the Hallman home: "Her right breast rose elastically under the white silk shirt. A nice machine, I thought: pseudo-Hollywood, probably empty, certainly expensive, and not new; but a nice machine. She caught my look and didn't seem to mind" (50). Archer and Zinnie reach a meeting of minds about male and female bodies and one language—sex—for relating them. Voyeur and pinup seem happily reconciled to their respective roles. Subtext, when Archer interviews Zinnie, is blissfully nonexistent, and their scenes together seem backdated a decade to the Chandlerian 1940s. Scenes between Archer and Mildred, or Archer and Rose Parrish, seem more heavily freighted with sexual issues still to be worked through.

Seeing Archer conflicted—"straightened out" with some female characters, conflicted with others—Macdonald unwraps another set of Freudian tools: Erik H. Erikson's. In *Young Man Luther* (1958), Erikson put Freudian psychoanalytic theory into practice on an historical figure, the young man emerging into historical importance as the type of all young male identity crises. Trusting to "the powers of recovery inherent in the young [male] ego," Erikson traces Martin Luther's youth as the archetypal "identity crisis."[10] Archer is similarly implicated in the identity crises of two young men of questionable recovery powers, Carl Hallman and Tom Rica (a new character who links Archer and Hallman further by being an acquaintance of both), and retroactively in his own.

The first young man, Hallman, presents himself to Archer as a case study. Archer and Rose Parrish actually discuss Carl Hallman as a "textbook" case of Freudian complexes (157). Cushioned by a textbook, Hallman's agonies seem manageable for Archer. Parrish summarizes the file:

> "Carl was devoted to his mother, deeply dependent on her. At the same time he was trying to break away and have a life of his own. She probably killed herself for reasons that had no connection with Carl. But he saw her death as a direct result of his disloyalty to her, what he thought of as disloyalty. He felt as though his efforts to cut the umbilical cord had actually killed her. From there it was only a step to thinking he was a murderer."
>
> It was a tempting doctrine, that Carl's guilt was compounded of words and fantasies, the stuff of childhood nightmares. It promised to solve so many problems that I was suspicious of it.
>
> "Would a theory like that stand up in court?"
>
> "It isn't a theory, it's fact." (156)

While *The Doomsters* is built on several versions (Horney's, Erikson's, and others) of the Freudian blueprint, its protagonist and prime analyst is skeptical that the blueprint alone, without the harrowing texture of historical experience, can explain human behavior. Macdonald was still struggling to integrate his intellectual grip on the Freudian model of behavior with the purgatory of his actual life in 1956–57.

The agonies of the second young man, Tom Rica, latch on to Archer more personally. Archer, coming to terms with himself as "young man Archer" by acknowledging his past-due debt to Rica, realizes what Erikson generalized from his clinical experience: "Young people in severe trouble are not fit for the couch: they want to face you, and they want you to face them, not as a facsimile of a parent, or wearing the mask of a professional helper, but as the kind of over-all individual a young person can live by or will despair of" (17). Macdonald uses the Tom Rica subplot (recycling and expanding the Bozey subplot of *Find a Victim*) to test Erikson's "young man" thesis and to expand the family romance beyond the nuclear family. Carl Hallman is far gone into a clinical case history, but Tom Rica is a young man who had sought out Archer as "the kind of over-all individual a young person can live by or will despair of." Rica's thwarted maturation, his ongoing "identity crisis," can be traced back to and linked with Archer's own crisis. The problem arising from the Rica subplot in *The Doomsters* is not simply that it has been included and adds another dimension to the Freudian design, but crucially that the talking through is placed at the protracted close of the novel, after the violent resolution.

A bloody shoot-out fails to bring a conclusion to *The Doomsters*. Instead, the case unwinds after the gunplay stops in a flat, nondramatic style that stretches out and eventually diminishes the impact of the novel. Mildred Hallman's confession to Archer does little to clear the novel of the clutter of textbooks. While they were still in high school, Mildred says, the two young people read books that gave Carl the fear of "going homosexual" (222). Which books these might have been is open to choice, but the popular books available on the subject of overprotective "moms" and effeminate sons were numerous. Philip Wylie's notorious indictment of "Mom" in *Generation of Vipers* was available in an annotated edition by 1955.[11] Wylie's diatribe was by no means the only book available for self-help and self-diagnosis. Because "the books said he had to have sex," Mildred obliged. But what many an analyst might have called their genital-phase sexuality never graduated to maturity. In *Childhood and Society,* Erikson describes in wooden, clinical terms what Macdonald tried to put into the doomed marriage of Mildred Gley and Carl Hallman:

> To put it more situationally: the total fact of finding via the climactic turmoil of the orgasm, a supreme experience of the mutual regulation of two beings in some way breaks the point off the hostilities and potential rages caused by the oppositeness of male and female, of fact and fancy, of love and hate. Satisfactory sex relations thus make sex less obsessive, overcompensation less necessary, sadistic controls superfluous.[12]

Good sex makes a good and healthy society, but the characters in Macdonald's detective novels seldom overcome "oppositeness." Mildred, as her confession continues, emerges as another candidate for analysis. Her father had decamped when she was a child, cutting off the textbook Freudian process of sexual differentiation. Mildred's mother is jealous of her daughter's sense of loss. "'She never gave me the love that a daughter owes her mother,'" Mrs. Gley whines. "'Mooning all the time over her no-good father—you'd think *she* was the one that married him and lost him'" (218). Archer's case expands, but only in one direction: the ever-complicating family romance. Corpses in the present come from botched family relationships in the past.

Mildred is, of course, both sinned against and sinner: the "normal" course of family experience that would have resulted in sexuality connected to an adult self—the whole being described by Erikson—eluded her. In *Three Contributions to the Theory of Sex,* Freud describes the case of the daughter whose outgrowing of the incestuous attraction to the father is negated by, among other factors, his absence.[13] Girls who withdraw love from their parents, Freud continues, often in married life "are incapable of fulfilling their duties to their husbands. They make cold wives and remain sexually anesthetic."[14] Mildred is a standard case. When she and Carl have sex before marriage, her participation is obligatory. After marriage Carl himself imposes abstinence in a neurotic plan to stop time and reset the sexual counter to zero. Mildred thwarts him using a plan pioneered by Lot's daughters: getting him drunk and seducing him. But "It didn't work, for either of us. The spirit rose up from me and floated over the bed. I looked down and watched Carl using my body. And I hated him. He didn't love *me.* He didn't want to know *me.* I thought that we were both dead, and our corpses were in bed together. Zombies. Our two spirits never met" (229).

The character of Mildred must have been particularly difficult for Macdonald to write; in doing so he was treading very close to his own father-daughter situation. In his narrative for the Menlo Park therapist, he went into candid detail about his relationship with his wife and their daughter's frequent witnessing of arguments, sometimes over sex, but also over professional ego. Margaret Millar had actually preceded her husband by introducing psychiatry into her own detective fiction in the 1940s. From 1941 to 1945 she had published six novels in whole or in part shaped by the psychoanalytic proclivities of her detectives. By the mid-1950s Margaret Millar was still writing novels but had switched to psychological suspense and other forms.[15] The married writers still competed for time. Macdonald frankly regretted his part in giving his daughter too much of the "hostilities" between male and female, and not enough of the harmony.

Sexual identities within the shifting framework of the family romance control the thematic ebb and flow of *The Doomsters.* Even though the case promises to reenact the textbook Oedipal story, it is not the son who kills the Father, although all of the evil in the plot stems from the failure of the Father to enable the lives of any of the family members under his power. The Tom Rica subplot helps to steer the novel away from a predictable Oedipal conclusion. Well after the various homicides in the Hallman empire and family have been disentangled from flawed explanations, Archer returns to his own failure to father Tom Rica through his identity crisis. He had, Archer remembers as the novel closes, spotted Rica as a young man in crisis, and he had made gestures indicating that he was ready to act the role of the father. But when the boy came to him at the crisis moment, Archer was too obsessed by his own sexual failures to meet the boy's psychological needs:

> It was a hot day in late spring, three years and a summer before. The Strip fluttered like tinsel in the heat waves rising from the pavements. I'd had five or six Gibsons with lunch, and I was feeling sweaty and cynical. My latest attempt to effect a reconciliation with Sue [his ex-wife] had just failed. By way of compensation, I'd made a date to go to the beach with a younger blonde who had some fairly expensive connections. (249)

Just at this moment Tom Rica approaches and Archer dismisses him. Rica was the son surrogate who sought face-to-face engagement not couch analysis, but the father/analyst could not rise above his own problems and rebuild the family romance. Macdonald is merciful to Archer, writing a cautious "happy" ending of *The Doomsters* in the form of Archer's reprieve from the sentence of Rica's ruined life. The "father's case" continues after the detective's official case is closed.

The protracted denouement of *The Doomsters* serves an extraliterary purpose. Macdonald had personal investments in the psychoanalytic process, and he had pledged his fiction to pay. *The Doomsters* is a split attempt to cover both debts: to mobilize an enormous mass of Freudian material circulating in the atmosphere of the times and in his personal situation to heal his own broken family, and to fulfill his formal obligations to the detective novel. *The Doomsters* left a balance due on both accounts.

Although the Millar family had made some progress toward healing after psychotherapy and exile, there was still a serious challenge facing the novelist. *The Doomsters* had not really succeeded in grafting the modern myth of psychoanalysis to the popular form of the whodunit. The action in Archer's cases still ran out of phase with the explanation of the case. Macdonald had Archer talking the talk, but the novel could not yet walk the walk. The next novel in the Archer series, *The Galton Case,* was written back "home" in Santa Barbara and for that simple reason seems to have been born under friendlier auspices.

Coincidences seem to have conspired to smooth the way. When Macdonald returned to live in Santa Barbara, he met Donald Davie, a British poet and critic who was teaching at the University of California, Santa Barbara, on a one-year appointment.[16] Davie, an admirer of Russian and Polish writers—a rarity among English-speaking academics—was immersed in the poetry of Poland's national poet Adam Mickiewicz (1798–1855), whose enormous narrative poem *Pan Tadeusz* (1834) became the Romantic epic of Poland. Davie was working on a collection of poems, eventually published as *The Forests of Lithuania* (1959), sparked by the story and images of Mickiewicz's poem. Davie and Macdonald would take long afternoon walks, the occasions for discussions of each other's work. Macdonald was working on a story in which a young man, of seemingly obscure origins, pursues the promise of a fated, golden patrimony: no less than riches, a girl, and his true identity in California. Macdonald and Davie must have had several moments of seemingly miraculous convergence, for the story of Pan Tadeusz, the young hero of Mickiewicz's poem, involves delayed guilt for his father's decades-old crime of murder, love and marriage to the daughter of the murdered man, the return of the father from exile and penance, and the elevation of the son to withheld patrimony.[17]

Father-son relationships must have dominated the conversation even when Mickiewicz was not the topic. One of Davie's recent poems in the late 1950s, published in *A Winter Talent and Other Poems* (1957), evoked his own dead father. "Obiter Dicta" begins: "Trying to understand myself, I fetch / My father's image to me." The father in "Obiter Dicta" is a version of Jack Millar; both seem larger than life, both are masters of bits: proverbs, "gems from Emerson," "maxims of the sages."[18] Most important, both fathers were "poets" whose figures hover in their sons' memories as role models retroactively confirming the son as the writer.

Being focused on one facet of the Freudian family romance, the son's journey back home after exile from the family—rather than feeling responsible for the entire library, as he seems to have been in *The Doomsters*—Macdonald surged through *The Galton Case* as "a breakthrough novel" (*Archer At Large,* ix). *The Doomsters* and the year of formal psychoanalysis had lowered the temperature of his autobiographical material. Now out in the open, not sequestered in private memory as failure at turning it into a novel, his past was ready for use—not for exorcism. Conversations with Davie about fathers and sons made him feel that his intuitions were not figments of his own psyche but traces of real structures out in the world. Other poets living and dead thought the same thoughts. *The Galton Case* might safely disperse the ghosts of childhood, redeem the writer from some of his massive guilt, and capture the essential structure of his experience.

Taking a proactive grasp of wit and the unconscious, Macdonald named the central family of *The Galton Case* after Sir Francis Galton (1822–1911), the Victorian gentleman-scientist who, following Charles Darwin, sought to take the hit and miss of natural selection out of the evolution of the human species and thus speed up the survival of the fittest by controlled breeding—eugenics. In fact, in Galton's scheme for selective breeding of human beings for racial and class superiority, there would be very little random chance: exceptional young men and women were to be deliberately selected for type. Not that a stunning individual might never rise from the lower orders, or a ne'er do well fall from the higher. Galton's eugenics did allow for a "sport," an anomaly. But his theory of directed breeding was calculated to strengthen the grip of the privileged race and class on social and economic power. The family romance, in Galton's eugenic fantasy, was purged of all turmoil and suspense, for allegiance to class overrode antagonism of personal wills within the family. His pioneering work in the science of fingerprint identification, for which he is most popularly known, was an offshoot of his scheme to certify and control membership in the higher order.[19] The Galton family of Santa Teresa implements the theory on a smaller scale.

The matriarch of the Galton family needs an investigator to locate her missing son, who, her intuition tells her, is still alive even though he had disappeared more than a decade earlier. Archer is called in on the advice of a local attorney, whose own family is in crisis: his too-young wife is near nervous breakdown. In fact, before Archer is well-launched on the Galton search he has the knifing of the attorney's houseman to solve. Peter Culligan, the dead man, had connections to a bootlegging gang decades in the past. Archer soon finds connections to the missing Galton scion, whose wife had had connections to the same gang.

Archer's search soon uncovers a skeleton that proves to be that of the Galton heir. But an apparent Galton grandson surfaces at the same moment, sending Archer on a second-stage quest to confirm the pretender's identity. This stage of the case sends Archer to Ontario and into the freighted memories of Kenneth Millar's past.

Unlike the opening of *The Doomsters*, which barges directly into the territory of the unconscious with Archer's dream of the hairless ape, the opening of *The Galton Case* firmly establishes the hard-boiled idiom as the novel's controlling language. Archer enters the well-appointed law offices of Wellesley and Sable, counselors to the higher orders of Santa Teresa, and immediately begins to undermine their pretensions to hushed superiority. Clearly, in a Galtonian society of ins and outs, Archer identifies with the outs:

> Audubon prints picked up the colors and tossed them discreetly around the oak walls. A Harvard chair stood casually in one corner.
> I sat down on it, in the interests of self-improvement, and picked up a fresh copy of the *Wall Street Journal.* (3)

In *The Doomsters* Archer moves tentatively in a case that, from its outset, is a minefield of repressed implications for his own psychological health; in *The*

Galton Case he is in control of the world and its symbols of power and meaning from the moment he enters. Hidden meanings do not ambush him; instead, he manipulates the signs and symbols.

The central symbolic system in the case is the Oedipus myth: the story of the son's search for the father who "abandoned" him, his subsequent dealings with an identity fractured by nature and nurture, and his attempt to put himself back together on the level of dream rather than expediency—that is, not to make himself an "in" but to find that, true to his inner conviction, he is and always has been an "in" by birth.

Archer is retained to find the lost son of a wealthy widow who had forsaken the family kingdom after an argument with his father. Archer's eye registers the signs of "kingdom" and dynastic (that is, breeding) pressure as he scans the Galton drawing room on his first visit with his client:

> I strolled around the room and looked at the pictures on the walls. They were mostly ancestor-worship art: portraits of Spanish dons, ladies in hoop skirts with bare monolithic bosoms, a Civil War officer in blue, and several gentlemen in nineteenth-century suits with sour nineteenth-century pusses between their whiskers. The one I liked best depicted a group of top-hatted tycoons watching a bulldog-faced tycoon hammer a golden spike into a railroad tie. There was a buffalo in the background, looking sullen. (13–14)

Archer's analysis of the Galton family pictorial archive gives him the subtext before he hears the actual text: obligations to social rank, approved breeding, and the consolidation of capital are handed down with the Galton name from father to son. The sullen buffalo in the background, soon to be hunted almost to extinction by the "sportsmen" carried west on the Galton railroad, is an undisguised figure of doomed masculine freedom.

Anthony Galton, the son, preferred the bohemian life of the sullen buffalo to hereditary wealth and position. He took to writing poetry, identified with the disadvantaged classes, and married (late in her pregnancy) a woman whom the hovering patron of the novel, Francis Galton, would have considered an inappropriate mate—an ex-prostitute with connections to a bootlegging gang. Hardly a woman to join the ranks of "bare monolithic bosoms" in the family gallery.

Before the novel is half complete, Archer is able to identify the remains of a human skeleton as those of Anthony Galton. At the same time, a boy by the name of John Brown appears near the site of Galton's fossils, searching for his lost family. Brown bears a striking physical resemblance to the long-dead Anthony Galton and, to compress the plot, quickly satisfies the longing grandmother that he is indeed her grandson. John Brown becomes John Galton, and, miraculously it seems, a family naturally heals itself after decades of dismemberment.

Archer has lingering doubts, exacerbated when he is beaten so badly by a criminal gang connected to the late Anthony Galton that he needs a week of hospitalization. But he has no scientific evidence to disprove the miracle of the boy's identity. The women in the Galton circle are convinced of John's authenticity by the strength of their emotional response to him, not by legal credentials. Perhaps remembering the buffalo in the family gallery, Archer himself feels drawn to the underdog, the prince in the pauper.

To represent the eugenicist position in the novel as a pseudo-scientific position (and, as the case progresses, to "neuroticize" it), Macdonald provides the character of Dr. Howell, the Galton family physician and a father obsessed with the proposed mating of his daughter with the pretender to the Galton fortune. To stigmatize the discovered grandson and heir, Howell explains Anthony Galton, the lost and dead son, in eugenicist terms:

> "Tony was a sport. I mean that in the biological sense, as well as the sociological. He didn't inherit the Galton characteristics. He had utter contempt for business of any kind. Tony used to say he wanted to be a writer, but I never saw any evidence of talent. What he was really good at was boozing and fornicating." (16)

Francis Galton's eugenics theory was founded on the "scientific" observation that the individual of the higher order or breed would always show forth among the lower by virtue of appearance, aptitude, and accomplishment. And vice-versa. John Galton's acceptance as the lost grandson becomes a test case. The women around John, his putative grandmother, Dr. Howell's daughter, and a childhood friend of his dead father accept him because he seems to satisfy their emotional need for the return of the lost son. Dr. Howell, the jealous father, is skeptical; he notices certain Canadian usages and inflections to John Galton's speech that—intensified by his own neurotic protectiveness of his daughter—persuade him the boy is an impostor. Archer leans toward the boy's side, even though the lingering effects of his beating tend to hint at a deeper explanation.

Autobiographical interests impinge on the plot at this point, the second stage of Archer's search—now to verify the identity of the son after finding the father—for Macdonald's own story is that of a poor Canadian boy who came to California and found his true identity. Macdonald used Kenneth Millar's life story as the pattern for John Brown. His most recent version was the text he had produced for his psychoanalyst just a few years earlier. Like his character John Galton, Macdonald was motivated to endure a wretched youth by the myth of his birth in California. Like his character again, Macdonald had a father who was absent for much of his youth, keeping his distance until old age and infirmity made him unable to fend for himself. Both fictional and actual fathers were poets. Like his character, education at the University of Michigan (in both novel and life) proved to be his visa to a life in the United States. Macdonald gives John Brown his birth month, December; a two thousand dollar bequest to match the one Millar received at his father's death; an Ann Arbor address down the street from a house Millar had lived in while a graduate student at the University of Michigan. Autobiographical facts that were too toxic for Macdonald to handle directly (for example, the memory of almost being left at an orphanage by his mother) could be handled indirectly as Archer follows John Brown's trail into the past.

The more Archer investigates John Brown, the more he discovers circumstances that pile up against his original gut feeling that the boy is in fact John Galton. John Brown's story leads Archer back east, to Michigan and on to Ontario. In Canada he meets one of John's women, the dark, lean, intense, and aptly named Ada Reichler, who not only knows the former John Brown but also knows his Oedipal fantasy (186). After a brief interview, Archer and Ada make love in a flower garden—an unlikely site for a detective to make love, but Ada Reichler is the right woman. Saturated as he was in Freudian theory, Macdonald probably adapted her name from Wilhelm Reich, whose writings led the sexual revolution: "It is sexuality that governs the structures of human feeling and thinking. 'Sexuality' (physiologically speaking, the parasympathetic function) is the life energy *per se*."[20] Archer proves himself, with Ada, a fervent disciple.

Less physiologically, he discovers in his interview of Ada Reichler the clues to a conspiracy, the origin of which long predates his involvement in the case, to groom John Brown for the role of heir to the Galton fortune and privileges. The conspiracy stretches back to the first missing son, Anthony Galton, and his involvement with a bootlegging ring. Up to the moment of reversal at the conclusion of the novel, Archer is, sadly, convinced that John Brown is indeed an impostor schooled by underworld forces who have pressured Arthur Sable, the lawyer who has hired Archer, to gain control of the Galton fortune.

As Archer pursues a young man he believes to be a Galton only by nurture, not by nature, back for a second time to the Canadian city of origin, Galtonian principles twist themselves back into relevance. The lost and banished son in John Brown's fantasy of himself proves to be a reality. Whereas Sophocles' Oedipus is doomed by a past that returns to become his bloody future, John Galton is rewarded by the verification of his dream. Like Gatsby, another of Macdonald's crucial literary characters, John Galton can become his dream; unlike Gatsby, however, there is no Jay Gatz to drag him back under an unforgiving past. Unlike the ending to *The Doomsters,* which unwinds in overlapping, analysis-like conversations between Archer and several characters (including himself), the ending of *The Galton Case* is swift and crisply paced. The novel ends on a dime as a fresh dawn breaks and John Brown is irrefutably proven to be the man he dreamed he was.

The *Doomsters* is structured like an album of Freudian snapshots, with characters and situations representing a wide array of popular and technical aspects of the theory: interpretations of dreams, theories of sex, fetishism, symbolism, wit, all loosely contained in the family romance. In *The Galton Case* Macdonald forecloses on this structure of serial dispersion by fixing the story within the stricter confines of the family romance with a minimum (for example, the Ada Reichler aside) of spillover. That the family romance also explained to Macdonald his own life story and enabled him confidently to occupy himself after decades of sorrow and insecurity—as man, as novelist, as father—was the personal breakthrough mirrored in the literary one.

Macdonald was careful to qualify the word *breakthrough* with the tiny, indefinite article, *a*. Ever the writer who defined himself in terms of oeuvre rather than by single title, Macdonald left a small wedge for the future. His plots, he well knew, never did and never would stray far from the Freudian family romance. The two novels of the late 1950s, *The Doomsters* and *The Galton Case,* thoroughly steeped as they are in the Freudian medium of the time and in the personal circumstances of the author, represent the high risks and mixed benefits of wedding two demanding systems—Freudian theory and the detective novel. Breakthrough in *The Galton Case* might, in the context of Macdonald's entire career, mean more for what it made possible for future work than for what it summed up of his past up to 1959.

But neither life nor fiction was finished with Macdonald. In May, 1959, just before final exams at the University of California–Davis, Linda Millar suffered a relapse. She broke one of the stipulations of her 1956 parole by beginning to drink, and disappeared from the campus. Her father took charge of a regional search that stretched from Reno to Los Angeles. Linda was found about ten days later, but worry, guilt, frantic and sleepless traveling took a deep toll on Macdonald. In June he was hospitalized for two weeks with hypertension, kidney stones, and heart damage.[21] To add to Macdonald's woe, *The Galton Case* failed to earn back his publisher's advance, a financial setback he could ill afford when his and his daughter's medical bills were several hundred dollars a week. He had only one way of making money: writing. The breakthrough was short lived.

Two novels came as emergency responses to the ongoing family crisis. Both explore the psychology of daughters by contriving extremely close, almost coinciding, identifications to their respective mothers. In *The Ferguson Affair* (1960), a non-Archer detective novel experimenting with a married detective, Bill Gunnarson, about to become a father, two half-sisters and their mother who could pass as triplets. Ian Ferguson, an emotionally limited Canadian millionaire living in a Santa Barbara-like California town, embodies much of Macdonald's own Canadian history: transition from the hard oil fields of Alberta to the "velvet playground" wreaks havoc with Ferguson's emotional balance. He falls in love with the good sister of the pair of twins, not knowing that the other sister is in fact his own daughter. There is a brief moment when he fears he has impregnated his own offspring. Blackmail, naturally, ensues, and Gunnarson sets out to clear up the "affair." *The Ferguson Affair* was by and large a mild failure, a dead end. Macdonald's experiment with a married detective never gels; the more Gunnarson vows to his pregnant wife that he can't wait to be a home with her, the more readers realize that he, a true brother to Natty Bumppo, prefers the chase to the hearth. A violent deus ex machina gets Macdonald out of the novel as a speeding car mangles the evil daughter—an eerie reprise of his own daughter's vehicular troubles and his paternal anxieties.

With not much more time to digest his daughter's second season of troubles, Macdonald wrote the next Archer, *The Wycherly Woman* (1961), a novel constructed of delayed paternal acknowledgement, the passing of daughter as mother, psychiatrists, and Archer's odd impersonation of the missing girl's father. Called in to locate Homer Wycherly's missing daughter, Phoebe, who has left college without warning, Archer decides that the key is her missing mother, Homer's estranged wife, Catherine. Homer Wycherly refuses to tell Archer anything about Catherine. Archer gets on the trail in spite of his client's refusal.

The hunt for the Wycherly women leads Archer to the corpse of a sleazy real estate promoter, the body of his equally sleazy accomplice in fraud and blackmail, and the body of a woman at first identified (by her uncle) as that of Phoebe Wycherly. Family "fraud" overtakes real estate fraud in the plot, and Archer eventually unearths the extended family secret: the dead woman is Catherine, Phoebe's mother, and Phoebe herself is the daughter of Catherine and her brother-in-law Carl Trevor. Trevor has committed the multiple murders out of cowardice and desperation. He kills himself in the final pages of the novel.

The Wycherly Woman is a neglected novel in the Archer series (never collected in a volume of three and ranked low by the novelist himself), but it operates as a subtle transition from the period of the breakthrough to the inevitable next stage—arguably Macdonald's strongest sustained production: the wholesale social breakdown of the 1960s epicentered more often than not in his plots on a troubled daughter.

Phoebe Wycherly has disappeared from college, and her father, just back from a self-indulgent Pacific cruise, has hired Archer to find her. The more Archer sees of the Wycherly family, the more he understands why the daughter might have sought relief away from it. Homer Wycherly, her father, bears a strong resemblance to his fictional predecessor, Ian Ferguson: both are irascible, domineering, yet essentially insecure men grown wealthy in oil. Wycherly has inherited his money and the land producing it: a "lost valley city" ironically named Meadow Farms. The landscape is desert and the only thing that grows is the field of Wycherly's oil derricks (3). Returning to his architectural vocabulary, Macdonald situates Wycherly in a house to mirror his domineering but distant personality: "The house stood high above the road at the top of a winding private drive. Its stone face was forbidding, like a castle built to dominate a countryside. From the old-fashioned verandah, I could look down into the town and out across the valley" (4). The ogre in the castle is Homer Wycherly, "a big man with wavy brown hair and a stomach" (4). In addition to the stomach, he has a temper: all the suffering in his life is the fault of his estranged wife, Catherine, who is also missing and who, Homer suspects, is responsible in some way for Phoebe's disappearance, too. These are two parents, Homer's brother-in-law Carl Trevor concludes, who "weren't meant to live together" (60). Such a statement, even by a fictional character, is extraordinarily close to self-laceration by husband/father in a parallel situation.

And yet Homer and Catherine have lived together and in the process apparently produced a daughter. Archer's search for the missing girl closely parallels Macdonald's search for his own daughter just a year earlier. It takes him first to Phoebe's campus apartment, where he meets her roommate, Dolly Lang, who is in the process of typing a sociology term paper on juvenile delinquency. Her theme: is delinquency a result of socioeconomic factors or "a lack of love"? (27). Macdonald's penchant for harrowing self-examination supplies this character and her college thesis.

Self-examination deepens a few episodes later when Archer, impersonating Wycherly in order to gain information about his client's missing wife and daughter, enters, via a kind of psychological transference, the identity of the parent. He realizes that the more often he repeats the lie that Phoebe is his daughter, the more it becomes a "provisional truth" (118). Meeting a woman in a bar he believes to be Catherine Wycherly, the missing girl's mother, he loses professional detachment to the provisional truth when he upbraids her: "'You're a strange mother, Mrs. Wycherly. You don't seem to give a damn if your girl is dead or alive'" (106).

As the Wycherly case leads to two murders, blackmail, and a long-concealed adultery, Archer's route to solving it turns away from physical evidence and into psychological territory. Archer eventually locates Phoebe at a psychiatric clinic run by a haughty professional whom Archer begins by loathing but ends by respecting for his blend of clinical expertise and genuine human concern for his patient (232). As with John Brown in *The Galton Case,* Phoebe's ordeal was ultimately caused by confusion on the level of parentage. Believing for most of her life that Homer Wycherly was her father, she learns from her embattled and doomed mother that her uncle, Carl Trevor, is in fact her father and that her natural parents have withheld the secret from her for twenty years. Learning of her true identity coincides with the death of her mother and the daughter's conviction that she is responsible. Two other deaths follow upon the first as Phoebe is quickly thrust into the torture of impersonating her dead mother in order to defraud parties to a real estate transaction. Indeed, the woman Archer had scolded was not Mrs. Wycherly but her daughter Phoebe, the object of his search. He was as close to the missing daughter as the next barstool but did not know it.

Identity and guilt seem inextricably tangled in the daughter's fate. Archer teams with Dr. Sherrill, Phoebe's psychotherapist, to disentangle the knot. Archer pieces together the facts: names, dates, sequences of events. Dr. Sherrill counsels Phoebe on how to absorb and live with both the bad and the potential good in her future. Phoebe is pregnant, and there is a boyfriend in the case who proves hardy enough to grow out of his mother dominance (206). Sherrill's therapeutic advice to his young patient seems aimed as well at the novelist: "'You can't incorporate yourself with your father—with either of your parents. This isn't entirely your tragedy. You tried to make it yours, but your part in it was really peripheral'" (255). Novelist and psychiatrist seem to want to have the daughter move on, shed family burdens like yesterday's newspaper, and, in the process, leave part of the guilt burden behind for no one to tend.

But guilt in Macdonald's world never evaporates; it takes up residence in another host. In *The Wycherly Woman* that host is Carl Trevor, one of Macdonald's infrequent male villains. Trevor has killed not only Phoebe's mother, his longtime lover, but also a pair of blackmailers. Archer extends him the stock Roman privilege of taking his own life at the end of the novel. Not before, however, Trevor diagnoses the times: "'You know, Archer,' he tells the detective midway through the search for Phoebe, 'whole strata of society seem to be breaking loose and running wild in this civilization—if civilization is the right word'" (121). The stratum that seems most at risk is youth, mostly daughters but also sons, who have been literally or psychologically cut loose by a failing stratum of mothers and fathers.

In the next six Archer novels, falling significantly in the turbulent decade of the 1960s and set in the capital of that turbulence, California, Macdonald pushed out from his personal guilt and used it as a vehicle for exploring the guilts of "this civilization—if civilization is the right word." Having grown out of conventional crime and into the thicket of family pathology, Macdonald pushed the family and its pathologies into the spotlight of the detective novel. Beyond its "nuclear family" boundaries, in the novels of the 1960s, the family romance in Macdonald's creative hands became a sensitive instrument in the examination of an entire social moment.

[6]

"I Wish They All Could Be California Girls"

Archer in the 1960s

The West Coast has the sunshine
And the girls all get so tanned.
I dig a French bikini on Hawaii island dolls
By a palm tree in the sand.

I been all around this great big world
And I seen all kinds of girls.
Yeah, but I couldn't wait to get back to the States,
Back to the cutest girls in the world.

I wish they all could be California—
I wish they all could be California—
I wish they all could be California girls.[1]

One "stratum" of the 1960s belonged to the Beach Boys. If their kingdom of summer days and nights had become detached from civilization—vexed by nothing more serious than fickle girlfriends in French bikinis—then so much the worse for civilization, where human beings grew old, faced debt, and worried about the future. The new madonna of this effortless slice of civilization was the California Girl. In 1959 she had been fetishized in the Barbie Doll. Eternally sixteen, white, blonde, sexy and sexless at the same time, she was a goddess and the beach her domain. An entire cultural system spun around her as wardrobes, cars, a boyfriend, and a narrative were created to ensconce her in a virtual reality, a myth. It was a tough reality to live up to, nevertheless, and the lyrics to the Beach Boys' chart-topping songs did not make it any easier.

The California Girl did not spring full-blown from the surfer's brow. In the decade before Barbie, Raymond Chandler had described her older sister, the golden girl, in *The Long Goodbye:*

She was slim and quite tall in a white linen tailormade with a black and white polka-dotted scarf around her throat. Her hair was the pale gold of a fairy princess. There was a small hat on it into which the pale gold hair nestled like a bird in its nest. Her eyes were cornflower blue, a rare color, and the lashes were long and almost too pale. She reached the table across the way and was pulling off a white gauntleted glove and the old waiter had the table pulled out in a way no waiter ever will pull a table out for me. She sat down and slipped the gloves under the strap of her bag and thanked him with a smile so gentle, so exquisitely pure, that he was damn near paralyzed by it.[2]

Trust Chandler to find the venom in the pudding: the paralyzing look. This golden girl, Eileen Wade, kills her husband in cold blood, and then herself. Beautiful almost beyond description, desirable but deadly, the golden girl is never just a person. Like Barbie and the California Girl of the Beach Boys' hymn, she is an icon, but cold.

Ross Macdonald knew the California Girl. At the end of *The Barbarous Coast*, Isobel Graff, maimed psychologically by a procession of men—her father who had married her off to a manipulative Hollywood climber, her husband who made love to a series of starlets in their cabana, and her erstwhile lover who had killed one of those starlets and let Isobel believe she herself was responsible—finally breaks down. Turning on the lover who had let her think she had committed murder, her scorn and hatred rain down on herself as well: "'So you did it all for me, you filthy liar! Young Lochinvar did it for Honeydew Heliopoulous, the girl of the golden west!' Her feelings had caught up with her. She wasn't crying now. Her voice was savage" (525). Isobel Graff takes the type back further than Eileen Wade, for her desperate outrage at all the men who have abused her brings to bitter focus "The Girl" of David Belasco's Broadway hit of 1905, "The Girl of the Golden West." Belasco's heroine "was beautiful, intrepid, passionate, vivacious; the soul of innocence; the incarnation of virtue; the blooming rose of vigorous health; and she could swear fluently, play cards, and shoot to kill."[3] She did it all in the overwhelmingly masculine world of the gold rush, where she steered her own course between two suitors, a lawman and a dashing Robin Hood, winning her lover in a poker game. Puccini adapted Belasco's script as an opera that debuted in 1910. Isobel's cry of sisterhood mocks both the myth and her failure to escape from it.

Like Chandler, Macdonald knew that the Girl of the Golden West was a volatile brew of indulged privilege and humanity denied and that her image had burrowed deep into the history of the West, making California a dangerous place for women. When the feelings in the icon catch up with the woman encased in the image, the results are "savage." In his novels of the 1960s, from *The Zebra-Striped Hearse* to *The Goodbye Look*, Macdonald created a series of California Girls around whom he built six novels reflecting a civilization in crisis, imploding from the weight of too much dream and not enough reality. In each novel, "The Girl of the Golden West" bears more than her share of thematic significance.

In cultural shorthand, the Golden West also goes by the name *California,* not just the thirty-first state, admitted to the Union in 1850, but the Golden West of fortunes just for the finding and new beginnings for everyone who can make it across the border. The California of American myth is our shrine to manifest destiny, the end and fulfillment of American idealizing.

It is a commonplace of U.S. history that the nation was discovered and settled under the protective guidance of Divine Providence—"under God." Beneficiaries of our (white) pilgrim ancestors, we are privileged to be a chosen people. And to confirm His choice God has granted us a new eden where we can restart human civilization—even recreate human nature—uncorrupted by original sin. Flawed beginnings were left behind, across the Atlantic. Americans moved westward across the continent carrying the same myth but with a new label, *manifest destiny,* until we came to California—"face to face for the last time in history," Fitzgerald wrote in his elegy to Gatsby, the quintessential American dreamer in pursuit of his own golden girl, "with something commensurate to [our] capacity for wonder."[4] That "something" was California, and our capacity for wonder made it mythic.

California has the dubious fate of being the last-chance eden of the Golden West. For generations, internal refugees have stood at the borders of California, like the Joads in Steinbeck's *The Grapes of Wrath* (1939), and beheld a land they took to be the last earthly paradise. Like all edens before it, California proved to be just another place once it was invaded by everyday history; like the California Girl, it could be as savage as it was beautiful once the capacity for wonder had surrendered to the necessity of simply being. Nonetheless, since the Pacific Ocean proved to be an insurmountable barrier to imagining a further eden, Americans have had to cling to California even though its mythic perfection came to be buried under housing tracts, freeways, oil wells, and—not least—movie studios, like the Helio-Graff studio that has so much to do with Isobel Graff's savage anger.

One of the many strategies in the struggle to uphold the myth of California against the assertion of its materiality is a kind of protective reflex: if the dream will not survive our waking, then the dreamers pretend to sleep on, clinging to the fantasy, like Dorothy in Oz, that they are not in Kansas anymore. Sleeping on transforms the dreamer, and the consequences of one's actions in sleep seem less real—as do the actions themselves. In California, especially in its concentrated core, Los Angeles / Hollywood, stars are born every minute and the mortal humans they were disappear like bad memories. Judy Garland is born; Frances Gumm disappears—and in *A Star is Born* (1954), Judy Garland plays the commoner Esther Blodgett, whom Hollywood turns into the California Girl Vicki Lester.[5]

Like bad memories, too, who we were always resurfaces to bedevil who we think we have become. Kevin Starr, in his history of California, now in its fifth volume—*Embattled Dreams: California in War and Peace, 1940–1950*—links the dream to a classic American novel. Los Angeles / Hollywood, he writes, is "the Great Gatsby of American cities," where everyone has come from somewhere else and lives a reinvented life.[6] Ross Macdonald was not immune to the dream of the reinvented life; he lived in Santa Barbara as both Kenneth Millar and Ross Macdonald, a Canadian by upbringing but a Californian by birth and, he thought, by destiny. With the "breakthrough" of *The Galton Case,* the theme of identity, harnessed to a geographical plot in which the old self is sloughed off in the dingy Midwest and a new one donned in the Golden West, proved a durable structure. The Archer novels of the 1960s, a decade in which California seemed to spread its velvet grip on popular culture, collectively bear signs of having been crafted in response to the contradictory attractions of mythical and real California. Macdonald revisits the east-to-west plot of *The Galton Case* in *The Chill* (1964), transplants Gatsby from Long Island to California in *Black Money* (1966), explores the downside of youth culture in *The Zebra-Striped Hearse* (1962) and *The Instant Enemy* (1968), and performs autopsies on the happy suburban family in *The Far Side of the Dollar* (1965) and *The Goodbye Look* (1969), published the year that Charles Manson and his murderous "family" brought an end to the decade and to the myth of sanctuary. Reviews of *The Goodbye Look* in the *New York Times Book Review* announced a new, overdue status for the writer, a critical plateau for himself and the genre for which he had long and anxiously been waiting. The 1960s was Ross Macdonald's best decade.

Certain images and themes identify the California of the imagination, and Macdonald used them all. California is a country of immigrants: first the Spanish friars and dons seeking a colonial empire of both the spirit and the flesh; then Americans first seeking gold (of which there was not enough to go around) and then land (of which, at first, there seemed plenty) came to California in the nineteenth century, drawn by the promise of paradise, which, fatally, their very intrusion obliterated. The foundation novel for this element of the California myth is Helen Hunt Jackson's *Ramona* (1884). The heroine, Ramona, is the daughter of a Spanish mother (herself the daughter of a landed aristocrat) and a Scottish father, a castaway of British coastal exploration. Together, Ramona's parents represent the first wave of European possession. Since both of Ramona's parents are dead, raising Ramona becomes the obligation of her aristocratic Spanish aunt. Mixed blood puts Ramona on the low end of the señora's esteem. The Girl of the Golden West falls in love with an Indian—a lover with forbidden blood—and the two marry, over the señora's objections. The romance plot is complicated by the arrival in California of swarms of Americans, mostly poor white southerners, whose rapacious ways dispossess both the dons and the Indians. Ramona's Indian husband goes slowly but inexorably mad and is finally shot—a sort of lynching—by a posse of Americans. Despite an ambiguously "happy" ending, which finds Ramona rich but exiled from

California, *Ramona* fixes mythic California in the popular mind: the beauty of the place, personified in a beautiful but vulnerable unparented "daughter"; mixed blood electrified by class and race fear; the infection of a pastoral paradise by American (that is, materialistic) exploitation; tension between "natives" and newcomers; visions of wealth close enough to kill for. Macdonald's California Girls are bolstered by all or part of this mythic capital; in *Sleeping Beauty* (1973) he makes the theme overt by naming a supporting character Ramona.

One of the shrewdest, and most mordant dissectors of the California dream embodied in the California Girl, the latter-day Ramona, is a native: Joan Didion. In her essay "Girl of the Golden West," clearly titled to ricochet ironically off the Belasco-Puccini original, Didion lays bare the pathology of the myth. Patricia Hearst's "captivity" by the Symbionese Liberation Army in the early 1970s, Didion claims, was more than a stunt, more even than the traumatic breakdown of one individual. It was the inevitable return of repressed guilt for human "kidnapping" of California itself:

> The extent to which certain places dominate the California imagination is apprehended, even by Californians, only dimly. Deriving not only from the landscape but from the claiming of it, from the romance of emigration, the radical abandonment of established attachments, this imagination remains obdurately symbolic, tending to locate lessons in what the rest of the country perceives only as scenery. Yosemite, for example, remains what Kevin Starr has called "one of the primary California symbols, a fixed factor of identity for all those who sought a primarily Californian aesthetic." Both the community of and the coastline at Carmel have a symbolic meaning lost to the contemporary visitor, a lingering allusion to art as freedom, freedom as craft, the "bohemian" pantheism of the early twentieth century. The Golden Gate Bridge, referring as it does to both the infinite and technology, suggests, to the Californian, a quite complex representation of land's end, and also of its beginning.[7]

Macdonald used two of these settings for their symbolic register: the bohemian coast in *The Galton Case* and the Golden Gate Bridge in *The Underground Man*. But more deeply his novels of the 1960s operate on an understanding he shares with Didion: that the heroines, like Didion's version of Patty Hearst, are representations of a complex and conflicted cultural history. Violent breakout is only a matter of time.

Didion's essay exposed the dangerously thin foundation under the facade of the California dream. "The romance of emigration," Didion concludes, left the California psyche with no permanent mooring, no "established attachments."[8] The hardships and dangers of overland migration—even and especially if the immigrant ended up as rich as Hearst's grandfather—produced a population that had left its feelings, with its furniture and its dead, at tight spots along the way. Just surviving to enter the Golden West produced a people who were "raised on a history that placed not much emphasis on *why*."[9] Macdonald used this subtext repeatedly, usually signaled by family art and portraits—for example, in the Galton family gallery, the paintings of Massachusetts ancestors in *The Zebra-Striped Hearse*, or the abandoned Idaho past of a murder victim in *The Far Side of the Dollar.*

What also makes Didion's essay useful as an interpretive key to Macdonald's novels of the 1960s is the assertion (in Macdonald only a suggestion) that racism is an essential element of the myth. The most prominent of the soldiers of the Symbionese Liberation Army who snatched Patricia Hearst were African American, assuming a racism that Didion's essay takes for granted in the post-Watts California of the early 1970s. Macdonald anticipated this aspect of the dream, but tracing the stress fractures of race in his novels is easier with Didion's help. Retellings of the California myth inevitably retrieve traces of the racism embedded deeply in its history. *Ramona* does not include African American characters, but as Mike Davis in *City of Quartz: Excavating the Future in Los Angeles* characterizes its power to incubate myth, Jackson's novel continues to fuel a white Anglo myth of California.[10] Indeed, Davis explains, the myth of California embedded in *Ramona* was invoked at the turn of the century to help sell California to small eastern and midwestern investors as "the utopia of Aryan supremacism—the sunny refuge of White Protestant America in an age of labor upheaval and the mass immigration of the Catholic and Jewish poor from Eastern and Southern Europe."[11] The refugee stream continued through World War II, making Los Angeles in 1949, in Kevin Starr's words, "the whitest big city in America."[12] This is Archer's orbit, and as early as 1952 in *The Ivory Grin* he was attuned to the dynamic of race relations.

California was also the place where the American suburb as a self-contained lifestyle was—if not invented—perfected, where the family car had its own room (the garage or carport), where the backyard barbecue was hallowed as a ritual site of family bonding and the sacred flame, and where that family assumed perfect symmetry in a dozen television series. The single-family home, with front yard for display and backyard for recreation and maternal surveillance in the endless California sun, rose with the myth of California as the object of all-American family worship. Macdonald's concentration on the Freudian family and their psychotherapeutic housing designs gave him a head start in exploring and deconstructing the hallowed myth of the family in the California of the 1960s. It is this cultural insight—that California packaged, but none too confidently, the American myth of family values in a race-free suburban utopia—that makes Macdonald's Archer novels *novels* rather than accomplished formula fiction.

The themes of many of his novels of the decade dramatize what Gwendolyn Wright, in her classic *Building the American Dream,* concludes about the contradictions literally built into the postwar suburb:

The architecture of the postwar suburbs was symptomatic of other problems, but it did not by itself cause those problems. One has only to consider the stifled frustration of women in the suburbs, their isolation from work opportunities and from contact with other adults; the limited experiences available to children and teenagers; or the emphasis on the man's role as the distant provider who should spend his time at home "improving the property." The setting for these psycho-sociological distortions was supposedly a "pure," "safe" suburb.[13]

Macdonald, with his bias toward "psycho-sociological distortions," was primed to capture the tensions of the moment. At the end of the 1960s, California also became the place where the suburban apotheosis of the family eden was ruined by Charles Manson, whose pseudo "family" murderously mocked the ideal and put a bloody end to the dream of the "'safe' suburb."[14] In *The Goodbye Look* (1969) Macdonald drew the 1960s to a close with a definitive, if less gory, requiem for the suburban family. Earlier in the decade, in *The Far Side of the Dollar,* he made "the stifled frustrations of women in the suburbs," the distance of fathers, and the frustrations of the children the fundamentals of his plot.

Over the full course of his career Macdonald's fiction addressed many of the fixtures of the California myth, but in the Archer novels of the 1960s, particularly, the "California aesthetic" plays a strong, shaping role. A series of estranged and vulnerable daughters reprise the fate of Ramona. On the level of cultural symbolism these daughters operate as figures for the abused land, the exploitation that is scarring California on the physical level. Macdonald's settings, for example, increasingly critique industrial and real estate development as disfigurement: Homer Wycherly's oil derricks in *The Wycherly Woman* (1961), for example, or the rampant freeway construction in *The Zebra-Striped Hearse* (1962). Mixed-blood romance in *Ramona* is reprised in the miscegenation and threat of mixed blood in *Black Money,* a novel that, while it owes much to Fitzgerald's classic *The Great Gatsby* (1925), also draws upon the explosive racial situation in Southern California in the 1960s. The blessings of youth, hymned in songs by the Beach Boys and other California and California-inspired music groups, touted the joys of the endless summer. In *The Zebra-Striped Hearse* and *The Instant Enemy* (1968) Macdonald exposed the anxiety and suffering of a youth culture abandoned to pleasure. And frustrated suburban wives trouble the plots of *The Far Side of the Dollar* and *The Goodbye Look.*

The Zebra-Striped Hearse, published in 1962, examines the pessimistic statement of Carl Trevor in the novel that precedes it, *The Wycherly Woman.* The youth stratum of "civilization" seems detached from the core, and Archer has been hired to put the parts back together. The case begins in conventional hard-boiled fashion with a mysterious but attractive female calling on the detective in his seedy office on Sunset Strip. The attractive woman is Isobel Blackwell, who has come to Archer in advance of her husband's appointment to head off what she fears will explode into a family catastrophe. Her husband's twenty-four-year-old daughter, Harriet, is engaged to marry a suspicious young man she had met in Mexico. This young man, operating under the alias of Burke Damis, claims to be a painter, one of the tribe that, in Didion's diagnosis, represents the belief in "art as freedom, freedom as craft." Not too deeply into the case, Archer concludes that Damis is more dangerous than benignly bohemian, that the kind of class-antagonistic violence later associated with Hearst and the Symbionese Liberation Army flows through Damis and threatens to convert Harriet from overprotected daughter into Tania-like rebel. He takes the case more in honor of and sympathy for Harriet and her stepmother, Isobel, than in deference to the father.

Isobel, Archer learns, is Col. Mark Blackwell's (ret.) second wife. He and his first wife, Harriet's mother, are divorced. Harriet's mother had moved to Mexico, to follow art rather than marriage, and it is on a visit to her mother that Harriet meets Damis. The trail of Damis leads Archer to Lake Tahoe, where the Blackwells have a lodge. In the Blackwell lodge worked a young girl, Dolly Campion, who has been found strangled. Her young child was moved from the scene in a tweed overcoat, and in his hand investigators found a button. Damis is Campion's husband, wanted in connection with her murder. Another corpse, that of a hapless private investigator, is found on Damis-Campion's trail as well; he has been killed with an ice pick.

Coincidentally, Archer encounters a band of surfers following the waves in a zebra-striped hearse and notes without recognition that one of the surfer girls is huddled against the chill in a tweed overcoat. Later in the case he will come back for the coat—the source of the missing button. Evidence against Damis-Campion for the murder of his wife, Dolly—and perhaps of Harriet Blackwell, too—fails to gel. Instead, Archer finds the trail of evidence, confirmed by the match of button to overcoat, leads back to the Blackwell household.

Before Archer reaches any firm conclusions, however, he confronts Harriet's father, a retired army colonel with ancestors stretching back, symbolically, to Massachusetts Bay. Their portraits hang incongruously in the Blackwell mansion in Bel Air, setting up the symbolic discord Didion probed: Providential founding, puritanical pride in "the City upon a Hill" opposed to expatriate California *ennui* and Damis's dark threat of antipuritanical anarchy. Mark Blackwell represents the deeply buried problems of emigrating: as Didion might claim, great wealth to go along with immense guilt, and no clue about how to deal with either in the absence of an indigenous place. Deeper in the national symbolic imagination, there is the level on which Mark Blackwell reenacts the role of John Winthrop and other Pilgrim fathers. Giving Blackwell an army past transforms him into a symbol of repressive discipline looking for a place to happen.

Damis's courtship of Harriet is a virtual savage kidnapping, as her father sees it, fundamentally no different from the seizure of a New England woman by a marauding Indian in colonial Massachusetts (or a member of the Symbionese Liberation Army with a sawed-off shotgun). But as in the actual "kidnapping" of Patty Hearst, the so-called victim turns her allegiance away from family and toward her wild captor. Harriet insists that she will marry Burke Damis, regardless of his past or her father's fulminations. The major antagonists come to a showdown in the driveway of the Blackwell home in verdant Bel Air. The shotgun that Mark Blackwell brandishes is eerily prophetic of the various assault weapons Patty Hearst displays in photographs of her as "Tania," her *nomme de guerre* as SLA militant, and functions equally well to recall a seventeenth-century musket and the vast disconnection between the drama Mark Blackwell thinks he is playing and the "ground" he is playing it on. In other words, by means of his careful, strategic economy of image and scene, Macdonald connects the Blackwell case to a deeper California cultural subtext.

The Blackwell case takes Archer to Mexico, where he spends a long night in a community of exiles from California, failed or fleeing one-time believers in the California dream who have created yet another dreamscape, where their money miraculously multiplies (thanks to a triumphant exchange rate for the dollar over the peso) and their failings seem to dissolve in the tropical rains and the cheap liquor. The fundamental unreality of this colony of exiles is slyly underscored in the novel by a nest of Macdonald's carefully placed jokes. One of the colonists whom Archer questions is a former movie star who made her name as a damsel in westerns; she had retreated to Mexico in order to prolong the glamour of her youth by marrying a man several decades her junior. Archer struggles to remember the actress's name, and when he brings it to the surface —Helen Holmes—she puts down her gun and invites him to have a drink. Exile, alcoholism, and a life on film that had fascinated a young boy (Archer) is the pattern of the life of Pearl White (1889–1938), the heroine of the celluloid serials Macdonald remembered from his childhood: *Plunder* (1923) and *The Perils of Pauline* (1914). Pearl White died in France of cirrhosis of the liver.

Macdonald tropes the silver-screen fantasy world of the exiles again. Soaked by a sudden storm, Archer attracts the attention of the American expatriate owner of the only hotel in town. This Samaritan, by the name of Claude Stacy, lends Archer some dry clothes, most notably a blue turtleneck sweater emblazoned with "a big monogrammed S" (71). Costumed as Superman, Archer makes his visit to the home of the former movie star, whose history of staged gunplay has spilled over into a real-life penchant for blasting away with live ammunition at anyone who annoys her. She takes a shot at Archer, but the bullet barely nicks the Superman sweater. The cohabitation of reality and fantasy, a tension that in various degrees characterizes the California psyche, dogs Archer throughout the entire Blackwell case. Sometimes, as with the kryptonite sweater, magic protects him; as his case breaks, however, ironic fantasy inevitably drops into sexual exploitation, murder, and ultimately suicide.

The pivotal clue of the Blackwell case, the overcoat with a missing button, is introduced by means of the title vehicle, a retired hearse painted with zebra stripes and used by a nomadic band of surfers, whom Archer meets at first accidentally and a second time by intent. One of the outcasts is wearing a Harris tweed topcoat with a missing button. Archer notices the fact; only later does the button itself turn up as a clue. Indeed, in light of the painful denouement of the Blackwell case, the stray button is not stray at all. Blackwell and his daughter match one another for stubbornness, as do Cordelia and Lear, whose dying request is "Pray you, undo this button" (5.3.309). The coincidence would fail as too far-fetched if Macdonald did not work hard to accommodate surfers, suspects, and victims into the same milieu, the milieu of the placeless in paradise. This apparently homeless band of four boys and two girls seems, from Archer's point of view, to be living the underside of the California dream. Social only within their own tribe, living on a poor diet of hamburgers and beer, heedless of their futures, they reject Archer's attempts at simple conversation. They prove out the diagnosis of the late Carl Trevor; in fact, they seem to know no other reality than being cut adrift. Like Blackwell's fragile identity as the displaced Puritan and the boredom and delusion of the colony of misfits Archer visits in Mexico, the directionless youth in the zebra-striped hearse reinforce the novel's theme of radical estrangement in the Promised Land.

Archer, of course, cannot claim complete immunity from the contagion of a disconnected myth. Only the case gives his wandering a purpose as the corpses mount: a strangled young wife, an amateur private eye stabbed with an ice pick. The trail takes him from Los Angeles to a small town farther south, to Mexico, back to Los Angeles, to Tahoe, to the Bay Area, back to Los Angeles, and finally to Mexico again for the sudden reversal at the end of the novel. Archer's physical mobility triggers a psychological restlessness, and he compensates by scrolling through much of his own background trying to place himself in a placeless civilization. In *The Zebra-Striped Hearse* Macdonald discloses comparatively more of Archer's biography than he does in other novels. And yet it is not the facts of Archer's pre-detective life that are important so much as the unrest that remembering them causes.

In Tahoe, tracking down Burke Damis (and fearing that Harriet Blackwell might be a "lady in the lake" like one of Chandler's victims), Archer connects with yet another nomad, a young woman using the name Fawn King. Archer uses her to lead him to places where Damis had holed up in and around Lake Tahoe. Repaying her with dinner, Archer succumbs to conversation. Fawn confesses that her real name is Mabel. Confession infects Archer, and he begins to tell the woman about himself. He stops when a kind of psychological alarm system goes off: "I'd begun to talk to the girl because she was there. Now I was there, too, more completely than I wanted to be" (139). Archer hurriedly pays the tab, leaves Fawn to become the prey of a drunk in a big white Stetson (154), and rushes to the airport to catch a flight to the Bay Area.

Finding oneself "there" presents the reinvented Californian, Archer included, with the entire bundle of issues he had left "there" to evade in the first place. Arnie and Phyllis Walters, the Tahoe husband-and-wife detective team whom Macdonald uses again in *The Chill*, represent the "thereness" of situated relationship and human meaning maintained in place and over time. Archer admires and perhaps even envies the Walters's "thereness," but he is far from adopting it. Indeed, as Didion diagnoses the California imagination, moving on is the first rule of behavior. As the principals in the Blackwell case demonstrate, nearly everyone is on the move, from place to place and from name to name.

A similar pathology runs through *The Zebra-Striped Hearse.* As the trail becomes more complicated, and unrelated corpses become more related in death than they were in life, Archer gradually comes to think that the Puritan Father is the dark nexus of the case—the "black well" from which the evil comes. Having run Blackwell to ground, Archer extracts a confession of sorts. Blackwell had taken sexual advantage of a house servant, Dolly, impregnated her, and the violence had spread from that point. Confessing the sin of seduction, Mark Blackwell uses the language of myth-as-pathology which ties the novel together:

> "I swear to heaven I didn't touch her when she was a child. I merely adored her from a distance. She was like a fairy princess. . . . I didn't see her again till we met last spring at Tahoe. She was grown up, but I felt as though I'd found my fairy princess once again. . . . And she was willing. She came back more than once on her own initiative." (253)

"The golden girl" undermines the myth in several ways: first, she shows sexual appetite, then she becomes pregnant, and finally begins to blackmail the Puritan father of her child. When Dolly—this version of Barbie—grows up, and grows human, she sprouts trouble.

Ironically, this brings another echo from Carl Trevor, the murderer of three in *The Wycherly Woman*: "'You start out with an innocent roll in the hay, and you end up having to kill people'" (272). Never that innocent. After Mark Blackwell kills himself, presumably in remorse for the killings Archer has been tracking down, the plot seems to have come to rest. But the California Girl has one more revolution; as the plot twists in the final pages it is Harriet, the other golden girl—too big, too much in looks like her father, too protected by the incest prohibition when the "fairy princess" was not—who is revealed as the murderer. Her motivation is that of the California Girl driven to desperation.

Tall and blonde, she unfortunately looks a little too much like her father (21–22), and the identification has burrowed fatally deep into her psyche. She explains the killings of her father's mistress (the mother of her half brother) and the men who have tried to reveal the secret as half-conscious attempts to keep the love of her father, to keep it all "in the family" (278).

The California Girl plays an important and diversified role in *The Zebra-Striped Hearse*. Embodied in Dolly, she is a direct allusion to the idealized "doll," the object of desire who, becoming human, brings chaos to family stability. Harriet, bequeathed a body scarcely doll-like, erupts with violence to reclaim her father's attention. Floating like a shadowy footnote beneath them both are the surfer-nomads, a dingy reality to counter the sun-and-sand myth.

In *The Chill* (1964) the moral and psychological decentering that occurs with emigration from the blighted Midwest to the Golden West (a trope Macdonald combined with the Oedipus myth in *The Galton Case*) is at the center of the plot, folded closely into Macdonald's signature Freudian drama, the family romance. Another Dolly appears—Dolly Magee Kincaid, a young woman traumatized by two murders she has seen all too closely. Female characters dominate the plot. In addition to Dolly there is Madge Gerhardi, an aging "Barbie" "engaged" to Dolly's estranged father who is, in fact, sponging on her; Helen Haggerty, a wandering academic, tanned and blonde, a murder victim and a blackmailer; Alice Jenks, Dolly's aunt and a sexually repressed spinster; and the Osborne sisters, nearing seventy, one of whom has come west and recreated herself in the new culture—with lethal side-effects.

As he did in *The Barbarous Coast,* Macdonald shoots Archer into a case when the detective agrees to find a missing wife for a young man, Alex Kincaid, whom the childless Archer intermittently imagines as his son. Like Mark Blackwell, Alex Kincaid's father in *The Chill* is a "heavy" father who threatens to unman his son by rescinding the younger man's power to establish his own ego and his sexual autonomy, by pressuring him to annul his marriage to the missing girl, Dolly Magee. In *The Chill,* the young husband suffers a wide range of difficulties in setting up his own psychological, sexual, and social household; even though Archer has tried and failed at this process himself, he still enlists to help other young men blocked before they get a chance to fail. With a boost from Archer, Kincaid survives his father's attempt to usurp his ego and annul his marriage to Dolly, the wife who disappeared on their honeymoon. Kincaid's social identity (unlike George Wall's in the earlier novel) is affirmed after he successfully fends off his father, when he makes a series of far-from-romantic medical and legal decisions. Archer's coaching seems vindicated, but the case is larger.

The marriage of Dolly and Alex is never consummated in the novel. But sex is yet again the burning fuse confirming Carl Trevor's deathbed wisdom that there is no such thing as an innocent roll in the hay. Reckless and desperate couplings from far back in the characters' pasts cause the problem of the present. The original sexual transgression happened in a fictional Illinois town that bears a general resemblance to the archetypal abandoned midwestern city of Macdonald's work—and life. The daughter of a U.S. senator is married to a local real estate and construction entrepreneur not unfamiliar with the shady side of life. The married woman seduces a college student many years younger than herself in retaliation for her husband's liaisons in the demimonde. When the cuckolded husband finds the lovers in bed, violence erupts. The husband is killed, the wife exiled, the investigating policeman forced into a cover-up, the policeman's daughter estranged from her father and eventually murdered, too. Archer starts from the present end of the skein—the fractured marriage of Dolly and Alex is his point of entry—and works backward in time and across mythic geography as he makes a trip to Illinois. Backward and inward is the path of the analyst.

The original, transgressive couple—the unfaithful wife and the college student—have emigrated to California, where they have invoked the dream to recreate themselves. They feign the roles of mother and son to cover the age discrepancy of their marriage. A youngish thirty-something wife is now the wrinkled sixty-something "mother." Her "son," now a youthful forty, has been on the lookout for younger women. The hint of Dorian-Gray age and sexual politics turns violent. Re-creation has limits, just as actions have consequences. Newness and youth are the currency of California, profusely minted in the 1960s. The campus where the son/husband serves as dean is itself so new that it has yet to mellow into the fabric of the residential landscape around it. And the rented house of a traveling academic whom Archer questions is so tangentially connected to the earth that it seems not grounded at all (227). In the register of psychotherapeutic architecture absorbed with Neutra designs, this house, with its walls of transparent glass, expose too much of what the doomed inhabitant wishes to keep concealed. This professor—daughter of the betrayed policeman in the original crime—is the latest, but not the first, victim of the compulsions of the "California Girl" driving the plot.

The son/husband can successfully recreate himself, if only in appearance, as a youngish academic because he started with an age advantage, and (as women in the novel complain) men have an advantage in the youth sweepstakes. The mother/wife, however, is less satisfied with her fate. Losing out sexually to two younger women who become her "son's" lovers exacerbates her deep-seated resentment. She identifies the younger women as threats and murders her sexual rivals. At the level of archetype, the character of the mother/wife is a study in maternal frenzy; she does not merely disapprove of her "son's" playmates, she kills them.

The mother/wife, whose periodic eruptions of homicidal violence are clearly linked to her rage at losing contests of sexual attraction over her younger husband, is paired in the narrative by the older, unmarried sister of one of the murder victims. This spinster, Alice Jenks, immediately impresses Archer as embodying the principle of denial that must be overcome for any woman to arrive at "normal":

> Close up, she wasn't so alarming. The brown eyes behind the glasses were strained and anxious. Her hair was streaked with gray. Her mouth was unexpectedly generous and even soft, but it was tweezered like a live thing between the harsh lines that thrust down from the base of her nose. The stiff blue dress that curved like armor plate over her monolithic bosom was old-fashioned in cut, and gave her a dowdy look. The valley sun had parched and roughened her skin. (99)

Generosity and denial, sensuous flesh plated with armor—Alice Jenks, like the more central character of the deranged mother/wife, represents a pathological misdirection of the female psyche. She may be seen as grotesque; Archer detects in the competing lines of control and sensuality in her face, the mask of a doll and the flesh of a woman.

Alice Jenks is clearly in the danger zone where banked desire and advancing age become volatile. Her private bedroom is a caricature of her psychological profile, suggesting a serious rift between private fantasy and public control:

> The blinds were drawn and she turned on the overhead light for me. It had a pink shade which suffused the room with pinkness. The floor was thickly carpeted with a soft loose pink material. A pink decorator spread covered the queen-sized bed. The elaborate three-mirrored dressing-table was trimmed with pink silk flounces, and so was the upholstered chair in front of it.
>
> A quilted pink long chair stood by the window with an open magazine across its foot. Miss Jenks picked up the magazine and rolled it in her hands so that its cover wasn't visible, but I knew a *True Romance* when I saw one. (106–7)

A clearer and more stereotypical rendition of repressed female sexuality can hardly be imagined. As overt as Macdonald is with the character of Alice Jenks, he hides the signs that eventually point to the killer.

This situation would seem excessively gothic, and not a little misogynistic, if Macdonald had not wrapped it in the California myth idealizing the Girl of the Golden West. The premium placed on youth in the California myth levies a surcharge for sexual attractiveness on women; they must hold on to enough of girlhood to preserve their attractiveness even as age takes an inevitable toll. The descriptions of the several women in the plot concentrate on faces etched with lines of age (26, 41, 177); only the younger are happy. Tension rises from this inequity in Archer's badinage with Helen Haggerty, the wronged policeman's daughter and not-so-young woman whose murder Archer fails to foresee or prevent:

"We academic people are such nomads. [Helen Haggerty says.] It doesn't
suit me. I'd like to settle down permanently. I'm getting old."
    "It doesn't show."
    "You're being gallant. Old for a woman, I mean. Men never grow old."
(43–44)

Haggerty, Archer learns, was not above blackmailing the son/husband with
disclosure of his marriage. But, factoring in her flaws, she is right about the
sexual politics. The overt Oedipal relationship in *The Chill* is bold enough to
provide its own interpretation. But Macdonald wraps it in a more nuanced cultural context than he uses in *The Gulton Case*, in which the Oedipal theme is
made to work with almost no context. When, in tracing the origins of present
crime into the past, he concludes that "History is always connected with the
present" (135), what connects moments in apparently divergent histories is
not the Freudian paradigm but the milieu of California. The more California
mythmakers allow themselves to be taken in by the present, the more they are
chewed up by their histories.

Eventually, Archer untangles the skein. All the corpses have one thing in
common: the woman driven by the mania of staying forever young has killed
them all. The fascination with eternal youth precedes serial murder. The aging
golden girl murderer in *The Chill* has allowed herself to become mesmerized by
the dream, and in her half-waking condition right and wrong, sane and insane
have lost all meaning.

If the pressure to be part of the cult of youth shapes crime and motivation
in *The Chill*, Macdonald's next novel, *The Far Side of the Dollar* (1964), puts
the sorrows and confusions of youth in the spotlight. The central couple in *The
Chill* are adults acting like children; in *The Far Side of the Dollar*, the kids have
to act like adults. But they have little guidance. Moving among so many disconnected generations, Archer despairs: "Generation after generation had to
start from scratch and learn the world over again. It changed so rapidly that
children couldn't learn from their parents or parents from their children. The
generations were like alien tribes islanded in time" (141). Set in Pacific Point,
Macdonald's "Massachusetts Bay" of the rich and privileged south of Los Angeles, *The Far Side of the Dollar* is a dark version of *Peter Pan* in which the Lost
Boys are never rescued, Wendy grows into womanhood without magic spells
to protect her, and Captain Hook does not turn back into the beneficent father.

The Far Side of the Dollar opens at Laguna Perdida School, a school for
"lost" boys on a lost lagoon. Archer has been called in to find a problem boy
who, like Carl Hallman in *The Doomsters*, has run away, chiefly from a father
whom he will not acknowledge as his own. Abraham is Abraham, but is the
son Ishmael or Isaac? Indeed, when Archer gets his first look at the school, he
concludes that he would have run away, too. To further underscore the theme

of lostness, Archer compares the boys of Laguna Perdida to German POWs he had seen toward the end of World War II.

Tom Hillman, the missing boy, has gone on a search for his real father. He is aided on his quest, in a sense, not only by intuition but by people from his titular father's past who convince him of another parentage. His father, a business executive and former navy officer, does not help matters by "adopting" a junior member of his management team as a surrogate son. Archer follows the trail of the missing boy into the father's past, and there he finds, with the help of Hollywood contacts, a liaison between the father and an aspiring actress— a California Girl of the 1940s with good looks and average talent—who had fled her arid Idaho home for bright lights and fame. Age is not the worst that happens to her; she is one of the dead Archer finds in his investigation. Other participants who shared the secret of the liaison also turn up dead. Suspicion hovers around Tom Hillman, but Archer soon dispels it.

Searching for the searcher, Archer has to think like an abandoned son. One of his first challenges is winning the trust of Tom Hillman's girlfriend, Stella Carlson, the daughter of the Hillman's neighbors in their protected suburban enclave. As he does in several of his novels, Macdonald spices the character of Stella Carlson with literary allusion. When Stella and Archer meet for the first time, she betrays a youthful combination of sophistication and naiveté by asking: "'Are they trying to cut out his [Tom's] frontal lobe like in Tennessee Williams?'" (44). Thomas was Tennessee Williams's christened name, and Rose Williams, the playwright's older sister, was lobotomized in 1943 as a cure for her "manic" behavior. Williams's portrait of Laura Wingfield in *The Glass Menagerie* (1944) was a tribute to his sister and penance for the brother's guilt for not being at home to intervene. Stella's conversation dramatizes a further meaning: the children of the suburbs are often too knowledgeable for the confined and protected lives they live.

Stella Carlson also asks Archer the same question the lost boys of Laguna Perdida had asked, "'Are you a parent?'" (46). His "No" elicits, at least initially, the potential for her trust. But Archer senses that the chemistry connecting over-thirty and under-twenty is too unstable for a simple "yes" or "no." As he continues to question Stella and the rain falls on his car, he begins to see Stella's essential bind: "Her lips were turning blue. I had a sudden evil image of myself: a heavy hunched figure seen from above in the act of tormenting a child who was already tormented. A sense went through me of the appalling ease with which the things you do in a good cause can slip over into bad" (45). Macdonald's regret for causing his own daughter's problems obviously seasons Archer's sense of the potential harm he might do simply in the course of his job. The interview with Stella comes to a close when her mother, calling out "Stella!" in the rain, another wink to Williams, ends the scene.

The search for Tom Hillman takes Archer into another briar patch of adult sexual angst, guilt, repression—and the consequences of the parents' sins on the lives of boys and girls. Tom Hillman's father, like Harriet Blackwell's in *The Zebra-Striped Hearse,* is a sexually hungry man whose military career serves as the unsteady governor on his passions. The uneven lurching of passion, shame, and denial creates bumpy havoc for the children of such parents. Even more so if, as in the case of Tom Hillman's putative mother, the wife is frigid: "I began to suspect that she[Elaine Hillman] didn't relate to men. It happened sometimes to girls who were too good-looking. They were treated as beautiful objects until they felt like that and nothing more" (139). Mrs. Hillman is the Girl of the Golden West who has become a mother without, as Archer eventually learns, childbirth. Worshiped or desired but never actually known, the golden girl becomes a lethal danger to society. Elaine Hillman, like the savage dolls in the two previous novels, turns worship into murder. In the ultimate scene of *The Far Side of the Dollar,* father and son attempt a reconciliation while the woman seeks, unsuccessfully, to buy Archer's silence and, failing that, stabs herself with her knitting needles.

Clearly Macdonald's experience with his own daughter, scarcely more than a decade old, shaped his somber view of the dangers of parenting. The youth-oriented culture of the 1960s, as it headed for flame-out in the 1970s, hewed closely to Macdonald's pessimistic course. Indeed, as Didion's essay on Patricia Hearst would claim ten years after *The Far Side of the Dollar,* what had begun in reparable alienation would end in violent rejection. Archer, however, re-pairs the broken relationship between Macdonald and his daughter Linda, and prophetically between Patricia Hearst and California, by earning the trust of Stella Carlson. She pays him the enormous compliment of admitting that he had never lied to her (166). The road to Tom Hillman's rescue runs through the Freudian family romance; one of the inmates of Laguna Perdida tells Archer that Tom's fantasy about being adopted is common currency in the school: "'A lot of the kids here want to think they're adopted. My therapist calls it a typi-cal Freudian family romance'" (169). Tom's intuition, like John Brown's in *The Galton Case,* proves to be true—in part: the woman he took to be his mother was not. Elaine Hillman, the legal but childless wife in this Abrahamic parable, has not only caused the expulsion of the natural mother; she has murdered her. And although her motivation sinks deeply into the psychology of sex and identity, where it merges with archetype, when it comes to the surface in place and time it does so as the California Girl.

Along with the collapse of the nuclear family, which Macdonald's investment in the family romance helped him to chronicle, California also provided the site for a larger social collapse. The Watts Rebellion of 1965 proved to be, because it exposed the dark side of the white utopia, a significantly more shocking collapse of the American dream than dogs and firehoses in Alabama. In American mythology, the South has always been dysfunctional, but the Golden West is supposed to be the place where we rise above our devils. L.A. noir, of course, is founded on a moral base, but the prevailing sins echo biblical absolutes: greed, lust, anger. Seldom had the detective novel, as "genre fiction," garnered any credit for addressing, or urging improvement to, moral dysfunction manifested in social problems.

Seldom, for that matter, had the genre even been called upon to be a part of the solution to problems of social injustice. Indeed, the novels of Hammett and Chandler, Macdonald's precursors, employ stereotype (racial and otherwise) so freely that they may be said to irritate racial, gender, and sexuality biases rather than soothe them. Macdonald's Archer novels have, by temperament and design, almost always eschewed crude stereotype, but not stereotype altogether. Archer himself has more than once patiently explained to a client—and to the reading public overhearing—that he is not "that kind" of detective, the kind who knocks back highballs before noon or consigns individuals to the depths of stereotype at a glance. And yet, with the exception of the Alex Norris subplot in *The Ivory Grin*, he had kept his African American characters (like Joseph Tobias in *The Barbarous Coast* and Sam Jackman in *The Far Side of the Dollar*) on the margins of the case. Race could be a valid undercurrent, however, as Tobias's story of being "profiled" for the murder of Gabrielle Torres in *The Barbarous Coast* illustrates.

Black Money (1966), the Archer novel published the year after the Watts Rebellion, is another "breakthrough" because, within the strict frame of the detective novel, Macdonald explores the racism clutching at the underside of utopia, using Fitzgerald's *The Great Gatsby* to do so. Often recognized as crucial to our cultural mythology, *The Great Gatsby*, the story of James Gatz's rise from obscurity in the Midwest to glamour and his inevitable fall in the East has not, until recently, been linked to our racial drama. It does contain some instances of anti-Semitism, but not overtly the racism of the era of Woodrow Wilson and the 1920s. The layering of two American obsessions—the utter freedom to remake the self balanced against the utter unfreedom of racial identity—makes *Black Money* one of Macdonald's most subtly powerful novels, a novel that—even more than the "breakthrough" *Galton Case*—stretched the detective novel beyond its formulaic limitations.[15]

In *Our America: Nativism, Modernism, and Pluralism*, Walter Benn Michaels locates miscegenation at the central juncture of the three "-isms" of his subtitle, driving the American writing that produced the "classics" of the 1920s, and shaped the definition of "classic" for decades. Only in a crudely overt but popular novelist like Thomas Dixon (author of *The Clansman* [1905], on which D. W. Griffith based his film *The Birth of a Nation* [1915]) is miscegenation (or the threat of it) the obvious pivot of plot, Michaels argues. Less overt, but no less urgent, is the fear of miscegenation in *The Great Gatsby* (1925): "For Tom [Buchanan] . . . , Gatsby (né Gatz, with his Wolfsheim 'gonnegtion') isn't quite white, and Tom's identification of him as in some sense black suggests the power of the expanded notion of the alien. Gatsby's love for Daisy seems to Tom the expression of something like the impulse to miscegenation."[16] For Michaels, provocatively, *The Great Gatsby* dramatizes the sum of all white, male fears: social displacement, miscegenation, and loss of economic privilege. These make up the undercurrents that Macdonald sensed in California and diverted into *Black Money*. It is not overt black skin that Macdonald uses in his novel, but the "in some sense black" threat embodied by the character of his inter-loper, Francis Martel.

The Great Gatsby was a crucial novel for Ross Macdonald. When the United States Navy sent him to Princeton, Fitzgerald's alma mater, to study communications in the 1940s, he felt he had gone to Princeton the same way Gatsby had gone to Oxford—a dream so vivid it had to be real (Kaye, 8-b-2). Fitzgerald was more than a biographical model of the young man fulfilling Ivy League hopes; he was a literary model as well:

Fitzgerald has been a kind of model of excellence for most of the writers of my generation. I started using him when I was in college and I've been reading him ever since. . . . Fitzgerald really said things about the North American experience that had never been said before, or if so, so well. He was a prose poet hero who lived out the American dream which, in his version and in our experience of it, is a somewhat empty dream when you get down to it. (Kaye, 1)

Gatsby was Macdonald's image of the fatality of growing up with no place but the place of your dreams, and he saw Gatsby's experience as parallel to his own: both were sons from marginalized regions, with large dreams and slender advantages, who saw the American dream "from the bottom" (Kaye, 1). Setting up *Black Money* as a novel in which a bastion of whiteness and wealth, the Tennis Club in Montevista, is breached by a stranger whose skin and money both carry suggestions of "black" makes this detective novel a mirror of its time and place.

The events of *Black Money* take Archer to the Tennis Club, an enclave of class and money within a larger gated enclave—the Montevista area of Pacific Point, Macdonald's Southern California version of Plymouth Rock. Archer's client at the Tennis Club is a young man, Peter Jamieson, whose fiancée, he insists, has been stolen from him by an intruder, a flashy interloper with the car, wardrobe, and house of a Gatsby but a swarthy skin and sex appeal that have swept away his California Girl, Virginia Fablon. Fitzgerald's Tom Buchanan is driven similarly hysterical by the mere idea of race mixing. "Have you read

'The Rise of the Colored Empires' by this man Goddard? [Tom asks Nick]. . . . The idea is if we don't look out the white race will be—will be utterly submerged" (12). It is Daisy, his golden girl, who wryly reassures him that everyone present is white. Macdonald lampoons Tom Buchanan's brute power and ignorance, too, by putting Peter Jamieson into a pudgy body bloated by an eating disorder. Both Archer's Jamieson and Fitzgerald's Buchanan have trouble articulating the "in some sense black" that they feel in the rivals for their golden girls—but the racial anxiety is the same.

The stranger threatening to "submerge" the Tennis Club in a rising tide of color, one of whose aliases is Francis Martel, makes his first appearance in the novel as the specter of racial pollution. Peter Jamieson is especially concerned:

> "This man is apparently wanted by the police. He claims to be a Frenchman, a French aristocrat no less, but nobody really knows who his is or where he comes from. He may not even be Caucasian."
>
> "Where did you get that idea?"
>
> "He's so dark. And Ginny is so fair. It nauseates me to see her with him."
>
> "But it doesn't nauseate her." (4)

Archer's arch reply to his white client's visceral racism and sexual hysteria shows that he can read a subtext. Being wanted by the cops does not make Martel dangerous; suspicion of his race does.

Peter Jamieson's hysteria only foregrounds the observable fact that the Tennis Club is already infiltrated by the ethnic alien. Who but the "other" would do the work? Marco the bartender is just another "*paisano*" (63), and Eric Malkovsky, with his Slavic profile, works around the clock taking and developing photographs (70). Kitty Hendricks is the daughter of Polish parents living, literally, on the wrong side of the tracks in Montevista (147). When the case takes Archer further into the darkness beyond the white Tennis Club, he encounters a symbolic trio of hoboes: a young black man, an Indian boy, and an old white man (73). The novel is ringed with literary reminders that the Caucasian enclave of the Tennis Club is anything but high and dry in the rising tide of color. Martel is only the first rivulet to seep under the door.

Martel, Archer learns, has bought his way into the Tennis Club with enough money to muffle the issue of his racial origin or his mating potential. "Swarthy" is tolerable, if it stays in its place and has enough money. Martel is currently impersonating a French outcast, but he has a more complicated past. The club photographer thinks he recognizes him as a former busboy. On the trail of the chameleon's identity, Archer encounters an overworked and self-important associate professor of French at the local college, Professor Tappinger. Martel and Virginia Fablon, the golden girl of the story, had met in one of his classes. The professor's own household is on the edge—his wife a desperate, borderline neurotic and his major career project stalled in his own excessive self-esteem.

The Tappingers mirror the Wilsons, who live in the valley of ashes in *The Great Gatsby*. In Fitzgerald's cosmos Wilson desires privilege and wealth through Tom Buchanan's car; in Macdonald's novel, Tappinger is more direct: he seduces Virginia Fablon. But more deeply Macdonald draws on the powerful anxiety stirred up by the character of Gatsby in the peaceful Long Island enclave of money. After Martel is introduced in the cultural imagery of the "Latin lover," a figure made popular in the 1920s by Rudolf Valentino whose screen roles combined sexual heat and ethnic taboo, he is recuperated as a Gatsby figure. Attempting to talk to the golden girl, Virginia, Archer first faces her "demon lover": "The driver of the Bentley got out facing him [Archer]. He was compact and muscular, dressed in English-looking sports clothes, tweeds and brogues, which didn't go with his swarthy sleekness" (14–15). Gatsby made a similar flashy impression on the staid Long Island rich with his shiny car and custom-made clothes.

Soon, bodies begin to accumulate. First, Harry Hendricks, a hapless amateur investigator, is killed when he gets too close to Martel's secret. Then there is the killing of Martel himself, followed by the death of Virginia's mother. Murders in the present lead Archer inevitably into the past, to the murder of Virginia's father. Suspicion initially leads to the resident mobster, a man named Leo Spillman who has skimmed money from a Las Vegas gambling operation (the "black money" of the title). Roy Fablon had fallen into debt to Spillman and was on the brink of selling his daughter Virginia to him in payment when he turned up dead in the Pacific. Spillman, however, has been incapacitated by a stroke; he cannot remember where his "black money" is, much less kill someone to get it back. Spillman's money, we gradually learn, finances Martel's invasion of the Tennis Club and has supported—in the form of blackmail payments—Virginia Fablon and her mother. Roy Fablon's death was not an accident, and his wife, knowing as much, has milked Spillman for years to keep his name out of the investigation.

The unseen trigger that brings Archer to the Tennis Club is the depletion of this blackmail money and the gangster's physical inability to pay any more. Spillman is Martel's Meyer Wolfsheim, his dark underworld connection, and for the novel the cold breath of the Midwest, for that is Spillman's original lair. Martel had risen from busboy at the Tennis Club to courier for Spillman, a Gatz-like past Martel struggles to disguise. He has less trouble than he anticipates because to the club members all nonwhites tend to look alike (53). Before he returned to the Tennis Club as the mysterious French aristocrat Francis Martel, he had indeed bused tables there as Felix Cervantes, and before that he had grown up in a Panama slum as Pedro Domingo. The aim of all his self-denials and reinventions is first California and then the golden girl, Virginia Fablon, the "lost" Daisy.

Macdonald rearranges the murder plot of The Great Gatsby, bringing the death of the dreamer from the end of the novel to the middle. This structural move gives Black Money time to explore the shared guilt of the white monolith of the Tennis Club, for the death of the intruder. Martel/Cervantes/Domingo threatens the enclave of the Tennis Club not because he is connected to the underworld and therefore figuratively "black," but because he is not white enough to marry one of the protected women.

Martel's racial otherness is the serious threat to the Caucasian preserve of the Tennis Club–Pacific Point–Southern California nexus. Money, no questions asked about its origin, had been the secret of admission to this high society until Martel's successful "passing" had exposed that hypocrisy. Peter Jamieson père, deliberately drinking himself into oblivion while reading The Book of the Dead, has been in a sense mummified by supporting the social hypocrisy by which the Tennis Club whitens all money but cannot whiten a body it perceives to be "not even . . . Caucasian." Talking to Archer, the elder Jamieson confesses:

> "There is something I should tell you, then, as an old Montevista hand. Almost anything can happen here. Almost everything has. It's partly the champagne climate and partly, to be frank, the presence of inordinate amounts of money. Montevista's been an international watering resort for nearly a century. Deposed maharajahs rub shoulders with Nobel prize-winners and Chicago meat packers' daughters marry the sons of South American billionaires." (27)

Martel is unassimilable and eventually killed, not because he has siphoned money from Spillman the gangster, but because he has challenged race and class hierarchy: he does not have enough money to whiten himself completely but just enough to expose the caste and race skeletons of the club. When Martel's covering identity is blown at the Tennis Club, he flees the gated community for a house in Brentwood, the Los Angeles neighborhood made famous for another crime story in which the word miscegenation did not appear in print but charged the public unconscious.[17] Surprised in the doorway of his Brentwood house (just as Gatsby is surprised in his pool), Martel is shot in the stomach and bleeds to death, but not before assuming a symbolic pose:

> Its [Martel's Bentley's] nose was jammed against the metal safety barrier at the dead end of Sabado Avenue. Beyond the barrier loose ground sloped away to the edge of a bluff which overlooked the Pacific Ocean.
>
> The Bentley's engine was still running. Martel's chin rested on the steering wheel. The dead eyes in his yellow face were peering out into the blue ocean of air. (157)

Martel's death not only reprises the shooting of Gatsby. Macdonald echoes Fitzgerald's powerful image of Dutch sailors spying the New World with Martel's lifeless eyes gazing at the Pacific: a more evocative way of saying that the American dream "is a somewhat empty dream when you get down to it." There is, strictly in terms of the mechanics of plot, no reason for Macdonald to fill in the character of Martel once he is murdered, except to use his life, as Fitzgerald does James Gatz's, as an allegory. What Archer finds out completes the assimilation of Fitzgerald's novel to *Black Money*. Like Gatsby, Martel is a product of his own fantasy. Martel, however, might legitimately have claimed French genealogy; it turns out that one possible forefather was a French emigré who went bust on a canal-building scheme in Panama.

> "Eventually he [Martel's grandfather] went more or less native, and spent his declining years with a girl in one of the villages. Pedro [Domingo-Martel] said she was descended from the first Cimarrones, the escaped slaves who fought with Francis Drake against the Spaniards. He claimed to be a direct descendant of Drake through her—that would explain the name Francis—but I think this time he was spinning a pure genealogical fantasy. Pedro went in rather heavily for fantasy."
>
> "It's dangerous," I said, "when you start to act it out." (211)

Claiming the Caucasian strain of blood merely calls more attention to what is denied. Martel not only functions as the racial other denied by a white utopia; he is a denier himself. Like Gatsby, who blithely skates on the emptiness of the dream when he tells Nick Caraway that he can repeat the past, Martel learns the hard way that there may be many fantasies of the self but there is only one history, one steel barrier between the limits of solid ground and the limitless blue of the Pacific.

What is more overt in *Black Money* than in its precursor *The Great Gatsby*, is that race is the arbiter of identity in American life. As Michaels sees it in his study of American novels of the 1920s: "And because (under Jim Crow) no black person could become a citizen, any white person could: for whites, becoming American required nothing more or less than learning to identify oneself as American, as opposed to a Northerner or a Southerner, an Italian or a Jew."[18] Macdonald's Tennis Club with its "champagne climate" is a Californian version of this durable American truth: belonging is a function of whiteness, and whiteness maintains itself by rituals of purification. The Watts Rebellion of 1965 exposed the unearned status of whiteness with civil unrest. Martel in the Tennis Club is something like a one-man insurrection and Archer his accomplice in pointing out the subterfuge.

As the decade ground on, the sense of civilization in decay, predicted in *The Wycherly Woman* in 1961, helped to shape Macdonald's darkest novel. Turning back to the chaos of youth, Macdonald produced *The Instant Enemy* in 1968, the fateful and chaotic year of the Tet Offensive in Vietnam; the assassination of Martin Luther King Jr. in Memphis and Robert Kennedy in Los Angeles; the occupation of the president's office at Columbia University; the disastrous Democratic convention in Chicago and the election of Richard Nixon; and the release of the Beatles' *White Album,* Charles Manson's enabling text. In the words of Todd Gitlin, activist and historian of the 1960s: "One can see the late Sixties as a long unraveling, a fresh start, a tragicomic *Kulturkampf,* the over-due demolition of a fraudulent consensus, a failed upheaval, an unkept prom-ise, a valiant effort at reforms camouflaged as revolution."[19] And 1968 was definitively the beginning of the end.

Whereas in *The Far Side of the Dollar* both Archer and Macdonald success-fully pick out a path through the minefield of adult/youth relationships and keep the children alive, in *The Instant Enemy* almost everything that can go wrong does. In fact, one of the killings is an "accident" that Archer witnesses but is powerless to prevent. Disconnected generations, between whom there is not merely a difference in outlook but outright violent resentment and distrust, disturb the background of the novel and powerfully mirror the "implosion" of the late 1960s. In previous novels boys and girls suffer psychological harm; in *The Instant Enemy* the harm is psychological and physical, and, in the case of the "accidental" killing, irreversible.

The novel opens on a symbolic landscape: "There was light early morning traffic on Sepulveda. As I drove over the low pass, the sun came up glaring behind the blue crags on the far side of the valley. For a minute or two, before regular day set in, everything looked fresh and new and awesome as creation" (3). As with creation in *Genesis,* human intervention ruins everything fresh and new and awesome. Archer's "awesome" day is short-lived. In the context of the California myth, "human intervention" means traffic and real estate development—the mixed blessings Mike Davis lists in *City of Quartz.* As Davis sees suburban development, builders and lenders view the landscape "as sim-ply another abstraction of dirt and dollar signs" (4). Postponed guilt for build-ing so much on so "fresh and new and awesome" an environment destabilizes the ethics and ecology—the "grounds" for moral decisions and for houses. It is as dangerous to live morally in this traduced ecology as it is to live physically; the ground is apt to move at any moment.

"For a minute or two," Archer sees beyond sin and penance, then "regular day set in" and he continues on a call to the house of a prospective client, Keith Sebastian, a mid-level officer in a savings and loan, whose own modern house, "an angular contemporary house cantilevered out over a slope" (3), not only underlines the hubris that nature is an abstraction to be overcome with enough money and engineering, but also serves as a symbol for the private lives of its inhabitants, Keith and Berneice Sebastian, whose finances and family psychology teeter over the slope of chaos. Archer has seldom met clients he likes less than the Sebastians.

Their seventeen-year-old daughter, Alexandria (Sandy), has run away, and Archer is not so sure that losing herself among the nomadic tribes of California youth is such a bad idea. The parents suspect her boyfriend, Davy Spanner, has taken Sandy to the wilds of West Hollywood, where disaffected young people wander the Strip to turn on and drop out. Archer watches silently as Sandy's mother scolds one of her daughter's friends for not preventing Sandy's disappearance, and he decides to take the case not so much to sooth the parents as to protect the children from the backlash of adult failure. The Sebastians' desperate attempt at suburban chic disturbs Archer, and his premonitions of disaster only grow stronger as he follows the trail of the lost kids.

The trail of Sandy Sebastian inevitably becomes the trail of Davy Spanner, a homeless and fatherless boy dangerously looking for both. Archer's first stop is the apartment of Laurel Smith, an impressive woman carrying vestiges of her handsome youth; she employs Davy as a kind of handyman. Laurel Smith, Archer learns, is herself under surveillance by a retired law officer, whose murder complicates the case later on. The trail of Davy also leads to his former high-school counselor, a man too earnest and overcommitted to his students and his pregnant wife.

The trail of Sandy, on the other hand, leads upward in the social hierarchy, to her father's employer, Stephen Hackett, the owner of the savings and loan financing new housing tracts like the one the Sebastians live in. Hackett lives in the hills of Malibu with his mother and her (younger) husband, his own overly psychologized German wife, and a malicious Mexican jack-of-all-trades, Lupe, a sadist who shoots mudhens out of sheer malice. The burden of sixties implosion is heavy in *The Instant Enemy*. Everywhere Archer turns another wounded human being presents his or her disorders. And several people die of them before he can stop the carnage.

The sense of impending disaster in the opening paragraph of the novel comes to fruition with the implacable pace of tragedy. Sandy proves relatively easy to find yet harder to restore to emotional wholeness. She is hiding a trauma, one she blames on her parents, who, in the first place, put her in sexual jeopardy and, in the second, would rather not face the enormity of the facts. Archer diagnoses the deep hurt but gets little additional cooperation from the damaged girl. He has to rescue her from attempted suicide in the Pacific before she will trust him with her secret. She needs the nurturing a family is supposed to give, but the Sebastians lack psychological as well as financial capital.

Sandy has, for good reason, adopted the mindset of Davy Spanner, who has decided that trusting adults is a losing proposition. He has reason: the adults who begot him refuse to acknowledge their son. All the harm he does, he does in the quest to know his father. He is a rebel like Tom Hillman and Stella Carlson in *The Far Side of the Dollar,* but unlike them he lacks even the facile sophistication to see his situation from the safe distance of precedent—in the terms of Freud or Tennessee Williams. His surname, Spanner, functions as a hint to his role: he is a wrench thrown into social machinery and about as supple intellectually and emotionally. Davy cannot think around and through the forces that pull him inside out, as Tom and Stella can. In the end, Davy is killed by a man who should have acted as his surrogate father, a casualty of knee-jerk defense of the suburban hearth and home. Davy's death is one of the most troubling in Macdonald's fiction. It echoes the death of another troubled and abandoned son crucial to the milieu of the 1960s: Plato in *Rebel without a Cause* (1955). Todd Gitlin, surveying the roots of the 1960s in the culture and society of the American 1950s, describes Plato as "errant, eventually martyred" in a society of failed and failing fathers.[20] In 1968, to Ross Macdonald, the late 1960s confirmed the worst predictions for the decade. Davy Spanner's death is one that Archer sees coming and cannot prevent; it simply happens as a result of civilization's breakdown.

To revise: nothing in Macdonald's plots "simply happens." The killing of Davy Spanner is only one of several acts of violence inflicted on parents and children in *The Instant Enemy,* pushing into and out of marriages and across three generations. The violence in this novel spills beyond the backward-rushing stream of guilt and confession that usually characterizes Macdonald's plots. Davy's death is prompted by mere panic when the adult who is charged with counseling him into some semblance of responsible maturity lets his own tenuous hold on adulthood evaporate. But the other murders were premeditated and covered up. Everyone in the principal cast is either perpetrator or accomplice.

If the death of Davy is a significant nadir in *The Instant Enemy* and in Macdonald's works as a whole, then the rescue of Sandy is a small step back from the brink of despair. Archer not only talks her out of committing a felony, he pulls her out of suicide. Even a decade after his own daughter's conviction for vehicular manslaughter and her later, temporary, disappearance from college in 1959, Macdonald still wrestled with his guilt for his daughter's troubles, externalizing it in Archer's dealings with fictional lost daughters. Pulling Sandy back from self-destruction is clearly a wished-for, retroactive rescue of his own daughter, which must have come onto the page at some considerable psychological cost. In *The Instant Enemy* her sufferings are deep and scarring—vaginal and anal rape by two men who had drugged her with LSD (her father's boss Stephen Hackett and the sadistic Lupe) and delayed, ineffectual protection by her parents (210–11). Sandy's testimony, like Davy's death, is as graphic as Macdonald ever gets in describing the crimes in his novels. The simple "roll in the hay" had become, in *The Instant Enemy,* sex crime. The difference is more than semantic, for multiple rape brings the Girl of the Golden West brutally into the real world and strips California of pretensions to myth.

Archer untangles the case, but any sense of achievement evaporates long before the final scene, in which he confronts the mother-and-son pair of evil-doers, Stephen Hackett and his mother Ruth Marburg. The mother, using her beauty to climb up the social rope, had two sons, an Isaac and an Ishmael. She conspired with one, after the fact, to cover up the killing of the father and the brother. Archer is worn out by the case and seems to feel sullied just to touch the check with which Ruth Marburg attempts to buy his silence on fratricide, parricide, rape, illegitimate birth, blackmail, and "justifiable" homicide. Returning to his mean office on the Strip, he gazes down on the sea of youth ebbing and flowing on the pavement:

> I had a second slug to fortify my nerves. Then I got Mrs. Marburg's check out of the safe. I tore it into small pieces and tossed the yellow confetti out of the window. It drifted down on the short hairs and the long hairs, the potheads and the acid heads, draft dodgers and dollar chasers, swingers and walking wounded, idiot saints, hard cases, foolish virgins. (227)

As the 1960s waned, the outlook for the future seemed confusing well beyond the view from Archer's office. For every liberation, there was a casualty. *The Instant Enemy* remains one of Macdonald's most powerful, and most melancholy, novels. It is also one of his most baroque plots, with several sets of legitimate and illegitimate parents, name and nickname puzzles, and as-sumed identities. It attracted Hollywood attention, and Macdonald labored on a screenplay off and on for a decade. No film has yet been made. Maybe the novel's cavernous melancholy warned producers away.

The 1960s came to a bloody end on the August night in 1969 when members of the Charles Manson family mutilated and murdered Sharon Tate, Abigail Folger, Jay Sebring, and everyone else they found at 10500 Cielo Drive in the privileged hills above Los Angeles. The Manson Murders shocked the beauti-ful people who clung to the myth of earthly paradise on Pacific shores. The dis-possessed Archer sees from his office window in *The Instant Enemy* walked right up the driveway and through the front door. What had been jettisoned on the way into the amnesia of myth, personified by the scrawny Manson and his misfit family of "lost" girls and boys, had "creepy-crawled" back. In his nov-els, Macdonald never dealt with violence so gruesome and apparently unmoti-vated. Macdonald's sense of evil had to have, ironically, more intellectual reach than Manson's ur-text: Lennon and McCartney's "Helter Skelter," released on *The White Album* in 1968. And yet Manson and the Macdonald who wrote *The Instant Enemy* identified the same ominous symptoms: an anesthetizing, suburban estrangement so numbing most of its victims never knew they suffered. But the children knew.

Although evil of Manson's senseless and vicious kind is not the raw material of Macdonald's fiction, parts of Manson's life cycle were. Charles Manson's fatherless birth in a midwestern city and his subsequent westward quest in search of reinvention and reconnection to "family" suggest comparisons with Macdonald's roster of California-yearning young men. The stories of Manson family members knit themselves into Macdonald's allegory, too, by virtue of such shared themes as parental disapproval of sons and daughters, expulsion from home and school, the seeming retreat of affluent parents into enclaves of their own construction—book-lined and liquor-stocked studies, subdivision cul-de-sacs, country clubs, careers. With an infinitesimal shift, Sandy Sebastian could have ended in Manson's family. By the end of the 1960s, the unraveling of the California of the imagination and Macdonald's cumulative masterplot, both deeply based on an idealization of the family, seemed poised to converge.

They did, in *The Goodbye Look* (1969), his last novel of the 1960s. *The Goodbye Look* is, in the rankings of many critics, Macdonald's finest novel, the novel that certified his metamorphosis from genre novelist to novelist. By interweaving the requirements of the genre with those of the novel, Macdonald proved that the detective novel was entitled to the status of the novel, that it could hold the kinds of meanings we expect of novels: not just the competent plotting of clue and resolution, but the mirrorings of the way we live now and how we think about how we live. That is, the genre (like an ice skating competition) was not just about completing the compulsory figures of the formula but also about the "free" program in which the novelist created a narrative artifact of his time and place.

The last Archer of the decade, *The Goodbye Look* was Macdonald's fifteenth novel in the Archer series and the first to be reviewed on the front page of the *New York Times Book Review.* A few months before publication of *The Goodbye Look* in 1969, John Leonard, an assistant editor at the *New York Times Book Review* and a Long Beach native like Archer, proposed to his editor that it was time to bring Macdonald's detective novels into the mainstream. William Goldman, another Archer admirer who had written an unused screen treatment of *The Chill,* agreed to write a review, and Leonard added an interview with Macdonald which put the writer and his novels in critical perspective. *The Goodbye Look* made the *Times* bestseller list, and Macdonald was acknowledged as a novelist—no longer a writer of "genre fiction."[21] William Goldman's review on the front page of the *New York Times Book Review* announced the Archer series as "The Finest Detective Novels Ever Written by an American."[22] Reviewing one novel, Goldman demonstrates, is reviewing the entire series. Like readers of William Faulkner, who find that his "postage stamp of soil," Yoknapatawpha County, is a universe, readers of Macdonald encounter a universe that swings around two poles, Pacific Point and Santa Teresa. The series as a whole and each novel within it operate as a mosaic of a moral and social landscape. John Leonard followed Goldman's review with an interview-based essay on Macdonald, in which he praised the writer's consistency and sense of structure and clearly placed him beyond the reach of comparison with Raymond Chandler.[23]

The Goodbye Look is, like all of Macdonald's novels, an examination of the complex entanglements of family psychology. But what he succeeds in doing in the last novel of the 1960s is what his novels of the decade had been striving for: a fully dimensioned portrait of family psychology in a specific moment of social history, the private in the public and the public in the private. The detective novel usually takes history lightly, leaving "great events" to espionage novels, which serve society as national rallying cries. The detective novel (Hammett's particularly) might posit a social or political context, but by and large the hero is left to operate in a mythic orbit—his charisma lifts him above social and class distinctions. Chandler's Marlowe, for example, impresses the megamillionaire of *The Long Goodbye,* Harlan Potter, when in the average run of events a man of Marlowe's class and station would never cross paths with a mandarin.

What brings Macdonald's *The Goodbye Look,* and his series, to such achievement in merging novel and detective genre is his sense of the mix of social conditions coming to the end of something at the end of the decade. He was the novelist of the moment. He pushes *The Goodbye Look* to the verge of the end of California by obliterating one of its constants: the myth of the happy family. In Macdonald's closed Freudian circle of meanings, the sins of the father are inescapable because, inevitably, being a father means inflicting harm. "Lost" sons and daughters might, with help, survive the trauma of being begotten, but of course they can never evade it. The boys and girls will need help, the parents will never provide it, and Archer can offer only so much. In the preceding Archer novel, *The Instant Enemy,* Archer's family therapy seems to begin to work, but its ultimate failure in the face of a mountain range of problems leaves him bitter and exhausted. As hospitals, drugs, and private clinics proliferate in his novels of the 1960s, the myth of the perfect family in the earthly California paradise stalls. In The *Goodbye Look,* it disintegrates of its own internal complications.

Sociologists who study the postwar American family agree on some common symptoms of the malaise. Domesticity, especially as it enforced strict gender roles, steamrolled psychological and sexual "problems" into conformity. Gwendolyn Wright was not revealing anything new when she wrote of "the stifled frustration of women in the suburbs."[24] As Elaine Tyler May sees it in *Homeward Bound: American Families in the Cold War Era,* the spread of suburbs and the spread of women's sense of crisis grew together:

In the popular media, women's sexuality became increasingly central to their identity. The promising as well as the troublesome potential of female eroticism found expression in the plots and genres of the decade. From the late forties to the fifties, subordination made the difference between good or bad female sexuality. Sexy women who became devoted sweethearts or wives would contribute to the goodness of life; those who used their sexuality for power or greed would destroy men, families, and even society.[25]

Critics agree as well that there is an intimate connection between what happens in the crucible of domesticity, the nuclear family, and where it happens: the suburban neighborhood. "In secure postwar homes with plenty of children," May continues, "American women and men might be able to ward off their nightmares and live out their dreams. The family seemed to be the one place where people could control their destinies and perhaps even shape the future. Of course, nobody actually argued that stable family life could prevent nuclear annihilation. But the home represented a source of meaning and security in a world run amok."[26] What Macdonald knew was that families as well as the world outside them might "run amok," too.

Gwendolyn Wright was more specific about the architecture of the suburban home, in a way that, we shall see, Macdonald uses as the tipping point of the case in *The Goodbye Look:* "Buyers wanted a big picture window or sliding glass doors to make the house seem larger and more open. Preferably, the glass wall was in the back, facing the 'outdoor living room,' where so many activities associated with suburban living took place. Here was the barbeque pit, the Junglegym, the flower garden, the well-mowed lawn" (254). What disasters might ensue if domestic surveillance should fail? If the adults in charge of insuring safety should themselves be agents of corruption, or simply weak? The instigating event of *The Goodbye Look* is the invasion of a privileged home in a protected suburban neighborhood. The invaders are never caught. Not as ruthless as the Manson family, these invaders steal a gold-trimmed Florentine box from the Chalmers family. Irene Chalmers brings Archer into the case without telling her husband. It is not long before Archer learns of (what turns out to be) one of the precedent "crimes" leading up to the theft of the box. Betty Truttwell, the "lost" daughter of the attorney who recommends Archer, and fiancée of the Chalmers's only son Nick, tells Archer of the killing of her mother by a hit-and-run driver almost two decades earlier on the same "safe" street. The vulnerability of the family fortress is a constant, low-level hum in *The Goodbye Look,* as it was throughout American subdivisions in the extended postwar era of the Archer cases in the 1960s.

Nick's mother, Irene Chalmers, who hires Archer to recover the stolen box without her husband's knowledge or consent, is redolent of problems when Archer meets her. "Her tone was both assertive and lacking in self-assertion. It was the tone of a handsome woman who had married money and social standing and never could forget that she might just as easily lose these things" (9). Inviting Archer into the study for a more detailed conversation, Mrs. Chalmers cannot resist the urge to flirt: she taps Archer on the cheek with an Olé rose, then drops it on the floor for a servant to retrieve. There are ample doses of sexuality, frustration, and insecurity in this suburban wife, and Archer is alert to them all.

As the case deepens, the family entanglements expand. The Chalmers, Truttwell, Rawlinson, and Swain families—whose tangled fates Archer is called upon to unravel—*should* be happy. They possess the essentials of the successful families idealized in the California of the imagination: more than adequate wealth to enjoy a consumer lifestyle, enviable social rank, membership in exclusive clubs, spacious and fine homes in desirable Southern California locales, good luck as pure and constant as the climate. Even factoring in some neighborly jealousy, there is enough of the ideal to go around: John Truttwell, well-fixed himself in Pacific Point, betrays a sliver of envy of his neighbor, Lawrence Chalmers, the owner of the stolen box and father to a troubled son. "'His mother left him a substantial nest egg,'" he tells Archer at their first meeting, "'and the bull market blew it up into millions'"(5). But the blessings of the bull market are powerless to protect the intertwined families from disaster. Money, like families, has a genealogy, and the Chalmers money goes back to a Pasadena bank owned by a man named Samuel Rawlinson. In addition to his bank, Rawlinson had a wife and a daughter. In addition to his wife, he had a mistress, Lawrence Chalmers's mother, who could not find domestic happiness with her husband, a "hanging judge" (44) whose temperament seems to have flowed from the courtroom to the bedroom. Rawlinson's legitimate daughter was married to the cashier of his bank, Eldon Swain. The bank had defaulted when Swain embezzled a half-million dollars. Swain stole the money with a plan to run away with a beautiful girl, Rita Shepherd, a friend of his daughter, Jean. Abandoned, Jean nurses a lifelong obsession to find her father and enlists the Chalmers's son, Nick, who has never been sure he belongs in the Chalmers home either.

Nick Chalmers is in and out of school and in and out of psychiatric care for a scarring memory having to do with shooting an older man in a hobo jungle when he was a boy. Swain's daughter becomes an alcoholic, and ultimately a corpse, on the futile quest to find her vanished father. Nick learns that his intuition is indeed valid; he is not the natural son of Lawrence Chalmers, although Irene Chalmers is his mother. Behind the facade of expensive homes, soft-spoken servants, rose gardens, purring Rolls Royce automobiles, and well-appointed psychiatric clinics, Macdonald's Pacific Point can claim no moral advantage over the local clinic where the Chalmers family spends a lot of time. Sexual discontent is rife, and the more nuclear the family, the more rampant. Archer even participates, bedding the wife of Nick Chalmers's therapist (152).

The sickness at the core of the idealized families of *The Goodbye Look* is exposed in a scene in which Archer and his client, Irene Chalmers, watch an old home movie featuring major players from each of the families. The scene is the comfortable Rawlinson home in Pasadena before embezzlement shattered the ideal, and the event is a backyard party around the pool. According to plan, the backyard is the zone of closest surveillance, and therefore should protect the most vulnerable members of the family, the children. Macdonald inverts expectations. Two women central to the plot—Jean Swain, who is by this point in the case dead, and Irene Chalmers—appear in the film as young girls. One, Archer notices, is a "young blonde with a mature figure and an immature face" (212). In the idealized California, the "Gidget" lives a charmed life—her "mature figure" is for the gaze, not the touch. She is Jean Swain, the embezzler's daughter, ultimately the victim of a murder. The other young girl is so beautiful Archer cannot break his gaze long enough to verify rationally what he has dreamed in troubled sleep a few scenes earlier: the girl has grown up to become Irene Chalmers. Later in the clip the girl mounts the diving board and, in a grotesque parody of sexual intercourse, allows future embezzler Eldon Swain to insert his head between her thighs and hoist her to his shoulders. The coupled pair dive into the pool and the camera loses them "underwater for what seemed a long time" (213–14).

The site of sin is the very zone where strictest supervision is supposedly most available. Macdonald uses the "sparkling surfaces netted with light and underlaid by colored shadows" (214) to conceal acts that cannot be mentioned, much less prevented by the adults who should be governing. Mapping the intricate genealogy of couplings, licit and illicit, is as complicated as a royal genealogy in the heyday of bastardy. It is so complicated in *The Goodbye Look* that Macdonald has Archer dream several of the connections. Indeed, the extreme tension Macdonald creates between the sparkling cover of idealized suburban family life and the sordid reality tunneling beneath it brings the entire myth of California to the breaking point. In *Hamlet,* the play is the thing to catch the conscience of the king, and Macdonald uses the home movie to unlock the truth behind the Chalmers facade. *The Goodbye Look* does what we expect novels to do: raise an ordinary moment of social history to extraordinary significance. We do not expect detective novels to propel us into our social history, rather to release us momentarily from it.

It is difficult to imagine where Macdonald could have taken the Archer series after the implosion of the California myth in *The Goodbye Look,* culminating his remarkable string of novels in the decade of the 1960s. The inner landscape of psychology in the Freudian family romance paradigm had been trekked and retrekked in the 1950s. The dovetailing of the family romance and the romance of California had proven to be a fertile territory for the next decade's worth of extraordinary books, capped in 1969 by recognition as a "legitimate" novelist.

In a sense, how to end became, in itself, the subject matter of Macdonald's last three books. All products of the 1970s. *The Underground Man* (1971), *Sleeping Beauty* (1973), and *The Blue Hammer* (1976) are apocalyptic novels obsessed with endings. The first two are centered on catastrophic events, a fire and an oil spill, which threaten to bring an end to the especially fragile and beautiful natural California. In them, Macdonald explored a new category of crime: environmental sin. The last published Archer novel, *The Blue Hammer,* was written by a man sensing unmistakable intimations of his own mortality. In *The Blue Hammer* artists die but the world goes on.

| 7 |

Love and Ruin

The Underground Man, Sleeping Beauty, The Blue Hammer

Long before Mike Davis, in *Ecology of Fear: Los Angeles and the Imagination of Disaster* (1998), dubbed Los Angeles "the disaster capital of the universe" as chronicled in a century of novels, short fiction, and films, Ross Macdonald traversed it as the landscape of love and ruin in which Lew Archer lived his final days. In *Ecology of Fear,* as well as in his earlier paean to the dysfunctionality of Los Angeles, *City of Quartz: Excavating the Future in Los Angeles* (1990), Davis revels in the cornucopia of Southern California's natural and political disasters: grotesque discrepancies in race and class and wealth; official malfeasance; racism; not to mention a full calendar of natural disasters—earthquake, drought, fire and rain. Through all the disasters, Davis sees the mind of California smiling: the apocalypse won't happen to me; old age, disease, sorrow, bad luck will skip over me like a wildfire hopscotching in a subdivision.

Davis describes a California mind with incredible lightness of being, hovering imaginatively, and literally, just a freeway exit or two from Disneyland or a movie studio. On any given day an assistant director and crew might show up to film a scene, and the actual place you live in could turn up on film as somewhere else. In the final novel of the 1960s, *The Goodbye Look,* Macdonald reversed the epistemological current of film, giving a home movie the power to release what the guilty had wanted to conceal. Evil happens in social history, and however light the mind of California, place and time are dense with guilt, a ball and chain.

From the beginning of the series, Archer observed the chiaroscuro realities and fantasies of his clients. Like his creator, he was a Californian by birth but a Scots-Canadian realist by temperament. In characters such as George Wall in *The Barbarous Coast* and Ian Ferguson in *The Ferguson Affair,* Macdonald understood that paradise was not for everyone. Endowing Archer with strong elements of his own divided character, he made him the ideal California detective: like Odysseus, he knows enough to lash himself to the mast with his fatalistic sense of justice as he tacks close to the island of the Sirens. Or as he mordantly tells a suspect in *The Goodbye Look*, "I have a secret passion for mercy. . . . But justice is what keeps happening to people" (127). In the three novels that came to be his final trilogy, Archer softens. Intimations of mortality, in the character and in the author, draw the unhoused, undomestic loner into a kind of nostalgia for the life he was too withdrawn and skeptical to plunge into in his prime. He is not himself a disaster in the final three novels, but natural and human disasters all around him seem to infiltrate his stoic defenses. In a late autobiographical notebook, containing thoughts from 1977—when there would be no more novels—Macdonald set himself a goal: "to seek out and describe that human vulnerability in which the possibility of love resides."[1] In the novels of the 1970s Archer had already set the itinerary.

Although Archer, like all serial fiction heroes, does not age with strict chronological inevitability, he does grow old in his work. The psychological and physical toll of case after case wears him out and wears him down. Macdonald, fifty-six when *The Underground Man* was published in 1971, had likewise been working doggedly and without lavish financial reward for a quarter of a century on the detective novel. Although he had attained a certain level of critical and financial success with the reception of *The Goodbye Look,* he knew the evanescence of fame and fortune. In a letter just before Christmas 1970 to Ashbel Green, his editor at Knopf, he noted that unsold hardcover copies of *The Goodbye Look* had been remaindered.[2] Twenty years of Archer, just to be remaindered. Big Hollywood money that had come his way in the 1960s with the sale of *The Moving Target* and *The Drowning Pool* and a deal to write a screenplay for *The Instant Enemy* did not come his way again until *The Underground Man* (1971) made the bestseller lists and was sold to television.

Personal sorrow had become a kind of writing partner, too, after the halcyon 1960s. In the fall of 1970, as he was working on the proofs of *The Underground Man,* his daughter and only child, Linda, died of a cerebral hemorrhage at the age of thirty-one. Macdonald's father had suffered a series of debilitating strokes and his mother had died of cerebral hemorrhage, both in their late fifties or early sixties. Macdonald himself struggled to keep gout and high blood pressure under control. The "lost" daughter was finally lost, it seemed, merely because she was *his* daughter. His own genetics must have exacted a kind of "justice" that kept happening to people close to him. In his world there were no "accidents."

Macdonald's final three novels explore this landscape of love and ruin: the first two against a background of environmental disaster, the third against the background of dying artists. The Southern California setting in which Archer moves is thick with omens of the end of the world. Not only natural disaster looms over every horizon. Working on *Sleeping Beauty* and *The Blue Hammer,* Macdonald was also aware of lapses in his own mental and physical capacity; his stamina for the physical work of writing, his powers of concentration and memory began to fail even as he monitored them. *The Blue Hammer* took him longer to plot and to write than any other work of his mature period; in a letter to a fellow novelist he called it "the longest Archer."³ Although he had begun to outline the next novel to follow *The Blue Hammer*, he was never confident he would finish it before his loss of memory became complete. Macdonald's last three novels, then, can be read as an extended requiem. Monitoring his diminished energy and running low on hope for the human species and the planet on which we live, Archer gradually relaxes his hard-boiled stoicism, not so much in acceptance as in exhaustion.

The Underground Man opens with a strong premonition of disaster: "A rattle of leaves woke me some time before dawn. A hot wind was breathing in at the bedroom window. I got up and closed the window and lay in bed and listened to the wind" (3). A dying world breaks in upon Archer's sleep, and when he closes the window to the death rattle it continues in his head, unabated. Once the day starts, his predawn dread is diverted when Archer meets a young boy in his apartment courtyard and invites him to help feed a raucous gang of blue jays. When the boy's mother, an attractive and vulnerable young woman, enters, the domestic scene is eerily complete: man, woman, child. Archer is almost desperate *not* to admit his interest in the possibility of connection. His interest is not simply erotic, for woman, Archer, and boy make a potential family, a social unit rather than a sexual pair, an ensemble made stable by its three-point stance. But portents flicker throughout his "light" conversation with Jean Broadhurst, the young woman and abandoned wife. A light, witty remark turns to lead; their conversation "dies" (7). In his bathroom mirror a few minutes later, Archer sees an old man—an "ancient mariner"—closer to the end of his days than to the fresh beginning: "I went into my bathroom and looked at my face as if I could somehow read his [Ronny Broadhurst, the boy's] future there. But all I could read was my own past, in the marks of erosion under my eyes, the mica glints of white and gray in my twenty-four-hour beard" (9). Archer has to face the inevitable disaster of his life; he is "a lonely man" (15) by accident and choice, and there is no time to reverse the trend. Enduring the end is more comfortable in twos or threes; alone, it is just the end. The "underground man" of the title is, ironically, both the corpse whose unearthing solves a fifteen-year-old murder and Archer himself who senses burial in his own solitude.

Premonitions of disaster with which *The Underground Man* opens develop quickly into actualities. Stanley Broadhurst, a young man in his twenties, barges into Archer's apartment courtyard and whisks his son, Ronny, away on a trip to Santa Teresa. Santa Teresa is the site of the Broadhurst ancestral home, a rancho that goes back, on Stanley's mother's side, to the nineteenth century. In the twentieth, much of it has been carved up for suburban homesites—the first of the environmental disasters in the novel. What's left is the hacienda itself, along with a smaller house at the head of a canyon (the "Mountain House"), and a few surrounding acres of avocado trees.

Stanley's marriage to Jean, like the rancho, is breaking up, and it is the echo of that disintegration that draws Archer toward the case in the first place. The action begins on a Sunday, and Archer is looking forward to a day of rest. But later in the initial afternoon Jean comes back to his apartment worried because she has not heard from her husband and son; she carries the news that a wildfire has been reported in the Santa Teresa hills. Geoffrey Hartman, linking Macdonald's work through *The Underground Man* to the history of the detective genre, rightly sees the fire as a natural disaster operating metaphorically. "By combining ecological and moral contamination," he writes, "Macdonald creates a double plot that spreads the crime over the California landscape."[4] The Broadhurst family has a long history of disintegration. Stanley's father, Leo Broadhurst, had vanished fifteen years earlier, presumably in a plan to leave his marriage and run away with another woman. Stanley has been searching for his father ever since. Indeed, the attention Stanley ought to have devoted to his own wife and son in the present he is investing in the father he has lost and the son he never was. Before Archer can find Ronny, though, he finds Stanley dead and a forest fire scorching the mountainside east of Santa Teresa.

The case of Stanley's murder leads through other disintegrating families. Fritz Snow, the Broadhurst's gardener, is a mentally and sexually arrested boy/man whose father had died when he was young: Fritz's mother has become too large and protective a presence in her son's life. Fritz might in fact be clinically "retarded," but his mother's smothering supervision is more problem than solution. The Snow triptych, like the Broadhurst one, proves the rule on which Archer works: families are the worst, but still the only, way humans can exist. Stanley's mother worshiped her own father so extravagantly that she was, according to her husband Leo, a frigid wife before and after the birth of Stanley. The Crandalls, another single-child family crucial to the plot, are similarly cobbled together of mismatched generations and (it turns out) mismatched DNA, and, accordingly, trembling on the brink of disintegration.

The Underground Man is a tightly woven pattern of theme and variation. Family and quasi-family groups of three merge into and out of focus. As Archer pieces together forensic and historical clues to the murder of the Broadhurst father and son, he also navigates a tight psychological terrain of basic (three-part) family units broken or breaking. He operates not only as a rational man seeking the explanatory unity of the various pieces of the story but also as an emotional man in part denying, and in part longing for, his own place in a tight, nurturing human triad.

Hartman laments—if only mildly—that Macdonald's novel is "somehow *too* understandable" in the Freudian formula, that the plot "moves deviously yet inexorably toward a solution of the mystery."[5] The deviousness of *The*

Underground Man springs from Macdonald's play with Archer's unacknowledged attraction to domestic groups. It is this latter "text" that genuinely shows Macdonald as the novelist who fought his way to making a fictional formula—bringing Freud to the detective novel—into an emotionally resonant basis for further growth.

Once highlighted, examples of the theme and variation structure abound. In the process of following leads, Archer encounters the exploded Kilpatrick family. The mother had left her husband and son more than a decade earlier to flee with Leo Broadhurst. Brian Kilpatrick, the cuckolded husband, has become a real estate developer, responsible for as much devastation to the Santa Teresa landscape as the fire. Kilpatrick's son, Jerry, is a disaffected drop-out who hates his father for losing his mother. At one point Archer, whose contempt for the elder Kilpatrick can scarcely be contained, finds a moment of solidarity. They are both men who have failed to hold families together:

> Kilpatrick looked at me levelly. A kind of angry brotherhood had been growing between us. It was partly based on the fact, which he didn't know, that my wife had walked out on me and sent me divorce papers through a lawyer. And partly that we were two middle-aging men, and three young people had slipped away over the curve of the world. (134–35)

The three young people are Jerry, Kilpatrick's estranged son; Susan Crandall, estranged daughter of the Crandalls mentioned above; and Ronny Broadhurst, whom the two kids have "kidnapped." Even in rebellion, humans form the basic family unit.

Archer retrieves the missing boy before he puts together fragmented clues to a history of murders. In fact, as a roving analyst he puts together people and families first, with the solution to the crime secondary. In a very intricate scene—one that has tangential importance for the solving of the crimes—Archer puts the Crandall family back together. He had predicted that the fleeing young people would turn up in the Bay Area, where Jerry's mother lives alone, having abandoned her husband and been abandoned by her lover, Leo Broadhurst. After almost losing Sue Crandall and Ronny when a stakeout is detected, Archer talks Sue out of jumping from the Golden Gate Bridge and takes her back to her parents. In the process of getting important information from Susan's mother, Archer puts mother, daughter, and father back together: a damaged but viable unit (chap. 29). For Archer himself, however, there can be no healing, only the glimmer of a promise that his innate loneliness cannot irrigate. The day, like most of Archer's, has been long and exhausting. Ellen Storm, Jerry Kilpatrick's estranged and lonely mother, invites Archer to share her bed. Archer declines. Ellen asks him what he is afraid of: "It was hard to say. I liked the woman. I almost trusted her. But I was already working deep in her life. I didn't want to buy a piece of it or commit myself to her until I knew what the consequences would be" (229). As consciously hard-boiled as his assessment of a night with Ellen might sound, the Archer of *The Underground Man* is a man ravenous for connection.

Archer is a survivalist among human and natural ruins. Generations of young people, he fears, have been "poisoned" emotionally (226). All around him families are collapsing. It is his bad luck to find the one cab driver in Santa Teresa who obsesses on natural disasters (82). As a recurrent metaphorical reminder, Archer returns to the wildfire that rings the town. Even when the fire is under control, the rain that knocks it out is too heavy for the fragile ecology (as real estate development has damaged it), and Archer must evacuate Jean Broadhurst and Ronny from an impending flash flood once the fire is out (261). If fire does not wipe out the world, then the deluge will. Their evacuation route traces the way back to Los Angeles and Archer's apartment building, where the plot began. Macdonald ends the novel (the crime has been untangled pages earlier) with a powerfully ambivalent image: a cobbled-together basic family unit poised on the edge of assent:

> I hoped it was over. I hoped that Ronny's life wouldn't turn back toward his father's death as his father's life had turned, in a narrowing circle. I wished the boy a benign failure of memory.
>
> As though she sensed my thoughts, Jean reached behind him and touched the back of my neck with her cold fingers. We passed the steaming remnants of the fire and drove on south through the rain. (273)

Macdonald exits *The Underground Man* with Archer poised dangerously between the vulnerability of love and the certainty of ruin. The Archer of the earlier novels owed more to the single-combat warrior convention of the detective genre, the last man standing in a field of perpetrators and victims. Not as egregious a sexual predator as some in the genre, Archer took his pleasure sparingly but always without fantasizing a future, without the sense that sex implied a social contract or a personal one that increased with each repetition. At the conclusion to *The Underground Man* Archer himself begins to emerge, but warily, from his own personal underground, suspended between isolation and connection.

The fine reviews that had welcomed *The Goodbye Look* hailed *The Underground Man* as well. Eudora Welty praised the novel on page one of the *New York Times Book Review*, Macdonald's second consecutive front page:

> Archer from the start has been a distinguished creation; he was always an attractive figure, and in the course of the last several books has matured and deepened in substance to our still greater pleasure. Possessed even when young of an endless backlog of stored information, most of it sad, on human nature, he tended once, unless I'm mistaken, to be a bit cynical. Now he is something much more, he is vulnerable.[6]

About a year later Geoffrey Hartman's essay appeared in the prestigious *New York Review of Books,* and financially and critically Macdonald had, apparently, made the definitive breakthrough.

In January 1969 disaster-prone Southern California was hit with a real, non-cinematic disaster. Union Oil's Platform A, in the Santa Barbara Channel about five miles from the shore (in federally controlled waters beyond the three miles under state authority), blew out, sending tens of thousands of gallons of crude oil up from fissures in the ocean bed. The initial blowout continued for ten days, until "wild well" experts could cap it. Seepage continued for several months. For the first few days of the spill, winds and currents kept the oil off Santa Barbara beaches and out of the harbor, but eventually the oil slopped ashore. Thousands of water and shore birds were fouled and eventually died. The Channel Islands, a wildlife preserve, were washed with oil and their sea lion populations put in jeopardy. The deaths of some whales that had migrated through the oil-choked channel were attributed to the spill. By any terms, the spill was an ecological disaster equal to a wildfire.

The oil spill was not the only disaster to welcome Southern California to the new year in 1969. For more than a week before the spill, the state from Santa Barbara south to Los Angeles had been drenched by rains, flooding, and the mud slides that inevitably follow. Snow even fell on the "sodden Southland," and lightning struck four airliners, all of which landed safely—one at the Santa Barbara airport. California governor Ronald Reagan toured Santa Barbara, but not to see the oil spill; he was there to visit flood and storm damage.[7]

Macdonald was an active protester, demonstrating against Union Oil and the U.S. Department of the Interior, which, he believed, had conspired to allow drilling in the channel without proper surveys and precautions and had continued in a conspiracy to minimize and cover up the magnitude of the damage and their own liability. He even got into a face-to-face confrontation with the CEO of Union Oil. In "Life with the Blob," one of the two essays he wrote on the spill, Macdonald took the meaning of the disaster beyond issues of legal liability and into the realm of environmental morality and philosophy. True, as ever, to his melancholy, "long" view of history, he thought that the natural world—birds, fish, habitat—would eventually renew itself." But the human damage," he wrote, turning philosophical, "is irreparable. Our ease and confidence in our environment has cracked, slightly but permanently, like an egg."[8] It is clear, in hindsight, that the spill, like the fire that permeates *The Underground Man,* lodged in Macdonald's creative imagination as the basic fabric into which he could weave a moral story. Maybe he even identified with the spill too closely. He used an image related to it in a letter thanking Eudora Welty for her review of *The Underground Man.* "To such a well-wisher as you," he wrote, "I can confess that I left the academic world to write popular fiction in the hope of coming back by devious ways and underground tunnels into the light again, dripping with darkness."⁹ The oil that spills across *Sleeping Beauty* is a complex and offset figure of guilt, a "darkness" that Macdonald admits to sharing. The combination of natural beauty (Santa Barbara, the channel, and its Islands), the fragility of its ecosystem, the arrogant exploitation of that ecology by technological, economic, and political forces (big oil, big government), and the problematic part played by the protesters who were implicated as both victims and victimizers of the environment (Macdonald might have cut up his Union Oil credit card but he, like Archer, never abandoned his car)¹⁰ provided a fertile mix for Macdonald's "late" and disaster-prone imagination. In a crucial way, the magnitude of the environmental disaster matched and even muted the overwhelming power of his psychological imagination.

In an article for the radical-Left *Ramparts,* Harvey Molotch, an urban ecologist at the University of California, Santa Barbara, tried to put the spill and protest into perspective. Without consciously intending to, he put Santa Barbara (the basis for Macdonald's fictional Santa Teresa) into a sociological context as well:

Santa Barbara seems worlds apart both from the sprawling Los Angeles metropolis a hundred miles further [*sic*] south on the coast highway and from the avant-garde San Francisco Bay Area to the north. It has always been calm, clean, orderly. Of the city's 70,000 residents, a large number are upper and upper-middle class. They are people who have a wide choice of places in the world to live, but they have chosen Santa Barbara because of its ideal climate, gentle beauty and sophistication. Hard-rock Republican, they vote for any GOP candidate who comes along, including Ronald Reagan.¹¹

Like the drilling platforms that seem, especially from a distance and at night, to float above the surface of the ocean like images in an animator's imagination, Santa Barbarans, according to Molotch, float in a privileged suspension above day-to-day concerns. In the grace periods between catastrophes, it might seem that the dream is the reality. When inevitable disasters do occur, such events become referenda on a wide range of beliefs and policies. Some of these issues are, of course, close-range and political. Macdonald enlisted in many of them by joining protest groups, attending rallies, and writing articles advocating change in federal environmental policy and assigning blame to big oil and its accomplices in government. But this was an excursion into a social context far less symbolic than the one Archer inhabits in *Sleeping Beauty.*

Other issues triggered by disasters in "the velvet playground" appear at longer range and seem embedded more deeply in the unconscious. This is Macdonald's primary realm, his "devious ways and underground tunnels." Molotch ventured part of the way toward this "other country," with a political edge: "The American dream is a dream of progress, of the efficacy of know-how and technology; science is seen as both servant and savior. From the start, part of the shock of the oil spill was that such a thing could happen in a country having such a sophisticated technology."[12]

The myth of the perfected paradise in California, of course, has always circulated in Macdonald's fiction, but with the "disaster" novels he admitted the worm of self-doubt to which Molotch refers. If there is an American dream, and an enhanced one in the Golden West of California, we are the dreamers and, consequently, responsible for the content and shape of the dream. We should not be surprised when we wake up.

Molotch saw a vision of waking nightmare in the work to contain the oil:

> The common sight of men throwing straw on miles of beaches, within view of complex drilling rigs capable of exploiting resources thousands of feet below the ocean's surface, became a clear symbol to Santa Barbarans. They gradually began to see the oil disaster as the product of a system that promotes research and development in areas which lead to strategic profitability—without regard for social utility.[13]

Macdonald repeated the image at the beginning of Chapter 19 of *Sleeping Beauty*. There is also a large photograph of oil-smeared men clad in full slickers cleaning the beach in the second of the two articles Macdonald wrote about the spill; "Santa Barbarans cite an 11th Commandment: Thou Shalt Not Abuse the Earth" was co-written with fellow Santa Barbara author Robert Easton.[14] Protective clothing to cover the entire body is not what one expects on the beaches of the "velvet playground." The particular sociological and political spin of Molotch and *Ramparts* may have been too radical for Macdonald, but he was not numb to the streams of meanings pushed up under pressure from deep below the surface of the dream of paradise. The "sleeping beauty" of the novel is the layered geological and mythical California: Santa Barbara shares the same initials, S. B.

As *Sleeping Beauty* begins, Archer looks out of the window of an airliner bringing him home from a vacation in Mexico as it banks over Pacific Point. The azure water is stained brown and black with an oil spill barely twenty-four hours old. Instead of driving home to his West Los Angeles apartment, Archer drives to the beach, where he sees and smells the oil close up. He is initiated into the early stages of disaster and subconsciously into the part he plays, for—like everyone in Los Angeles—he is nothing without his car. Indeed, mobility is a central part of his identity. Chasing leads puts him in his car and on the road, a movement-based life with which he is not altogether displeased:

> I lapsed for a while into my freeway daydream: I was mobile and unencumbered, young enough to go where I had never been and clever enough to do new things when I got there.

The fantasy snapped in my face when I got to Santa Monica. It was just another part of the megalopolis which stretched from San Diego to Ventura, and I was a citizen of the endless city. (84–85)

The oil fouling the Pacific enables both the daydream and the waking disillusion, and Archer finds that he might solve the case but not the underlying moral dilemma: to live by oil is to kill, slowly, the earth.

The smell of spilled oil, like the decay of the earth's body, becomes a motif in the novel, a recurring olfactory image for the pervasive sense of a damaged equilibrium between humans and the natural world. In "Life with the Blob," Macdonald reported that the odor of spilled oil had begun "to flavor our lives" on the charmed coast of Santa Barbara.[15] In the novel, the smell infiltrates closed rooms just as wind-borne droplets of oil smear picture windows. Sight and smell function as the sensory equivalent to the shared anxiety of catastrophe and the creeping acknowledgment of guilt that Archer senses among the spectators on the beach: "They looked as if they were waiting for the end of the world, or as if the end had come and they would never move again" (4). From cracked egg to the end of the world, Macdonald transforms the oil spill from natural event to objective correlative, an image to coordinate theme and action in something larger than an essay: a novel. In a quick succession of verbal and visual images, Macdonald reinforces the connection between spill and end of the world. A dramatic, crimson sunset leaves Archer feeling as if he is walking "under the roof of an enormous cave where hidden fires burned low" (9). A band of surfers comes ashore ahead of the spill: "They looked as if they had given up on civilization and were ready for anything or nothing" (10–11). The CEO of the oil company gruffly complains about critics of the spill: "'People are blaming the spill for everything that happens. You'd think it was the end of the bloody world'" (25). In a sense, it is.

In the atmosphere of final catastrophe, the human sleeping beauty of the novel enters: Laurel Russo, the only granddaughter of the founder of the oil company whose well has blown out. Archer meets her on the fouled beach, where she has gone in a vain and self-tortured effort to save oil-drenched birds. When a grebe dies in her arms, staining her white blouse with oil, Archer makes the mistake of telling her the truth: a lot of birds are going to die because of the spill (10). Laurel, for personal reasons Archer is fated to learn, feels personally guilty for the dying birds, and Archer's bald remark inches her psychologically closer to her own end. Archer intuitively senses the nudge and Laurel's fragile psyche, and so he follows her down the beach, apparently hoping to undo the damage. Her fragile psychological state mirrors the dangerous moral position most in the novel deny: we are all to blame.

Feeling a sense of responsibility and guilt himself, Archer offers to drive Laurel to her home. Before he can get her safely back to her husband, Laurel— like the nymph for whom she is named—escapes from Archer's care with a bottle of his sleeping pills, enough to kill herself. Archer is thus obligated to find the woman, for whom he is now responsible, and awaken her to the mixed pleasures of a post-disaster world. Archer, by implication, can live with the idea of his own death (his sleeping pills), but Laurel is liable to use them before she grows a husk to cover her vulnerability.

The search for Laurel Russo takes Archer into the Lennox family. Laurel's grandfather, William Lennox, founded the oil company. Her father, Jack, now runs day-to-day operations. Her uncle, former navy captain Benjamin Somerville, is in charge of cleaning up the spill but is compromised in his efforts by his parallel responsibility to control the "spill" of information on the seriousness of the blowout. In the choice of "Somerville" as the name of the compromised corporation man, Macdonald hints at his thorough understanding of the spill story. In the long second act of lawsuits and dueling experts, a professor of petroleum engineering at UC Berkeley inadvertently showed his co-optation by the oil industry when he admitted that he could not jeopardize his relations with that industry by testifying against it. His name was Somerton.[16] Like all families in Macdonald's novels, the Lennox family and its extensions balance the appearance of stability against the actuality of deep psychological fissures. Jack Lennox is a choleric and tyrannical husband and father; his wife, Marian, is a well-coiffed trauma. Elizabeth Somerville, Laurel's aunt, competes with the oil company and her husband's former navy steward for his attention and takes some measure of revenge by sleeping with Archer. Septuagenarian William Lennox has abandoned his first wife for a much younger woman, setting off dynastic tremors. The first Mrs. Lennox is anything but a wounded old lady; toward the end of the novel she places a curse on all men for all the disasters, personal and public, in the world (148). As is also the case with Macdonald's family-rooted plots, the sin in the current generation can be traced back several decades.

Not only oil washes ashore at Pacific Point. Archer pulls the body of a wizened, scarred man from the surf. This man had not been killed directly by the spilled oil in the present, but his death is related to an avatar of the blown well: spilled gasoline aboard an aircraft carrier in World War II. Laurel's uncle had been in command, her father the communications officer, and the scarred dead man the witness to a murder thirty years old, the victim of which was the mistress of both father and uncle. Sexual sin repeats biblical original sin and spills forward into the environmental sin. Guilt and delayed retribution for long-past sins in the Lennox family saga bubble up from far beneath the surface of the present and make it possible for Macdonald, in *Sleeping Beauty,* to realize guilt on the monumental scale of the oil spill. In the end, the scorned wife is the murderess, and she kills herself melodramatically, as does Elaine Hillman the scorned wife of *The Far Side of the Dollar,* before Archer can lay a hand on her. The disjunction of the ending, retrieving the conclusion of a different kind of case for a new kind of crime, makes *Sleeping Beauty* less successful than *The Underground Man* at reforging the linkage of conventional novel and detective novel.

"Santa Barbarans Cite an 11th Commandment: 'Thou Shalt Not Abuse the Earth'" bears an overt, biblical title. The spill set Macdonald to work to build a bridge between one moral structure established over centuries of practice in what he often called "the Christian West," and a new morality in which the ways of God to humanity and of one person to another were joined by the ways of humanity to nature. The "nature" he had in view, of course, was specifically Southern California. This identification is made more than obvious in a short scene squeezed into *Sleeping Beauty*. Tracking down a suspect in the disappearance of Laurel, Archer interrogates a beer-swilling woman who used to drink with the suspect he seeks. "She had a broad handsome face, jet-black eyes, tar-black hair. Her body looked swollen in its tight black dress but, like her face, it had a heavy beauty" (169). Grotesque but reminiscent of beauty and slightly ethnic—when the woman tells Archer that she has accepted the name Ramona as a "joke," we get the punch line (171). Helen Hunt Jackson's fictional embodiment of prelapsarian California in *Ramona* (1884) has been abused; she bears only the traces of former innocence and beauty, blackened now as if with oil.

On the principle that no good deed goes unpunished, the *New York Times Book Review* turned on *Sleeping Beauty,* giving it a page 55 review and a less-than-marquee reviewer who seems to regret that previous reviews had ever connected Archer and literature. Macdonald, the reviewer scolded, "has fallen prey to the exuberance of his critics and is now writing in the shadow of a self-regard that tends to play his talent false."[17] The review illustrates the tug-of-war that defines the detective genre: one side strains to pull the genre "upward" to the "legitimate novel" while the other side is more comfortable with a serviceable formula. In *Sleeping Beauty* Macdonald tried to use the oil spill as Hemingway had used war—as a cataclysmic background for the assessment of the basic moral character of the species. The *Times* reviewer was not having it; the detective genre, he seemed to say, was a minor genre and ought to stay that way.

The next novel in the Archer saga was not intentionally the last, but it is, nevertheless, saturated with valediction. Even while working on *The Blue Hammer* (1976), Macdonald began to see the end of the road. In twenty-five years of writing the Archer series, he had settled into a groove: each year or two a new novel would be ready for the publisher. After *The Goodbye Look* (1969), Macdonald's production slowed. He was growing older, and niches on the best-seller list had enhanced his income from first trade publications, movie options, and paperback rights—he could afford to take a bit longer to produce the next novel. But the novels themselves were becoming more complex as he grew beyond the confines of the genre. As Macdonald repeated and internalized the voice and form of the genre—as it merged more intimately with the voice and form of his own imagination—some stylistic tics (inside jokes, asides, cameos) became less frequent, and more comprehensive structural and thematic literary goals, like the permutations on groups of three in *The Underground Man* or the merging of environmental and sexual guilt in *Sleeping Beauty,* seemed not only possible but obligatory. In his later books, from *The Goodbye Look* through *Sleeping Beauty,* Macdonald accomplished what he had aimed at from the outset: to take a popular form, thought capable of little more than temporary escape *from* serious thought ("a neglected stepchild of literature," one critic called it)[18] and make it the legitimate vehicle for serious moral and cultural stock-taking.

Perhaps it seemed to be the right time for a self-referendum after more than a quarter-century at work. Macdonald signals his intention by including a scene he had used in the first Archer, *The Moving Target:* a visit to a mountaintop occupied by a spacey religious guru and his followers. Whatever the case, Macdonald described *The Blue Hammer* as a summing-up book, a project through which to gauge his work as one whole achievement, a body of work. One of the results of the critical praise for *The Goodbye Look,* Macdonald wrote to his Knopf editor Ashbel Green, was that he (and, he hoped, his readers) could see the Archer series, not just an individual novel in it, as his achievement.[19]

The central idea of *The Blue Hammer,* he said, was not new; rather, it stretched more than a decade into his writing past (Nelson, 12A-4). Indeed, a central premise—a Cain-and-Abel situation in which one brother has artistic talent and the other none, leading to jealousy and fratricide—informs *The Instant Enemy* (1968). Macdonald refurbished the central situation for *The Blue Hammer* but changed the surround. The pivotal motif, not surprisingly given the self-appraising purpose of the book, is a portrait of the lifelong artist in old age. It is as if in writing *The Blue Hammer* Macdonald created characters like mirrors; as Macdonald walks by each one he cannot resist the temptation to see and judge himself.

With life and work situated nearer the end than the beginning, *The Blue Hammer* echoes with the valedictory lines common to much of Samuel Taylor Coleridge's poetry. Coleridge's late poem "Work without Hope" (1826), for example, sets the tone of work as life: "Work without hope draws nectar in a sieve, / And Hope without an object cannot live." In a sense, the detective genre without the solid addition of cultural significance heftier than escape is the sieve of Coleridge's metaphor. But Macdonald had "worked" the sieve into a solid vessel, and he used *The Blue Hammer* to pay tribute to artists—himself included—who had given dry bones life.

The late works of Coleridge are apt for Macdonald, who thought of himself in similar, nearly valedictory, terms in the early 1970s:

> Over a long period of time [he replied to an interviewer], the novelist writing a book is a man who is willing to wait for his effects, wait for his payoff and make the reader wait too. This has been characteristic of my life and I've spent

a great deal of my life waiting and working towards a distant goal. The tendency has been to pick up loose ends and complete circles that have been begun. An arc of a circle leaves me unsatisfied. I ultimately want to complete the full circle and of course I'll complete the fullest circle of all when I die. (Kaye, 73)

Like Coleridge's Wedding Guest, to whom the Ancient Mariner tells his melancholy story of dead albatross, ghost crew, and a life of guilt without parole, the Archer of *The Blue Hammer* is surrounded by images of "forlorn" or lost sense, wasted or wasting bodies, and a wedding of sorts (Archer's late-life love for Betty Jo Siddon, a woman he meets in the course of the case). The wedding festivities in Coleridge's poem, Macdonald would have known full well, are heard offstage; the mariner's obsessive confession interrupts the guest's journey to the party, and it is clear he listens with a sense of anxiety that the fun might be over before the mariner concludes his tale. As tender as Archer's feelings for Betty Jo become, his relationship with her is truncated, postponed, and like the Wedding Guest in the poem,

> He went like one that hath been stunned,
> And is of sense forlorn:
> A sadder and a wiser man,
> He rose the morrow morn.

In his opening conversation with prospective clients Jack and Ruth Biemeyer, whose stolen painting (the early work of Richard Chantry, who disappeared at the apex of his talent) Archer is asked to recover, Jack Biemeyer, no older than Archer (who is "more like fifty" [136] in this novel) misremembers a simple fact about why he built his palatial house in Santa Teresa and reacts with "a stricken look in his eyes . . . [realizing] that his mind had slipped a notch" (6). With this moment as a kind of password, the novel unfolds as a script illuminated with images of "slipping" down into physical and mental dissolution. Archer's response to Francine Chantry's gallery of her missing husband's paintings, for example, is to see them as variations on the theme of humans "devolving" into animals (16). Olive Street in Santa Teresa, the second stop on Archer's voyage into the case, is dissolving toward demolition after its heyday as a solid bourgeois neighborhood. One of his early interview subjects, Gerard Johnson, is an "invalid husband," addled by obscure war injuries and alcoholism. To end their first interview, Johnson taps the side of his head and remarks, sadly, "'Nobody home upstairs'" (38). A formerly beautiful woman who modeled in the nude for the missing painter simply "got old," and when Archer finally locates her she looks back over the continent of her life as if it were another country (165, 216). When Archer visits a nursing home in search of the missing model, he hears behind closed doors the querulous sounds of old people at night (67). Still another character claims to have an overactive "forgettery" when accused of not telling Archer all she knows (247). *The Blue Hammer* is crisscrossed with omens of mental and physical dissolution brought on more often than not by age.

Almost everyone Archer meets, as the case spirals back into the past, and almost every site he visits used to be healthier, intact. And nothing—not youth, not the earth, not honor—can be restored. At certain intersections in the case, the *mementi mori* are underlined with self-referential importance. Following the path of the Biemeyer's missing portrait, Archer encounters the dead body of a mediocre painter about his own age. Jake Whitmore would never have become a good painter, but he worked at it and hoped for more. Presumably, he died of a heart attack while swimming in the surf off a Santa Teresa beach. Frequent, almost daily, swims in the Pacific were a habit Macdonald saw as primordial: "The sea, like my lost father, is one of the recurrent themes in my life. . . . In recent years, particularly after I had a little bit of heart and circulation trouble. . . . I formed a habit of swimming in the sea every day all year round and I still get perhaps my greatest pleasure in physical sense out of wading into the sea and taking my daily swim" (Kaye, 76; ellipses added).

To balance the image of the dead painter's "blue body with its massive hairy head and shrunken sex" (58), Macdonald follows up his private wake for the dead Jake Whitmore with a vigorous, septuagenarian artist. Simon Lashman has important information about a prime witness in the tightly woven case of art, murder, and stolen identity. But what is almost more important in Archer's interviews with Lashman, in person and by telephone, is that Lashman represents the persistence of the aesthetic drive in the waning days of the mortal body: hope with an object, in Coleridge's terms, or, in Macdonald's, enduring for the payoff. Lashman cuts short the initial telephone call from Archer to return to his painting: "'I am seventy-five years old. I'm painting my two-hundred-and-fourteenth picture. If I stopped to attend to other people's problems, I'd never get it finished'" (88). When the painter and the detective meet in person, Lashman has almost as much to say about the life of the artist in a world of dissolving minds and bodies as he does about the missing model whom Archer seeks. Although he speaks with "pride and nostalgia and regret," Lashman is reluctant to postpone his work to indulge in nostalgia for what cannot be relived. Work is life; stop the one and the other ends too. Even though the missing painter, Richard Chantry, had been his pupil decades in the past and had even eclipsed the teacher in a blaze of early talent, Lashman is proud that he, not Chantry, is still painting. "'He [the pupil] lacked the endurance to stay the course. In this work, you really need endurance. . . . I expect to die myself the day that I stop working'" (98). There is more to the character of Simon Lashman in *The Blue Hammer* than plot mechanics: He is one of Macdonald's array of alter egos, the artist on the long arc completing "the fullest circle of all." As he did in his other "late" novels, *The Underground Man* and *Sleeping*

Beauty, Macdonald imagines Archer out in the open, unprotected by the gum-shoe's requisite cynicism. The ancient detective is closer to love in *The Blue Hammer* than ever before. Risking a blatant violation of the predatory conventions of "love" in the detective genre, and in some of Archer's earlier hit-and-run one-night stands, Macdonald takes Archer's relationship with Betty Jo Siddon much further than those with Jean Broadhurst (*The Underground Man*) and Beth Somerville (*Sleeping Beauty*). Like Coleridge's wedding as the offstage counterpoint to the ancient mariner's woeful tale of death and guilt, Archer's future with Betty Jo operates as a tantalizingly delayed counterplot to the obsessive, solitary investigation. Archer's affair with Betty Jo Siddon is a carefully calibrated indulgence in the memory of the intact, youthful body and a life horizon seemingly limitless and bright.

Betty Jo Siddon, a feature-writer for a Santa Teresa newspaper, is introduced as a hale and straightforward woman who has escaped the handicap of being beautiful. She is, like Macdonald's wife Margaret Millar (they had been married thirty-eight years in 1976), a tough, professional writer, who struggles against male-chauvinist editors to write the Chantry story. Compared to her recent sisters Jean Broadhurst and Beth Somerville, she is self-reliant rather than vulnerable, eroticized, for Archer, by her work rather than by her body or by the fact that she is the "property" of another man. She passes a kind of initiation test that Archer himself administers. As she and Archer approach the closed door of the house occupied by Chantry's "widow" and her house man, Rico, they hear "the sound of a woman moaning in pain or pleasure." "'Women all sound the same under certain circumstances,'" Archer deadpans just before a lipstick-smeared Rico opens the Chantry door (77). Betty Jo bends but does not break.

Even though the lovers make it to bed once in the course of the case—a lovemaking that leaves Archer feeling almost young again (82)—their second time is delayed by Betty Jo's stubborn, professional pursuit of the Chantry story. A little like the wedding guest who cannot drag himself away from the mariner's tale, Archer tastes love strongly seasoned by dread and ruin. Before he sees Betty Jo again after their first night together she disappears, and he breaks cool by allowing others to see his concern. His worst fears are almost fulfilled; Betty Jo had indeed found Richard Chantry, only to be trussed up nude in a chair and compelled to "sit" for her portrait—Chantry's last work. Once rescued from that danger by Archer, she does not swoon into the hero's manly arms but takes herself away again to write the story of her own captivity.

Macdonald's personal reports of struggling long and hard with *The Blue Hammer* can be verified in the style as well as in the thick pattern of imagery of dissolution and the nostalgia, through love, for youth. Gilbert Sorrentino comments that *The Blue Hammer,* though more complex than *The Moving Target,* is "less rhetorically gaudy."[20] He also finds more metonymy and correspondingly less metaphor. The things in the plot, in other words, represent themselves; they are not worked into a dense and multi-referential pattern (like the fire in *The Underground Man*).

Symbolic texture is not the only stripped-down aspect of the novel; verbal texture echoes the symbolic texture in its spareness. The prescribed, stiff-jawed voice-over narration of the detective genre is reduced more than once in *The Blue Hammer* to a kind of telegraphic simplicity. In one passage, early in the novel, Archer visits the art store and gallery of a former friend and teacher of Richard Chantry, the missing painter:

> A bell tinkled over the door as I went in. The interior had been disguised with painted plyboard screens and gray cloth hangings. A few tentative-looking pictures had been attached to them. On one side a dark woman in a loose multi-colored costume sat behind a cheap desk and tried to look busy.
>
> She had deep black eyes, prominent cheekbones, prominent breasts. Her long hair was unflecked black. She was very handsome, and quite young. (14)

The rules of the detective novel as a genre, of course, forbid lapses into fine writing. Chandler usually stands in sparse company with his preference for style: lengthy asides, brilliant similes, elaborate descriptions of rooms and clothing. But this passage from *The Blue Hammer* is stark: short, uncomplicated sentences in a repetitive pattern that seems to strain just to get itself said rather than to hold itself in. The effect of several passages in the same reduced style is to mute everything but the central narrative concern: the problem and the unraveling.

The Blue Hammer was published in 1976, three years after *Sleeping Beauty*—more than double the usual interval between Macdonald novels. Macdonald was sixty-one in 1976, an "old" sixty-one by his own account, and worn down, if not out, by more than three decades of steady, heavy professional writing. He must have been aware, too, that he was about at the end of the Millar lifespan. In Coleridgean terms, both he and Archer were feeling like "ancient mariners." Soon after publication Macdonald began to register lapses of concentration and memory and confessed that the habitual return to work on the next novel might never take place. In a 1977 notebook entry he saw his loss of memory not as a physical symptom but as a psychoanalytic one: his attempt to escape from himself.[21] When he could not deliver a new novel in the clockwork two years, his publisher filled the void with an omnibus volume, *Archer in Jeopardy* (1979). A cruelly ironic title: within a year Macdonald began to tell friends and associates that he could not concentrate well enough to write—not even personal letters—and that he could not remember past events well enough to construct a plot.

Macdonald's friend and coauthor of "Santa Barbarans Cite an 11th Commandment: 'Thou Shalt Not Abuse the Earth,'" Robert Easton, thought he could detect the loosening of Macdonald's stringent creative hold on his novels when he read *The Blue Hammer.* Macdonald dismissed it as simple mellowing, but Easton suspected later that it was "Alzheimer's disease, beginning subtly." During the years Easton had known him in Santa Barbara, Macdonald's health had been precarious but his stamina for writing miraculous. Easton saw: "hypertension, heart trouble, gout."[22] At times, Macdonald told him, he was taking nine different medications daily. Psychological stress became a serious problem with his daughter Linda's troubles in the 1950s and her death in 1970. His wife, novelist Margaret Millar, began to suffer macular degeneration in the mid-1970s as well, tightening the noose of emotional stress just as his own health was breaking down. Millar's family health history was not encouraging: both parents had died in their sixties. Macdonald died of complications of Alzheimer's disease in 1983, at the age of sixty-seven.

| 8 |

The Genre after Macdonald

It is tantalizing to imagine the next Archer, the one Macdonald could not finish. In the 1970s the detective genre was on the brink of great change. In 1970
Joseph Hansen introduced Dave Brandstetter, the first frankly gay private investigator; the novel *Fadeout* presents gay male emotions and some scenes of
intimacy as candidly as "community standards" allowed. Robert B. Parker's
Spenser series began with *The Godwulf Manuscript* in 1973, gradually developing Spenser into a macho champion who can also choose the correct wine to
accompany a Coquilles St. Jacques he prepares himself from ingredients on
hand. The early 1980s saw the debuts of several series with women detectives:
notably Sue Grafton's Kinsey Millhone and Sara Paretsky's V. I. Warshawski.
Clearly, the genre of Hammett, Chandler, and Macdonald was no longer the
exclusive property of heterosexual, white males.

Having introduced Betty Jo Siddon and having linked her sexually and emotionally with Archer, Macdonald seems to have sensed an evolution in the genre
and his own work. Betty Jo is not just a casual sexual conquest. If he were to
have included her, Archer and Siddon might have become a 1970s version of
Nick and Nora Charles, the married sleuthing couple, with which Hammett
brought his active writing career to an end. Chandler, too, arrived late at the
married detective: when he died he had started a novel in which Marlowe mar-
ries Linda Loring, the sister of the murderer and suicide Eileen Wade of *The
Long Goodbye*. Two of Macdonald's self-conscious heirs, Robert B. Parker and
Michael Connelly, make their loners' relationships (in and out of marriage) as
prominent as the pursuit of the killer. As one critic says of Connelly's Harry
Bosch, "he's actually rather soft-boiled . . . he has a past and a personal life."[1]

Archer has a past and personal life, too; but not until *The Blue Hammer* does
"relationship" become a theme. If Macdonald had left Betty Jo out of the "next"
Archer novel, then the viability of Archer in the genre as it was molting would
have been severely damaged. The old-style private eye could get away with
being a serial lover, but only in a genre dominated by the straight, white male.
In former relationships, Archer had held himself on the far (if only just so) side
of emotional commitment to any woman. He might sleep with a willing witness

once, but neither he nor the woman sought a second meeting. Both seemed to understand the rules: between independence and codependence there was no middle ground. With Betty Jo, however, Archer had thrown himself into her life as well as her bed. It is clear that their intimacy is more than sexual.

In working notebooks dated from 1974 and 1977 Macdonald experimented with an Archer novel in which the detective learns he has a daughter. He played with the idea that the daughter is Archer's with a friend of Sue, his estranged wife. The mistress knows that Archer still loves Sue and mulls over the idea of uniting the original but flawed couple by using the "lost" daughter as a catalyst. Macdonald apparently was shut off from further exploration by his illnesses. From preliminary pieces of "The Painted Cave," one of his working titles, it seems clear that Macdonald was being drawn away from the isolated, cool, wary Archer and toward imagining the detective in something loosely resembling a family. What the speculations in his late notebooks mean is impossible to say with certainty; none of his experiments grew beyond hypothetical suggestions to himself. Merely considering Archer in a household, rather than alone on mean streets, seems to verify tendencies in the last trilogy, in which overwhelming images of ruin are countered with guarded indications of Archer in—or moving toward—love.

A novelist as accomplished as Macdonald could have invented ways out of the character "problem" he had with an aging Archer longing for some form of domestic connection. Indeed, Macdonald had had some experience with married detectives while writing "The Hunters" in the 1960s, a projected television series featuring a husband-and-wife team. No pilot was ever made, but surviving scripts and treatments suggest an updating of the Nick and Nora Charles stories. But there were other elements of the changing environment that Archer (and Macdonald) might have found more challenging.

As the 1970s merged into the 1980s and then into the end-of-the-century period, Macdonald's ability to absorb a new ethos into the Archer saga might have suffered uncharacteristic stress. Homosexuality is one illustrative example. Gay-bashing, overt or covert, had been a staple of the detective genre as a macho stronghold. Earlier Archer novels were not innocent of some degree of the bias. In *The Barbarous Coast,* for example, gangster Carl Stern's homosexuality is portrayed as a form of morbidity, and his murder is a kind of "bonus" in the plot. He is a shadowy presence, held just inside the frame of the plot until he is killed. In *The Blue Hammer* Archer confronts homophobia in others (the missing painter Chantry and his teacher Paul Grimes are lovers, and the cops express distaste when they find out), but Archer keeps his tolerance to himself, addressing the reader but not another character. As gay and lesbian liberation movements accelerated into the public consciousness after the Stonewall riots of 1969, the routine gay-bashing in Hammett's and Chandler's novels became increasingly difficult to tolerate. In fact, the exquisite and extraliterary pleasure Parker's Spenser takes in pummeling a gay bodybuilder in the second novel of the Spenser series, *God Save the Child* (1974), seems anachronistic in the same decade in which Joseph Hansen's gay detective, Dave Brandstetter, made his first appearance in *Fadeout* (1970), the first of five Dave Brandstetter novels in the decade.[2] In Michael Connelly's Harry Bosch series, the most stable and enduring relationship in Bosch's circle is between a male assistant district attorney and his partner, and Bosch looks with some longing on the difficult but faithful lesbian relationship between his married captain and her female lover: he goes out of his way to keep their fragile secret. The genre, clearly, adapts to the temper of its times, and a novelist of Macdonald's powers could have adapted, too.

Certain forms of violence, especially the more savage, do not appear in the Archer novels. Although Chandler disparaged the "vicar's rose garden" murders of the English wing of the genre, the violence Marlowe witnessed falls short of the carnage the genre would soon feature. Dismemberment, evisceration, torture—the catalog of evidence in the case of the Black Dahlia in 1947, for example—seldom find their way into Archer's or Marlowe's cases. In *The Barbarous Coast*, again, a woman is killed, transported in the trunk of a car, incinerated, and left in a desert pit; but usually Macdonald's killers are economical with bullets, stab wounds, and the time-honored blunt-force trauma. Increasingly in the 1980s and 1990s, as the work of Patricia Cornwell and others illustrates, grand guignol is more easily taken for granted, and the perpetrator is often a deranged genius, like "The Dollmaker" in Michael Connelly's *The Concrete Blonde*, or the murderer in T. Jefferson Parker's debut novel, *Laguna Heat* (1985), who incinerates two victims with turpentine and slices off the eyelids of one so she will have to watch. The Tate and LaBianca murders by the Manson family are frequently "credited" with ushering a new level of violence—wholesale, random, bloody—into the American imagination and the California myth. Corpses do accumulate in Archer's cases, but there is a reason for each killing. Murder is nothing if not intensely personal for Archer.

As Sue Grafton's appropriation of Santa Teresa in her Kinsey Millhone series illustrates, the rise of a generation of women detective novelists—Grafton, Cornwell, Sara Paretsky, Nevada Barr, and others—threatened to mothball, or soft-boil, the hypermasculinized private eye, even one as wary of violence as Archer. Women writers have long held prestigious places in the history of the detective genre, especially in the British tradition; and Macdonald's wife Margaret Millar had begun (and then abandoned) a detective series in the 1940s.[3] But, even in most of these cases, the authors were women but the detectives were men—often with smart, attractive female companions. The male narcissism and proprietary sense of agency deeply embedded in the genre were not measurably shifted until the late 1970s and early 1980s, when Marcia Muller, Sue Grafton, and Sara Paretsky began to publish their respective series with female detectives.[4]

Even the most muscle-bound of hard-boiled detectives felt some leavening. Robert B. Parker's Spenser tempers his hard-knuckle approach with smooth expertise with a wine list or at the range in his own kitchen. In *The Godwulf Manuscript* (1973), the novel in which Spenser debuts, the heir apparent to Archer sleeps with a mother and her daughter, kills three people, and, to redress the balance, expertly prepares Coquilles St. Jacques (for one), choosing a crackling Pouilly Fuissé to accompany his solitary meal. A font of self-deprecating wisecracks, Spenser is a "lite" version of Archer, an interesting attempt by Parker to graft a more sensitive and socialized male to the stock of the self-reliant killer and thereby to extend the tradition in which he self-consciously places Spenser. In his doctoral dissertation, Parker not only affirms the centrality of the male trinity but asserts the necessity of violence.[5] He repeats with approval the verdict of D. H. Lawrence in *Studies in Classic American Literature* (1923):

> True myth concerns itself centrally with the onward adventure of the integral soul. And this, for America, is Deerslayer. A man who turns his back on white society. A man who keeps his moral integrity hard and intact. An isolate, almost selfless, stoic, enduring man, who lives by death, by killing, but who is pure white.
>
> This is the very intrinsic-most American. He is at the core of all the other flux and fluff. And when *this* man breaks from his static isolation, and makes a new move, then look out, something will be happening.[6]

Parker's design on the heavily masculine tradition underlined by Lawrence is to "move" the killer out of his "static isolation." Spenser may have achieved only limited success. Archer was his own muscle (when, with decreasing frequency, he needed force), and (more crucially) he was his own psychologist who questioned the benefits of stoic isolation. Parker might know too much about structural skeleton of the genre. In Spenser's second case, Parker introduces Susan Silverman to function as Spenser's romantic relationship and to perform the psychological counseling he is too macho to do himself. The woman performs by proxy the move beyond isolation that Parker's alpha male will not or cannot complete. In a later addition to the series, he introduces Hawk to help Spenser mitigate his whiteness; yet relegating Hawk to muscle and the underside of the law only reinscribes Spenser as white. Parker's division of the labor in the Spenser novels—a self-conscious attempt to follow Macdonald and Chandler in the genre—paradoxically reveals his failure to advance the genre as Macdonald had—and as Parker himself had set forth in his dissertation.

Parker's inconclusive "progress" in the American detective genre indicates that Macdonald remains the modern master. In retrospect it seems that the detective novel merged closest to the mainstream of American literature when there was a consensus mainstream: in the decades presided over by Hammett,

Chandler, and Macdonald himself from the 1930s and into the 1970s. The social upheavals of the 1960s—the rise of feminism and women's liberation from roles and behaviors imposed on them by others, the breakthroughs in civil rights, the emergence of gay and lesbian cultures following the Stonewall riots of 1969—produced institutionalized changes in the following decades as the demonstrators, inevitably, became the establishment and wrote themselves into power. When the mainstream diversified in the 1970s—a fragmentation that has not yet been reversed—the detective novel diversified with it. Macdonald's immediate successors have tried to follow.

Following Parker's Spenser, but situated in Southern California, are T. Jefferson Parker and Michael Connelly. Parker's first novel, *Laguna Heat,* is deeply resonant of Macdonald. Set in Newport Beach and Laguna Beach, the novel's murders revolve around a gated resort community, and the trail of the crimes in the present leads the detective, Tom Shephard, into the past and his own father's past misdeeds. Parker's Shephard is, by the end of *Laguna Heat,* a private detective rather than a professional officer but has yet to reappear in a second novel.

He did, however, give his protagonist an "art collection," one print of Edward Hopper's "Nighthawks," which makes its way into the collection of Harry Bosch, the troubled anti-hero of Michael Connelly's series of police procedural novels set in Los Angeles in the chaotic 1990s. The Bosch novels begin with *The Black Echo* (1992) and continue to the present. Arguably the most successful of the series, so far, is *The Concrete Blonde* (1994).[7] Bosch, a detective on the robbery-homicide desk in Hollywood, bears many superficial similarities to Archer. Both are loners. Even though Bosch works as a policeman and is partnered on most of his cases, he is essentially the lone and flawed "saint with a gun" that D. H. Lawrence identified in Cooper's novels and in the American frontier character generally.[8] Harry is an orphan; Archer's childhood vital statistics mention a grandmother but no other adults. Bosch is in and out of romantic relationships and once was married; Archer has a similar, if less explicitly detailed, romantic record. Bosch even dresses like Archer: suit, dress shirt, tie. Like Archer but unlike Spenser, Bosch's culinary skill seldom rises above making a sandwich and opening a bottle of beer.

On one level, of course, the hero of the genre inhabits a general pool of characteristics, and similarities such as those listed above do not establish continuity or influence. But Connelly takes Bosch further back into Archer; like both Parkers, Connelly self-consciously reaches for the Macdonald legacy. Bosch's house, on steel stilts perched in the hills with a view of Los Angeles freeways, is a clear tribute to the use Macdonald made of domestic architecture in his novels. Harry's life is continuous with the disaster-defying engineering of his house: before the house is damaged in an earthquake and condemned as uninhabitable, it functions effectively as a symbol for the detective's unsteady hold on "grounding" in his job and belief in the honor of his colleagues in police headquarters.

In *The Concrete Blonde,* the centerpiece of Connelly's Harry Bosch series, the genealogy of Archer to his descendant in Connelly's work is most clearly evident. As the novel opens, Harry is on trial in civil court, the defendant in a case of wrongful death: in the line of duty he had shot and killed a man linked by layers of circumstantial and forensic evidence to a series of murders of prostitutes in Los Angeles. Each woman was garroted and her body made grotesque by lavish application of her own makeup. In the course of the trial another woman's body is found, encased in concrete and discovered during the demolition of a building burned out during the Rodney King riots. Police had been tipped off to the location of "the concrete blonde" during Bosch's trial: clear and damaging evidence that the man Bosch had killed might not have been "the Dollmaker," the press's name for the serial killer. To defend himself in the civil suit, Bosch must find the answer to "the concrete blonde."

Several direct and indirect gestures link Connelly's novel with the body of Macdonald's Archer work. Indeed, there is even a hint of a three-way connection from Macdonald to Parker to Connelly: the offbeat lawyer, Vince Haller, whom Spenser recommends to a client in *The Godwulf Manuscript* passes his surname to Harry Bosch's father.[9] In addition to the broad agreement within the genre outlined above, Bosch and Archer share an appreciation for L.A.'s mystic network of freeways and the almost Zen-like therapy of knowing how to navigate the roads. Closer ties between Connelly and Macdonald surface in several deliberate particulars. The attorney for the plaintiffs in the wrongful death lawsuit is named for Macdonald's nemesis, Raymond Chandler. Honey Chandler, known by the nickname *Money* because she always wins her lawsuits against the LAPD, specializes in cases of excessive force—an ironic gesture to Chandler's Marlowe who suffers so many beatings himself. Harry's current lover, a teacher, has assigned *The Big Sleep* to her class of middle-school students. More deliberately still, a disaffected attorney whom Harry meets on cigarette breaks during the trial, washed out of the profession when he lost a case of police brutality. "'Justice is what happened,'" the ruined lawyer tells Bosch when Harry asks why he no longer practices; the echo of Archer's "'I have a secret passion for mercy. . . . But justice is what keeps happening to people'" is unmistakable (*Goodbye Look,* 127). The case that drove the lawyer out was "the Galton case."[10] Connelly could have used any name, or no name at all, for this aside to the main plot. Choosing to echo the title of Macdonald's "breakthrough" novel is more than homage; it is a deliberate reach for writerly connection.

Clearly, Michael Connelly intended some gesture of respect to his predecessor, but the Harry Bosch series in its span so far represents a departure from the world of Archer. For all the similarities both circumstantial and intended, there is a radically different presence of violence: savage, graphic, repeated. The moral universe represented by Los Angeles / Hollywood in Connelly's work is well beyond any hope of healing. Riots lurk in the background of all crime and punishment, suggesting that the defenders of order are themselves deeply compromised and that bringing one malefactor to justice is less than insignificant among such widespread cynicism and malfeasance. Bosch's own character as a loner, as the series lengthens, verges on pathology. In *The Last Coyote* (1995), for example, his rogue behavior gets a fellow policeman tortured and killed.

It is, of course, central to the nature of artistic influence that the beneficiary of the influence carry the "burden" onward, demonstrate its value as an expressive and interpretive form for a moment and set of circumstances beyond the original. Macdonald did this with the heritage of Hammett and Chandler. By acknowledging Macdonald as their precursor so openly, writers like Robert B. Parker, T. Jefferson Parker, and Connelly perhaps inadvertently indicate the difficulty in living up to him. Evil may indeed have expanded exponentially, and our tolerance for images of it, too, but our moral agent—now Harry Bosch —like his namesake Hieronymous Bosch reflects a world of chaotic grotesques. The world of Harry Bosch is far more lethal than Archer's, in the deeply terminal stages of self-destruction measured by the Vietnam war (Harry's first stop out of the orphanage) and the Rodney King riots, in the shadow of which he tries to close the books on murder.

During the 2000 presidential campaign, candidate George W. Bush traded favorite detective novel titles with a reporter. The reporter recommended Michael Connelly's *The Concrete Blonde;* Bush's contribution was *The Zebra-Striped Hearse.*[11] As Macdonald might have said, the politics of the readers doesn't matter; the politics of the genre is democratic (small *d*), moving freely into all ideologies. Detective novels, as novels, serve as primers on their society's notions of good and evil, virtue and malice, pollution and cleanliness.

Novels are not the same as the historical record, and there is perennial debate about their status in that record. But because novels in the detective genre are produced by so many hands and at flood-tide pace, they can respond to alterations in the historical metabolism much more nimbly than literary novels. If we had to wait for a *Madame Bovary* to register the temper of the age, for each age, there would be many ages with no record at all in fiction.

Of course, much of this nimbleness derives from the formula: The narrative wheel need not be reinvented for each detective novel. For Sue Grafton, for example, Santa Teresa is already a made literary environment; she works to change its topography from male to female. Indeed, often the author's challenge is to find the proper balance of familiarity and originality. The detective novel is not the most original story every told, but the most basic; the most useful because it can be told again and again, registering even slight readjustments to the cultural status quo along the way. No writer who chooses the detective novel chooses originality, except for the accessories. Macdonald knew that his choice obliged him to achieve something much more difficult than originality (in which, probably, he did not believe anyway): to make the instantly familiar seem fresh and unprecedented, to make moral and psychological reality immediate. His audience is everyone who can read.

Ross Macdonald's novels succeed more often than they fail. Of his eighteen Archer novels, some work better than others. But, as a professional novelist who lived on his writing income, he did not have the luxury (like Flaubert, whose name appears in both Macdonald and Chandler as the signifier of literary finesse) of honing each individual novel until it was perfect. Some, such as *The Drowning Pool* and *The Wycherly Woman,* he wished he could have rewritten. Others, like *Black Money* and *The Underground Man,* can stand up to the toughest critical standards the literary novel has generated. His great decades were the 1950s and 1960s, as Hammett's were the 1920s and 1930s and Chandler's the 1930s and 1940s. He fashioned the detective genre to the ethos of those times, as Hammett and Chandler had done before him. He translated the crime and corruption of Hammett, the melancholy stylizing of Chandler away from the often artificialized wilderness of "mean streets" and into the heart of the family, where crime could be seen not as the anomalous product of extraordinary individuals but as the inevitable offshoot of flawed human nature. His Lew Archer began literary life as a detective and evolved into a psychologist, taking crime and punishment with him.

Macdonald was always in ambiguous territory: definitely far from the vicar's rose garden but also at arm's length from the mean streets. Aficionados of the traditional hard-boiled detective novel decry the ambiguity; others see it as fertile. As Geoffrey Hartman perceptively stated, "the shrinking embrace of an overprotective family" in Macdonald's fiction is as lethal as any maximum security prison or dark street. Reynolds Price put it more succinctly in his poem "The Core: For Ross Macdonald": "The mother did it."[12] Dorothy Sayers, outlining the history and format of the detective story, wryly commented "It is fortunate for the mystery-monger that, whereas, up to the present, there is only one known way of getting born, there are endless ways of getting killed." Although in 2004 there is probably already a detective story involving birth by cloning, what Sayers wrote confidently more than seventy years ago locates Macdonald: whereas his American precursors Hammett and Chandler concentrated on ways of getting people killed, Macdonald found the seeds of crime and evil in being born and being reared. Murder victims in his fiction usually die in mundane ways: they are shot or stabbed or bludgeoned. No curare-tipped darts, sliced brake lines, or postage stamp adhesive laced with arsenic. Archer has no need of a police lab to tell him how someone died; the question is always "why?" and, even more tantalizing, "when?": for in Archer's cases he searches not for the moment when the fatal blow was actually delivered but rather the moment in the collective life of the family when the mark was inevitably set. In Archer's world we share our humanity in sharing its doom. Archer, and his readers, can never stand back at an antiseptic distance from the evils in his cases. Increasingly, as his career develops, Archer is weighted down by the dead and the living he would rather understand than punish.

Archer knows one very large, universal, and melancholy truth: we only get one life, but we can dream of many others we would like better. He approaches each case with a kind of foreboding: he will have to deal with a roster of people who desire to be something other than what they are, and they will have committed crimes to achieve their dreams and further crimes to hold on to them. The crimes, Archer knows, are only the minuscule tip of the iceberg. To map the unseen mass of discontent Macdonald deployed the Freudian model of consciousness when the seven deadly sins proved inadequate, and he did so with a convert's faith. The Freudian outline of act and motive was not one of several strategies Macdonald could use; it was the only one. He knowingly ran the risk of repetition and predictability; indeed, several of his novels clearly recycle earlier plots: much of *The Barbarous Coast* and *The Galton Case* is repeated in *The Chill*; much of *The Far Side of the Dollar* is reprised in *The Goodbye Look*; the Cain-and-Abel plot emerges in both *The Instant Enemy* and *The Blue Hammer*. Macdonald, as a person and as a writer, had faith in the Freudian paradigm; it explained what was objectively there, although unseen. Repetition was not his biggest worry; in the end, a certain consistency became his signature, just as the repeated face of Raphael's madonna became his.

As a novelist and a critic, Macdonald could do what those of us who are only critics can't do: he could think about literary history and *be* it at the same time. By embracing a popular genre *for* its popularity rather than *in spite of* it, he nourished culture from its midst rather than from the problematical and outnumbered avant garde. If every artist were Picasso, he seems to have said, where would our culture be? "I think a piece of writing doesn't have to be written on a very high, serious level in order to be valid, or in order to support the culture," he said in one of his last interviews. "I would simply go on from that and examine the many, different ways in which culture can be spread and fed in the presence of an already existent culture which has its values, but which has to be continually fed, refed and taught and assisted in all the different ways that we pay tribute to art."[13]

Like the DNA he inherited as a physical fate—circulatory systems that broke down in his father and mother and in his only daughter—Macdonald inherited a literary DNA with the detective genre he embraced and committed himself to refresh and nourish. He fulfilled his commitment. He expanded the moral range of the genre beyond the narrow field of crime that his acknowledged predecessors, Hammett and Chandler, had furrowed. He deepened the literary resonance of the detective novel, not only by ornamenting his with literary allusions but more importantly by grafting the detective novel successfully to the main branches of the American novel and more thoroughly to the Freudian paradigm. *Black Money,* as an example of the former, does not merely echo Fitzgerald's classic novel *The Great Gatsby,* it assumes a dialogue with it. Macdonald drew powerful undercurrents from Fitzgerald's novel and adapted them for a retranslation, not simply a recostuming. And he took enormous risks with the Freudian paradigm, so precariously balanced on the lip of cliché, over and over again exploring the family romance as the incubator of sin and self.

What Macdonald strove to do in his books was to close the divide between life lived and life thought. He could not do that; no one can. And that is why there was always another case for Archer and why the next case was always already the previous one. By surviving in his work for so long—as long as he could, like his alter ego Simon Lashman in *The Blue Hammer*—Macdonald made the detective novel series an ongoing philosophical work. That is why we can read his novels over and over again.

NOTES

Prologue

1. Barzun, "Aesthetics of the Criminous," 563, 564.
2. Barzun, "A Catalogue of Crime," 568.
3. Wilson, "Who Cares Who Killed Roger Ackroyd?" 390–97.
4. Barzun, "Why Read Crime Fiction?" 574.
5. Ibid., 576, 578.
6. Cawelti, *Adventure, Mystery, and Romance*, 1, 18, 13.
7. Grella, "Murder and the Mean Streets," 6–15.
8. Pepper, *The Contemporary American Crime Novel*, 5.
9. Bertens and D'haen, *Contemporary American Crime Fiction*, 113.
10. Cawelti, *Adventure, Mystery, and Romance*, 18.
11. The most recent and thorough biography is Nolan, *Ross Macdonald*. Critical/ biographical studies include: Wolfe, *Dreamers Who Live Their Dreams*; Speir, *Ross Macdonald*; Bruccoli, *Ross Macdonald / Kenneth Millar*; Bruccoli, *Ross Macdonald*; Schopen, *Ross Macdonald*. Two extensive but unpublished interviews, among the Millar Papers in the University of California–Irvine Library, also support this study: Art Kaye, 1970; Paul Nelson, 1976.
12. Barzun, "A Catalogue of Crime," 569.

Chapter 1: Constants

1. Dashiell Hammett to Blanche Knopf, March 20, 1928. In Hammett, *Selected Letters*, 45–47.
2. Kenneth Millar used two pseudonyms. Very early published work appeared under his christened name, Kenneth Millar. For a short time he used a pseudonym based on his father's name, John Macdonald: John Ross Macdonald. The similarity of this pseudonym to the name of the author of another series of crime novels, John D. MacDonald (1916–86), caused a "dust up" in 1953—mostly involving agents and publishers. John D. MacDonald, who had published his first hardboiled novel, *The Brass Cupcake*, in 1951, wrote to John Ross Macdonald in 1953 that he was happy to be confused with a newcomer who could write so well. The John D. MacDonald letter (September 5, 1953) is in the Millar Papers, UCI. The majority of Millar's work appeared under the name Ross Macdonald. I observe a simple convention here: In the very few instances when I refer strictly to the

historical person, I shall use the name Millar; in the far greater number of instances I shall use the name Macdonald, on the grounds that the man himself bled life into art.

3. Cooper-Clark, "Interview with Ross Macdonald," in *Designs of Darkness,* 84–85.

4. Welty, "Foreword," in Macdonald, *Self-Portrait,* i.

5. Davie, "On Hearing about Ross Macdonald," in Sipper, *Inward Journey,* 95–96.

6. For an excellent recital of these constants, see Leonard, "Ross Macdonald, His Lew Archer and Other Secret Selves."

7. See, for example, two recent essays reviewing and reevaluating the stature of Dashiell Hammett: Atwood, "Mystery Man," and Pierpont, "Tough Guy." Atwood, a fellow Canadian, does not mention Macdonald; Pierpont mentions his name but adds nothing by way of comment.

8. Hammett, *The Maltese Falcon;* see chap. 7 for the Flitcraft story and Brigid's reaction.

9. Macdonald, "Farewell Chandler," in Sipper, *Inward Journey,* 41.

10. Blotner, *Faulkner,* 2:1171; McCarthy, *Howard Hawks,* 380–82.

11. Macdonald, "Farewell Chandler," in Sipper, *Inward Journey,* 47.

12. See Cowan, *John Inness.*

13. Macdonald, *Self-Portrait,* 13.

14. Ibid., 14.

15. Ibid., 35.

16. Ibid., 5.

17. Millar, "Approximate Chronology," Millar Papers, UCI.

18. McWilliams, *Southern California.*

19. Davis, *Ecology of Fear.*

20. Bloom, *Anxiety of Influence,* 5.

21. Norris, *The Responsibilities of the Novelist,* 7.

22. Macdonald, "The Scene of the Crime," in Sipper, *Inward Journey,* 11–34.

23. Ibid., 30.

24. Norris, *The Responsibilities of the Novelist,* 7.

25. Macdonald, *Self-Portrait,* 110, 118.

26. Ibid., 110.

27. Ibid., 16.

Chapter 2: "An Unhappy Childhood Is Practically Indispensable"

1. Tolstoy, *Anna Karenina,* 3.

2. Macdonald, *Self-Portrait,* 3.

3. Signed "J.M.M." Millar Papers, UCI.

4. Cowan, *John Innes,* 7–15.

5. "Down These Streets a Mean Man Must Go," in Macdonald, *Self-Portrait,* 6.

6. Millar Papers, UCI; *Winter Solstice,* 5:11.

7. *Plunder,* starring Pearl White (1889–1936), is a serial in fifteen parts, released in 1923. See the discussion of Macdonald's *Zebra-Striped Hearse* in chap. 6 for more of his homage to White.

8. Millar Papers, UCI.

9. Anderson, "The Crime Corner," 12.

10. Millar Papers, UCI.

11. Originally published under the name Kenneth Millar, citations are from the 1987 reprint edition, Macdonald, *Blue City.* This novel has also been adapted for the screen (1986).

12. Millar Papers, UCI.

13. Cerf, "Trade Winds."

14. Macdonald, *Self-Portrait,* 35.

Chapter 3: Literary Fathers and Archer's Debut

1. K. M.'s statement to his analyst (1957), Millar Papers, UCI, 9.

2. Donald Davie to Ken Millar, March 4, 1960, Millar Papers, UCI.

3. Like the current reigning king of the genre, Michael Connelly, who learned the trade as a police reporter for Fort Lauderdale (Fla.) and Los Angeles newspapers. See Weber, "Watching the Detectives," 38–41.

4. Millar, "The Inward Eye," 73.

5. Ibid., 438.

6. Ibid., 192.

7. Ibid., 112, 181, 185.

8. Ibid, 117.

9. Miller, *Auden,* 2, 29; for Miller's description of English 135, see 22–29.

10. Kenneth Millar's class notes to English 135. Courtesy Donald Pearce.

11. Class notes, English 135.

12. Millar, "The Comic Hero" (paper for English 135), 1, Millar Papers, UCI.

13. Auden, *The Enchafed Flood,* 13.

14. Millar, "The Comic Hero," 11.

15. Nolan, *Ross Macdonald,* 55.

16. Auden, "The Guilty Vicarage," 147.

17. Ibid., 149–50.

18. Ibid., 153.

19. Ibid., 151.

20. Ibid., 154.

21. Auden, *The Enchafed Flood,* 92.

22. Ibid., 111, 90.

23. Ibid., 108.

24. The first edition of *The Moving Target* was published under the name John Macdonald. Millar's next six books—four novels in the Archer series, a collection of short stories with Archer, and one non-Archer detective novel (*Meet Me at the Morgue*)—were published under the name John Ross Macdonald. Most are now available under what became his lasting pseudonym, Ross Macdonald. To minimize confusion, I will use Ross Macdonald as the author's name from this point on.

25. Oates, "The Simple Art of Murder," 36.

26. Goodall, *Yasuo Kuniyoshi,* 40, 41.

27. Macdonald, *Strangers in Town.* William Faulkner won the second prize for "An Error in Chemistry."

28. Sipper, *Inward Journey,* 39.

29. Macdonald, *Self-Portrait,* 102.

30. Ibid., 18.

31. Brophy, "Detective Fiction," 123.

Chapter 4: The Rock and the Hard Place

1. Raymond Chandler to James Sandoe, April 14, 1949, in *Raymond Chandler: Late Novels and Other Writings,* ed. Frank MacShane (New York: Library of America, 1995), 1035.

2. Sipper, *Inward Journey,* 37.

3. Ibid., 38.

4. Ibid.

5. Ibid., 10–11.

6. Ibid., 11.

7. Chandler moved to La Jolla when he could afford to leave Hollywood, and Macdonald lived in Santa Barbara.

8. Starr, *Embattled Dreams,* 238.

9. Ibid., 236–38.

10. Ibid., 213.

11. Macdonald, *Self-Portrait,* 110.

12. Chandler, "The Simple Art of Murder," in *Raymond Chandler: Later Novels and Other Writings,* 987.

13. Ruehlman, *Saint with a Gun,* 5, 90, 105.

14. Hammett, *Crime Stories and Other Writings,* 711, 729.

15. Kenneth Millar to Henry Branson, November 28, 1953, Millar Papers, UCI. Branson wrote seven John Bent novels between 1941 and 1953.

16. R. T. Bond (Dodd, Mead) to Kenneth Millar, December 28, 1955, Millar Papers, UCI.

17. Wolfe, *Dreamers Who Live Their Dreams,* 118.

18. *Mom* is Philip Wylie's term of opprobrium. See Wylie, *Generation of Vipers,* chap. 11.

19. Nolan, *Ross Macdonald,* 21.

20. Subpoenaed to testify in a Justice Department inquiry into the Civil Rights Congress in 1951, Hammett declined to give even his own name. See Hammett, *Selected Letters,* 451–52.

21. Millar Papers, UCI Library.

22. Ibid., *Winter Solstice,* 4.

23. See Ellison, *Invisible Man* and "Twentieth-Century Fiction and the Black Mask of Humanity," in *Shadow and Art.*

24. Boucher, "The Ethics of the Mystery Novel," 385.

25. Macdonald, *Strangers in Town,* 42.

26. Chandler, *The Long Goodbye,* 562.

Chapter 5: Freud and Archer

1. Schwartz, *Cassandra's Daughter,* 191.

2. Neutra, *Life and Human Habitat,* 20; see also Lavin, "Open the Box."

3. Leslie A. Fiedler, *Love and Death in the American Novel*, xii–xiii.

4. For a more detailed account of Linda Millar's accident and the aftermath, see Nolan, *Ross Macdonald*, 160–79.

5. Freud, "On Beginning Treatment," 372.

6. Pateman, *The Disorder of Women*, 20.

7. Freud, *Basic Writings*.

8. Macdonald, "The Angry Man," in Nolan, *Strangers in Town*, 121–64.

9. Horney, *Self-Analysis*, 25. Horney draws a direct line between the analyst and the detective:

> In some ways his [the analyst's] work might be compared with that of the detective in mystery stories. It is worth emphasizing, however, that whereas the detective wants to discover the criminal the analyst does not want to find out what is bad in the patient, but attempts to understand him as a whole, good and bad. Also, he deals not with several people, all under suspicion, but with a multitude of driving forces in one person, all under suspicion not of being bad but of being disturbing. Through concentrated and intelligent observation of every detail he gathers his clues, sees a possible connection here and here, and forms a tentative picture; he is not too easily convinced of his solution, but tests it over and over again to see whether it really embraces all factors. In mystery stories there will be some people working with the detective, some only apparently doing so and secretly obstructing his work, some definitely wanting to hide and becoming aggressive if they feel threatened. Similarly, in analysis part of the patient co-operates—this is an indispensable condition—another part expects the analyst to do all the work and still another uses all its energies to hide or mislead and becomes panicky and hostile when threatened with discovery. (126–27)

10. Erikson, *Young Man Luther*, 8, 14.

11. Wylie, *Generation of Vipers*; see also Strecker, *Their Mothers' Sons*; Erikson, *Childhood and Society*, 247–57, also includes a commentary on *Mom*.

12. Erikson, *Childhood and Society*, 230.

13. Freud, *Basic Writings*, 553–629.

14. Ibid., 618.

15. Margaret Millar was the author of two overlapping series of detective novels with psychoanalytic accents. *The Invisible Worm* (1941), *The Weak-Eyed Bat* (1942), and *The Devil Loves Me* (1942) feature amateur sleuth and "consulting psychiatrist" Dr. Paul Prye. In *The Devil Loves Me*, Prye is joined by Inspector Sands, a more empirical policeman, who continues in *Wall of Eyes* (1943) and *The Iron Gates* (1945). For an evaluation of Margaret Millar's work, see Demarr, "Margaret Millar."

16. Nolan, *Ross Macdonald*, 185–87.

17. For a summary of *Pan Tadeusz*, see Weintraub, *The Poetry of Adam Mickiewicz*.

18. Davie, *Collected Poems*, 36–37.

19. For an overview of Galton's theory of eugenics, see Tucker, "For a Twentieth the Cost."

20. Reich, *The Sexual Revolution*, xix.
21. See Nolan, *Ross Macdonald*, 204–13.

Chapter 6: "I Wish They All Could Be California Girls"

1. "California Girls," Brian Wilson (Mike Love uncredited), Irving Music, Inc. BMI. Released on the Beach Boys, *Summer Days (And Summer Nights!!)* Capitol Records (T-2354), June 28, 1965.
2. Chandler, *The Long Goodbye*, 490.
3. Winter, *The Life of David Belasco*, 2:197.
4. Fitzgerald, *Three Novels*, 137.
5. *A Star is Born*, dir. George Cukor, prod. Sidney Luft (Warner Bros., 1954).
6. Starr, *Embattled Dreams*, 227.
7. Didion, "Girl of the Golden West," 100.
8. Didion extends and elaborates this theme in *Where I Was From*.
9. Didion, "Girl of the Golden West," 108.
10. Davis, *City of Quartz*, 26, 330.
11. Ibid., 30.
12. Starr, *Embattled Dreams*, 230.
13. Wright, *Building the American Dream*, 258.
14. See Bugliosi, *Helter Skelter*.
15. Michaels, *Our America*. Walter Mosley's "Easy" Rawlins novels have emphasized the strength of a tradition in African American detective fiction. The linkage of genre, race, and place (Southern California) runs through the novels of Chester Himes, notably *If He Hollers Let Him Go* (1945). See the first chapter of this book for some commentary on the part race plays in the California of the imagination.
16. Michaels, *Our America*, 25.
17. See Toobin, *The Run of His Life*.
18. Michaels, *Our America*, 33.
19. Gitlin, *The Sixties*, 286–87.
20. Ibid., 33.
21. See Nolan, *Ross Macdonald*, 284–92.
22. Goldman, Review of *The Goodbye Look*.
23. Leonard, "Ross Macdonald," The critical ritual continues in the present generation of crime writers. See Weber, "Watching the Detectives": Michael Connelly's series of crime novels featuring LAPD detective Harry Bosch is praised for producing, in Bosch, "a hero for our age," 40.
24. Wright, *Building the Dream*, 258.
25. May, *Homeward Bound*, 63.
26. Ibid., 24.

Chapter 7: Love and Ruin

1. Kenneth Millar, notebook, variously dated in October 1977. Courtesy Ralph B. Sipper.
2. Kenneth Millar to Ashbel Green, December 17, 1970, Millar Papers, UCI.
3. Kenneth Millar to Mike Avallone, October 18, 1975, Millar Papers, UCI.

4. Hartman, "Mystery of Mysteries," 32.

5. Ibid., 31.

6. Welty, Review of *The Underground Man,* 258.

7. Torgerson, "Third Storm Rips Sodden Southland"; Gillam, "Reagan Urges Help for Victims of Flood."

8. Macdonald, "Life with the Blob," 77.

9. Kenneth Millar to Eudora Welty, January 18, 1971, Millar Papers, UCI.

10. Nolan, *Ross Macdonald,* 283.

11. Molotch, "Oil in the Velvet Playground," 44.

12. Ibid., 47.

13. Ibid., 48.

14. Macdonald and Easton, "Santa Barbarans Cite an 11th Commandment."

15. Macdonald, "Life with the Blob," 71.

16. Molotch, "Oil in the Velvet Playground," 49.

17. Woods, Review of *Sleeping Beauty,* 55.

18. Sokolov, "The Art of Murder," 101.

19. Kenneth Millar to Ashbel Green, July 19, 1970, Millar Papers, UCI.

20. Sorrentino, "Ross Macdonald," 148.

21. Millar, notebook (see n1, above).

22. Sipper, *Inward Journey,* 53.

Chapter 8: The Genre after Macdonald

1. Weber, "Watching the Detectives," 40.

2. See Baird, "Hansen, Joseph," 481–84.

3. See n15, ch. 5. Millar returned to a series detective, lawyer Tomas Aragon, three decades later: *Ask for Me Tomorrow* (1976), *The Murder of Miranda* (1979), and *Mermaid* (1982).

4. See the discussion of these authors in Bertens and D'haen, *Contemporary American Crime Fiction,* 17–38.

5. Parker, "The Violent Hero."

6. Lawrence, *Studies in Classic American Literature,* 62–63.

7. Connelly, *The Harry Bosch Novels,* 519–793.

8. Lawrence, *Studies in Classic American Literature,* 62–63.

9. Parker, *The Early Spenser,* 24.

10. Connelly, *The Harry Bosch Novels,* 645.

11. Brookhiser, "Close Up," 62–63.

12. Hartman, "The Mystery of Mysteries," 32; Price, "The Core," 97; Sayers, "The Omnibus of Crime," 380–81.

13. Cooper-Clark, *Designs of Darkness,* 96.

BIBLIOGRAPHY

A Note on Sources

In the interest of reading convenience I have cited passages from Macdonald's novels in the text in parentheses. Bibliographical citations appear here, in the bibliography. His novels exist in first edition, book club editions, English editions, three omnibus collections of three novels each, and several paperback editions. Vintage Crime / Black Lizard editions are the most recent paperback editions. In pagination they correspond to the Knopf first editions, so I have used Vintage / Black Lizard editions for the following: *The Moving Target, The Drowning Pool, Find a Victim, The Doomsters, The Zebra-Striped Hearse, The Chill, Black Money, The Far Side of the Dollar, People Die.* I have used first trade editions (Knopf) for the following: *The Way Some People Die, The Barbarous Coast, The Ivory Grin, The Instant Enemy, The Galton Case, The Goodbye Look, The Underground Man, Sleeping Beauty, The Blue Hammer.*

Kenneth Millar's unpublished papers are held in the Special Collections of the University of California, Irvine, Library. I quote from them with permission of the library and of the Margaret Millar Charitable Remainder Unitrust, holders of the literary rights. Transcripts of two lengthy interviews with Millar have been of particular help. Art Kaye, in preparation for a video program on the life and work of Ross Macdonald, interviewed Millar in 1970. Excerpts from transcripts of this interview are denoted "Kaye" in this text and use the transcripts' pagination. Paul Nelson prepared a lengthy transcript of his interviews with Millar, preparatory to an unpublished magazine article. Excerpts from this document are denoted "Nelson" and follow his pagination.

Kenneth Millar published under his own name and three pseudonyms during his career. Those works that have been published only under the name Kenneth Millar are so listed in the bibliography. Since reissued works have been regularized under the name Ross Macdonald, the bibliography uses that name for all other titles. *Meet Me at the Morgue* (1953) has not yet been reissued; it appears in the bibliography under the pseudonym John Ross Macdonald.

A.B. Review of *The Moving Target*, by John Ross Macdonald. *New York Times*, April 3, 1949.

Anderson, Isaac. "The Crime Corner." Review of *The Long Tunnel*, by Kenneth Millar. *New York Times Book Review*, October 1, 1944, 12.

Allen, Dick, and David Chacko, eds. *Detective Fiction: Crime and Compromise*. New York: Harcourt Brace Jovanovich, 1974.

Atwood, Margaret. "Mystery Man." Review of Dashiell Hammett. *New York Review of Books*, February 14, 2002, 19–22.

Auden, W. H. "The Guilty Vicarage." In *The Dyer's Hand and Other Essays*, 146–58. New York: Random House, 1962.

———. "Ishmael—Don Quixote." In *The Enchafed Flood: Three Critical Essays on the Romantic Spirit*, 90–151. Page-Barbour Lectures, University of Virginia, 1950. New York: Vintage, 1964.

Axelrod, George. *The Seven-Year Itch*. New York: Random House, 1953.

Baird, Newton. "Hansen, Joseph." In Klein, *St. James Guide to Crime and Mystery Writers*, 481–84.

Bargainnier, Earl F. *Ten Women of Mystery*. Bowling Green, Ohio: Bowling Green State University Press, 1981.

Barzun, Jacques. "The Aesthetics of the Criminous." In Barzun, *A Jacques Barzun Reader*, 563–64.

———. "A Catalogue of Crime". In Barzun, *A Jacques Barzun Reader*, 567–71.

———. *A Jacques Barzun Reader: Selections from His Works*. Edited by Michael Murray. New York: HarperCollins, 2002.

———. "Why Read Crime Fiction?" In Barzun, *A Jacques Barzun Reader*, 571–78.

Bergman, Robert L. "New Training Group Formed in Los Angeles." *American Psychoanalyst* 25, no. 2 (1991): 25–26.

Bertens, Hans, and Theo D'haen. *Contemporary American Crime Fiction*. Hampshire, U.K.: Palgrave, 2001.

Birmingham, Stephen. *California Rich*. New York: Simon & Schuster, 1980.

Bloom, Harold. *The Anxiety of Influence: A Theory of Poetry*. New York: Oxford University Press, 1973.

Blotner, Joseph. *Faulkner: A Biography*. 2 vols. New York: Random House, 1974.

Bontemps, Arna. *God Sends Sunday*. New York: Harcourt Brace, 1931. Reprint, New York: AMS Press, 1972.

Bontemps, Arna, and Jack Conroy. *They Seek a City*. Garden City, N.Y.: Doubleday, Doran, 1945.

Boucher, Anthony. "The Ethics of the Mystery Novel." In Haycraft, *The Art of the Mystery Story*, 384–89.

———. Review of *The Ivory Grin*, by Ross Macdonald. *New York Times*, May 4, 1952.

Brookhiser, Richard. "Close-Up: The Mind of George W. Bush." *Atlantic* 291, no. 3 (April 2003): 55–69.

Brooks, Cleanth, and Robert Penn Warren. *Understanding Fiction*. 2nd ed. Englewood Cliffs, N.J.: Prentice-Hall, 1959.

Brophy, Brigid. "Detective Fiction: A Modern Myth of Violence?" In *Don't Never Forget: Collected Views and Reviews*, 121–42. New York: Holt, Rinehart & Winston, 1966. Originally published in *Hudson Review* 18, no. 1 (Spring 1965): 11–30.

Bruccoli, Matthew J. *Ross Macdonald*. New York: Harcourt Brace Jovanovich, 1984.

———. *Ross Macdonald / Kenneth Millar: A Descriptive Bibliography*. Pittsburgh: University of Pittsburgh Press, 1983.

Bugliosi, Vincent, with Curt Gentry. *Helter Skelter: The True Story of the Manson Murders*. 1974. Reprint, New York: Bantam, 1975.

Caughey, John, and LaRee Caughey, eds. *Los Angeles: Biography of a City*. Berkeley: University of California Press, 1977.

———. "A New Force—the Blacks." In Caughey and Caughey, *Los Angeles*, 461–65.

Cawelti, John G. *Adventure, Mystery, and Romance: Formula Stories as Art and Popular Culture*. Chicago: University of Chicago Press, 1976.

Cerf, Bennett. "Trade Winds." *Saturday Review of Literature*, May 1, 1948, 4–6.

Chandler, Raymond. *Later Novels and Other Writings*. Edited by Frank MacShane. New York: Library of America, 1995.

———. *The Long Goodbye*. 1953. In *Later Novels and Other Writings*, 419–734.

———. "The Simple Art of Murder." In *Later Novels and Other Writings*, 977–92.

Cohen, Michael. "The Detective as Other: The Detective *versus* the Other." In Klein, *Diversity and Detective Fiction*, 144–57.

Condon, Richard. *The Manchurian Candidate*. 1959. Reprint, New York: Jove, 1988.

Connelly, Michael. *The Harry Bosch Novels: The Black Echo, The Black Ice, The Concrete Blonde*. Originally published 1992, 1993, 1994, respectively. Boston: Little, Brown, 2001.

Cooper-Clark, Diana. Interview with Ross Macdonald. In *Designs of Darkness: Interviews with Detective Novelists*, 83–100. Bowling Green, Ohio: Bowling Green State University Popular Press, 1983.

Cowan, John Bruce. *John Inness: Painter of the Canadian West*. Vancouver, B.C.: Rose, Cowan & Latter, 1945.

Davie, Donald. *Collected Poems, 1950–1970*. London: Routledge & Kegan Paul, 1972.

———. "On Hearing about Ross Macdonald." In Sipper, *Inward Journey*, 95–96.

Davis, Mike. *City of Quartz: Excavating the Future in Los Angeles*. 1990. Reprint, New York: Vintage, 1992.

———. *Ecology of Fear: Los Angeles and the Imagination of Disaster*. New York: Metropolitan Books–Henry Holt, 1998.

Demarr, Mary Jean. "Margaret Millar." In Winks, *Mystery and Suspense Writers*, 679–87.

Didion, Joan. "Girl of the Golden West." In *After Henry*, 95–109. New York: Simon & Schuster, 1992.

———. *Where I Was From*. New York: Knopf, 2003.

DuBois, W. E. B. "Colored California." *The Crisis*, August 1913, 192–96.

Erikson, Erik H. *Childhood and Society*. New York: W. W. Norton, 1950.

———. *Young Man Luther: A Study in Psychoanalysis and History*. New York: W. W. Norton, 1958.

Ellison, Ralph. *Invisible Man*. New York: Random House, 1952.

———. "Twentieth-Century Fiction and the Black Mask of Humanity." In *Shadow and Act*, 24–44. New York: Random House, 1953.

Fiedler, Leslie. *Love and Death in the American Novel*. New York: Criterion, 1960.

Fitzgerald, F. Scott. *Three Novels: The Great Gatsby, Tender Is the Night, The Last Tycoon*. New York: Charles Scribner's Sons, 1953.

Freud, Sigmund. "An Autobiographical Study" (1924). In Gay, *The Freud Reader,* 3–41.

———. *The Basic Writings of Sigmund Freud.* Translated by A. A. Brill. New York: Modern Library, 1938.

———. "On Beginning Treatment" (1913). In Gay, *The Freud Reader,* 363–78.

———. "Recommendations to Physicians Practicing Psycho-Analysis" (1911–15). In Gay, *The Freud Reader,* 356–63.

Gay, Peter, ed. *The Freud Reader.* New York: W. W. Norton, 1989,

Gillam, Jerry. "Reagan Urges Help for Victims of Flood." *Los Angeles Times,* January 29, 1969.

Gitlin, Todd. *The Sixties: Years of Hope, Days of Rage.* Rev. ed. New York: Bantam, 1993.

Goldman, William. Review of *The Goodbye Look,* by Ross Macdonald. *New York Times Book Review,* June 1, 1969, 1–2.

Goodall, Donald B. *Yasuo Kuniyoshi, 1889–1953: A Retrospective Exhibition.* Austin: University of Texas at Austin, 1975.

Gordon, Richard E., Katherine K. Gordon, and Max Gunther. *The Split-Level Trap.* 1961. Reprint, New York: Dell, 1964.

Gosselin, Adrienne Johnson, ed. *Multicultural Detective Fiction: Murder from the "Other" Side.* New York: Garland, 1999.

———. "Multicultural Detective Fiction: Murder with a Message." In Gosselin, *Multicultural Detective Fiction,* 3–14.

Grella, George. "Murder and the Mean Streets: The Hard-Boiled Detective Novel." *Contempora* 1 (March 1970): 6–15.

Hammett, Dashiell. *Crime Stories and Other Writings.* Selected by Steven Marcus. New York: Library of America, 2001.

———. *The Dain Curse* [1929]. In *The Complete Novels of Dashiell Hammett.* New York: Alfred A. Knopf, 1942.

———. *Selected Letters of Dashiell Hammett, 1921–1960.* Edited by Richard Layman with Julie M. Rivett. Washington: Counterpoint, 2001.

Hartman, Geoffrey. "The Mystery of Mysteries." Review of *The Underground Man,* by Ross Macdonald. *New York Review of Books,* May 18, 1972, 31–34.

Haycraft, Howard. *The Art of the Mystery Story: A Collection of Critical Essays.* 1946. Reprint, New York: Biblo & Tannen, 1976.

Himes, Chester. *If He Hollers Let Him Go.* 1945. Reprint, New York: Thunder's Mouth Press, 1986.

Holton, Robert. *Jarring Witnesses: Modern Fiction and the Representation of History.* London: Harvester Wheatsheaf, 1994.

Horne, Gerald. *Fire This Time: The Watts Uprising and the 1960s.* Charlottesville: University Press of Virginia, 1995.

Horney, Karen, ed. *Are You Considering Psychoanalysis?* 1946. Reprint, New York: W. W. Norton, 1962,

———. *Self-Analysis.* New York: W. W. Norton, 1942.

Kafka, Franz. *The Castle.* Translated by Mark Harman. New York: Schocken Books, 1998.

Kennedy, Liam. "Black Noir: Race and Urban Space in Walter Mosley's Detective Fiction." In Klein, *Diversity and Detective Fiction,* 224–39.

Kilpatrick, Elizabeth. "What Do You Do in Analysis?" In Horney, *Are You Considering Psychoanalysis?* 159–85.

Kingra, Mahinder. "The Forked Root of Evil." Review of Vintage reissue of Macdonald novels. *Baltimore City Paper,* December 25, 1996.

Klein, Kathleen Gregory, ed. *Diversity and Detective Fiction.* Bowling Green, Ohio: Bowling Green State University Press, 1999.

————. *St. James Guide to Crime and Mystery Writers.* 4th ed. Detroit: St. James Press, 1996.

Lavin, Sylvia. "Open the Box: Richard Neutra and the Psychology of the Domestic Environment." *Assemblage* 40 (Dec. 1999): 6–25.

Lawrence, D. H. *Studies in Classic American Literature.* 1923. Reprint, New York: Viking Press, 1964.

Leonard, John. "Ross Macdonald, His Lew Archer and Other Secret Selves." *New York Times Book Review,* June 1, 1969, 2, 19.

Macdonald, John Ross. *Meet Me at the Morgue.* New York: Alfred A. Knopf, 1953.

Macdonald, Ross. *Archer in Hollywood.* New York: Knopf, 1967. Includes *The Moving Target, The Way Some People Die, The Barbarous Coast.*

————. *Archer in Jeopardy.* New York: Knopf, 1979. Includes *The Doomsters, The Zebra-Striped Hearse, The Instant Enemy.*

————. *Find a Victim.* New York: Alfred A. Knopf, 1954.

————. *Archer at Large.* New York: Knopf, 1970. Includes *The Galton Case, The Chill, Black Money.*

————. *The Barbarous Coast.* New York: Alfred A. Knopf, 1956.

————. *Black Money.* New York: Alfred A. Knopf, 1965.

————. *Blue City.* New York: Alfred A. Knopf, 1947. Reprint with an introduction by Robert B. Parker. Boston: Hill & Company, 1987.

————. *The Blue Hammer.* New York: Alfred A. Knopf, 1976.

————. *Ceaselessly into the Past.* Foreword by Eudora Welty. Santa Barbara: Capra Press, 1981.

————. *The Chill.* New York: Alfred A. Knopf, 1964.

————. *The Doomsters.* New York: Alfred A. Knopf, 1958.

————. *The Drowning Pool.* New York: Alfred A. Knopf, 1950.

————. *The Far Side of the Dollar.* New York: Alfred A. Knopf, 1965.

————. *The Ferguson Affair.* New York: Alfred A. Knopf, 1960.

————. *The Galton Case.* New York: Alfred A. Knopf, 1959.

————. *The Goodbye Look.* New York: Alfred A. Knopf, 1969.

————. *The Instant Enemy.* New York: Alfred A. Knopf, 1968.

————. *The Ivory Grin.* New York: Alfred A. Knopf, 1952.

————. "Life with the Blob," *Sports Illustrated,* April 21, 1969, 50–52, 57–60. Reprinted in Macdonald, *Self-Portrait,* 69–79.

————. *The Moving Target.* New York: Alfred A. Knopf, 1949.

————. *The Name Is Archer.* New York: Bantam, 1971.

————. *Sleeping Beauty.* New York: Alfred A. Knopf, 1973.

———. *Strangers in Town.* Edited by Tom Nolan. Norfolk, Va.: Crippen & Landru, 2001. Contains "Death by Water" (1945), "Strangers in Town" (1950), and "The Angry Man" (1955).

———. *The Underground Man.* New York: Alfred A. Knopf, 1971.

———. *The Way Some People Die.* New York: Alfred A. Knopf, 1951.

———. *The Wycherly Woman.* New York: Alfred A. Knopf, 1961.

———. *The Zebra-Striped Hearse.* New York: Alfred A. Knopf, 1962.

Macdonald, Ross, and Robert Easton. "Santa Barbarans Cite an 11th Commandment: Thou Shalt Not Abuse the Earth." *New York Times Magazine,* October 12, 1969, 32–33, 142–49, 151, 156.

May, Elaine Tyler. *Homeward Bound: American Families in the Cold War Era.* New York: Basic Books, 1988.

McCarthy, Todd. *Howard Hawks: The Grey Fox of Hollywood.* New York: Grove, 1997.

McWilliams, Carey. *Southern California: An Island on the Land.* 1946. Reprint, Salt Lake City: Gibbs Smith, 1973.

Michaels, Walter Benn. *Our America: Nativism, Modernism, and Pluralism.* Durham, N.C.: Duke University Press, 1995.

Millar, Kenneth. *The Dark Tunnel.* New York: Dodd Mead, 1944.

———. "The Inward Eye: A Revaluation of Coleridge's Psychological Criticism." Ph.D. diss., University of Michigan, 1951.

———. Review of *Love and Death in the American Novel,* by Leslie Fiedler. *San Francisco Chronicle,* July 24, 1960.

———. *The Three Roads.* New York: Alfred A. Knopf, 1948.

———. *Trouble Follows Me.* New York: Dodd, Mead, 1946.

Millar, Margaret. *The Iron Gates.* New York: Random House, 1945.

Miller, Charles H. *Auden: An American Friendship.* New York: Charles Scribner's Sons, 1983.

Minter, David. *A Cultural History of the American Novel: Henry James to William Faulkner.* Cambridge: Cambridge University Press, 1994.

Molotch, Harvey. "Oil in the Velvet Playground," *Ramparts,* November 1969, 43–51.

Moss, Robert F. "Ross Macdonald." In Winks, *Mystery and Suspense Writers,* 2: 633–50.

Nelson, Paul. Obituary, Ross Macdonald. *Rolling Stone,* September 1, 1983, 60.

Neutra, Richard. *Life and Human Habitat.* Stuttgart: Verlagsanstalt Alexander Kock GmbH, 1956.

Niebuhr, Gary Warren. *A Reader's Guide to the Private Eye Novel.* New York: G. K. Hall, 1993.

Nolan, Tom. *Ross Macdonald: A Biography.* With an introduction by Sue Grafton. New York: Scribner's, 1999.

Norris, Frank. *The Responsibilities of the Novelist and Other Essays.* New York: Greenwood, 1968. Originally published in 1902.

North by Northwest. Produced and and directed by Alfred Hitchcock. MGM, 1959.

Nugent, Walter. *Into the West: The Story of Its People.* New York: Alfred A. Knopf, 1999.

Oates, Joyce Carol. "The Simple Art of Murder." Review of Raymond Chandler. *New York Review of Books,* December 21, 1995, 32–40.

Orwell, George. *Homage to Catalonia.* With an introduction by Bob Edwards. London: Folio Society, 1970.

Parker, Robert B. *The Early Spenser: The Godwulf Manuscript, God Save the Child, Mortal Stakes.* New York: Delacorte / Seymour Lawrence, 1989.

———. *The Violent Hero, Wilderness Heritage and Urban Reality: A Study of the Private Eye in the Novels of Dashiell Hammett, Raymond Chandler, and Ross Macdonald.* Ph.D. diss., Boston University, 1971.

Pateman, Carole. *The Disorder of Women: Democracy, Feminism, and Political Theory.* Stanford: Stanford University Press, 1989.

Pepper, Andrew. *The Contemporary American Crime Novel: Race, Ethnicity, Gender, Class.* Edinburgh: Edinburgh University Press, 2000.

Pierpont, Claudia Roth. "Tough Guy: The Mystery of Dashiell Hammett." *New Yorker,* February 11, 2002, 66–75.

Poe, Elizabeth. "Nobody Was Listening." In Caughey and Caughey, *Los Angeles: Biography of a City,* 426–31.

Price, Reynolds. "The Core: For Ross Macdonald." In Sipper, *Inward Journey,* 97.

Reich, Wilhelm. *The Sexual Revolution: Toward a Self-Governing Character Structure.* Translated by Theodore P. Wolfe. New York: Orgone Institute Press, 1945.

Reid, David., ed. *Sex, Death, and God in L.A.* New York: Random House, 1992. Reprint, Berkeley: University of California Press, 1994.

Reilly, John M. "Margaret Millar." In Bargainnier, *Ten Women of Mystery,* 223–46.

Rosenthal, Henry M. "The Religious Novel and the Detective Story." *Partisan Review* 15, no. 7 (July 1948): 839–43.

Ruehlman, William. *Saint with a Gun: The Unlawful American Private Eye.* New York: New York University Press, 1974.

Sayers, Dorothy L. "The Omnibus of Crime." In Allen and Chacko, *Detective Fiction,* 351–82.

Schopen, Bernard A. *Ross Macdonald.* New York: Twayne, 1990.

Schwartz, Joseph. *Cassandra's Daughter: A History of Psychoanalysis.* New York: Viking, 1999.

Sipper, Ralph B., ed. *Inward Journey.* Santa Barbara: Cordelia Editions, 1984.

Sokolov, Raymond A. "The Art of Murder." *Newsweek,* March 22, 1971, 101–8.

Sorrentino, Gilbert. "Ross Macdonald: Some Remarks on the Limitation of Form." In Sipper, *Inward Journey,* 148–53.

Speir, Jerry. *Ross Macdonald.* New York: Ungar, 1978.

Spellbound. Directed by Alfred Hitchcock. Produced by David O. Selznick. United Artists, 1945.

Spiller, Robert E., et. al. *Literary History of the United States.* 3 vols. New York: Macmillan, 1948.

Spock, Benjamin. M.D. *The Common Sense Book of Baby and Child Care.* New York: Duell, Sloan & Pierce, 1946.

Starr, Kevin. *Americans and the California Dream, 1850–1915.* New York: Oxford University Press, 1973.

————. *Embattled Dreams: California in War and Peace, 1940–1950.* New York: Oxford University Press, 2002.

Steiner, Wendy. "The Diversity of American Fiction." In Emory Elliott, ed. *Columbia Literary History of the United States,* 845–72. New York: Columbia University Press, 1988.

Strecker, Edward A. *Their Mothers' Sons: The Psychiatrist Examines an American Problem.* Philadelphia: J. B. Lippincott, 1946.

Symonds, Julian. *Bloody Murder from the Detective Story to the Crime Novel: A History.* London: Faber & Faber, 1972.

Tolstoy, Leo. *Anna Karenina.* New York: Modern Library, 1930.

Toobin, Jeffrey. *The Run of His Life: The People v. O. J. Simpson.* New York: Random House, 1996.

Torgerson, Dial. "Third Storm Rips Sodden Southland," *Los Angeles Times,* January 29, 1969.

Tucker, William H. "For a Twentieth the Cost: Sir Francis Galton and the Origin of Eugenics." Chap. 2 in *The Science and Politics of Racial Research.* Urbana: University of Illinois Press, 1994.

Weber, Bruce. "Watching the Detectives." *New York Times Magazine,* May 9, 2004, 38–41.

Weintraub, Wiktor. *The Poetry of Adam Mickiewicz.* The Hague: Mouton, 1954.

Welty, Eudora. Review of *The Underground Man,* by Ross Macdonald. In *The Eye of the Story: Selected Essays and Reviews,* 251–60. New York: Random House, 1977. Originally published in *New York Review of Books,* February 14, 1971, 1, 28–30.

Wilson, Edmund. "Who Cares Who Killed Roger Ackroyd?" In Haycraft, *The Art of the Mystery Story,* 390–97.

Winks, Robin, ed. *Mystery and Suspense Writers: The Literature of Crime, Detection, and Espionage.* 2 vols. New York: Charles Scribner's Sons, 1998.

Winter, William. *The Life of David Belasco.* Vol. 2, 1918. Reprint, Freeport, N.Y.: Books for Libraries Press, 1970.

Wolfe, Peter. *Dreamers Who Live Their Dreams: The World of Ross Macdonald's Novels.* Bowling Green, Ohio: Bowling Green State University Press, 1976.

Woods, Crawford. Review of *Sleeping Beauty,* by Ross Macdonald. *New York Times Book Review,* May 20, 1973, 55.

Wright, Gwendolyn. *Building the Dream: A Social History of Housing in America.* 1981. Reprint, Cambridge, Mass.: MIT Press, 1983.

Wylie, Philip. *Generation of Vipers.* 1942. Reprint, New York: Holt, Rinehart & Winston, 1955.

INDEX